HOMEGOING

HOMEGOING

MICHELLE MARKEY BUTLER

Book I of The Tall Ships of Saradena

PINK
NARCISSUS
PRESS

This is a work of fiction. All the characters and events portrayed in this book are fictitious or are used fictitiously.

HOMEGOING
© 2014 Michelle Markey Butler

Cover illustration & design by Duncan Eagleson

Published by Pink Narcissus Press
P.O. Box 303
Auburn, MA 01501
pinknarc.com

Library of Congress Control Number: 2014948233

ISBN: 978-1-939056-08-5
First trade paperback edition: December 2014

For my parents.

We learned *sabidur gerva eng protege* before we ever set foot in school.

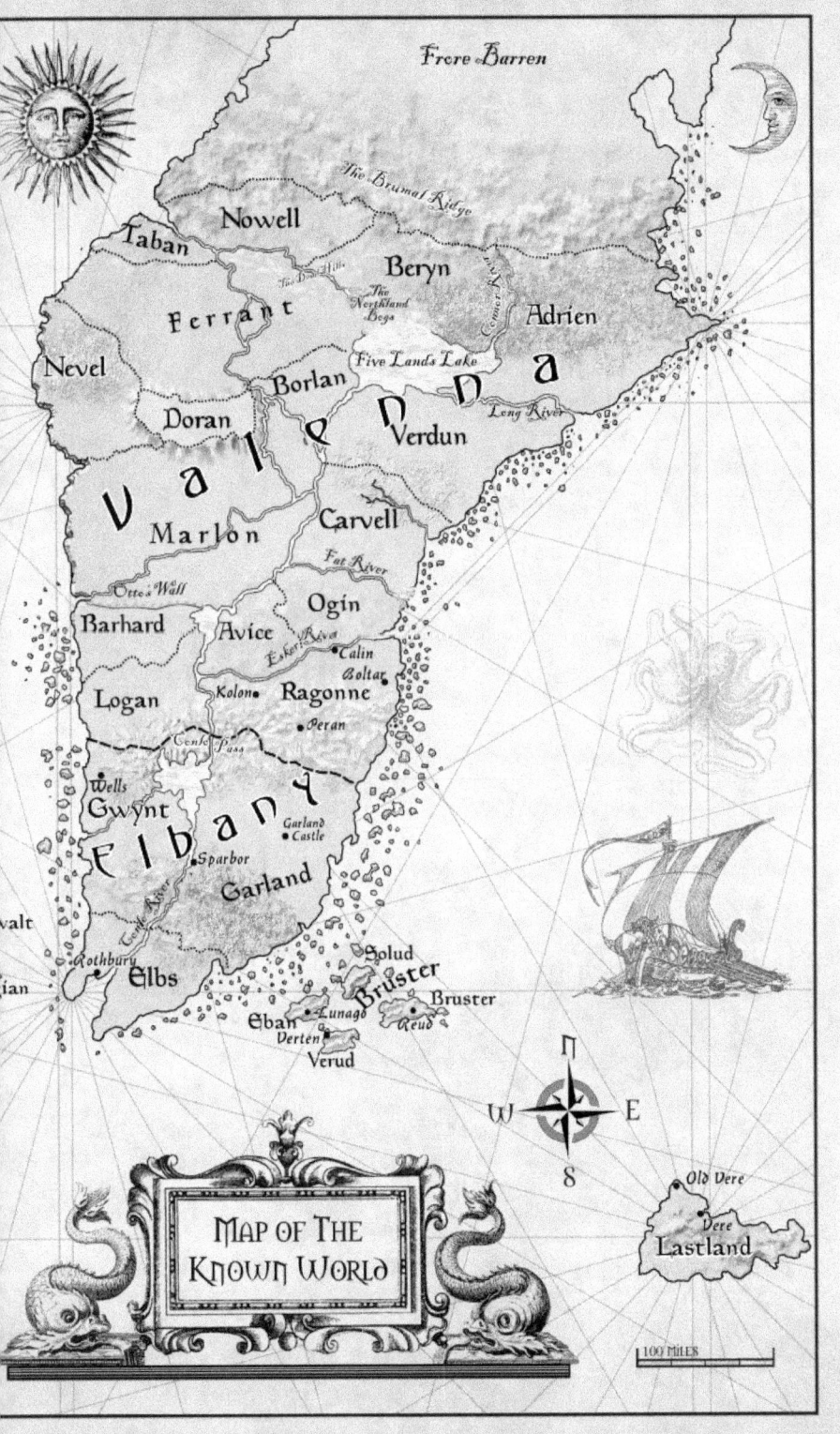

Map of the Known World

EPIGRAM

Geðenc hwelc witu us ða becomon for ðisse worulde, ða ða we hit nohwæðer ne selfe ne lufodon ne eac oðrum monnum ne lefdon!

Remember what punishments befell us in this world when we ourselves did not cherish learning nor transmit it to other men! –Alfred the Great, from the preface to his translation of Pope Gregory the Great's *Pastoral Care*.

BOOK I

CHAPTER I

One did not swear, even under one's breath and in Brusterian, before one's adopted lord. No matter what nonsense he spouted. I seized a hanging fold of my skirt in each hand. A letter had come—to people who could not read? From a country we'd never heard of? Foolishness. It had to be a trick of one of our known enemies. Of which we had no dearth.

The Roth glanced down at the page. "The messenger said it was brought by a ship half as tall as the cliff of Elbsridge."

His wife, sitting beside him, made a noise that would have been rude if it were louder. "That's impossible."

"A dozen men saw it."

"The cliff's two hundred feet high. No boat's that big."

Doubt tickled the back of my neck. She was right. No ship could be so large. There must have been a ship, though, one that seemed bigger than normal. That would be harder to feign. Any kingdom's Vere-trained clerk could produce a letter. Boats were built only in Bruster, and were small. But one could be hired, and perhaps made to seem bigger from a distance, and strange, as if from an unknown country. Trickery still seemed most likely.

"Lord." I clasped my hands behind my back. "Lady Elsbeth is correct. But surprise exaggerates." I flicked a finger towards the curling parchment sheet. "This is meant to surprise. And frighten. Your interest in reading is widely known—and mocked. It must be a ploy."

"I'm surprised." Lady Elsbeth folded her hands. "But by your mistrust, Doctora Bann. I've read that letter. You taught me yourself. Do you doubt your skill, or mine?"

I squeezed the fingers of my left hand with my right until they ached. "Neither, lady. But —"

"*You* have read it." The Roth shared a look with Lady Elsbeth. "Doctora Bann has not." He handed me the letter. "Your pardon."

"And mine." Lady Elsbeth spread her hands, not quite

concealing her impatience. "It's unfair to ask your thoughts before you've seen it."

I barely heard her. I read the letter, and then again, more quickly:

Douglas, son of Ailred, Roth of Elbany:

Greetings.

Saradena has not spoken in many years but our gaze has never left you. We have watched you grow lax in the behaviors and expectations of Carolingian tradition, and been troubled.

We have been patient with—not blind to—the transgressions of Elbany. Our patience is at an end. Restore the neglected Henrican observances and show your compliance to us in Estane within one year. Else we shall enforce your obedience with all the might of Saradena.

His Eminent Lord, Spenser, Prester-General.
From his own hand.

What did any of that mean? Saradena? There was no Saradena among the kingdoms of the Three Lands.

The document itself was even more perplexing. I could count on one hand the times I had touched a manuscript so ornate. The parchment was creamy soft, so fine the hair-side was only slightly darker than the flesh-side. Most of the words were in a crisp, true black, but the Roth's name was gold. Red and gold interlacing framed the first letter of the message, one strand ending in a green beast's head with gold eyes, a tiny red tongue curling from the open mouth. The signature—*His Eminent Lord, Spenser, Prester-General*—was interwoven with blue.

Green, gold, red—rare, costly inks. Fear rippled my thought. Given time and materials, any kingdom's clerk should be able to produce the letter but it would take months and be expensive. Who would make such an effort for a trick?

My doubt grew, and with it, concern.

That *blue*...

The blue that curled among the signature was a deep, bright blue, the color of the afternoon sky on the first warm day of spring. Not the watery green-blue I learned in Vere. My hands shook, making the page quiver. The oldest scholars in Vere could not have made that ink.

"It says what we thought," the Roth said. "And—it is real."

His words brushed my ears lightly, as if he whispered from across a courtyard. Better, far better, if the letter were the stratagem of a known enemy. Elbany had been attacked many times but never conquered. The blue ink dispelled that hope. "Yes," I said.

"Hmm." Worry mingled with pride in his growl. I heard it even as I read the letter again. Its source was not difficult to guess. He had accepted me as his clerk, but his aim was higher: to create a library and bring literacy back to his people, starting with himself and his wife. He still struggled with simple words, but Lady Elsbeth had had better success. She had worked the message out before they summoned me to confirm it.

"What do you know of Saradena?"

I struggled to lift my gaze and did not succeed. "Lord?"

"The question was plain enough." Lady Elsbeth's voice was cold.

I snapped my eyes upward, turning the page over.

She leaned forward. "You were at Vere. What if anything did you learn there about Saradena?"

Even with the writing out of sight I did not dare glance down. I held the letter out to her. "I know no more than you do, lady. What *this* says."

"All Vere's books but nothing about Saradena?"

I raised one shoulder. "Perhaps there would be. I didn't read every book in Vere's library." There was no need to tell them many of the manuscripts had been kept from me. The scholars had taught me under compulsion; they had never accepted me. "That would be the work of a lifetime."

The Roth looked at his wife. Her eyes went to the door.

Chapter II

I stood before the door to the library, or what would become the library if my fool students ever learned enough to copy books, trying to quiet myself before entering. My displeasure was unjust. Of course the Roth had dismissed me. I could tell him nothing more. I was no princess here.

Nor anywhere, now.

The thought bit deeper than it ought. Six years. How many more must pass before my disgrace would scar over? Not heal—some hurts never did—but cease to weep through and knit closed, however blemished. All wounds must, or putrefaction would settle in.

Or perhaps the rot had already taken hold.

Once I overheard a Brusterian fosterling explain the oddity of my presence in the Roth's household to another boy. "Everything has a use. Even throw-away things. The kitchen midden warms the pig shed. You can spread cow dung on the fields, or dry it to burn as fuel. But a barren princess..." He spat on the floor, as he had seen the men do. "A barren princess has no worth. She should have jumped from the highest window of the Black Keep. That much was left to her at least, to lessen the family shame."

Perhaps I should have. But I had not. I left, and could not return.

Did not have to return. My breath huddled in my chest, startled at the sudden notion. How strange it had not occurred to me in that light before. The Roth had given me a new home, and a purpose. I need never go back. Not to Ferrant, whence my husband had cast me. Not to Vere, which had taught me unwillingly and would not keep me. Most of all, not to Bruster. Outrage had fled but I was far from settled, and I stood at the door, pulling a shuddering breath.

After a dozen heartbeats, I felt calm enough to go in.

My students looked up as the door opened, Edgar, Agyfen, and Godric nodding respectfully and Alban nervously, but he

always seemed nervous. They were at their writing desks practicing scripts, as I'd left them.

They were not, in fact, fools. All were capable when they
worked hard, even Agyfen, whom I'd nearly sent home last
month when it seemed he'd never master the difference between
'd' and 'b'. When I'd first come to Elbany I'd hoped to have a
dozen books copied and bound within five years. More than a
year later, with none of my students having moved beyond practicing on wax tablets, I doubted I'd ever see that many books on
our shelves. They *were* making progress. Just slowly. Alban was
almost ready for parchment, both making it and practicing
writing on it, the next steps in the long process of learning to
create books.

Given the writing desks and shelves the carpenter—who truly
was a fool—had produced, it was just as well no books would be
ready soon. Looking around the room, I felt a growl rising. I'd
explained what was needed. The carpenter had nodded but it'd
been clear he wasn't listening, used to having his judgment asked,
not directed. But he'd never built a library before. No one in
Elbany had even seen one. He made the shelves too small, posi-
tioned them in front of the windows, and integrated two of the
writing desks into them, where they were shadowed by the
shelves. He could scarcely have done worse if he'd tried.

When he built them, I was away from Rothbury choosing the
sheep for our first parchment from amongst the Roth's flocks.
When I returned, I had demanded an audience, but more than a
week later, he had yet to come. Uncertain of the extent of my
authority towards him—he was the Roth's own carpenter, which
would usually outrank the clerk, but the Roth valued me more
than most kings did their clerks—I stretched my patience to its
uttermost, and waited. I had resolved that morning to speak to
the Roth, before the strange ship with its stranger letter arrived,
wiping away all other thought.

That letter...

I walked among the writing desks, correcting my students'
errors more from habit than attention. Godric held the stylus like
a blacksmith's hammer again. Agyfen looked up, fear etched
across his face, when I tapped the 'b' he had written instead of
'd'. But he was improving; the rest of the passage was fine. I
nodded at him to continue, suppressing a smile as he tried to hide

a relieved sigh. Edgar's letters were neatly formed and legible, but still varied too much in size. He scowled at my tell-tale fingertip, but then sat up straighter, smoothed the wax, and began again. Alban looked as if I were coming at him with an axe. But his script was perfect, as it had been for the last three weeks.

"Well done," I said. "If your work remains this good, you can begin practicing with parchment and ink next week."

Even his smile, broad as it was, was nervous.

"Just scraps to start, mind you." I had brought parchment trimmings from Vere for this purpose, although I'd hoped to put them to use six months ago.

He bowed his head. "Of course. Thank you, Doctora Bann."

I went to my own desk, although I knew I wouldn't be able to work.

That letter...that blue...

Saradena...

Could it be? An unknown country? It seemed absurd. But I knew better. I'd seen that brilliant blue ink.

And why not? Who could say what lay beyond the curve of the sea?

My breath caught. Not unknown. *Forgotten*. It must be. They sent us a letter, assuming we could read it. They remembered us, and presumed we remembered them. Somewhere in our history, now lost, lay the key to understanding Saradena's demands.

We had to find that past. How? I'd never heard of Saradena, not in any Brusterian song, not during my years in Ferrant. It was true I hadn't read every book in Vere, but if the scholars knew of a country the rest of the Three Lands had forgotten, I'd have heard some hint of it. If knowledge of Saradena was preserved at Vere, it was buried deep among scarce-read manuscripts. But where else could we hope to find anything?

I shied away from that question, one hand twitching as if to ward off an insect. That there were other books, in Ferrant, no one knew better. But no one knew less what they might contain. I took out my wax tablet and stylus, writing a passage from memory of the story of Ethelda the Weaver for Alban to copy, tracing the words of the letter in my mind.

I had to find these people. And, once Elbany was safe, learn how they made that blue ink.

***

"Doctora Bann?"

Alban's voice held a deeper grade of anxiety than usual. I turned, pretending not to notice his hasty step backward. "Yes?"

"The carpenter is here."

"Carpenter...?" My mind, brimful of the letter, sputtered.

"You wanted to see him. About the shelves."

"Yes." I felt my lip curling as my head cleared. Alban took another step back. "Thank you. Show him in."

He bowed and went to the door, returning with the carpenter, who greeted me with neither bow nor honorific. Alban glanced at him in concern, which the carpenter either did not see or ignored.

I was used to people stumbling over their greetings. I had been Maudlin, princess of Bruster, then Tedora, queen of Ferrant, before I became Doctora Bann, clerk to the Roth of Elbany and the only woman the scholars of Vere had taught. To many mouths "lady" seemed to feel odd for a noblewoman cast off by both husband and family. Most people only rarely encountered a Vere-trained clerk, and of course never a woman. For them "Doctora Bann" proved a bar too high. But the approach the carpenter took was uncommon—no address at all. Most people mastered their discomfort and uncertainty when they realized silence was worse. Clearly there was no question in his mind whether the Roth's carpenter outranked his clerk.

I rose. If he was expecting an inferior's bow, he was disappointed.

"You wanted to see me?" His gaze did not meet mine, resting instead on the shelves, satisfaction oozing.

His preening snapped the last threads of my patience. "Yes."

Alban, eyes swiveling between us, bowed and hurried back to his desk.

"You built these?" I flicked a fingertip at the shelves.

He smiled. "Yes. A good—"

"Useless."

His mouth opened but no sound crept out.

"They're too narrow. None of our books will be this small."

He collected himself. "Now listen here—"

"*You* listen."

His eyes narrowed. "I am the Roth's head carpenter, and I say these are beautiful shelves."

"They are lovely," I said. "But they aren't meant to be looked at. They're for holding books. Ours will be quartos, this big," I held up my hands, "by this wide. They would hang over the edge. They would bend. They would be knocked off."

"I'm busy. My work is in demand throughout Elbany." He sniffed. "If you're going to be particular, you should have been clear about what you wanted."

I felt my hands clench. "I did tell you. Are you deaf or merely stupid?"

He paled. "You can't speak to me like that."

"Then there is the sunlight."

His haughtiness returned. "Now you expect me to change the sun?"

"There must be light, of course, but on the tables. Too much is bad for books. It fades them. It dries them. They crack, and then they crumble. As I told you. On your shelves sunlight would bake them all day." I stepped closer. The carpenter was not a tall man; I had no difficulty meeting his gaze without looking up.

"Make do with what you have," he said, attempting to look down his nose at me. "Your library's not important."

"It's not my library. It's the Roth's," I said. "Books kept on *your* shelves would not survive ten years. The Roth expects his library to last a good deal longer." Although the Roth's interest in reading was laughed at throughout the Three Lands, only he, Lady Elsbeth, and I knew the full extent of what he hoped his library would do for Elbany. It was a bold plan. It might not succeed. But it would not fail because of a carpenter's laziness.

Rage burned in his eyes but he said nothing. Good. We were getting somewhere.

"Perhaps we should ask the Roth his preferences? Leave the shelves as they are and ruin his books? Or rebuild, correctly this time?"

"I could put doors on the shelves. Lady."

I was unimpressed by his late-come courtesy. "Doors that would not close? I already told you the shelves are too shallow for our books."

The man's face flushed but he bit down on whatever came into his mind first. "No, lady. I meant I could build new shelves of the proper size, but with doors to protect them from the sunlight."

"No."

"But—"

"No. You must do it again. Properly. Books have to be kept out of sunlight but it's too damp to keep them behind doors. The air must move freely around them or they will rot."

"But if I have to make the shelves again, to fit elsewhere, I'll have to rebuild some of the writing tables as well."

"So? They're not right either. The shelves shadow the work surface."

"But—"

"You did not listen before," I said. "Listen now. Carefully."

I waited.

Finally he realized I expected a response. "Yes? *Lady?*"

"Books live on shelves of the right size, out of sunlight but in open air. How big will our books be?"

Panic bloomed in his face. He hadn't listened this time either. His hands half-lifted, fluttering uncertainly. I muttered a few of the Brusterian words I'd been thinking as I stood before the Roth that morning.

He did not understand but the substance must have been evident. "I'm sorry, lady," he said, more contritely than anything since he arrived. "If you would tell me once more?"

"Quartos." My hands inscribed a book-sized square. "About this high. This wide." His attentiveness cooled but did not quell my irritation. "You should have done your work right the first time. Now build what I need, not what you think best. Or easiest."

"Yes, lady. They'll be what you want."

"They had better."

"Yes, lady." He bowed, and I nodded his dismissal.

I went to the window, hearing the door close as he left. It was late afternoon, when the low-arching sunlight burnished the brown stones of Rothbury castle until they gleamed like bronze. This was not the Black Keep of Bruster, the elegant pale gray stronghold of Ferrant, or the shining white city of Vere. But it had its own beauty, that of a well-balanced, keen-edged sword, unadorned at the hilt but not diminished by that lack of embellishment. Rather its own grace seemed the more evident in the plainness of the design.

As I was about to turn away, sudden movement caught my eye.

A messenger galloped through the gates, hardly drawing rein though he had entered the courtyard. It was too far to hear the rapid clatter of hoof beats or his feet upon the stones as he flung himself down. But I could see the rolled parchment in his hand.

CHAPTER III

As I watched, the messenger strode towards the doors, passing beneath the raised portcullis. He must not have been a messenger long, or else had not been sent to Rothbury before. I saw him catch himself as his foot snagged on the uneven paving stone before the doors. Perhaps the tread of many men had pushed it askew. Perhaps its slight lopsidedness was intentional, one of the many unobtrusive defenses built into castles. I had nearly pitched over the same stone myself my first pass through those doors.

I turned from the window and left the library, heading for the Roth's audience chamber. Another written message had come. Why wait to be summoned again?

A second, arriving so soon after the first...surely they were related. Perhaps Saradena had sent letters by an overland route as well as by ship to ensure at least one arrived?

Rothbury castle was bigger than the Black Keep but not by much, which made the Roth's giving half the third floor for his library all the more noteworthy. A short walk took me to the staircase, which spiraled downward as steeply as either of the Black Keep's. On the second floor, passages led from the small landing to a public reception hall, a smaller audience chamber, and the Roth's private rooms.

I had come from the library so quickly I wondered, as I approached, whether the rider had brought the letter yet. As soon as I drew near enough to see the doorward, I knew he had.

The doorward stood before the entrance to the audience chamber, as he did any room when the Roth was present. The most trusted retainer, the last man between an enemy and his lord, the doorward was as suspicious as a Brusterian under-king and as watchful as a gossip-hound. I had never seen emotion in his face any more than in the stones of the wall beside him. Today, he shifted as I came closer, one side of his mouth twitching. His evident worry shook me almost as much as the letter had.

I was admitted as soon as he announced me.

The Roth and his wife sat, as they had earlier, before a brazier in which a small pile of charcoal glowed. It was chilly enough in Elbany and Bruster to warrant a fire for another month. The audience chamber was in the castle's only tower, about fifteen feet across at its widest. I could see Elbs Bay through the windows in the curving wall behind them.

"Forgive my impertinence," I bowed. "I saw the messenger from the library window."

"Which messenger?" the Roth said.

They let me braise in surprise for half a dozen heartbeats.

"Probably the first," Lady Elsbeth said. "We sent Seamus to fetch you. He'd scarcely left before the second arrived. You didn't see him?"

I shook my head. Two messengers? Had they both brought letters?

Her eyes narrowed, not boding well for the fosterling who had dallied in bringing the summons.

"More letters?" I said at last.

"One, at least. We have not received either rider formally yet, but the first was seen holding a scroll."

"They're taking hospitality," Lady Elsbeth said. "Then they'll come before us."

That was customary. Carrying news and messages from kingdom to kingdom, particularly in spring, was difficult, dangerous, and filthy. Messengers were given time to eat, drink, and have a rudimentary wash, before delivering their burden.

"They're from Logan and Ragonne," she said.

"Ah." The soft exhalation drew out as I considered the implications. Elbany's only two allies in Valenna. Perhaps Saradena's aim was wider than we'd assumed.

Lady Elsbeth nodded. "You guess our thought."

"If you suspect Saradena threatens not just Elbany but her friends, then yes," I said.

There was a rap on the door. "Enter," the Roth called.

The doorward appeared. "The messengers are returned."

"Show the Logane in."

I moved to the side, clearing the reception space before the brazier. The messenger was splattered with mud from shoulders to boots, but his face and hands were clean. He made a deep bow.

"I am James, lord, son of Methel. He has served the King of Logan since he came to the throne, and his father before him."

"I remember him. Good man. One of the quickest hands with an axe I've seen. Almost as good as Lord Garland himself."

"Thank you, lord." His credentials accepted, the messenger's stiff stance eased. "The king of Logan and his lady, your sister, send their greetings. Something strange has happened. They ask your help." He drew something from his belt pouch. A scroll, somewhat squashed. "This was...brought by...a very large...ship." He spoke as if he did not quite believe what he was saying. "Vere has not yet sent Logan a new clerk. My King asks if you could have your clerk read it."

A ship? To Logan? If the letter were from Saradena, we should be even more worried. Brusterian longboats never ventured into the western sea, where mountains studded the waters thick as acorns in fall. If a ship got to Logan, it had been made and steered by hands more cunning than ours. Which meant their weapons probably outstripped ours as well.

The Roth stretched out his hand. The messenger stepped closer long enough to give him the scroll. From where I stood, the seal looked identical. The Roth looked it over and passed it to Lady Elsbeth, who studied it before breaking the seal and unrolling it. She nodded to him, then gestured for me to take the letter and confirm her assessment.

I scanned it. Except for the greeting, it was the same. I dipped my head to them in confirmation.

"James of Logan," the Roth returned his gaze to the messenger. "I thank you for your service. Elbany can aid our neighbor in this matter. But first we must give ear to a second rider. Step aside and wait."

The Logane looked bewildered, almost certainly wondering why he would be allowed to hear another kingdom's message. But he bowed again without speaking.

As he straightened, he glanced at me, standing to the Roth's left. Puzzlement, and then realization, swept over his face, and he pointedly crossed to the other side of the audience chamber. I looked down at the letter, grappling humiliation and rage, not just because of the insult but because I felt it.

I looked up as the second messenger was brought in. He was the man I had seen, who nearly fell headlong over the paving stone. He was as road-worn as the other but it was evident he was a different class of man, and no mere messenger. Though grimy, his clothes were well-cut from good cloth, and the brooch closing his cloak was gold inlayed with garnet. He stood straight before the Roth, not bending slightly in unconscious subservience, and his bow was respectful but not deferential. "I beg your forgiveness in coming before you so unseemly. I bring grave news. I am Orlo, son of my lord King Philip's sister Rosara."

The Roth's eyebrows rose. "Lord of Kolon. You honor me, cousin. It has been several years since I saw you last."

I stumbled over that 'cousin' until I remembered the Roth's mother had been a sister of King Philip as well.

"Yes, lord. But since you call me by that title, you know why. King Philip's affairs in Kolon keep me well occupied."

"Some pressing need must call you from that duty."

"Indeed." He let his gaze travel the room, lingering meaningfully on myself and the Logane messenger.

"I think I can guess your errand." The Roth motioned for the doorward to bring forward another chair, then dismissed him. "Sit, cousin. Elbany also received a letter."

Glancing around again to register his concern about continuing this discussion with others present, Lord Orlo sat beside Lady Elsbeth. "From...the same source?" In his wariness he did not say the name. He was a handsome man, more striking than the Roth, black hair and eyes, or so dark a brown they appeared black. His gaze went again to the Logane messenger in growing comprehension. "Perhaps more than our two countries?"

The Roth looked at me, then flicked his gaze towards Lord Orlo. I stepped around the brazier to hand the Ragoni lord the letter the Logane messenger had brought. Lady Elsbeth drew out the other and gave it to him. He raised his hand and showed a curling, but no longer sealed, scroll. Laying all three on his lap, he looked between them. He couldn't read, of course, but he needn't to examine whether they were the same. "I see. What is your counsel, lord?"

"Most immediately, we must send word to Logan of what the letter says. And that they were not alone in receiving it." He summoned James of Logan with a gesture.

"Go now. My doorward will direct you to the steward. When

you've slept and are ready to leave, I will tell you what message to deliver to the King of Logan." The Roth's voice dropped. "Messengers are chosen, among their other skills, for discretion. We—your King, the King of Ragonne, and myself—rely upon yours in this matter."

"Yes, lord." He bowed, and was excused.

"Logan's clerk died, and has not yet been replaced," the Roth said after the door closed. "The strangeness of receiving a written letter was obvious but they had no idea what it said."

Lord Orlo pursed his lips, considering. "So a trusted, but not noble, messenger was sent."

"Have any other kingdoms received them?"

He shrugged. "There's no way to find out. Ragonne will not tell her neighbors she lies under such a threat." He leaned towards the Roth. "You believe it?"

"Yes." His hands, resting on the arms of his chair, twitched with some suppressed passion. "Does Philip?"

"Oh, yes," the Ragoni lord breathed. "I saw the ship myself. I was in Boltar when it arrived. It was too big to land. It carried another boat the size of a Brusterian longboat. Half a dozen of them rowed to shore in that, but only one got out." He shook his head. "They left as soon as he gave me the letter. They didn't stay to hear that I could not read it. I rode to Peran immediately. Domon, Philip's clerk, was well into his day's bottle when I got there, but it sobered him up in a hurry."

I tried not to stare, shocked by his calling a Vere-trained clerk by his given name. Vere scholars and clerks chose a second name, and were called by that name and their title. I'd picked my great grandfather's, who'd defeated Ludlow, under-king of Eban, to become High King.

But I could understand the clerk's reaction.

"What are Philip's thoughts?" the Roth asked.

"Gather a force, sail east, and attack them first."

East...a tendril of memory stirred.

"What is it?" Lady Elsbeth asked.

Silently I cursed my indiscrete face and her inveterate quickness. "East...sounds right, lady."

"Why?"

I looked out the windows. Beyond Elbs Bay, south and east, lay Bruster. Beyond Bruster, lay Vere. Beyond Vere...who knew? I recalled, now, stopping short in the passage, straining to listen as two scholars chattered around the corner, gossiping about a story the cook's oldest son had heard from one of the new boat slaves about a place far in the eastern waters, somewhere even colder and more mountainous than Bruster. In Vere, eavesdropping had proven a crucial skill. "I overheard the story. I was not told it."

The Roth's forehead creased. Lady Elsbeth was nodding. Lord Orlo was on his feet.

"This is Doctora Bann?" He froze for a moment, then bowed. "Lady, I am pleased to meet you." He paused, again looking at me so intently it might justly be called staring. "I had hoped it would be sooner, and under other circumstances." He moved closer, one hand stretching out towards me. "When your father was arranging your marriage I wanted to offer for you. King Philip would not allow it."

I stepped back, unable to decide if he were serious. "It is as well for you he did not."

"Maybe." His gaze met mine. "But I am not in need of heirs. My lord Philip has plenty of nephews." Black fire glinted in his eyes.

Mockery, then. He wasn't the first to amuse himself by prodding my injuries. "Lord—" I began, trying to contain my annoyance.

"Is there a chair, cousin?" he interrupted. "It's not right to leave her standing like a servant."

The Roth looked both irritated and abashed. I'd never been invited to sit in his presence. Princess and queen I had been but now I was a clerk. A valued, trusted clerk, but a clerk. The Ragoni lord did not wait for an answer. He went to the door, returned with a fourth chair, and brought it to where I stood.

He smelled of travel—horse sweat and saddle leather and half-dried mud, and his own sweat, a muskier, softer scent than the horse's. Beneath all, something else. Like cloves or ginger, but honey-laced. I thought of feast-day dishes, savory and sweet. *Him,* I realized the next moment. It was the aroma of the man himself. I felt myself flushing and took another step back, nearly bumping against the windows.

Strange. His eyes laughed at me but he insisted on greater courtesy than the Roth, whose graciousness towards me was undeniable. It was vexing. But I had more important concerns than trying to plumb the mind of a Ragoni lord. I waited until he returned to his own chair before glancing sidelong at the Roth for his quick nod. With that permission, I sat.

"East makes sense," Lady Elsbeth said.

"Oliver," Lord Orlo said. "That was our thought."

"Yes," the Roth said after a moment.

I looked between them. Who was Oliver?

If my confusion was visible, as was likely, Lady Elsbeth gave no sign. Neither did she explain. "'East' is better than nothing," she said, sliding her toes closer to the brazier and crossing her ankles, "but not much."

"The letter came five days ago," Lord Orlo said. "Philip has already begun preparations for our attack."

The Roth stroked his beard. "That is not an approach I would recommend."

"It's a plan good for nothing but stoking my lord king's pride."

This time I stared openly, at his blunt assessment and that he spoke it to us.

"Is he being discrete?" Hot concern spilled through Lady Elsbeth's outward calm. "If the other kingdoms of Valenna..."

"My lord king says he will ready our forces in secret." Lord Orlo's gaze sought a corner of the room. "But..."

"Subtlety is not known to be a strength of Philip of Ragonne," the Roth said. "You must persuade your king against this foolishness."

"I saw the ship. He didn't." Lord Orlo spread his hands. "If we take the battle to them, I fear they'll cut us down like grass." His fingers tapped his leg. "They may anyway."

"Or we may attack people who have no quarrel with us," Lady Elsbeth said. "If there's land to the east, why should Saradena be the only country in it?"

"The same worry has troubled me." His eyes avoided theirs again. "It does not trouble my king." He looked back at the Roth. "What will Elbany do?"

"Prepare to defend ourselves." The Roth's jaw tightened. "While trying to prevent the attack."

"How?" Lord Orlo got the question out before I did.

The Roth turned to me. "You are going to find Saradena."

Chapter IV

I stiffened, watching for a sneer beneath the Roth's words. His expression was smooth, but nobles were taught from birth to cloak their thoughts in disinterest. Unlike me, most learned the skill. He might mean what he said. Or he might be following Lord Orlo's example and indulging a fit of mockery.

To search for Saradena. To help Elbany. To show my new lord that his trust in me was justified—and my father's rejection hasty. I clenched the arms of my chair, grasping what might be grasped, as if to sit unmoving would mean I did not desire it enough. Surely my lord Roth would not make such an offer in jest.

I clicked my tongue in irritation, but self-directed. The Roth had never made sport of me. Why would he start now? The Ragoni lord had galled my nerves.

Lord Orlo narrowed his eyes. "How?" he said again.

"We must have had contact with them before. Years ago," Lady Elsbeth said. "Otherwise their letter makes no sense."

I gave a quick nod. I'd walked this path already.

The Ragoni lord's head tipped as he considered. "That stands to reason."

"We've forgotten them. But they don't know that."

"Their ships left too quickly. We had, and have, no way to tell them," Lord Orlo said.

"We might remember them...somewhere." The Roth waved a hand at the letters, which Lord Orlo had collected after they'd scattered when he stood. "Something must have been written down. Doctora Bann is no ordinary clerk. If anything survives, she will find it."

"Vere," Lord Orlo said. "You're sending her back to Vere."

"Yes," Roth Douglas said.

Go back to Vere? That was as unwelcome as returning to Ferrant. Or Bruster. I hoped my face did not show my dread, or at least not the depth of it.

"I gather you haven't heard of Saradena before, even at Vere?" Lord Orlo shifted in his seat so that he might look at me full-faced.

"No. But I wasn't looking for it." I would not flinch beneath that crackling gaze. *I would not.*

He tapped his chin, thinking. "Lord...may I propose a change?"

The Roth gestured that he should continue. Lord Orlo's eyes snapped back to me. "Do you trust anyone at Vere?"

An odd question. He must know, or could guess, the scholars had not welcomed their enforced female student. If I loathed them less than Francis of Ferrant—or my father—it was because there were more to divide my attention among. All but one. "Yes. But—"

"Good." He swiveled back to the Roth. "They've only given us a year. Let Doctora Bann ask a scholar she trusts to search Vere so she can look elsewhere."

"Where?" Lady Elsbeth leaned back. "The only books are at Vere."

"As everyone knows. Or at least everyone in the south." He flung a hand at me. He sat across the brazier, well beyond arm's reach, but I jerked back. "Everyone is wrong. As you know."

The Roth looked but did not speak his question. Lady Elsbeth followed his lead but appeared to be chewing her tongue to do so. I felt my face burn. "Yes." I fought the impulse to rise. Standing would seem as if I were guilty of something. "Ferrant." I indulged a furious sidelong glance at the Ragoni lord. "It's not widely known, but Ferrant holds a number of books in the king's palace." *And that bastard Francis would not let me read any of them.* How had Lord Orlo known? Even in Ferrant only a handful of people did.

"I would have thought," the Roth said coldly, "you would mention something that might help us."

"Ferrant's books might—or might not. I have no idea what they contain. I was never—allowed—" I spat the word out like a gristly bite I'd almost choked on, "to read them." It had been the most infuriating of the affronts, large and small, Francis had amused himself by inflicting. He'd taken me to see the three chests, each full of books so old their white leather bindings had gone brown, relocked the chests, and ordered me never to read them, never even to enter the room. I knew better than to try; that was, of course, what he wanted. I should have anyway. But it was a long while before I learned I had no means of pleasing Francis, longer yet before I stopped trying.

And *that* had been the man my father had given me to, and been shamed by when he cast me off.

The Roth was stroking his beard again. I'd been in Elbany long enough to recognize the gesture. He believed himself less clever than his lords and the movement gave him something to do while he deliberated. "No," he said at last. "Since we do not know if Ferrant's books would help, I am not willing to reveal our danger to an old enemy to study them."

"Neither is Ragonne," Lord Orlo said. "Later, if we find nothing..." He shrugged. "We may decide we have no choice—"

"If we find nothing, Elbany might as well risk Ferrant as wait for Saradena," Lady Elsbeth said.

"I had a different suggestion," he went on, eyes sparking like a shoot of fresh flame from seemingly burnt-out coals. "My lord Philip has begun a library for Ragonne."

"Why?" I got the word out half a heartbeat before Lady Elsbeth. "Most nobles disdain reading, but King Philip has said openly that books are good only for kindling."

Roth Douglas raised his eyebrows at the bluntness but did not contradict me.

"Because you are," Lord Orlo said. "My lord king does not wish to be outdone by his backward Elbish relations even in something he scorns." He gave the Roth a small bow. "Pardon the slight, lord. I speak my king's thoughts, perhaps more candidly than I should."

"We were aware before now of Ragonne's opinion," the Roth said. "My mother was allowed to marry an Elbish lord only because no Valenian nobleman would have her."

"I've heard that." The Ragoni lord's gaze flicked towards me, then downward, surprisingly long lashes veiling his eyes. "Not all of us would disdain an indomitable woman."

"Two months ago," he went on before my irritation at his continued teasing had time to flare up again, "my lord king directed his clerk to search his holdings, and inquire discretely among the nobility, to find whatever books were to be found. Domon has been more successful than anyone would have supposed." His gaze stayed pointedly away from me. "He has found forty already."

Forty?

I would not live to see forty books grace Elbany's library, and Philip's clerk had found them scattered around Ragonne like wild turnips. Hope whipped through me. If I began poking through the recesses of Rothbury castle, sent messengers to the lords of Elbany, might there be books to seed our library?

I knew the next moment it was false hope. Books were the products, and now the relics, of calmer, wealthier times. Ragonne had always had more of both. It was no surprise Ragonne had had books; only, perhaps, that so many survived. Elbany had never had the peace or prosperity that would reap a crop of manuscripts. Moreover, the Roth's embryonic library had been gossiped about for a year. If any of the lords had found a book, they would have presented it to him to curry favor.

Lady Elsbeth raised a hand, palm upward. "Philip's clerk found the books. Why can't he search them?" The question, *Why should Elbany's clerk do the work of Ragonne's?*, was implicit, but since they were allies, left so.

"By rights he should," Lord Orlo said. "But it wouldn't be wise."

I remembered what he'd said earlier about Domon being well into his daily bottle when he'd given him the letter. She seemed to recall his words as well. "I see."

"Yes." His voice fell. "I would prefer someone whose brain was not floating in wine."

Or inattentive in any way. He was right. This search would brook no woolgathering. Even the dullest scholar would recognize a book about Saradena. But we were unlikely to find one. A picture of our enemy would have to be pieced together from marginal comments, occasional offhand references, casual comparisons. Just the things an unfocused mind would miss.

"They must be old books," I said.

His eyes glinted with bright, soft fire, the kind that coaxed you to stick your hand in amongst the flames. "Yes."

He understood the temptation he spread before me. He must. This, too, was amusement for him. But his enjoyment at laying the bait did not mean I could ignore it. Books spoke, if you knew how to hear them; carefully kept, they could be read long after their makers had lived, died, and crumbled in their graves. Those voices called to me, made me push my way into Vere despite difficulty and good sense, to hold in my hands the thoughts of dead men. Ragonne's books would not have told their secrets to anyone in living memory. *Assent to the Ragoni's plan and I could read them.*

A smile prowled his lips as he watched me squirm with longing for something so ridiculous, to a nobleman's mind, as dried sheepskin stained with dyed water.

I took a slow breath. "What say you, lord?"

Roth Douglas stroked his beard. "Is there someone you trust at Vere?"

"Yes."

"Send a messenger to him."

I hesitated. "May I write to him instead? A messenger, trusted as he must be, is someone else who would know about the letter, and Saradena."

"Of course." Both his voice and the wave of his hand were brusque, but his impatience was directed at himself. I supposed he found it hard, despite his commitment to his library, to think of sharing information in the unfamiliar method of writing.

"Lord," Lord Orlo said suddenly, "what of Bruster?"

My gaze swiveled to the Ragoni lord.

"What do you mean?" the Roth said.

"Did Bruster receive a letter?"

"We've heard nothing from Bruster," Lady Elsbeth said.

"Strange." Lord Orlo tapped his fingers on the arm of his chair. "Why the three of us, but not our fourth ally?"

I was surprised by the fear, then relief, that sluiced through me. I hated my father. I was never going back. But I was glad, it seemed, that Saradena's threat had overlooked my homeland.

"Maybe we'll understand when we know more about Saradena." Lady Elsbeth looked at me. "We don't know what they want. We could hardly expect to understand why they demand it of Elbany, Ragonne, and Logan, but not Bruster."

Lord Orlo turned his gaze to me as well. "We'll leave at daybreak."

I realized, too late, that riding to Ragonne with him would necessitate *days* in his company.

The books had better be worth it.

Chapter V

Traveling overland to Ragonne usually took a week. We rode into Peran late in the afternoon of the fourth day. Lord Orlo set a brisk pace as we left Rothbury and only quickened it as we went. I was glad. It kept him quiet.

At first, during the necessary slower intervals, he tried to talk to me. I stared over his shoulder, pretending I hadn't heard. It was rude but better than the alternative. For Elbany's sake I could not afford to let him provoke me into saying something unwise and unforgivable.

Avoiding his gaze, turning away when he tried to speak and affect not having noticed, required effort and vigilance. I was glad when we reached the city. Once through the gates, we rode at a walk, but the narrow streets enforced single-file progress. For a time, twisting my head like an owl as I tried to look everywhere at once, I almost forgot about him. I'd never been to Peran and there was plenty to see—and look forward to. King Philip's *palais* was famous. Notorious, to some minds.

No other nobility, let alone a sitting king, made his primary residence in anything but a castle. The *palais* had been planned by Philip's father but left unfinished at his death. Even his detractors acknowledged Philip's loyalty and perseverance in finishing his father's work and living in it. But the warriors of Bruster snorted with laughter whenever they spoke of the *palais*, proof of the madness of Valenians in general, the Ragoni in particular, and Philip above all. I smiled, remembering Anhud's scandalized hiss ("The Ragoni king lives in a house within the city, like a common merchant!"), and examined it as soon as it came into view.

It was certainly one of the most beautiful buildings I had ever seen. Philip's palace would not have been shamed by comparison with the Ferranti castle. Three stories high, of pearl-gray stone that glinted rather than shone in the sunlight. Every protruding surface was carved, as if the building were a sculpture or a banquet subtlety. The corners, the stones between each story, the lintels of the windows and doors, the parapet running along the top were covered in a profusion of curves and spirals. Smiling faces and dancing bodies peeked out among the burgeoning vines of stone.

A second look revealed what the first missed, distracted by the lush decoration. The graven walls were thick and strong. The windows' ornate casings made their small size seem an aesthetic choice. The palace was set back far from the street, a high, guarded wall surrounding its grounds. Despite his neighbors' snickers, the King of Ragonne's home was not defenseless.

As we rode closer, I saw signs of heightened vigilance. More men watched from the wall than would be typical. At least two canvassed the grounds on foot. The main gates were closed. The wicket door in them was opened, but guarded by an armed man on either side. An air of tension hung over all, as if the warriors were waiting for something but weren't sure what or how to recognize it if it came. In the surrounding streets people continued their normal lives; Philip had been successful so far in keeping the letter secret. Ultimately this would be impossible, for Elbany and Logan as well as Ragonne. Rumors would already be brewing. People had seen the ships; they would feel the worry. But the longer the secret held, the better.

The guards recognized Lord Orlo and hastened to open the gates. I found myself holding my breath as we rode through. The jittery atmosphere was contagious. And not surprisingly: anxiety bred more of itself. I scolded myself when I realized, exhaling slowly and deliberately. Doctore Mustorn's voice rang between my ears. 'You cannot govern others until you can govern yourself.' My father had prevailed upon his clerk to teach himself and his children to read, write, and figure. The clerk had been reluctant, but my father gave him to understand that it was not a request to be granted but a command to be fulfilled, and furthermore, he was Reud-born before all else. Once he'd grappled with his conflicting loyalties, he became a faithful teacher, instructing us not just in letters and numbers, but in what he could remember from Vere's books, while my father discretely acquired a few volumes of our own. In the end, my father had been so pleased with Doctore Mustorn's work that when the clerk died he was honored with a high noble's burial. I was glad he had not lived to see my forced, failed marriage and shameful homecoming.

Lord Orlo touched my mare's neck. I hadn't seen him dismount, and I twitched back involuntarily, trying to ignore his distracting honeyed-clove scent. "Wait here. Let me see my lord Philip alone first."

I nodded and he left. I patted the mare's neck. If Lord Orlo managed to persuade Philip, it'd be useless if I couldn't settle to work.

'You cannot govern others until you can govern yourself,' This time it was Utor's voice I heard reciting the lesson. *Utor.* After our mother's death, my oldest brother cared for me. He made sure I washed, dressed in clean clothes, ate properly. He braided my hair, and later, taught me how to do our family braid myself. He showed me how to ride, and practiced knife fighting and throwing with me until by the time of my marriage only he could best me in a bout, although often not by much. When I went to Ferrant for the triumphant—for Bruster—match our father had arranged, it was Utor I missed most profoundly—and after my humiliating return, him I faced most reluctantly. "There will always be a place for you in Reud," he had said. But they had in no way wanted me there, cause and reminder of the mortification of Bruster's pride.

What was taking Lord Orlo so long?

I leaned back in my saddle, stretching. My legs and back were tattling that my library work left less time for riding than when I'd lived as a Brusterian princess. I suspected I wasn't feeling it in my rump yet only because it was numb. I tipped my head, trying to ease my stiffening shoulders, but straightened when I saw Lord Orlo across the courtyard.

No matter what Philip decided, I'd be away from Lord Orlo soon. *Good.* He was undeniably a comely man, almost as handsome as Francis. It was a pity his manners were nearly as bad. *Francis.* Dangerous waters, and pointless to venture into. If I closed my eyes, the warm May breeze on the back of my neck could almost have been his breath.

I did not close my eyes. I hardly dared blink until the moment passed.

"My king is not enthusiastic." He put a hand under my mare's nose and she crunched a carrot he'd acquired during his time in the *palais.* "But he will allow it. He will not halt his other preparations."

"But—"

"I know." His voice became even quieter. "It's enough for now. I'll return to that problem later. I must get back to Kolon. It's not good to be away so long." He took the reins of his horse from his retainer.

"I hope we meet again." He bowed his head. "My best wishes for your stay in Ragonne." He clicked to his horse and moved away, his men following.

***

"Ah. The Doctora." Philip did not rise.

"Lord." I bowed, linking my fingers tight behind my back. Without a doubt Philip of Ragonne was going to harrow my patience.

It had already been chafed. I had been hustled into the king's presence without time to wash, without refreshment, without hospitality of any sort. The *palais'* front doors opened onto wide stairs leading to the upper floors. I had tried not to stare. To my knowledge, nothing like it existed anywhere else in the Three Lands. As broad as I was tall, the stairs occupied a staggering amount of space, angling up to the next floor rather than spiraling compactly. Here, the builder had allowed style to over-ride sense. You would need twenty men to defend those stairs!

My astonishment had turned into irritation as I was led past them to a much smaller set of stairs at the rear of the palace. The servants' stairs, I realized as we climbed.

This room was Philip's working space. Another snub. The *palais* had a lovely reception hall. I had walked through it on the way to the back stairs. Was the insult meant for me personally, or for the Roth? I inhaled, reaching for control if not real calm. Maybe he was hoping I would react badly and give him an excuse to send me back to Elbany, shaming both myself and the Roth, and denying me the chance to see his books. I thought of those manuscripts and shut my teeth.

He sat silent, apparently watching for signs I had taken offense. Knowing that made my annoyance easier to suppress. At last my fingers relaxed.

A full minute passed before he spoke. Much as I would have liked to examine the room more closely, I did not dare look away from him; it would have given graver insult than anything he had offered me, perhaps enough to demand my departure. But his chair alone provided ample distraction. It was rich, even gaudy: high-backed, its arms formed like stalking panthers, with Ragonne's device carved into its back above his head, brightly painted in green and red. It was not his throne; I had seen that in the formal reception hall. But this humbler seat was grander than any the Roth owned.

"Lord Orlo requested that I allow you to search the books Domon found for information about our new adversary." He was cannier than I'd expected, not saying 'Saradena' unnecessarily although no ears but ours were present.

"Yes, lord. Lord Orlo and my lord the Roth decided it could add valuable knowledge to our coffers."

He waved a hand. "Our new enemy means to attack. What more do we need to know?" He glanced towards the windows as if his thoughts were wandering. It would be foolhardy to trust that, but I allowed a portion of my attention to go to the windows as well. The palace enclosed an interior courtyard and this room overlooked it. The windows, larger than those on the lower and external walls of the palace, were open. A light wind feathered in, and I could smell apple blossoms.

"We must attack them first."

I bit down. It wasn't my place to debate the merits of this plan with him. "Even so, lord, surely it would be helpful to know as much as we can about the enemy."

He shrugged. "Perhaps. What is certain is that the stronger we are, the better. If we attack in surprise and in strength, we can overwhelm them before they realize what is happening."

My patience splintered. "I have heard Lord Edwy used to say the best battle is one you don't have to fight. By learning about our enemy we might avoid a war with them."

"Edwy was not as clever as many believed. The Roth is new to his station. It makes him hesitate where a stronger man would strike." Philip drew himself up. "I will strike."

Behind my back my hands curled into fists. "Yes, lord."

He looked surprised. I took advantage of his silence. "When may I begin, lord?"

"As soon as you like." His smile said he believed he'd bested me. "Someone will show you to your room, then to the library."

"Thank you, lord."

The smile broadened. "Given how anxious you are to get to work, your presence will not be required at dinner tonight. Or any other night."

Another insult. I was to eat in the kitchen with the servants. I clung to the shreds of my temper with both hands. "That will be most convenient, lord."

"One more thing. Our clerk has become...indisposed—"

I suppressed a snort with difficulty, doubting I managed to keep my face even. Lord Orlo had said the clerk was a drunkard.

"—and is not always able to keep our records properly. While you are here, I expect you to assist him in these duties." Philip folded his hands.

From that smooth movement I knew he understood how offensive his demand was and he reveled in making it. I was there on a desperate search, trying to save his home and mine from an unknown but obviously powerful enemy. He insisted I keep his drunken clerk's accounts. If rage could set a man ablaze, Philip of Ragonne would have burnt where he sat. I nodded stiffly.

"Very good," he said, satisfaction full in his voice. "I am glad we understand each other. But know this: war is coming. I will tolerate my cousin's foolishness so long as it does not interfere with my preparations." His eyes flicked away, dismissing me with more completeness than simply giving permission to leave. "You may go."

CHAPTER VI

I followed the servant, humiliation and wrath squeezing my throat. My fingers leapt to my belt knife but I pulled them away. The Roth would not thank me for killing his cousin. Even this one.

Besides, if I were to kill a king...

***

I had not believed what was happening, even as I watched it happen. I had marked the woeful anniversary of our marriage by sitting up alone, wondering what would become of me. The five childless years required to show barrenness were complete. I watched the moon rise, wane, and set, saw the change of the guards on the wall at middle night. Later, the eastern sky sprouted light like mold on week-old bread, misplaced and forgotten behind the water jug.

The sun had been up for two hours when a maidservant came to pack my belongings. I had not summoned her. She bobbed an uneasy bow and did not look at me. She worked with care, folding my things neatly, but only those items I had brought with me. Every shift and gown Francis had given me remained. I wondered which of his mistresses he meant to bestow them upon.

Not long after noontide, there had come a rap upon the door. Francis' steward stepped inside without waiting to be called. The arrogance of the action was customary. The compassion on his long face was not. Dread that had been fermenting in my gut since the night before foamed and rose as I wondered what Francis had planned that moved his haughty steward to pity. "You are sent for, lady."

Lady. Not *Queen.* I knew what was coming, what I had expected since the maid packed my things.

I thought I knew. I didn't.

We did not go to the stable but the hall, and I understood then that I had been wrong. I was not to be sent home quietly.

The hall was full when we arrived. It seemed as if every noble in Ferrant, his wife, and heirs, every wealthy merchant and his apprentices, every servant who could slip away from his duties and pretend to wait upon the king's guests crowded Francis' formal feasting hall, three times as large as my father's.

The steward took me to the court herald and disappeared from my side like a shadow at noon.

"Maudlin of Bruster," the herald intoned, the high ceiling booming my name—my old name—through the hall like drumbeats.

"Let her approach," Francis called.

I heard the whispers of a thousand garments, but no throats, as the crowd drew apart to let me pass. The burden of their eyes dragged like a wet cloak.

Francis wore a gold-embroidered silk tunic and fine linen trousers. An ermine-lined cloak hung over all, so long it draped the arms of his throne and brushed the floor. His left hand rested on the head of a boy of about five, standing at his knee. Another boy, perhaps three, held the older's hand. A woman, as lavishly dressed as the king, sat to his right. On her lap, she held a third boy, more than a year old but not quite two.

"Sire." I gave him a queen's bow. Small foolhardy gesture of rebellion.

Francis said nothing. His eyes met mine like sword upon shield. There had never been love within them. Contempt, always. Derision had never left his look, not even when he came to my bed to take me in duty and his own vile amusement. When his eyes darkened in his pleasure, disdain stayed.

I would like to think I fought him then, stare to stare, fought him though we stood unmoving, a clash of wills alone. But in truth, few heartbeats passed before I let my eyes drop. There was no path to triumph for me here, not even a way to leave with my honor intact.

I knelt, as any supplicant before the king, as he clearly wanted.

"What do you wish, Maudlin of Bruster?"

He summoned me before him, then spoke as if I had come to beg a boon. *That you might fall dead where you sit, you bastard son of a goatherd.*

"As the king wishes, sire." I spoke in a normal voice, and from my kneeling position, it was unlikely anyone, perhaps not even Francis himself, heard me.

"To be released from our marriage bonds?" His words reverberated through the hall. "That is well. It is good we are agreed. I also wish this. Five years have passed, and you have not given me an heir. Your barrenness is proven. More—" His voice rose. "I take it as a sign that my lords who urged against this alliance, whose advice I ignored in favor of the Brusterians' enticements, spoke true. This match was so unfit that the royal blood of Ferrant refused to mingle with base Brusterian. A horse might more easily produce offspring with a sow."

Murmurs ran through the crowd, like the rush of water in a rill after a sudden rain. I strained to listen, wondering if he had gone too far and lost the temper of the hall.

One burst of open laughter. Then another. The hall burst, a torrent of approving mirth echoing from the walls, the arching ceiling ringing with it.

Francis rose, the oldest boy stepping aside hastily. The crowd quieted. He held out his hand to me.

I dared enough to look up, feeling my eyebrows pull together as I tried to guess what shame he meant to inflict now and make it seem my choice. Finally he seemed to comprehend my confusion. He pulled the ring I had given him, the one my mother had presented to my father upon their marriage and he had worn until her death. Understanding at last, I fumbled to slide his from my finger.

I dropped it on his outstretched palm. It hit the other with a small clang I saw as much as heard. He lifted his hand.

"The ill-conceived," he paused to allow the crowd to chuckle appreciatively, "marriage between Francis, King of Ferrant, and Maudlin of Bruster, is at an end, through the just cause of her barrenness. The fault is hers, and hers alone." One hand gestured expressively at the boys beside him. They bore his stamp like so many silver pennies. "I am free to take another wife. Upon the urging of my lords, I choose Hilde, daughter of the lord of Nilsom—"

In the tail of my eye I saw a red-faced man nodding vigorously, smiling. The new-made lord of Nilsom. Yesterday he had been a fishmonger, happy to pander his daughter to the king. Francis turned, holding out his other hand to her. She rose, settling the smallest boy on her hip. He took up his ring, yet warm from my finger, and slid it onto hers, then gave her my father's ring to put upon his own.

Holding her hand, he drew her forward. "Queen Hilde."

At his gesture, the boys stepped to his side. "Prince Henri. Prince Georg." He jostled the babe on Hilde's hip. "Prince Magne."

"Our queen! Queen Hilde of Ferrant!" the crowd shouted, and continued to shout. "Prince Henri. Prince Georg. Prince Magne!" Francis let them, until the walls and ceiling rang once more. Finally he held up his hand. They quieted. He directed the new queen back to her chair, and her sons followed.

"You have leave to depart," he said to me.

"As soon as my lord wishes," I said. "Are horses and attendants ready?"

"Why should I spare either horses or attendants to guard that which has no worth?" he said.

Why should I spare either horses or attendants to guard that which has no worth? His words echoed in my head like the crowd's shouts had echoed in the hall. I had heard them every day since, had seen them behind my eyelids when I tried to sleep, had thought of them when I dressed each morning as if they were written on the soles of my boots.

I rose slowly from numbed knees, bowed, and left. I had enough wit remaining to slip back to my rooms to take my best boots although they had been made in Ferrant, empty the bag that had been packed for me, and visit the storerooms to fill it with cheese, apples, and twice-baked bread.

It was a long walk from Ferrant to Logan, the closest of our allied nations, where I begged a Brusterian boat captain to take me to Reud.

★★★

Francis had been eminently worth killing. And, perhaps, my father...?

I had grappled that question before but was no closer to an answer. He had made the match with Francis to strengthen Bruster from a provincial power to a force within the larger political world of the Three Lands. The failure of the marriage, *my* failure, had shattered my father's ambitions.

My attention jerked back to my surroundings. Why were we

still going downstairs? The Black Keep could have fit into one of the palace's upper floors, and there were lower levels too? What did they do with it all?

The first underground level clearly held the kitchen. My nose filled with the smell of the palace's approaching supper, and I remembered I hadn't eaten since morning. So close to our destination, we had decided not to stop at mid-day. If the aroma was anything to judge by, the household's cook was excellent.

The servant went on, descending the odd angled stairs. They were narrower than the ostentatious set at the front of the palace, less than half their width, but they would still be more difficult to defend than proper spiraled steps. I began to be alarmed. They could *not* keep books down here. "Where are we going?"

The woman looked around. "To your quarters, lady."

Ah. I let my breath out. A room in the lower levels was annoying but unsurprising. "Where are the books?"

"They're here too." I followed her into a passage. "For your convenience King Philip assigned you a room on the same floor as the library." She opened a door. "Your room." She indicated another door to the left, slightly open. "The books are in there." She twisted her hands together. "May I go, lady? It's almost supper time. I'm needed in the kitchen."

I took two steps towards the second door, sniffing.

The woman repeated her question. Not really listening, I nodded, taking another step. I smelled mold coming from the library.

***

Inside, seated at a table, was...the clerk?

When Brusterian bards word-painted a fat and slovenly fool, they might have been thinking of this fellow. A manuscript lay before him, an open wine bottle and a loaf beside it, the piece in his hand dropping crumbs. Onto the book. For this offense, eating or drinking at a table where a book sat, any student in my library, as in Vere, would have been switched.

He belched. "What do you want, girl? You lost?"

Anger, roused by Philip and banked rather than extinguished, burst back into open flame. It was almost a relief to have this deserving and non-kingly target. "I am Doctora Maudlin Bann, Vere-trained clerk, and librarian to the Roth of Elbany. I have been sent by my lord to consult Philip of Ragonne's books. You will show me to those books and," I let my voice drop, "you will cease using them as table linen."

He scratched his belly with his free hand. Something rumbled. I felt my nose wrinkle when the stench reached me. I waited, watching him, thinking of how hard I'd fought for the learning he shunted away.

He blinked, saying nothing. Finally he pushed his chair back and stood. "Be off, wench. You're lost. And a liar." He moved around the table. "Vere does not teach girls. Everyone knows that."

His speech was clearer than I'd expected. I narrowed my eyes, not taking my gaze from him.

He leered, stepping closer. "Long as you're here..." His hand was at his belt.

As was mine. My knife was out, the blood pounding hot in my ears. One more step. Even Philip could not object. It would be a favor. Ragonne could request a real clerk.

"The scholars taught *me*. And before them, my father's arms-master." The point of my blade hovered between us. "Everyone also knows Brusterians are unmatched with the knife."

Some caution seeped through. He took a step back. "Now, listen..."

I held my knife steady. "The books?"

Footsteps and a shuffling of parchment startled us both. Through a doorway to my left came a much younger man, carrying a pile of books and loose pages.

His lips rounded in surprise but the next moment his expression smoothed. "Good day, lady."

I was impressed. Even in Bruster, a bared knife was usually worth mention.

"King Philip sent word you had come," he continued, "but I didn't expect you today."

"Get your own, Hal," the older man growled.

The younger man set his armload on the table. "I see you've already met Doctora Bann." He stepped closer, looking into Domon's eyes. "You remember. The clerk from Elbany? The king sent word she's to have access to our books." He touched his elbow, guiding the larger man back to his chair. "Finish your supper, Domon. I'll see that the king's commands are fulfilled."

"The king." Domon allowed himself to be seated. "The king

my brother wants me to find books." His hand went to his bottle. "And read them." He patted the other's hand. "You're a good man."

Hal tapped the book. "How is this one?"

Domon shrugged. "Another history." He turned back to the book. With some difficulty, I resisted slapping the bottle out of his hand. The drunkenness was unsettling but not appalling: in Vere the scholars were known to indulge. But endangering a manuscript was unforgivable.

The young man picked up his pile again. "If you would follow me, lady."

***

I stood in the doorway, speechless at the sight and smell of that inner room.

There were no windows. The whiff of mildew I'd caught outside the first door was a choking reek here. The stench of rot mingled with the smell of damp stone and candle smoke. An astonishing amount of smoke from two flickering candles. Dark and damp. The slow death of books.

I scanned the room once more, horror ebbing somewhat as closer attention revealed efforts to preserve the books despite their surroundings. The room was neatly arranged, and neatly kept. Shelves lined the walls. Shelves of the proper size. The carpenters of Ragonne, at least, knew their craft. I'd not seen any like them before, but they were well designed for their location, made not of solid boards but narrow slats, minimizing each book's contact with the surface. The volumes lay well apart, touching neither each other nor the wall. Air circulated as freely as possible. Nonetheless, the books were suffering. I could see warped leaves.

So many...

Lord Orlo's estimate had been low, or his information old. Shelves stood along each wall except for a portion occupied by a worktable, sixteen sets in all. Each held about twenty books. Three hundred and twenty. A grandson, more likely a great grandson, of the Roth might see as many books in Elbany's library. It was nearly one tenth of Vere's.

It was dreadful but understandable that books might be scattered through the castles of Ragonne's lords, moldering in neglect and ignorance, but to have searched for them, only to put them in the cellar like last year's apples...Philip had gathered them to say he had a library before Elbany's had even begun. That accomplished, he let them rot. I began to mutter in Brusterian, then stopped. I didn't know anything vile enough to call him.

"May I speak plainly, lady?" The young man set his pile on the table.

"Please do," I managed.

"My lord Philip collected these because the Roth is creating a library—"

"That's what Lord Orlo said."

"Then you already knew..." he paused, weighing his words, "it was unlikely they were kept well."

Or should have, I admitted inwardly.

"My lord Philip does not want his library to cost anything. He laughs at how much the Roth has spent and doesn't have any books yet." He held up a hand as I sputtered. "Doing a thing properly is costly. I know. But King Philip does not desire to do this properly. Merely to have it. More truthfully, to *say* he does. This is one of the reasons my lord is irked by your arrival. He wants to boast of his library abroad, not have anyone read the books."

I glanced towards the outer room. "He said Philip told him to read them."

"Yes." He smiled but it was not a pleasant smile. "That is my lord's other reason for his library. To keep Domon busy."

"He's incompetent. Why does Philip keep him?"

"You heard him..." He let his words dribble away.

The King my brother wants me to find books... I sighed. "A natural brother?"

"The old king must have been..." He deliberated, then shrugged, apparently not finding words both accurate and tactful. "My lord has a number of bastard siblings. The head cook is another. The resemblance is there, if you look. But my lord makes no secret of it." His gaze dropped. "He seems to be proud of his father's...prowess."

I thought of Francis, flaunting his mistresses, preening as they presented their sons. "I see."

"Do you?"

I gave him a sharp look.

"Forgive me, lady," he said. "But I saw your face just now. You wanted him squealing like a speared boar."

I met his gaze. Domon was a pig. I didn't repent of wanting to stick him like one. I should, I knew. *Not such a safe target after all.* Good thing I'd checked my temper. Good thing Hal had arrived when he did.

"I understand," he said. "He's arrogant, slovenly, and demanding. He's been known to strike the servants." His chin ticked up. I saw a fading bruise high on his cheekbone. "He's worst to the women, free with his hands and willing to do more. He's not as drunk as he usually seems."

I remembered how anxious the servant woman had been to leave.

"It will be tricky for you," he continued, "here in the library, where he typically is."

"Where does he sleep?"

"Domon is family. He has a room upstairs." He tapped his fingers, rustling the parchments. "But he prowls the lower floors, looking for servant women. Lock your door."

I fingered the hilt of my belt knife. "I can take care of myself."

He looked startled. "So I assumed. But whatever provocations Domon offers, you must not kill him."

"Why not?" I knew why, but the question burst out anyway. "Philip doesn't deserve the favor, but favor it would be."

"I've been told he wasn't always like this. Despite Domon's embarrassments, and there have been many, my lord loves his brother, or at least the brother he remembers. He wants to give him every chance to change."

I sniffed. "I doubt he will."

"Probably not, but it speaks highly of the king that he hopes for it."

I uncurled my fingers. "Very well. But if Domon tries to touch me again, he will not live to think better of it."

"I know how difficult he is. But the family sent him to Vere for good reason. When he is clear, he is clever." He went quiet. "I feel sorry for him. Sometimes I even like him. I would not see him killed." He shrugged. "But I like most people. Even you. I think."

Was he laughing at me? "Who are you?" I asked, more curtly

than I'd meant.

"My apologies." He bowed. "I should have said earlier. I am Hal, lady. Domon's assistant. And his keeper."

"He needs one."

"Yes. As his drinking worsens, so do his problems. Most recently he stole a horse."

"Philip has no horses for his brother to ride?" My gaze wandered over his shoulder, back to the shelves of books.

"This wasn't just any horse. The King of Avice sent a messenger to my lord king. A favored messenger. He rode a Verduni stallion."

My attention returned to him in an instant. The fastest horses in the world—the *known* world—grazed in the green pastures of Verdun. "Domon stole a *Verduni stallion?*"

"And rode him until he dropped."

I winced. The Verduni did not part readily with their horses, particularly stallions. No one in Bruster, not even the High King, owned a Verduni horse. I couldn't imagine how the King of Avice had acquired one. Let alone what he paid for it. I felt sorry for the stallion—I'd never even seen a Verduni-bred horse up close—but not for Philip.

A worrisome thought wriggled. What message had the King of Avice wanted to get to Ragonne so quickly? Did it have something to do with the Saradenian letters? Had other kingdoms of Valenna received them? Had they heard rumors?

"There was an uproar," he said mildly.

"I should think so," I said, not mildly.

"It was best to get Domon out of sight. So my lord created the library." One finger flicked dust from the topmost parchment sheet in his pile. "If Domon makes more trouble, the king will have to send him away. Only so much can be smoothed over. This is his last chance. I am to help him."

I barked a laugh. "Your task is even less likely to succeed than mine."

His gaze went keen. "What is your task?"

I shut my teeth, too late. "My responsibility."

He held up his hands. "As you say, lady."

I let my breath out slowly, grateful his control was better than mine, and looked around again, wondering where to begin. "Has Domon taught you something of reading? Do you have any idea what is here?"

"I already knew how to read," he said, so casually I had to listen to his words again in my head to catch what he had said. "My orders are to keep Domon out of sight and out of trouble, but when I'm here, I may work with the books." He gestured towards the shelves. "The king allowed me to have his carpenters build these."

"Your pardon, Doctore—" I began.

He made a brushing motion. "I'm not Vere trained."

Fascinating. I fought the urge to ask where he had learned. If there was a secret school somewhere, as the Roth desired for Elbany, it wasn't my concern. Nor was he likely to tell me.

He pulled one of the chairs back from the table. "Would you like to sit, lady?"

When I had, he seated himself as well. "Domon can be difficult to keep track of." His fingers rustled the parchment sheets. "The work has gone slowly."

"What are those?"

"Leaves that have come loose from their books. I've been trying to find the ones they belong to."

"Why were you carrying them around?"

"Domon is often ready to leave by this time of day. I was straightening up when I heard you." His gaze flicked to a cupboard, standing beside a doorway I hadn't noticed in the gloom. "I was about to put them away. It's best to not leave loose parchment lying around." He gave an embarrassed cough. "There's a privy by the storeroom."

Using leaves torn from books in the jakes? Such things were spoken of in Vere in the same hushed tones Brusterian children told one another tales of the *leoyong*. But while rarely seen, and hence often assumed to be legendary, our mountain cats were real, as I had reason to know.

As was this nightmare, apparently. I shuddered, thinking of hands ripping pages from their binding, fouled parchment falling down the garderobe shaft.

"Until Mistress Baynor became head cook, the kitchen staff used to pull out pages to wrap pies. And fish."

"You're making that up."

He lifted one shoulder. "Sometimes I'm surprised they had any pages left."

I sat up straighter. "Wait. Did you find some of the books here? In this room?"

"Domon did. That room," he pointed to the second doorway, "was being used as an unofficial wine cellar. The real one is two floors down. Domon discovered this, of course. Among the bottles were books. Old, he said. Very old."

I felt my tongue flick out to wet my lips.

"They're in bad shape, lady," he said. "The damp is worse in there, and the books were on the floor."

Philip, Francis, Lord Orlo, the Roth, my father. Ragonne, Elbany, Saradena. All fled. Thought and vision narrowed to the width of that doorway. *Very old books.*

"—found them but could not read them," someone was saying.

"What?" I pulled my mind back. A fear too horrible to fully grasp iced through me. I swore in Brusterian. "Are you saying he threw them away?"

"No. They're here. But—"

Relief flooded me. "That's enough for now."

He cocked his head. Listening for Domon, I realized after a moment's puzzlement. Satisfied, he nodded. "I put them aside to work on after I catalogued the others —"

"Cataloguing? You've been cataloguing? Using what method? How—"

"I—"

"Start at the beginning," I waved a hand. "It'll be faster. What was it like when you arrived?"

He closed his eyes. Was he recalling the library's earlier state or seeking the patience to deal with me? "All the rooms on this floor were used for storage. At least one still is. If the harvest is particularly good, so is the room you've been given for sleeping."

I nodded, remembering what he said earlier about a storeroom.

"After Domon found the books and my lord decided to create his library, I was assigned to Domon. How King Philip learned I can read, I don't know."

My estimation of Philip grudgingly rose a notch. In this at least he showed competence. *You must know your men's strengths before you can use them.* I heard Utor's voice again. It had been one of our lessons.

"I took the books outside to dry—"

There was a noise from the outer room, like a bottle dropped but not broken.

It was several minutes before he returned.

"I'm sorry, lady. I need to escort Domon to his room. Once he's settled, I can see to our supper. You must be hungry, and the head cook is a good woman to know."

Another royal bastard, I remembered. And I was ravenous, I realized once my attention had been diverted from the manuscripts. But everyone in the Three Lands, nobility included, had known hunger often enough to learn to ignore it when necessary.

I looked at the shelves. One hunger bowed before a greater. If he left, I would be alone with the books. Many, many books. "I'll wait. Take your time."

Chapter VII

A lightning chill flashed down my back.

I could count on my thumbs the times I'd been alone with a book.

I picked up the nearest with hands that were steady only because I stared at them sternly until they stopped trembling, not wanting to risk dropping a manuscript.

I untied the thongs holding the book shut. The binding, probably once the creamy white of undyed leather but now aged to autumn brown, creaked as it opened. My fingers savored the feel of leather and parchment, and I inhaled, pulling in the warm smell of the binding, the musty aroma of long-closed book, the acrid underscent of ink. Three deep breaths passed before I turned my gaze to the words, letting the moment linger.

One saved the tastiest dish for last, even on a feast day.

In theory, scripts were standardized for easier reading. In practice, every scribe had his own quirks, varying enough that coming to an unfamiliar hand was difficult. Hands differed most in the letters 's' and 'r', and in abbreviations. A new manuscript always gave a moment of panic, the page looming with meaningless marks.

The moment passed, the sea of ink settling into recognizable words. The fear heightened the thrill as meaning returned. It was, perhaps, how warriors felt, staring across the field as they ran towards their enemies.

I turned over a leaf, then another. Fascinating. Strange, but fascinating.

Not so much for what it said, but what it was. Records of the king of Ragonne's means. What he had collected at harvest time, what goods and cash-money had been paid in taxes, what the King's household spent.

How old was it? Each kingdom's clerk kept accounts, but on wax tablets, to be wiped clean and reused at the end of the season. Sheep were to shear, and, sometimes, to eat; even then, only the skins too damaged for other uses were given for parchment. Here, too, I knew the depth of the Roth's commitment to his library. For our parchment he let me choose healthy, undamaged animals from his flocks.

I put it back and reached for another. It also held accounts. Returning it, I stepped to the next shelf. The volume I chose there also contained accounts. A quick look into another manuscript confirmed my suspicion: both shelves were full of account books.

Amazing.

Written records, kept for years...a new king could know what had been collected before, what spent. Lords often sent a new king less revenue, and merchants tried to charge more. With these a new king could prevent such trials of his authority. A king could tell if his steward skimmed money. He could see if a part of his holdings produced less than it was wont, and rest the land for a year.

And these treasures were of no worth here but as jakes wipes.

I moved on, suddenly urgent, wanting to touch as many manuscripts as possible before Hal returned.

Vitae. The next shelf, as well as the three after, held bio-graphies. Of Ragoni lords, if my cursory search told true. Vere held few *vitae*, perhaps fewer than Domon had collected from scattered corners and stored in the cellar. Dual pangs of loss and envy prickled. *We have become barbarians.*

The next two shelves, angling together into the corner, held histories. If I were going to find information about Saradena, it would be here. I flexed my fingers, trying to still the giddy whirl behind my eyes. So many books, but they might yield nothing. If the ones I'd glanced at were representative, they were Ragoni history. I saw no mention of other countries of the Three Lands; how likely was it Saradena would be discussed?

But hope warms quickly, and cools slowly.

I froze, a book in my hand. Much as I would have liked to begin reading the histories at once, it made better sense to continue exploring the library, to understand how Hal had divided and shelved the astonishing collection, before embarking on that search. Reluctantly I lowered the book.

The next two shelves proved a disappointment. Lengthy and poor verse tributes to the victories of Ragoni lords. The sort of

thing preserved now only in the memories of harpists, and mercifully forgotten if they died before taking an apprentice. The two
following seemed to be the 'everything else' section. Each book I
picked up was different. The first volume contained proverbs a
nobleman collected to instruct his son. Another was a bound
volume of letters from a husband, away with his lord at war,
giving his wife advice about managing their lands. In another a
mother described to her soon-to-be-married daughter the
running of a household. One told about the making of medicines
and the healing properties of herbs. Two were volumes about
how to cook various dishes.

Recipes. Written down! I tried to imagine it: A book in the
kitchen, with the cook, spoon in hand, reading what to add next
to the pot. Ludicrous.

Yet here was the book, open to a page describing a lentil and
mushroom stew. My stomach rumbled plaintively in response.
What wonders were here! For these books to have been made...in
the past, many people must have been able to read and write, not
just scholars of Vere and Vere-trained clerks.

I was almost grateful enough to be civil to Domon.

How long had Hal been gone? There were shelves left. I
stepped to the next one and picked up a volume.

Oh.

Ragonne's books had already exceeded my expectations,
indeed surpassed my wildest hopes. I'd been intrigued by the
account books, impressed by the *vitae*, inspired by the histories,
and stunned by the miscellany section—but this book, if the
whole shelf were like it, was almost painful in its possibilities.

It was a description of a man's travels.

I put it back and took up another.

It was also a narration of a journey.

Travel books...

Even more than the histories, *here* was potential. Not for a
marginal reference or an offhand comment either. There could be
whole sections, maybe an entire manuscript, about Saradena. The
hope that had uncurled like a spring seed sent down slender
white roots.

How many? The more there were, the more likely one
among them would have something about Saradena. I hurried to
the next shelf.

What...?

Stepping back, I exploded in my native language, castigating the lineage, intelligence, and personal habits of those responsible for wasting parchment on...*this*. Only years of training ensured I did not pitch the manuscript across the room.

I closed the cover, breathing in. I didn't know books like this existed. Disgusting. And someone had drawn accompanying pictures in the margins! I put it back, reaching hesitantly for another. Surely not? But it was just as lurid. And the pictures were bigger. Foul misuse of literacy. I felt the affront as an almost physical blow.

I moved to the next shelf, the last before the doorway into the third room. It, too, was filled with books of vile nature and questionable value.

I hurried away from the shelf as if it were a contagion that might spread. Hal must have looked at *every one* as he catalogued. My stomach twisted, hunger fled. At least I wouldn't have to. These books could have nothing to offer my search.

On the other side of the doorway into the third room stood the cupboard where Hal said he kept loose parchments. I moved towards it, shuddering again at the idea of them finding their way to the jakes. *Barbarians.*

Then I thought of the books filling the two shelves I'd just left. More worthless books than I would live to see good ones in my library. Perhaps the past, or least parts of it, was not as civilized as their literacy implied.

I reached for the cupboard door but did not open it, my attention caught by the shelf on its other side. Hal said he put the first books Domon had found there, the ones so badly damaged they were unreadable.

Were they really?

Domon was Vere-trained but worked hard to drown his learning. Hal could read, but how thoroughly had he been taught?

Maybe...

I lifted one as if it were a basket of eggs. The cover was brown, cracked, and in places, flaking. The leather strap resisted, then creaked in startled protest as I loosened it to open the cover.

Mold and water had ravaged. Bugs and mice had bitten deep. The outer leaves were mangled beyond hope. But the inner were more or less intact.

Years had faded the script and darkened the parchment. It was difficult to tell where writing ended and bare page began, particularly in the shadowy light of the stingy candles. Writing unlike anything I'd seen before, miniscule, close together, with little space between the words. There had been illuminations but the gold was almost gone, revealing the ink dots beneath showing the pattern for the painter.

Gradually the unfamiliar script began to uncurl. Tangled ink separated and became letters. Letters grouped and became words. *I can read it...*

But merely words. My mind clattered as I grazed my fingers along the lines of script. Individual words, here and there, I could read. But I couldn't understand the meaning. The sense of the language stole away like a fox through the underbrush.

I frowned, trying to remember what Hal had said. I'd thought he said they were too damaged to read but, thinking back, realized otherwise. *Domon could not read them.* I looked at the book again, and burgeoning thrill crowded out annoyance. These books had been written so long ago the very words of the world had changed. To study them, to learn to read them...it was a challenge worthy of a scholar of Vere. Not just a clerk, the *doctore* sent to kings to keep what few records they desired, but a *magistre*, the scholars who spent their lives reading and learning at Vere.

If I could figure out how to read them, what might they contain?

The thought was as breathtaking as the task. How old were they? Hundreds of years? How many hundreds? They were written in an earlier form of the language now known as Valenian, but they might well be older than Valenna itself, their covers browning before Otto forged the northern kingdoms into an empire.

Older than Otto...

I closed my eyes, fighting the need to sit down. These were not just the words of dead men, calling across the years. They were all that remained of a lost world, one in which the name of Otto Tyrannus had never frightened an Elbish child nor emboldened a Valenian lord, when Elbany did not exist because it had not yet been required.

A horrid thought struck. Maybe only this one was not thoroughly destroyed. Maybe the others were damaged beyond all reading.

I returned the manuscript as quickly as care would allow, and with the same rushed caution looked through others. They were the same, cover and first quire rotted or gnawed away, but the inner gatherings remained legible. Indeed, many were in better condition than the first, their ink still dark and crisp.

The book was in my hand. I could take it to the table. Maybe the language would not be difficult to unravel. Maybe Domon's wine-addled brain couldn't sort it out but a clear mind could seize hold soon enough. Maybe the information we needed was there. The books *must* have been written when we still had contact with Saradena.

Temptation bit like strong herb on the tongue, but I did not move.

The age of the books did not guarantee they would contain information about Saradena. It would take time to work out the older language if I could, after which I might well find the ancient books were more *vitae* of forgotten lords. Or more cookbooks. It would be indulgence, not productive search. Knowing that did not make walking away from them any easier.

I put the book back and turned, fleeing as if they might grab me, and began to pace. I'd start with the travel narratives, then move to the histories. It was the only course that made sense. Tomorrow—

I stopped.

One year. Less than a year. Casting a last glance at the unreadable, ancient books, I went to the travel narratives and took a volume to the table. The Saradenians surely were not waiting until tomorrow.

Chapter VIII

The script seemed to swirl like mist when I opened the cover. But soon enough the strangeness ebbed, letters and then words emerging like rocks when the tide goes out. As I became accustomed to the script, I read more quickly. The book described a minor scion of the Ragoni noble family as he journeyed to Nevel to marry a member of their royal family, probably equally minor. It was a delightful little volume, engrossing, even droll at times, but unlikely to yield information about Saradena. I skimmed faster. When his party encountered Magari, raiding from the northern mountains into Beryn, I slowed my pace. I'd heard of such raids, but this name for the mountain men was unknown to me, and I hoped more new knowledge would be forthcoming.

No luck. The narrative ended not long after. The young lord reached Nevel, married his intended, and presumably lived happily ever after. Or not. I knew—who better?—the perils of arranged marriages.

I put the manuscript back, pausing to stretch before taking up another. Flexing my shoulders, I studied the shelves, indulging a surge of mingled disbelief and envy. So many books, *so many books,* and they had been casually collected by a drunkard to keep him out of bigger trouble on the order of a king who valued dung more highly.

At least his assistant seemed to grasp their value—

Wait—shouldn't Hal be back by now? I turned towards the door, as if looking could make him appear. I'd explored the library and read an entire manuscript. More than enough time, surely, to get Domon settled for the night. So where was he? Hunger returned in a gnawing rush, and in its wake, irritation. Had I been abandoned, Philip's disdain encouraging his servants to treat me likewise?

But Hal hadn't seemed the sort to snub a guest, despite his lord's implicit consent to do so. A wisp of concern curled through my hunger-stoked annoyance.

As I stood, considering, the shelves inevitably drew my attention. I could eat later. When would I be alone with so many books again? I reached for another volume.

The outer door opened and hurried footfalls approached.

"My profound apologies for leaving you here so long, lady," Hal panted. He looked flustered. His bark-brown hair was as mussed as the short Valenian fashion would allow, his eyes blazed embarrassment, and creases crisscrossed his tunic as if he'd been sleeping in his clothes.

"Something's happened." I was glad of my fragment of worry, lessening the guilt of my irritation and suspicion.

"Yes," he said, more calmly. "But it's better now. I'll tell you about it over supper, lady."

I set the book back in its place. "Are you all right?"

"Yes." He drew a shuddering breath that belied the claim. "Thank you for asking. And thank you for your patience."

I didn't manage to suppress a snort as I followed him back to the stairs.

"Did I say something amiss?"

"I am not generally known for my patience."

"I've heard that." He smiled. "I suspected leaving a scholar among so many books would be a light hardship, no matter how hungry you were, but I didn't intend to be gone so long."

Always alert for slights, I eyed him, wondering if he meant what he said. Vere-trained I was, true, but the scholars did not consider me one of them. "I kept busy."

★★★

I could have found my way with my eyes shut. The smell of fresh bread had filled the air since we reached the stairs, but as we stepped into the kitchen, I caught other aromas: roast pork, lentil stew, carrots-and-cabbage, apple pie. Two tables were laden and occupied. The royal household had finished their supper, and now the kitchen staff could eat. They glanced up, growing quiet, but one woman was already halfway across the room to meet us.

I stared. Head cooks tended to be short, plump matrons, all red cheeks and floury skirts. The woman whose cool gaze met mine was slender and tall, her dark hair streaked with white. She had the same black-brown eyes as Philip and Domon. Had I seen her elsewhere in the palace I would have taken her for one of the royal family.

Which, of course, made perfect sense.

However much she did not look the part, she clearly was the head cook. Her authority showed in the others' behavior as well as her own.

"Doctora Bann." She inclined her head. I was surprised, but realized a heartbeat later that my presence must be common knowledge through the palace. "Hal."

"Mistress Baynor." He bowed. "Can you provide our guest supper, lady? Doctora Bann has traveled far and not eaten since she arrived."

"I am no one's lady," she said. From her tone, this was a long-running point of mock-dispute between them. She eyed him shrewdly. "When was the last meal *you* had, busy as you are with my worthless brother?"

He lifted one shoulder. "I wouldn't say no. Lady."

She inclined her head again, as if conceding this bout, and led us to a table.

Her staff finished their meal and moved to their next tasks, cleaning the kitchen and preparing for the morning. She joined us as we sat, although a portion of her attention always remained on her workers. The servants' faces suggested they believed she saw all that occurred. I saw no undue fear in them, just the careful attention of those who knew their work was held to a high standard and the pride that accompanied meeting it. They surreptitiously watched to see if the outsider apprehended how well their kitchen ran. I wondered about the ethics of advising the Roth to hire away his cousin's cook.

A young woman, the same one who had guided me to the library, brought bowls of lentil stew and a loaf of bread.

"Philip should have sent Domon away years ago." Mistress Baynor's gaze flicked to the servant as she set down the bowls. "He trapped Ina in the stairway not two weeks ago. Thoroughly pawed her and tore her dress. Fortunately Torrell happened along." Another quick glance pointed him out, a bulky-shouldered young man by the hearths. Anger blazed in her voice. I suspected the cook's temper might kindle less quickly than mine but once roused would burn as hot.

Hal looked aghast. "I'm sorry."

She waved a hand. "I don't blame you. No one could keep Domon from trouble all the time. He's too eager to find it. I spoke to Philip." Her lips thinned. "He won't listen. I don't know what Domon will have to do before Philip will see reason. But I bet sooner or later we will find out." She glanced at Hal. "By all means, do your best. But he will too."

"King Philip hopes his brother will improve."

Her mouth twisted. "We've discussed this before, Hal. Nothing has changed. You know, I know, everyone but Philip knows, Domon is getting worse, not better. He has gone from being a nuisance to an open threat." Frustration steeped her words. "The best I can do is to keep him out of the kitchen." Ferocity radiated from her like the heat from the fires. "He doesn't try to come here anymore."

I very much wanted to know how she accomplished that but squelched my desire to ask.

Hal raked a hand through his hair, which did nothing to improve its order. "I must do as my king commands."

Mistress Baynor smoothed the strands above her ear, as if attending to Hal's dishevelment by proxy. "And what brings the famous Doctora Bann to Ragonne?"

My temper flared but in the next heartbeat I pushed it down. Her tone had been curious not unkind. "Lord Orlo was in Rothbury and mentioned King Philip's library." So far, the truth. But truth would only work so far. "He suggested, and the Roth agreed, that I should look through King Philip's books to see if we would like to copy any for our library."

She was quiet for a moment. "I heard Orlo had been sent to Elbany. The king's nephew. Not a common messenger. Yes, I *very* much wondered about that. Then he returned with you, too quickly for anything but desperate riding." She folded her hands. "You've come to examine Philip's moldy books? I doubt it."

"It's true."

Her glare was relentless and, ultimately, irresistible.

"Mostly," I raised my hands, part concession, part entreaty. "You are royal enough to know secrecy is often necessary."

"And royal enough to know it rarely bodes well." She gestured, urging us to return to the food we had barely touched. "I wish you luck with whatever your real purpose is. Despite what my brother thinks, Ragonne's alliance with Elbany has benefited Ragonne as much as Elbany. We need to keep our friends."

I spread a thin smear of butter on a piece of bread. "Is Ragonne acquiring new enemies?"

"Not that I know of." She rapped her fingertips on the table. "But there are rumors. As always. No one knows what Tomas of Marlon intends. He claims to be content with his throne. But he is Richard's brother, and no one has forgotten." A mournful note shivered in her voice. Thinking through the family relations, I realized Edwy of Elbany had been her nephew. The Roth's brother had been the last death of the Ricardian war. "Philip's lords won't admit it but Edwy's plans are what kept Marlon out of Ragonne so long."

"I didn't know him. I wish I had. I was at Vere then."

"Vere." Her gaze curled inward like a cat. "Would they had sent me instead of Domon." The light of the outward world returned to her. "What was it like?"

I hesitated, surprised to have found another woman who wanted to go to Vere. Reluctant gratitude trickled through me. My father, unlike Mistress Baynor's, had been willing and able to demand my admittance. But he had owed me that much and more. "I am grateful to have learned from the scholars." I kept my voice as even as I could. "But they did not teach me gladly."

A deep shadow of understanding pooled in her eyes. "I can read a bit. I bullied Domon into teaching me when he returned."

"Well done." I wished I could tell her the Roth's wider plan for his library. He wanted more of his people literate, and not just men. But there *was* something I could offer. "Has Hal mentioned that at least two of the books contain recipes?"

"Recipes?" She leaned back, her apparent disbelief equaling what I'd felt when I found them. "In a book?"

Hal wiped up the last drops of his stew with a bit of bread. "It's true. I'm sorry I did not tell you about them before."

"If you have a free moment, come to the library," I said. "We'll show them to you."

"I'll do that." Her eyes unfocused as she considered the prospect, then narrowed as her attention returned to her staff. "If you would excuse me?" Following her now-riveted look, I saw a washing boy set aside a still-dirty but supposedly clean pot.

"Of course, lady," Hal said. "Thank you for supper."

She stood, turning her attention from her imminent victim long enough to mock-glare at Hal. "Don't let Domon get to you.

I hazard the earlier uproar was related to him?"

"He asked me to get him a cup of water, then slipped away while I fetched it. It was quite a search before I found him again."

She snorted, her gaze on her underling once more. "You should have known he was up to something when he asked for water. Domon hasn't drunk water in years."

"As you say, lady."

Her gaze flicked to me. "How long will you be in Peran?"

"As long as needs be."

"Of course. I will come to the library as soon as I can. Good evening, both of you."

***

I blinked awake, wondering at the scent of apples. Then I remembered. I was in Peran, sleeping in an erstwhile storeroom, working in a rotting library, and trying to avoid killing a royal drunk.

I sat up, yawning. After supper I'd returned to the library and continued with the travel narratives. It seemed prudent, with Domon safely away, to work as long as I could.

Or maybe I simply couldn't resist the pleasure of being alone with so many books.

I'd searched three more manuscripts but found nothing relevant to Saradena. In my mind I heard wind whistling past like our time before their promised attack.

All the more reason to begin early today.

CHAPTER IX

I was on my second book before Hal and Domon arrived. Its script was a wretched, wandering hand that formed 'h' and 'b' indistinguishably. I could make sense of it but only with determined attention. I heard Domon settle at his table and nodded a greeting to Hal without looking up when he came to collect the loose parchment sheets from the cupboard. Once he rejoined Domon in the outer room, I promptly forgot them both in the intensity of my task. It seemed no time at all before Hal slipped back into the room at mid-day to ask if I'd like dinner.

The offer was welcome. I hadn't had breakfast. I thanked him and put the manuscript aside. Strange little book. I was nearly halfway through. It was a description of a fosterling's travels with his lord, the writing undertaken, as he explained, at his tutor's instruction, for practice while he was away. Given the state of his script, he certainly needed it. Fascinating, but nothing to do with Saradena.

When I stepped into the outer room I found Mistress Baynor herself had brought our meal. Hal lifted the cloth covering the basket. "Rye bread, green cheese, and apples. Oh, and fresh butter. Thank you."

She caught my puzzled look. "The books you mentioned. I wanted to see them so I brought the basket myself." Steeped in my reading, I'd forgotten the recipe books. I'd wondered why the head cook had come on such a small errand. She waited while we ate, sitting as far away from her half-brother as the small room allowed, and was on her feet as soon as we brushed the last crumbs from our fingers.

We settled ourselves in the second room. Hal presented Mistress Baynor the recipe books with a flourish, then stood beside her as she sat in the room's only other chair. I fought the urge to put my hands over my ears as she slowly read aloud, one fingertip following the words on the page. It would be discourteous. But the distraction was maddening.

Finally she looked up. "Astonishing. Truly astonishing."

"I knew they were here," Hal said, chagrined. "I should have told you."

Her lip curled as her eyes flicked towards the outer room. "You have enough to think about."

"As you say, lady."

Her attention returned to the book. The whispered, staggering reading was excruciating. My fingers twitched. Rude. And unkind. It was tortured reading, but she *was* reading, and she'd fought as hard as I had to obtain the skill. Harder. I'd pushed my way into Vere to get away from a family who no longer wanted me. Mistress Baynor had wrested reading from a drunken, despised half-brother.

Hal glanced towards the front room. "It's rather quiet out there, lady. Would you mind if I...?"

"With Domon, quiet is bad." Mistress Baynor gave him a hard look. "Go, by all means." After he left, she turned to me. "So you are examining the books."

"Yes."

"What are you looking for?"

"I can't tell you."

"Then let me tell you."

I slapped my hands down on the table to either side of the book. "I can't discuss this with you."

"Of course." She scrolled one hand in the air. "So just listen."

I glanced at the doorway but Hal did not return. No help there. "Go ahead." She was going to anyway.

"Something has happened, something so fearful even my brother is forced to consider looking in books for help."

"Ha." It slipped out. "You know your brother better than that."

"Forced to tolerate others looking, then."

I said nothing, but my face must have told tales. She gave a brisk nod.

"Rumors followed Orlo from Boltar. Stories of an enormous ship." She leaned closer. "Most people laugh at them. For now. I do not. Not when Orlo rode in all haste to Elbany." She closed the recipe book. I held my breath, watching, but she handled the volume as gently and carefully as a clerk. "He returned with you. And left you here with these books. I think—" she lowered her voice, although there was no one to overhear—"we have reason to fear..." One shoulder lifted in a half-shrug, almost apologetically. "...something. An attack, perhaps." Her face set, as if expecting me to argue with her or dismiss what she'd said. "And —our enemy must be one we've not faced before." Her gaze flicked to the books surrounding us. "That we know."

I sat, silenced by surprise and admiration. She had puzzled it out, from so little. As well or better than the scholars at Vere, and she was in a kitchen. "You are right, princess of Ragonne."

"I am no princess. I am not even anyone's lady, despite Hal's courtesy." Her voice had not grown louder. "I prefer it. I married a man I love. What princess can say as much?"

I jerked back as if slapped.

She looked baffled. Then contrition flooded her face. "I did not mean...I apologize."

My anger dispelled. The mortification proved more difficult.

"Do we know...when?" she asked at last.

"One year." My voice was almost steady. "They've given us a year."

"A year?" Her eyebrows climbed. "Why would they give us a year to prepare?"

I mentally threw up my hands, deciding to share what I knew and hoping Mistress Baynor was as trustworthy as she seemed. This did not improve my mood. I'd sworn to keep the letter secret and the Roth had not excepted his aunts. But she would be a greater danger with incomplete information, seeking more elsewhere. "You've already guessed much. But you must keep this secret."

"That goes without saying," she snapped. "I ask not to satisfy my curiosity but because I try to give my brother cooler-headed advice than he gets from the battle-hungry retainers he surrounds himself with."

"Philip asks your opinion about political matters?"

"Of course not!" Her voice was frigid. "But I give it. It is difficult, as you might imagine, to do so without him realizing."

I thought of my interview with Philip. "Yes."

"I take it you are searching for information about our new enemy," she said.

"Not just Ragonne's enemy. They sent letters to Logan and Elbany as well. Perhaps others. There's no way to find out without revealing our danger."

"I can see that." Moving the book from her lap to the table, she went to the doorway to look out at Hal and Domon.

"The Roth sent me to learn anything I could. Where it is. Why they would attack us—"

"Isn't it obvious?"

I glared, annoyed at the interruption, even more at the insinuation. "The letter—"

"What did it say?" she demanded, coming closer.

I pulled a deep breath. Was I this imperious? Probably. "I saw all three letters." I held up a hand to forestall another intrusion. "Elbany's, obviously, came to us. Lord Orlo brought Ragonne's as proof. Logan's clerk recently died and he sent the letter to Rothbury to be read. All were the same except the greeting." I recited the message.

Her fingers rapped her forearm. "Interesting."

"Yes. The demands, and the delay, suggest conquest is not their aim. Or not their sole aim."

"If you've described it accurately—"

"I described it exactly," I said with heat. "I memorized it."

She glanced down, noticed her tapping fingers, and stilled them. "Of course. It's just odd. *Restore the neglected Henrican observances.* Saradena's," her mouth formed the new word but did not voice it, "quarrel seems to be philosophical. Or perhaps religious." She paced towards the far wall, turned, stalked back. "Do you suppose...the Cynric?" It could scarcely be called a whisper. "Could they know?"

"How could they?" I shuddered. It was not clear even to me whether my question was directed towards the Saradenians or the Cynric. I knew that the stench of blood and iron had not flooded the room like a fast tide, but I smelled them nonetheless. "The Cynric have been gone so long. We don't know much about them."

But what we did was enough. More than enough. More like a memory than an imagining, I heard weeping, the sing of a blade as it arced downward, the shrieks of a child bound too tightly to flinch. They caught every drop in wide silver basins, gleaming beneath the half-moon required for their doings. From that blood, moon-bathed and shadowed both, could be called forth *cyfargrym*, power that moved sideways to the world, effecting things contrary to nature and beyond craft. Or so it was said. That name was nearly forgotten, but whispers yet ran about wicked magic, although more commonly now to deny it once existed than to fear it might return. "The Roth's sister, who married the king of Logan not long before I came to Elbany—"

"I know," she interrupted dryly.

I ignored her. Certainly she would be aware of her niece's marriage. The location, not the marriage itself, had been my aim in mentioning it. "—says that in Logan there are noblewomen who do not believe the Cynric existed."

She looked so outraged I blinked in the sudden heat of it. "They are utter fools."

"I did not say I was among them," I said. "We have long memories in Bruster."

"But not so long as to remember Saradena."

"No." I looked down at the table. "Your thought about the Cynric is a good one. Something Saradena knew, or thought they knew, prompted these letters. Perhaps the Cynric. Perhaps something else. I'll watch for information about the Cynric as I read." But I rather hoped I wouldn't find any.

She cocked her head as if struck by a sudden thought. "Why are you here, and not Vere?"

"The Roth was going to send me to Vere." I looked towards the doorway as if hearing a noise from the outer room but really trying not to show my relief at being in Ragonne instead, despite mistreated books and Domon. "Lord Orlo suggested I write to someone I trust, asking him to check Vere's library while I came to Ragonne and searched Philip's."

"You're here, so I take it there was someone at Vere you trust?"

"Magistre Poll."

Her lips pursed. "Your *maestro?*"

Even if I'd mastered a noble's formal disinterest, I couldn't have concealed my shock.

She went on. "The more Domon figured out I envied his time at Vere, the more he bragged about it. He explained how the tutoring system works. It makes sense you would trust your mentor."

The scholars would not have been pleased to know Domon had told an outsider about Vere's internal workings.

She laughed. "Domon was not supposed to tell me such things, was he?"

"No."

She crossed the room. "I suspect you did not mind not returning to Vere."

"No," I said again, then went on without thinking. "It could be worse. If I find nothing here, I may be sent to Ferrant." The next instant I clamped my teeth. I sounded mithering and frightened. The Roth's clerk could be neither.

Her brow furrowed. "Other than abject cruelty, of which I have never suspected him, what reason could the Roth have?"

I was surprised by the sympathy and abashed at having seemed to solicit it. "Ferrant has books."

"*Do* they? Interesting." Her fingers began tapping again, this time against the bookshelf closest to her. "I assume you do not already know what is in them?" She continued without waiting for a response. "No, certainly not. Francis is not a man to allow his wife to read. Particularly if she would enjoy it. Hmm. Douglas would have to ask a favor of Ferrant and risk revealing our trouble, which he will not care to do until he has no other choice. Yes, I see."

She noticed her fingertips beating a rapid pulse, scowled, and stopped. Clearly inactivity did not suit her. Just as clearly, she'd been taught it was not ladylike to fidget. The façade of calm I'd seen in her kitchen must have been the result of practice and occupation, but nonetheless a façade. "Let me give you my advice, more straightforwardly than I give it to my brother." She flashed a brief smile. "Get Hal to help. You can trust him." She glanced around at the shelves. "My suspicion is there's nothing here to find. You need to eliminate this possibility as quickly as possible, return to Elbany, and ask the Roth for his next command. Then, almost certainly, go to Ferrant. I am sorry," she said, sounding as if she were.

"I swore to tell no one. I've already broken that oath. I don't care to again."

"Secrecy is not as important as success. The Roth will forgive if you do what is necessary."

One hand stole to my braid, fingering the tuft at its end. "I am a clerk, not a politician. I *hate* this."

She laughed. I looked up. She laughed louder, apparently at

the look on my face. "You may not like it. I'll believe that. But you are a princess of Bruster—"

"Were."

"*Are.*" She strode back. "No one can efface your blood. You dislike the politics but you can't say you don't understand them." She leaned closer. "Right now, you are whatever the Roth needs you to be. Most of all, he needs you to be fast. Use Hal."

"I'll think about it."

She nodded crisply, as if I'd agreed. She sat again and turned her attention back to the recipe book.

Be fast. Do the search. Use Hal. I trusted Mistress Baynor enough to tell her my task. At least when she'd already guessed most of it. Did I trust her enough to take her advice about how to conduct it?

CHAPTER X

I spent the next two days reading as quickly as possible, for as many hours a day as I could keep my eyes open. Unasked, Mistress Baynor arranged for meals to be sent to the library.

I found nothing. Not a passing comment, a snippet of a sentence, or a marginal notation referring to Saradena, let alone a full flood of information clarifying their grievance.

The weather did not help. Low-lying Ragonne, like the rest of Valenna, was warmer than Elbany or Bruster, which were mountainous. On the third day after my arrival, Ragonne's spring turned unusually hot, and the library sweltered. I heard myself growl as I once more wiped away sweat trickling down my forehead before it could fall onto the book.

It was just as well I was doing much of my work late into the night, when no one was around for me to snap at.

***

The heat had an unexpected benefit: Domon spent less time in the library. Most days he arrived barely in time for noon-tide and left well before supper. It meant I saw little of Hal, but I considered that an acceptable sacrifice.

The hot misery was also worth enduring to spend so much time alone with so many books.

By the morning of the fifth day after my arrival, I'd finished half the travel narratives. I'd risen especially early and was well into my second manuscript before breakfast arrived. I heard the door open, a tray sliding onto the outer table, and the door closing again. Then, after a few moments, a sound like an ox-cart bumping along a cobbled street.

I looked up, around, and finally down to find the source. "Ah." I leaned in my chair to scratch the cat's head. "You have the loudest purr I've ever heard."

Thus encouraged, she jumped up onto the table. Not onto the manuscript. "Good girl." I slipped my hand under her chin. The purr rumbled louder. "How many mice have you killed today?"

When at last I turned back to the book, she stepped into my lap, turned a graceful circle, and settled down, tucking her tail neatly over her front paws.

The library was stifling, my shift and dress sweat-sticky already. Too hot for a furry, living blanket. But I liked cats. They were common around a castle, boon companions in the fight against vermin. They were particularly encouraged at Vere, helping keep the page-nibblers away. This one looked enough like Magistre Poll's favorite to be its twin: long body, flat face, shaggy gray fur that puffed out its tail to the width of my hand. "Liath," I murmured, pulling a final stroke down her back, using the name of my *maestro's* cat since I did not know her own.

★★★

Philip did not forget his demand that I provide clerical work during my stay. He sent word early the next morning that I was to attend him presently, and kept me all day and the next two as well, accompanying his steward through every room in the palace, taking stock of their foodstuffs, assessing the winter's damage to the roof, determining which retainers needed new clothing.

Like the demand, the work was about putting me in my place, showing me how useless he considered my search. In his reckoning, counting bags of flour and missing slates were a better use of my time. My annoyance grew at finding the steward perfectly competent, neither desiring nor requiring my notations to remember what work was needed.

Philip joined us for the inspection of his weapons stores. He mused aloud about increasing his stockpile, unsubtly demonstrating how he thought the Saradenian threat should be handled. I silently noted all on the wax tablet, avoided looking at him, and pressed my teeth together until my jaws ached.

★★★

A week later the weather had not improved, but I had finished the travel narratives. I moved to the histories, regretting it immediately. The travel narratives had at least been interesting. The histories were longer, and they were dull, copious descriptions of Ragoni regional happenings. Liath returned as I finished the fourth manuscript, following the kitchen servant bringing supper. I scratched her ears as she kneaded my lap.

"You know how I know no one's read these books for years?"
I progressed to her chin. She licked a paw and cleaned her disor-
dered ears. "If anyone had, they'd have scraped the parchment
and reused it for something worthwhile."

It wasn't entirely true. Verbose and boring they were, but if
someone wanted to write a history of Ragonne, these books
would be a valuable source. I didn't. I needed Saradena. But I
doubted I'd find it among these books. So far the histories had
scarcely mentioned any country outside Ragonne.

Liath sat with me as I worked late into the evening. When at
last my head began to pitch forward, she found the movement
unsettling and leapt down. Giving up for the night, I followed her
out, scavenging whatever remained unspoiled from the supper
basket on my way past.

***

The next day's second manuscript was mercifully interesting,
particularly compared to the one I'd just finished, which should
have been called *An Interminable History of the City of Boltar.*
The new book covered the building of fortifications in Conlo.
Conlo was the closest Ragoni city to Elbany and had regular
contact with it.

Towards noon I heard the outer door open. Low voices told
me Hal and Domon had arrived. I heard a chair creak as Domon
settled into it, and was returning my attention to Conlo when
Hal stepped through the doorway.

Conlo, Elbany—even Saradena—all fled.

A gash arced across his forehead, and bruises purpled the
right side of his face. The cut, although long, was probably not
serious. Blood had trickled down, matting his eyebrows, but the
wound had already clotted. More worrisome, but less immediately noticeable, was the blood oozing between the fingers of his
left hand, tightly clenched on his right arm just below the elbow.

I seized his shoulders and steered him to a chair. "What
happened?"

"Domon, lady," he grunted. "My lord Philip allows his
brother a bottle of wine a day."

I was surprised by Philip's tangible, and expensive, generosity
towards his brother. Or perhaps he thought Domon would be
more manageable if he were tipsy most of the time. If that *were*
his strategy, it seemed unsuccessful. "That doesn't sound like a

reason to attack you."

"He finished today's. Hours ago. He did not take well to me refusing to demand another from the steward."

"Let me see."

He shook his head. "No need. It's deep. It'll need to be stitched."

I drew my hand back. "Don't move. You'll make the bleeding worse. I'm going for supplies." Given how tightly his fingers pressed the wound, he clearly knew. "It'll be a few moments. Will you be all right?"

"What's Domon doing?"

I peeked through the doorway. "Eating." I hadn't heard the mid-day meal arrive.

"He should be busy for a while."

"I'll be right back."

Domon scarcely glanced up as I ran past to my room. Like most people, men and women alike, I traveled with needle and thread. You never knew when you might have to sew up your clothing or other belongings. Or if you were unlucky, yourself. I started back to the library, then changed my mind and headed for the stairs.

"It's Hal," I told Mistress Baynor. "He's hurt. I need water and cloths, maybe some cooking wine to clean the wound."

"What happened?" she asked as she gathered them.

I gestured at my arm. "He cut him." No need to specify who. "Wanted more wine. I don't know any more."

"Philip *must* see reason," she hissed, putting a small bottle of cooking wine in my hand. "It goes without saying you should keep that out of Domon's sight."

I tucked it into the pouch hanging from my belt beside my knife sheath. "Thank you."

"I'll send soup."

"Thank you," I repeated, and hurried back down the stairs as quickly as I could without slopping water out of the bowl.

★★★

"How are you?" I dropped the cloths onto the table but set the bowl of water on the floor.

"Well enough." He watched as I returned the manuscript to its shelf. Only then, with the book safely away, did I move the bowl to the table. "You always remember to protect the books, no matter what is happening?"

"Training." I dipped a cloth into the water. "I was only switched twice in Vere before I learned."

"Harsh."

"Necessary." I reached for his arm but he shied away. "Start with the one on my head, please, if you don't mind, lady."

"All right." We wouldn't be able to avoid the real injury, not for long, but if he wanted to work up to it, that was fine. Maybe he wanted to know I was competent before trusting me with it. Fair enough. I washed away the dried blood, patted the cut dry with a clean cloth, then watched it for a few moments. It did not start bleeding again. "You were lucky. Just a scratch."

He glanced down. "Not so lucky with this one."

"No." I picked up a dry cloth. "Move your hand now."

When he uncurled his fingers, the bleeding quickened. I pressed the cloth down. His lips thinned.

"Can you move the hand? The fingers?"

He wriggled them gingerly. "Seems so."

"Good." I reached for his torn sleeve and began to roll it up one-handedly, the other hand still compressing the wound. "Might as well save your shirt as much as possible. It can be mended." I kept talking, trying to hold his gaze, to distract him. "You should mend all right too, as long as it doesn't fester. You *were* lucky, even with this one. An arm is full from wrist to elbow of things that work much better unsevered."

"I know."

"I see you do." His forearm lay exposed beneath my fingers. I hadn't noticed, until that moment, that no matter how hot the weather, he never rolled up his sleeves. The scars were fearsome. Two were so thick I was surprised he still had the arm below. "Did he do this?"

"No." He glanced uncomfortably at the scars as if he'd rather I roll the sleeve back down. "That was before I came to Ragonne."

I considered him more closely. He *must* be older than he looked. At least I hoped so. Not even in Bruster would someone who seemed barely eighteen come by such scars fairly. But he offered nothing more, and it was not my place to pry. "Very well," I said. "Let's get it stitched while Domon is safely occupied."

I threaded my needle. Holding it in one hand, I peeled back the cloth with the other. The bleeding had slowed but not stopped. I sluiced the wound with wine, then jiggled the bottle at him, offering the remainder, but he shook his head.

"Ready?"

He took a deep breath and nodded. I pushed the gaping edges together. It was not the first time I'd done so. Like all nobles I'd been taught to clean and care for wounds. I also knew how to cut a man's throat if his injuries were beyond help or hope. This I had not yet had to do.

"At least the sides are smooth, not jagged," I said, trying to give him something to think about beside the bite of the needle, the strange sensation of thread sliding through flesh. "What did he get you with?"

He looked bemused. "His belt-knife, of course, lady."

I stared. "After everything he's done, Philip lets him wear a belt-knife?"

He shrugged one shoulder. "How else would he eat?"

I washed the now-closed wound and bound a clean cloth over it. "Wait here." My knife was in my hand before I reached the doorway. Behind me, I dimly heard Hal call. I ignored him.

I flicked my wrist. My knife thudded into the table between Domon's hands. His head snapped up.

"He can read," I said. "He can *read.*" I stepped forward, and then my knife was back in my hand, its tip inches from his nose. "He is not a common boat slave, to lash at your whim."

His eyes narrowed, suddenly much more lucid. "The King my brother allows me to discipline my servant as I see fit."

My knife did not move. "The King your brother cannot make you less dead. Which is what you will be if you take your knife to him again. Philip may allow you to waste your own training, but you will not waste someone else's."

I was not Valenian, and its tongue was not the language of my heart. I switched to Brusterian. From the way his eyes widened, he must have understood part of it, as he should after his years at Vere.

"As you wish," he sneered. "*Doctora.*"

Chapter XI

Hal was standing when I stalked back. "That was a kind impulse, lady," he said. "But...unlikely to be effective. And I suspect you have made Domon eager to settle accounts with you."

I shoved my knife into its sheath. "I can take care of myself."

I blinked as a knife appeared in his hand. "So can I, actually. I would not have let him kill me." He put up his knife as quickly as he'd drawn it. "Unless there was some good reason."

I wondered what he would consider a good reason. A person only gets one life, after all, coming from dark unknown and soon enough returning to dark unknown, like a sparrow flying from the night into a well-lit hall and out again. Then I shook my head. No doubt it was just dark humor.

"It's better for us who have to deal with Domon to...allow a certain amount of ill-temper. It keeps him from striking harder. I'm not sure now what he'll do to the next person he goes after."

"You can *read*," I said stubbornly. "No one should be allowed to strike you."

"With Domon, it's unavoidable, lady."

I paced to the end of the room. "Philip should not tolerate this."

"But he does," he answered. "It cannot be changed, so it must be managed."

"Someday—"

He held up a hand. "I know, lady. Mistress Baynor and I have spoken about this many times. Domon will, at some point, do something the king cannot excuse or ignore. But this is not it. Until then, my lord Philip gives Domon wide allowance. It is my job to keep him out of trouble as much as possible."

I stopped by my worktable, both hands pressing its surface, trying to check impotent rage. I could not save him any more than I had been able to save myself from Francis' derision or my father's. The unconcerned smirk on Domon's face even as he'd feigned acquiescence...my warning had accomplished nothing. At least nothing good. "It will be worse for you. I'm sorry."

"Don't be, lady. I appreciate your concern." He flexed the fingers of his injured arm appraisingly. "I should get back to Domon. Thank you for your help."

★★★

As May sweated into June, I worked on the histories, spending long hours in the library, except for two days when Philip again demanded clerical work. By mid-June, only half a dozen remained.

Liath took to lying on the table as I worked, flopped flat on hot days, curled into a ball on the rare cooler ones. Closing a completed manuscript, I rebound the strap, then ran a hand down the cat's back before rising to put the book away. "I believe I now know more about the history of Ragonne than anyone else in the Three Lands." She gave her loud, gravelly purr. "Or anywhere else." Every time I finished reading a manuscript and looked around at the well-stocked shelves, I was awed by the knowledge preserved there, and angered by how little it was esteemed.

She tensed under my hand, then sprang down to stalk a mouse that was ill-advisedly trying to sneak into the outer room, no doubt lured by the ever-present crumbs under Domon's table.

"It is shameful that a palace cat cares more about these books than the king." I went to the shelf, exchanging the book for another. "You at least try to protect them."

★★★

A week later, I finished the histories and began the verse manuscripts, hoping to return to the speed with which I'd searched the travel narratives. I could read two travel manuscripts in the time it took me to get through one history. After the verse manuscripts, only one section would remain. The *vitae*. But it was the most extensive, five shelves, and would take at least three weeks. More likely a month. Then—

I didn't want to think about *then*.

But to my simultaneous consternation and fascination, I discovered many of the verse manuscripts were *compilatios*.

Compilatios were common in the library of Vere, and I'd been surprised by their absence here. It was much cheaper to bind several manuscripts together, resulting in a collection of works, sometimes related, sometimes not, within the same codex. The lack of *compilatios* suggested such wealth expended on these books it made me want to howl in frustration at their neglect.

It also made me even more curious about their origin. Who in Ragonne's past had valued reading enough to create these books?

All my scholarly instincts were itching to dig through the library and learn whatever there was to be found about these patrons. But as I'd done with the unreadable manuscripts, I suppressed the impulse. It wasn't what I was here for. But it was difficult. Even if the books, not to mention Ragonne, were still here in a year, I doubted I'd be allowed to return to study them.

★★★

I shook my head to clear it, forcing my gaze back to the book. Were there a window to be looked out, it would still be dark despite the early rising of the summer sun. I'd been in the library three hours already, and had gotten halfway through one verse manuscript. Like most of its peers, it was a *compilatio*.

I'd left the library the previous night after midnight. Sooner or later, the short nights would catch up to me, but not yet. Or at least not much. The books were too fascinating, and time too dear. It was nearly the end of June and I'd managed scarcely a third of the verse manuscripts.

By the time the library began heating up to its normal sticky unpleasantness, I'd finished the *compilatio* and moved on to the day's second book.

It was not a *compilatio*, but that was little enough to be thankful for. The writing looked as though the scribe had worked left-handed and with his eyes closed. He had an infuriating tendency to make up his own abbreviations, which he used copi-ously. He also knew Brusterian. If a Brusterian word conveyed the thought better, he used it instead. I'd worked with macaronic composition in Vere, but it took time. This book might well consume the rest of the day.

But by the time Hal and Domon arrived, I'd partially forgiven the manuscript's idiosyncratic clerk. It was the first book I'd found in the library that was not about Ragonne. It was, in fact, about Bruster.

Saradena slipped to the back of my mind, fascinating as it

was to see an outsider's description of my homeland. Unsurprisingly given the scribe's—or perhaps, author's—familiarity with our language, he wrote from the experience of having visited the clustered islands.

He had even included Vere. I was impressed. Few outside Bruster knew Vere lay on land belonging to Bruster, although the island of Lastland had been lent to the scholars since before anyone could remember. Which did not stop periodic grumblings among Brusterian nobles. I could not entirely blame them. Lastland was bigger than any of the clustered islands. The interior was a rocky, treeless waste, but many Brusterians did not know that.

His description of the Black Keep was properly admiring. I thought of the castle, glinting like a gem, the city of Reud at its feet, the black sand shore rich and deep as velvet, and my breath sat captive in my chest. *I would never see it again.*

***

I looked up as I heard the outer door open. There were murmurs, then the sounds of Domon settling himself at his table. I glanced back down at the manuscript as Hal walked into the room, as if not wanting to be caught paying attention to their arrival.

"Good day, lady." He toed the other chair. "May I?"

I gestured assent, realizing I hadn't seen him or Domon since the day Hal was wounded. What was Domon up to? Keeping Hal away so he could damage him unobserved? "How's your arm?"

His fingers brushed the site. "It's healing, lady."

"May I see?"

He hesitated, then shrugged, presumably recalling I'd already seen the scars he kept so carefully concealed. I pushed up his sleeve and loosened the bandage. The wound was clean and cool, with none of the redness that would indicate the dreaded putrefaction.

I nodded, pleased. If a wound soured and cauterization failed to stem the festering, the only way to save the person's life was amputation. Half still died. I'd heard the screams of men held down while their rotting arms or legs were cut off. Even these had a better chance than the gut-stung. Belly-wounds were nearly always fatal; rot settled far too easily into such injuries.

"It looks fine. You were fortunate." My gaze slid uncontrollably to the scars, wondering again what had happened to him, but I did not ask. He would not hide them if he wanted to speak of them. I tapped his arm. "Those stitches could come out now, if you like."

He nodded. "If you would, lady. I don't think the wound will reopen, and it's better not to wait." He sounded as if he'd been through this before, which given the evidence of his body was certainly true. I pulled a small, sharp pair of scissors from my belt-pouch. I'd begun carrying my needle, thread, and scissors with me at all times. Just in case.

I cut the stitches, then began pulling out each piece, one by one. It was a strange sensation, I knew, to feel thread being drawn through your skin below the surface, and it did not help to do it quickly. But the discomfort was minor compared to the wound that had necessitated it, or the stitching itself, and Hal sat unmoving until I finished and rebound his arm.

"Thank you, lady."

"What are you doing here?" I asked.

He laughed, his eyebrows rising, but replied before I could clarify. "Domon has been busy. You got his attention."

"Good." *Better me than you.* My fingers twitched but I kept them from straying to my belt-knife.

He continued, low-voiced. "He is intrigued. He wants to know why you're spending so much time here, reading these books. What's here? Specifically, what's here that he does not know about?"

I felt my lip curl. "Almost anything, since he hasn't read them."

He inclined his head. "He is reading them now, lady." His voice grew even softer. "He believes you are looking for something. He wants to find it first. He has been searching when you are not here. He doesn't want you to know."

I looked at my hands. Mistress Baynor advised confiding in him but the Roth wanted the letter kept secret. "King Philip must have told you. I am looking for books touching upon Elbany's history. My lord Roth might want them copied for his library."

"As you wish, lady." He rose. "Domon does not believe that." He paused. "Neither do I, although I do not discuss it with Domon." He glanced towards the outer room. "Domon knows you arrived with Lord Orlo. He assumes you are here on his behalf."

"What?" I sprang from my chair.

"Domon has been uncharacteristically circumspect, which in itself is worrisome. He seems to suspect that Orlo approached Elbany about supporting a bid to challenge the king, that Elbany agreed, and that you are here to find evidence Orlo's claim is superior to the king's."

I stared, startled both by Domon's logical thought process and his conclusion. It was wrong, but nonetheless a concern. False rumors can damage as much as true. If the suspicion came to Philip's ears—and it would—it could bruise his trust of Orlo although Philip knew the real reason for my search. Orlo was his strongest lord, and the relationship between a king and his second-lord was vexed. Real trust between such men was impossible. There was too much power to be had.

"There is more." Hal leaned closer. "Domon remembers Orlo wanted to make suit for you but King Philip refused." He was silent for a moment. "Did you know?"

"Orlo told me when we met in Rothbury. Before that, no."

"Domon believes Orlo went to Elbany in part to offer for you. Now that your marriage would be..." he hesitated, "less politically advantageous, he could press his suit without consulting either the High King or King Philip. If he *were* planning to challenge the king, he wouldn't be concerned about his permission anyway."

I remembered Orlo's dark eyes, burning into mine. *I am not in need of heirs.* He had been in earnest?

It was of no importance. I did not want to marry again. Did I?

I recalled how waspishly I'd behaved in Rothbury, and on the ride to Peran. Orlo had most likely returned to Kolon with his odd fascination exorcised.

It was not a loss, not really. My world for the next year was Saradena. After that, it was not likely to matter.

CHAPTER XII

"I..." I steadied my voice. "I am not here on Orlo's behalf.
Nor is he planning any move against King Philip. Not," I added
hastily, "that there's any reason I would know. If he were. But I
suspect not."

Hal blinked. "I believe you. Domon will not."

Mistress Baynor had urged me to confide in him and enlist his
help with the search, but I had hesitated, unwilling to break my
oath again. Should I tell him my real purpose now, to defuse
Domon's suspicion? Not to protect Orlo, but Ragonne. Internal
conflict would be disastrous in the face of the Saradenian threat. I
chewed my lip, Brusterian epithets flitting through my mind. I
didn't like the idea of casting aside my vow of secrecy a second
time, but Domon could easily cause a great deal of trouble. "You
said Domon has been searching the library. When? I've been
working from before dawn until after midnight every day."

"He has been getting up in the middle of the night and
coming down here."

"You've been with him?"

He inclined his head. "Oh, yes, lady. It is not safe to leave
Domon unattended. Although he has been drinking less."

"What do you do while he searches?"

"I've been working again on restoring the loose pages to their
books." He cocked his head. "Why?"

"Hold." I turned, pacing up and down the length of the
room. Mistress Baynor trusted him. I had every reason to
presume her judgment was sound; it was clear she was an
eminently sensible woman. Breaking my oath again was vexing,
but the Roth would expect me to encounter trying situations
along my way and to do as I deemed best. What mattered was
Elbany's survival. I was to find or do whatever necessary to that
end.

I walked back to stand before him. "I am not here on behalf
of Orlo," I repeated. "I *am* here, as I said, as a representative of

the Roth. But not to find books to copy for his library."

He sat, folding his hands.

I swallowed the last crumbs of reluctance, and began.

***

He nodded as I spoke, a rapid torrent of words, as if it were better, if I must break my oath, to do so quickly. To my surprise and some disgruntlement, he seemed unperturbed to learn the Three Lands were not alone in the world.

"That fits," he said. My face must have spoken clearly. He went on, "There have been rumors, since lord Orlo returned from Boltar."

I frowned, irritated for a different cause. Mistress Baynor had mentioned rumors as well. That was troubling. We didn't know how many of the kingdoms of Valenna were included in the threat. If Marlon or Ferrant had escaped Saradena's notice and our danger came to their ears, Elbany could be long conquered before any outsiders arrived. Unlike the stories about Orlo, which originated with Domon, and which I could perhaps defuse by setting Hal straight, I had no way to cool the whispers of those who had seen the massive, outlandish ship.

He leaned back in his chair. "Saradena," he said more to himself than aloud. He looked up. "There have always been scattered stories of other lands, lady."

At his age, he had precious little business making statements about what had 'always' been. He looked barely old enough to have armed for a sheep raid in Bruster. I pressed my knuckles against my lips, holding in amusement, thinking of my younger brothers earnestly instructing me about knife attacks I'd learned years earlier.

He gave me a level look, as if he guessed my thoughts. "Most such tales claim the other lands lie east. Perhaps their creators knew more than we thought."

I moved back to my chair. "I don't suppose you remember seeing anything that looked like, say, *A Compendium of Saradena* during your categorization of the books?"

He gave a rough laugh. "No."

"We have one year. Less than a year, now," I said. "Mistress Baynor suggested I ask you to help."

His eyebrows shot up. Having started, I pressed on. "With Domon spending time here, actually reading the books, you might be able to."

He sat silent for a moment. "I am honored by your trust, lady, and Mistress Baynor's." His thumb rubbed at the bandage beneath his sleeve. "Domon must be my first concern, as King Philip has commanded. But I will be glad to help as much as I can. What are we looking for?"

"*Anything.*" I flung both arms out. "Anything related to Saradena." I drew my arms back, cupping my hands as if shaping my words. "Ideally, of course, we'd find a full description. Where it is. What the relationship between it and the Three Lands used to be. What their grievance is. But any mention, however slight, would help." I tapped the manuscript lying open on the table before me. "Off-hand comments. Marginalia. At least it would confirm the Three Lands did once know about Saradena and more information might exist." I turned my head as I glanced towards the shelves, the end of my braid flying over my shoulder. "I've searched the travel narratives and the histories, and have begun the verse manuscripts. I haven't found anything yet."

"There are many *compilatios* among those," he said.

"So I've discovered." My gaze flicked to the *vitae*. "Would you like to begin there?"

He spread his hands in wordless assent. "If that would be most helpful."

"Thank you." I felt my gaze begin to creep back to the open book. "I should work."

"Of course." He rose.

I remembered something. "Why *are* you here, now? You said Domon was searching late at night."

He smiled wryly. "He found a book he was so interested in, he wanted to come back and continue it as soon as he'd slept."

Funny how parts of his training held true, despite everything. Domon was master here; he could have taken the volume with him. But in Vere, books did not leave the library.

Hal tipped his head, listening to the low sounds from the outer room. "He seemed deeply engaged, but even so, I should get back." He stopped at a *vitae* shelf long enough to pick one up. "I'll get started."

"Thank you," I said even as I allowed my attention to return to the manuscript.

Leaning on my elbows, I pressed my fingertips together.

Even with Hal's help...another week at least...maybe two, if more of the *compilatios* proved difficult. It would be July before I returned to Elbany. Two months of our year gone. I began to read.

***

With Domon's nocturnal library searching, I didn't expect to see either of them soon. I was surprised therefore, only four days later, to hear the outer door open.

The verse manuscript I was reading was thankfully not a *compilatio*, but neither was it deeply engaging. Or perhaps I was just having difficulty focusing. I'd worked late, and when I finally went to bed I dreamed of my father, the gray set of his face when I returned from Ferrant. I woke quivering away from his stare. So it was a heartbeat or two before I realized I heard Domon's voice —but not Hal's.

Concern cut through the fog in my mind. Hal was certainly correct that Domon would seek to settle scores with me, and I didn't care to be surprised by him. Armsmaster Anhud would have been pleased with how quickly my knife was in my hand.

Then I did hear Hal's voice, intermingled with the sounds of Domon settling at his table. I had my knife sheathed before my young friend came in. "What are you doing here?"

He went wearily to the cupboard. "And good day to you too, lady."

He had spoken lightly but the rebuke stung. I frowned at him. "Hello, good morning, and how are you? Fine, thank you. And yourself? Well? Good." My fingers drummed the table. "That addressed, now may we consider the question of saving our countries from annihilation?" The thump of my fingertips against the table had not driven away the remembered iron pallor of my father's countenance.

Hal shifted in his chair. Whatever irritation had touched his face had fled. "Lady? Are you well?"

"I'm fine," I said, more calmly. It took an effort. I'd overreacted, I knew, lashing out in the perturbation of my dream, but knowing that did not make it easier to dampen my annoyance. "How is your arm?"

He held it out, sleeve down as always, but I could see it was lying flat, with no bandage beneath. "Nearly healed. How are *you*, lady?"

I ignored his real question. My temper had always been short, but since Francis, it had become more and more ungovernable. That was none of his concern, however. "I've finished three more verse manuscripts. Nothing there."

He let it go. "I've gotten through ten of the *vitae*. Nothing there either."

"So why *are* you here?" I asked again.

His fingers scraped the edge of the table, idly worrying at a gouge. "Domon is not as interested in what you're doing anymore."

"Why not?"

"He found something more intriguing."

"In the library?" I half rose. Could Domon, impossibly, have stumbled onto something about Saradena?

"Not about your task."

His eyes flicked away. I tracked his gaze as I dropped back into my seat. The lewd manuscripts. A disgusted sound escaped me. "Those? He's reading *those?*"

He sighed. "It was only a matter of time." He leaned back in his chair, crossing his legs at the ankles. "He means to read all of them before going back to searching the library. He doesn't think it necessary to conceal this reading, so I expect we'll be here in daytime for a week or two."

I tried to imagine reading *all* of those books. Every one of them. From beginning to end. Nauseating.

Chapter XIII

Disgusting as was the thought of anyone reading the unsavory books, Domon's discovery of them was, ironically, the beginning of my most pleasant time in the Ragonne library.

Domon ensconced himself at his table every day, stirring only to turn folios and eat. Hal felt comfortable leaving him alone while he worked in the second room with me, where the manuscripts were safely away from Domon's bottles and plates. Liath would sit on the table between us, purring like a turning millstone.

Hal made good speed through the *vitae*. I continued with the verse manuscripts more slowly because of the *compilatios*, which at least yielded an intriguing and unpredictable variety of works. His presence at my elbow, working side by side, was...companionable, it surprised me to realize. I'd never worked in partnership in a library. In Vere, I sought the most isolated tables, finding the scholars' resentment distracting. In Elbany, I taught my students; they were not my peers.

By the end of June, I had finished the verse manuscripts and joined Hal in the *vitae*. It was a jarring transition. Unlike the *compilatios,* the *vitae* were typical of what I'd come to expect from the Ragoni library—insular, predictable, boring. But faster.

One more week, and my search would be finished.

I tracked Domon's progress through the risqué manuscripts almost as carefully as I followed my own. The current arrangement would last only as long as they did. He too was moving steadily. One more week...there should be enough for one more week.

Usually Domon and Hal arrived two or three hours after I did. But on July 3rd, early morning and then mid-morning came, and they did not. I was not too worried. Once before they had been past time, and it turned out Philip had summoned his brother. Another day they had not come at all. I later learned the king had given Domon a gift—the day out, riding.

By noon I was beginning my third manuscript of the day. The

first had been a particularly tedious *vita* of a Ragoni minor lord; the second, for a change, the tedious life story of a Ragoni lady. It, at least, had the merit of being short. The third was better, a lord obsessed with a minor border dispute between Ragonne and Avice. He was interesting, even if he was, as was evident the further I read, quite mad. His biographer was skilled, I noted appreciatively, in presenting the events of the lord's life while concealing his madness as much as he could. The lord was evidently also a kinsman of the king, who was at some pains to prevent a war with Avice over the contested two acres.

My luck held with the next as well. It proved the most intriguing *vita* yet. The book purported to be a woman writing her *own* life story, explaining to her granddaughters the sort of things they should not do. It was outrageous and fascinating. I doubted its veracity. The Ragoni noblewoman said she eloped at age thirteen with an Adrienne stableman, only to return ten years later with three children, pretending to have been kidnapped in order to be accepted back into her family. Perhaps it was a tale intended to frighten its young readers down the right path.

Not to mention the idea of a book written for *children*... Deep in thought, I heard the outer door open but noted it only in passing. There had been another manuscript, supposedly written by a child. Could literacy really have once been so widespread that children both read manuscripts and sometimes were given the precious gift of parchment to preserve their own thoughts? I'd been at Vere two years before I'd been allowed to write on anything besides a wax tablet—

"So."

The small word, hissed slowly, cut through my thoughts. I sprang up, whirling and backing away, my knife leaping into my hand. Belatedly I realized my ears and nose had been sending a warning that in my scholar's preoccupation, I'd pushed aside. Anhud would have been mortified.

Where was Hal? Had he killed him this time?

Domon watched me, satisfaction etched across his face. "Threaten me? Throw your knife at me?" His head jerked as he sneered, as if his lips moved so fiercely they jostled his entire face. "In Ragonne, women know their place." He took a step towards me.

"I am a princess of Bruster." Startled fear and anger flamed up, burning red hot until only fury remained. But within it, a sliver of wonder at hearing the words I'd said unthinkingly. I wasn't. Not any longer. Or so I'd believed.

My knife was level with his gut. He was not yet in reach. I spat on the ground between us. "That is what your life is worth if you try to touch me."

"*Princess.*" Derision squatted heavy in the word. He spat also. "Barren bitch. That is what your life is worth *now.*"

That this assessment was generally accepted throughout the Three Lands did not lessen my rage at hearing it from him. My fingers tightened on the hilt. "Go. Before I kill you."

His hands went to his belt. "I will laugh at your complaints with my brother the King."

I could barely hear him. Drums. I could hear the battle drums of Bruster. I'd told him to go, but I wanted him to stay and give me reason to kill him.

He advanced, smiling. I stepped back. His smile broadened, then seemed to crack as I crashed my left hand against the side of his head, simultaneously stabbing for his heart.

He twisted when my hand hit, saving his life. The blow meant to finish him grazed across his ribs, tearing his shirt and leaving a long, shallow wound. He staggered back, one hand pressed against the bleeding.

"You...!"

This time I had the chair in my left hand, the knife in my right, and compensated for the resulting twist.

Better. But not perfect.

He backed away, blood dripping.

"I'll kill you!" he shouted, his face red as the blood on his fingers.

I did not respond. His blood was on my blade, my own blood was singing, and this time, I knew, I would have him.

When he charged again, it seemed to me he was moving through mud. I saw clear and big as a full moon the opening for my knife. I hefted the chair, ready to place it before me at the last instant, stopping him, while reaching through the legs for the fatal lunge.

But as I swung it into place, I remembered, like a shout in my mind, what Hal had said: *Philip likes his brother...do not kill him!* His advice, forgotten in my wrath, drowned for an instant the drumming in my blood. My knife thrust was a second too slow. Domon seized his chance, grabbing the chair and jerking it aside. It hit my hand, stuck between its legs, and knocked my knife away.

Vile Brusterian filled my head but I had no breath to utter it. I did not draw my boot knife. Yet. Should I decide to heed Hal's warning, *was* there any way to avoid killing Domon?

There was no time to think. He lunged. I dodged. He hit the table hard, grunting and panting as he got back up, holding his side, blood still dripping from his chest.

He backed away, and almost without pause, lowered his head and charged again, snorting like a bull. His haste and undirected rage made it an easy matter to lower my shoulder and let his movement toss him over it. He hit the floor hard and skidded into the doorway of the third, unused room.

He took his time getting to his feet and stood eyeing me warily. Too bad. If he kept bellowing around, I could probably avoid killing him. Reason fought instinct. Hal was right. In addition to his affection for his half-brother, Philip would relish an opportunity to denounce me to the Roth. The relationship between Ragonne and Elbany would be strained, which neither country needed. Philip might have me killed. I exhaled, feeling aggrieved, and in grim perversity, amused. This was why I hated politics. You couldn't kill even someone like Domon without having to worry about the consequences.

Domon panted, his cheek beginning to bruise where he'd hit the floor. One hand pressed against his chest wound.

Watching him, I assessed my situation. My belt knife had skidded all the way under the table, against the wall. I doubted either of us could retrieve it quickly enough. Not being Brusterian, he might not know about my boot knife. He might think me weaponless. I was between him and the outer door, but I did not believe I could walk backwards through both this room and the front room without glancing away from him, which I did not dare do. My empty fingers flexed, but I left my boot knife sheathed for now. I'd do my best not to kill him, but I would not risk falling victim to his intentions. I would sooner return to Ferrant to be Francis' washerwoman.

His gaze flicked, as if he were planning his attack. I was ready. I couldn't let him get too close. He was stronger, and if he got a firm grip on me, even Anhud's training might not help.

He tensed, eyes narrowing. His waiting, his sudden, unexpected patience, made me uneasy. Should I draw my remaining knife? That would be tantamount to deciding I had no choice but to kill him.

Perhaps not. If I could get him in arm's reach, carefully...it might work. I straightened, putting my hands on my hips, seeming to relax.

Domon, as I'd hoped, took this as a sign I was warming to his advances. He perked up, a smile beginning, engaging whatever charm he believed he possessed. "That's better. I am noble, after all." He moved closer, slowly, arms outstretched as if approaching a balky horse. "It's been a while for you, too, hasn't it." He winked. "I won't tell Orlo."

I smiled as encouragingly as I could.

He relaxed, and walked toward me more quickly. I smiled in earnest. Honestly, the arrogance of the man! To believe I'd go in the blink of an eye from fighting his attentions to welcoming them...I'd *stabbed* him!

I watched him for signs that he, too, was feigning, meaning to attack when he'd come close enough. *No.* He walked with caution but no tension as if readying for a move. I hadn't really expected this ploy to work. But it was. Years of drowning his brain in wine had obviously not benefited his thought processes.

I held my indignation and disgust tightly, trying to look approachable while readying my attack. As long as he came at that pace...

When he took his final step, I reached down. I pulled out my boot knife, swiveling it in my hand as I drew back, and brought the hilt down with all my strength on his head. It connected with a satisfying, solid *crack.*

He fell like a dropped stone. I paused long enough to check that he was still breathing. Boot knife in one hand, I scooted under the table to retrieve my belt knife.

Sheathing both, I ran for the door. Then I stopped, sprinted back to the *vitae* shelves, and scooped up half a dozen. Even with Domon unconscious, I did not care to be alone with him, but I didn't want to lose any more time to him. He was not stirring, yet I ran as if he were chasing me, out the door and up the steps to the kitchen.

CHAPTER XIV

"What has happened?" Mistress Baynor was at my elbow before I'd closed the door.

"Domon came to the library," I said, pleased my tone was even, almost calm. "Without Hal." The fear I'd pushed down reemerged, roaring. Stupid, I thought, feeling my shoulders quake. The danger was already past.

Someone gasped. Ina, the girl Domon had accosted.

Mistress Baynor squeezed my shoulder. "So Domon's dead?"

"No." I sounded sulky and defensive. I swallowed and tried again. "Knocked out. I hit him with the hilt."

Ina began to sob. A broad-shouldered young man left the hearth, brushing past the others, and folded her into his arms. His shirt, light against the heat of the kitchen, was soon patchily damp with her tears.

"Torrell," Mistress Baynor said. There was no reprimand, but neither was there encouragement. Managing relationships among staff could be thorny. "When Ina is calm, everyone will return to what they were doing. I expect the king still intends to eat this evening."

I waited while she put her domain back in order. After a while, satisfied her underlings had settled to their tasks, she led me to the farthest table. I put down the books I'd brought, too appalled by the rest of the day to be astonished I'd done so. One of her staff brought wine, bread, and a bowl of stew.

"Thank you, Jock." She waited to say anything further until he'd stepped away. "So he lives? That is regrettable."

"I wanted to kill him," I said, defensive again. "But Hal had said killing Domon, no matter what the provocation..."

"He's right." She sighed. "Philip would react badly, if only because it gave him a reason." Her voice slipped lower. "Where's Hal?"

Both my hands clutched the closest manuscript. "I don't know."

She pursed her lips. Collecting Torrell, she led him to the door, speaking softly. He nodded and left.

"Torrell will find him," she said as she returned. "I hope Domon hasn't killed him." She sat again, fingers tapping the table. "My idiot brother," she said, in a voice pitched low enough to reach only my ears. "Wasting a good servant on Domon."

She pushed a bowl toward me. "You should eat."

I stifled a smile. Uncook-like as her appearance was, Mistress Baynor held to the core belief of all head cooks that most troubles could be solved with good food. Many could, I supposed. It smelled wonderful, a dish meant for the king's table, swimming with costly beef, barley, and carrots drowning in the thick broth.

She saw my appraisal of the stew. "If we run out, he can have salted herring tonight," she snarled. "Maybe if I start feeding him what he deserves, he'll see reason about Domon."

I picked up a spoon. She curled her lip, clearly still thinking about her brothers. "Have you found anything?"

"No." I pulled the spoon through the stew, savoring the scent. "And I've almost finished searching. You were right."

"You need to return to Elbany." She slid the loaf closer. "If there's anything that will help us, it's not here."

"You know why the Roth sent me," I said, prickled on my lord's behalf by the undertone of criticism in her voice.

"I do," she replied, "but it might have been better to swallow his pride and go to Ferrant at the beginning."

"It wasn't pride that stayed him," I protested, my voice hot although remaining low.

She held up a hand. "Peace. It's done now. Perhaps I'd have agreed to the strategy if I'd been there. Conquered by an ambitious Valenian neighbor would be no better than conquered by...someone else."

We sat in silence. I thought about Torrell and what he might find, and suspected Mistress Baynor's thoughts ran along a similar path. I sipped at a spoonful of the stew. I hadn't eaten since early that morning, but it was too good to wolf down, and it gave me something to do while we waited.

The door opened. Torrell entered, and behind him, walking slowly but on his own, was Hal. There was a lump on his head so large I could see it from where I sat.

Mistress Baynor was there in an instant, grasping his arm

despite his protests. "Come. Sit."

I started towards them, but she had him halfway to the table before I'd taken half a dozen steps. She waved me back into my seat, steering Hal to the bench opposite. He sank into it shakily. Jock brought a bowl of cool water and a cloth. Mistress Baynor thanked both her servants, and they returned to their work.

"What did he hit you with this time?" She bathed the mass on his head.

"Wine bottle." He grimaced at her touch but did not move. "I'd just come around when Torrell arrived."

"Well, he ended up unconscious himself." She shot me a fiery glance. "I hope you gave him as pretty a lump." Her fingers probed. "I don't think the skull's cracked."

I blew out a breath, craning my neck for a better view. As soon as I'd seen the swelling I'd worried about the bone.

She noticed my scrutiny. "Want to check it yourself?" I stiffened, but the tone was one of professional consultation, not challenge. I stood, coming around to their side of the table.

"I agree," I said after examining the damage. It was a relief to know that if Hal was going to be injured regularly at least he had someone competent to care for him. Mistress Baynor, I felt certain, could have stitched up his arm as well as I had.

I tapped Hal's shoulder. "You should come to Reud and take service with the High King. It's safer being a Brusterian warrior."

Mistress Baynor snorted appreciatively and snapped her fingers. Jock brought another bowl of the exquisite beef stew. "Eat," she told Hal, even more firmly than she had me.

Hal, still very pale, picked up the spoon and sipped broth.

"This cannot go on," she said. "I'm going to Philip."

He looked up. "It won't do any good."

"What good will it do to let Domon keep at you?" she barked back.

I watched, intrigued by the display of her wrath. Her hands clenched and unclenched. Finally she strode across the room, not raging aloud as I would have, but crackling with anger fearsome in its control. "Stay here," she snapped as she shut the door behind her.

Hal met my eyes, then looked away. His face was almost colorless. I said nothing. What was there to say?

Mistress Baynor's rage seemed to quell mine, and I could feel relieved weariness creeping into my body. But there was work to do. No matter what Domon did, Saradena was coming. Scooting down the bench, away from the food, I took the first book from the top of the pile.

Despite my best intentions I had difficulty settling to my task. I hadn't read outside a library since I was a child. Even then, Doctore Mustorn had always conducted our lessons in the same quiet, tidy room, his stern silence reminding us how odd our instruction was. No noble but our father had his children taught to read. We were certainly never allowed to take books from our study room, let alone into the kitchen.

The bustle of servants provided continual, distracting movement. Hal's strained face reminded me of the day's troubles. But gradually, as he ate, he gathered himself, and I got used to the blur of activity. When I turned my attention to the book again, I found myself able to read, the kitchen now seeming warm and companionable. The scrapes and clattering as vegetables and meat were prepared, the smells as the food cooked, and the low talking of the staff created a background noise very like that of a scriptorium. With better smells. Scriptoriums usually tended toward the clean, crisp scents of ink and parchment. But sometimes, if one were seated too near a particularly forgetful scholar, pungent sweat and unwashed body.

"Lady?" Hal whispered presently.

"Hmm?" I did not look up immediately, snarled in a dicey passage of scribal obfuscation.

"Why are you here? In the kitchen?"

"Oh!" I blinked, realizing he did not know what had happened. In an equally low voice, I told him. When I finished, we sat in silence again. My fingers rapped the book but I did not return my attention to it, riveted by his slight smile. Was he *amused?* Pleased at having his prediction proved right? How *dare* he!

"What is it?" I spat.

"Lady?"

"You find it funny anyone would try to accost me?" I hissed. Domon's taunts still rang in my ears. "Or are you gloating? You were right. He wanted revenge."

He stiffened. "Neither, lady. But I confess I rather like the thought of him nursing a headache as good as he gave me. Yet he lives, so the king's anger will not be dangerous. It was well done."

Shame scorched like hot water down my back. My fingers curled, anger not lessening but changing its target. "Perhaps I should have killed him. He's a menace."

"You know King Philip—"

"I remembered," I said curtly. "Mistress Baynor agrees with you." I glanced towards the door, wondering how her discussion with Philip was going.

He shook his head. "She won't get anywhere." He sopped up the last of the broth with bread. "When Domon wakes, he'll go first thing to complain to his brother. About both of us, if I guess rightly. I may as well stay here. It will be a little while longer before he is looking for me." He moved down the bench, wiping his hands on his shirt. "Hand me a book, please, lady?"

I passed one across and went back to my own. We had not read long before Mistress Baynor returned, unsated fury crackling as she stalked in.

"Domon was there," she hissed between her teeth.

I exchanged looks with Hal.

"You," her flashing eyes caught Hal, "are unruly and uncooperative, and Domon has been far too lenient with you already."

This time, I felt certain, the glow in his eyes *was* amusement, albeit grim amusement, at hearing himself so characterized. "I expect I am to report to my lord Philip?"

"Immediately."

He rose, suppressing a weary sigh. "Very well. Thank you for the stew, Mistress Baynor."

"Hal—" she stopped.

I understood. She had to be tired of apologizing for her brothers. As a natural member of the Ragoni nobility, she felt responsible for their actions even when she could not influence them. Frustrating beyond endurance.

"You." Her gaze snapped to me. "It doesn't matter what you claim happened. Philip could not possibly believe a word you say. 'Everyone knows the dry-wombed are mad.' She raised a shoulder in apology, but it was no surprise Domon had called upon that adage. "And probably in league with Orlo. What was *that* about?"

I swore viciously in Brusterian. Domon's slander had come to Philip's ears despite my efforts. I told her what I'd learned from

Hal.

She sat. "It makes a certain amount of sense, I suppose." One hand cupped her chin, considering. "I would not have thought Domon capable of such complex reasoning, not with the amount of drink he downs, and has done for so long. I'll have to keep closer watch on him."

I made a noncommittal noise. It might be better for Mistress Baynor's own well-being to stop arguing with her brother about Domon, since Philip was resolved not to hear her.

"He knows Domon is lying." She stopped her hands before they slammed down on the table. "But he pretends to believe him and says he will do nothing. What will Domon have to do before Philip sees sense?"

I remained silent, hearing again the drums that had beat in my blood, demanding to drain Domon's life like a cup. I understood why it had been better to spare him, but it rankled to eat the insult and leave him alive to tell false tales.

"Ah, well. Nothing more I can do. Domon will fix himself soon enough. He's careening towards disaster." Mistress Baynor grimaced. "Soon, I hope."

Slowly her eyes refocused on our surroundings, and began darting around the kitchen, taking in what her staff was doing. She must not have liked what she saw. She rose, her tongue clicking. She started away, then turned back, tapping the table by my hand. "You will stay, for the rest of the day, won't you?"

I considered. It was probably safe to go back to the library. But I had *vitae* to read, the day was already far gone, and I was settled in comfortably. Nor did I mind people around, just now. I nodded.

She returned the nod briskly and went back to her work. I turned my attention back to mine as well. Later someone brought me a pot of dark mead. Mistress Baynor came back to say I could work as long as I liked, even after the kitchen servants had gone to bed, but I left when she and her staff did, feeling more exhausted than since arriving in Peran.

CHAPTER XV

I worked steadily but anxiously the next morning, waiting for Domon and Hal's arrival, wondering what would happen.

To my surprise, nothing did. At least nothing aloud. Assured of his brother's support, Domon returned to the dirty books with a smug smile. Moving so stiffly I knew Domon had taken his fists to him, if not more, Hal came into the second room only long enough to fetch a chair and a book. Apparently his punishment included Domon's constant, immediate presence. I bit down on a surge of white-hot anger but said nothing to either of them. There was nothing to say. Three days passed, long days of mingled tedium and frenzy as I continued the *vitae*. More long-winded accounts of more insipid Ragoni nobles. It was astounding the Roth was a competent ruler, given *this* was his mother's bloodline.

The next morning, Domon must have decided he'd shown his absolute authority over Hal long enough. He preferred to be alone with his reading, and allowed Hal to return to the second room while they were in the library.

I was glad to have his calming presence at my elbow again. I was reminded of sitting with Cedrick and Birnan, my two younger brothers, learning to read under Doctore Mustorn's watchful attention. Surprisingly for such an old man, he had sight and hearing like a hawk and about as much interest in humor. So it was no wonder that on the rare occasions our teacher stepped from the room, Cedrick prodded Birnan's ribs with a finger while Birnan elaborately ignored him, keeping his eyes riveted to his book. But most times, we sat quietly, studying in companionable silence. I sneaked a sidelong glance at Hal. He was probably Birnan's age, or near enough. I wondered if Hal had older brothers he tried to live up to, like Birnan had, always worrying he would never be as good.

Liath seemed cheered by Hal's return as well, spending most of the first day he was back stretched out beside him, her paw on his left hand.

We read until our eyes ached, but found nothing.

Nothing *really* about Saradena, that is. The morning of July 6th, I came across the name Sari de Nanin. I looked up, excitement tingling. It was close, the sort of variation well within the bounds of possibility. Could it be, finally...? Breath catching, I read the passage again. Hal caught my gaze, eyebrows arching. *Find something?* I half shrugged. *Maybe.*

I returned to the top of the leaf, going over it again slowly. Bitter disappointment pooled.

It *was* a name, but not a country's name. Merely a noble-woman from Verdun who married the brother of the lord whose *vita* it was, and a coincidental similarity to what I sought.

I shook my head at Hal and continued reading.

★★★

By the end of the week, we began the last shelf of *vitae*.

Domon's interests did not change, but his methods did. Either the manuscripts had begun to contain lurid lyrics, or the books had always included songs but he only recently decided to sing them. We often heard him caterwauling now, always to the same tune, humming when he couldn't read the words or make them fit his music. Some were so risqué I found myself blushing, despite my age and years of marriage. Some were apparently worse; they contained Valenian words whose meaning I did not know. Hal must have; in the midst of one such rendition he went absolutely crimson and kept his eyes riveted to his book, looking so uncomfortable I decided not to needle him about his misspent youth.

I had just started my current *vita*'s description of the birth of its subject's first son when Domon once more burst into song. I'd become adept at shutting out the noise, after the first surprise when a song began. But this one was lengthy, and as it continued, I found it harder and harder to ignore. It was so long it must be written in the text itself, not scribbled in the margins.

His volume increased as he went on. I put my hands over my ears, but I could still hear him. I hunched over the book, trying to focus, but found myself staring at the page, seeing not the words but a vision of myself standing behind Domon, ready to knock him senseless—and blessedly silent—again. I pressed my ankles against the legs of my chair, forcing myself to stay seated.

Unwanted, the words began to seep into my consciousness. There were many verses, each about a new place the speaker traveled to, a woman he met there, and the attentions she lavished upon him before he continued his journey. Between the verses was a refrain:

> *Girls the world over will roll in the clover*
> *With a man with a strut and a swagger.*
> *Purse above of gold and below of stone,*
> *I was well met by the girls of Marlon.*
> *The girls of Bruster pass muster,*
> *In Carvell, they are swell, as fine in sweet Carlomond.*
> *But the girls of Sera Serdent—breasts, sides, and eyes —*
> *Even Martin de Kolone would not pass them by.*
> *Even the Founder would have found them divine.*
> *But the eagle ladies let be, for all the ships in the sea,*
> *Else her purse will take your stones in fee.*

After several repetitions, Domon was belting out the chorus with lurid if atonal enthusiasm, but I heard nothing but the words themselves.

Sera Serdent! My hands fell from my ears like the last leaves of autumn. After the false hope of Sari de Nanin, I was wary, but...it was possible. It was dreadful doggerel, of course. Poetic genius was rarely found writing bawdy tales. But here was, perhaps, a mention of Saradena. The repetition of initial syllables was very common over the course of several copyings —

I pictured Domon eating and drinking as always while he read (and sang). I thought of the unsteadiness of his hand when he lifted the bottle. Maybe this was, like Sari de Nanin, a dead end, but...I met Hal's gaze. "Get the book!"

Without a word he ran to the shelf for another manuscript. Even in my distraction I admired his quick thinking. With surprisingly few complaints, he successfully traded it for the one Domon had been reading. It was not long before he handed the book to me, but my mind had already chased possibilities and implications through the Three Lands and beyond. He gave it to me open to where Domon had been reading, and there it was.

I scanned both leaves, turning over the few following. A full eight pages of bawdy travel lyrics. No title for either the poem or the book, but that was usual. Books were so rare their owner would know what each was about without notation. Even in the more literate past, this appeared to have been true. I'd found no books in the Ragoni library with formal titles. In Vere, important books were marked on their binding to make them easier to locate on the shelf, and books read frequently tended to be referred to by implicit titles referring to their content...

I forced my mind, skittering in excitement, back to the book. It was a *compilatio*. The poem was the fourth item in the codex. I leafed through the other works. As near as I could tell from a hasty inspection, they were unrelated. They were prose and about Ragoni lewdness rather than that encountered in travel. *I might have to read them more closely later.* I winced at the thought, *if the reference were real.*

I moved to the poem. I'd been hesitating, steadying myself to be disappointed again. I took a deep breath, touching the first lines. It began with the speaker boasting he would tell of his travels throughout the whole world and the women he 'met' along the way. There certainly were a lot of them, I thought wryly, noting again the length of the poem. As was typical, the chorus was written after the first verse, but after each additional verse its repetition was indicated by a mark.

I studied the refrain, the piece that had caught my attention during Domon's singing. Marlon, Bruster, and Carvell were all part of the Three Lands. Carlomond and Sera Serdent were not, nor did those resemble names for any region of Valenna, Bruster, or Elbany. They could be other countries, outside the known lands. Sera Serdent could be a variation of Saradena...

I checked rising hope. Better to eliminate other possibilities first. I did not want to spend time tracking down this reference only to discover that Sera Serdent was a minor town in Adrien.

"Are there maps?" I asked Hal.

"In the library?" His lips pursed. "Not that I've found. There might be something sketched in one of the unread *vitae*, but no formal, full maps."

I nodded. I'd expected as much. I'd glanced through nearly all the books and found no maps, formal or marginal.

I rose to pace. The Roth had a map, a large tapestry hanging in his audience chamber. It was solely pictorial, of course. His mother had made the tapestry for her husband, and neither of them could read. She was Ragoni...might Philip have one? If he did, could I manage a look at it? *No good.* Philip could not read either. If he did have a map, it too would be pictorial. What I needed was a detailed, labeled map. Where was I going to find that?

I stalked back and forth along the narrow room. Did I really need a map of the Three Lands before investigating the poem as a possible Saradena reference?

I did. I must. The refrain implied Sera Serdent and Carlomond were countries. The other places mentioned were countries. But perhaps they weren't. I would not give precious time to another false lead. Where was I going to find what I needed?

Vere had such maps. For all the help that was.

And—Martin de Kolone...

I rubbed my forehead. Why was that name familiar?

"A *map*," I muttered aloud as I approached the entrance to the outer room. "A *good* map."

"My brother the king has maps."

I stopped short. Deep in thought, I'd forgotten both Hal and Domon. I stepped to the doorway.

"My brother the king has maps," Domon repeated, eyeing me. "As good as Vere's. Better, I'd say. Why do you want them?"

I eyed him back. I'd never trusted him. I trusted him less now. Could I afford to assume he was lying? If the maps existed, he could get them. If he wanted to.

"The...song...you were singing," I said. "It mentioned places I've never heard of. I'd like to know where they are."

His gaze met mine, suddenly clear, then unfocused again. But I recognized *this* glazed look, and was intrigued rather than troubled. For the first time, I saw the Vere-trained clerk in him.

"Yes," he said slowly. "Marlon, Bruster, and Carvell, fine...but what are Carlomond and Sera Serdent? Hmm." His gaze sharpened. "I'd like to know that too." His leering smile returned. "This fellow thinks he's found the most beautiful women in the world. *And* accommodating. Yes, I'd like to know where they are. Hal!" He bellowed this last.

"Hal," Domon said again as he appeared. "Let's go see my brother."

CHAPTER XVI

I paced the library furiously. *Domon* was going to consult Philip's maps. I had not asked, nor been invited. He would have refused, and enjoyed refusing.

If he claimed neither Carlomond nor Sera Serdent could be found, could I trust him? He might steer me wrong for his own amusement. Or he might simply overlook the names. He had no real reason to search carefully.

And *why, why, why* was I certain I had seen the name Martin de Kolone before?

It was three hours before they returned. It felt longer. I'd paced until my legs ached. Then, lacking other options, I returned to the *vita* I'd been working on before Domon began singing.

I had more self control than I would have supposed. I was able to concentrate enough to read.

At length I finished it, finding nothing about Saradena. I felt weary and disgruntled, persuaded I should not have told Domon why I wanted the maps. Mistress Baynor could perhaps have convinced Philip to let me see them. I was not at all certain that was true. Still, maybe she and I could have thought of something.

I was trying to force myself to face the next *vita* when the door opened. I heard the now-familiar sounds of Domon settling himself at his table. I growled Brusterian epithets. He wasn't even going to tell me what he'd found.

Hal stepped through the doorway. Three large rolls of parchment lay cradled in his arms.

I jumped up. His eyes crinkled as he smiled. "My lord Philip's maps. All of them."

I silently withdrew the insults I'd hurled at Domon. Some of them.

He set them on the table. I pounced, unrolling the first with almost-shaking hands. Domon had not exaggerated. Or not much. It was a handsome map, nearly as fine as Vere's. It was

large, the width of a full skin, a detailed portrayal of the provinces and cities of Ragonne, beautifully illuminated.

And *labeled.* The writing was small and neat, a brilliant black,
but the letters were so archaically formed I had trouble reading
them. These maps were *old.* Not Philip, nor his father, nor his
grandfather, had commissioned them. Like the books, they were
an inherited treasure. But recognizing the maps' practical worth,
Philip and his predecessors had valued them more than the
books. Of course, they could scarcely have valued them less.

"Domon did not find Carlomond or Sera Serdent," Hal said
as I opened the second map.

Just as beautifully drawn, its writing equally old fashioned, it
showed the sixteen kingdoms of Valenna. I pressed my knuckles
to my lips. Every province. Every city.

"I convinced Domon to ask the king for leave to bring the
maps here so you could look as well." His voiced lowered. "I am
not certain if Domon is interested because you are or because of
the song's claims about the women there. But he wouldn't mind
if you found them for him."

I unrolled the third, which showed the southernmost kingdoms of Valenna, along with Elbany, and to the south and east,
Bruster. I brushed my fingertips across the clustered islands,
trying not to think of the glinting beauty of the Black Keep in the
afternoon sun, the feel of the black sand shore beneath my boots,
the touch of my brother Utor's hand correcting my grip on a
knife hilt.

"We have to search quickly," Hal continued. "King Philip
wants his maps back before his evening meal. That gives us just
over an hour."

"Well done," I murmured, gently pulling the map of the
kingdoms of Valenna towards me. *One hour.*

★★★

A difficult task and little time to accomplish it can make
hours fly. But sometimes, focused attention on that task makes
time seem longer. As I studied the map, the moments drew themselves out, like rain dripping from the eaves. Hal sat beside me
and began searching the map of lower Valenna, Elbany, and Bruster.

I worked systematically, difficult as that was since I knew
time was short. All my instincts clamored to scan the parchment
wildly, as if the names would leap out at me if my gaze fell upon

them. Training overmastered the urge. I ran my fingers, lightly and slowly, over the map from left to right, moving a little further with each pass. Time stretched like a cat in summer.

Hal finished his map and moved to the one of Ragonne, but when I finished the Valenna map, I began again. If they were anywhere, they would be here. It was more detailed than I had dared hope. Each kingdom's provinces, their few cities, all but the most minor villages, even informal local nicknames for certain areas, were included. But none were *Sera Serdent* or *Carlomond...*

Hal touched my arm. "Lady? It is time. I need to return the maps now."

*No—just a few more minutes—*one *minute—*

"Lady..." His tone held reproach.

I looked up. *I hadn't found them.* That was, I supposed, a good thing. If neither appeared in maps of the Three Lands, they might well be other countries. Elsewhere. But at that moment, it didn't feel good. I had to give the maps back.

I stood, looking over the map of Valenna once more before I must roll it up. Focusing on the words, I'd not appreciated its sheer loveliness. Vere's were scarcely finer. Brusterians made maps, but they were pragmatic, sketchily drawn in black ink, pictorial only, although my father had had one made that included wording. The Ragoni maps underlined in gold the name of the city where each king made his home, and the names of the provinces in red. The sea-mountains, running along the sides of the southernmost kingdoms, were drawn in dark grey, not the black ink the names were written in. They jutted up from the blue sea, their low peaks looking nearly as ragged and sharp as the real mountains—

I felt my mouth fall open. That *blue.*

Brusterian exclamations, both sacred and profane, trickled out. How could I have stared at the map for an hour, and not seen it?

The names of the seas were written not in the pale blue-green any Vere-trained scribe could make, but the spring-sky blue I had seen only once before. On the Saradenian letter. I touched it, with the barest tip of one finger. Strictly speaking the Vere ink was a better match for the real color of the sea, but no scribe would ever use it if *this* blue were at hand.

We were right.

I leaned heavily on the table, hands braced on either side of the map. They were right, the Roth and Lady Elsbeth. And me.

We'd supposed the wording of the Saradenian threat meant we had once known of and had dealings with Saradena. The letter also implied that from the Saradenians' perspective there had been an offense committed by us for which they now demanded redress or revenge. The map gave no indication, of course, what that offense might have been. But it proved our deduction. *We did know them. Well enough to have learned the secret of making this ink from them.*

Or perhaps they learned it from us! The Saradenians knew more now, but that might not have been true in the past. Someone in the Three Lands had made this exquisite map.

Hal touched my arm again. "I *have* to take the maps back. Did you find anything?"

"No," I said slowly, weighing whether to tell him about the ink. "And yes."

His head tipped inquisitively.

"I didn't find Carlomond or Sera Serdent." I tapped the illuminated water. "But this blue—this is Saradenian blue." I explained the distinctive ink on the Saradenian letter, and what it meant, finding it here.

"So now you know your search has something to find."

"Maybe." With a last long admiration of the blue, I rolled up the map. "We knew them. Now we *know* that. Surely something was written about them. But have any of those books survived?"

He gathered the maps up. I followed him into the outer room. I couldn't keep them but I didn't want to lose sight of them before I had to.

Domon looked up. "Did you find them?"

I shook my head. "No." I paused, deciding what to tell him. Something untrue might be best, given his wagging tongue. "Perhaps they're made-up places, for the purposes of the poem."

His derisive laughter interrupted me. "That could be true. But you don't think so."

"I assure you—"

He sneered. "You lie badly. Princess."

It was a well-chosen shot. I blinked, eyeing him with new caution. He was disturbingly cogent when his brain was drier than usual.

He laughed again, enjoying my consternation. "I'd say it means Orlo's ship was real. And the letter it brought."

I gaped. Was the Saradenian letter still a secret from *anyone?* But the next instant I remembered what Orlo had said. *Domon— Philip's clerk—was well into his day's bottle when I got there, but it sobered him up in a hurry.*

"Yes," I said, grudgingly acknowledging what he already knew. I did not mention the blue ink. Then I recalled his other conclusion, the false one. "Orlo plans no move against Philip."

He tipped his head back, studying me. "Perhaps. Or perhaps you *can* keep your own counsel when you choose. Any decent tactician knows an outward threat is an excellent time for an inward challenge. Orlo is a very good tactician."

"But—"

"Enough. Orlo may be planning nothing, as you claim. I suspect otherwise, as I have told my brother."

I resisted the urge to speak. No words of mine could dissuade him, and really, what proof did I have of Orlo's fealty but the impression, upon short acquaintance, of a man who planted his loyalties so deep no swirling winds of fortune would shake them?

He moved towards the door. Hal followed, the maps in his arms.

"Wait," I said, as Domon's hand touched the latch.

He looked back.

"The maps," I said. "Does Philip *know...?*" I let my voice trail off, unable to put into words the depth of what Philip should realize, and most likely did not.

I saw the clerk's gleam in his eyes once more. "No. He values them for their usefulness. They're much older than he supposes." His voice rang with scholarly confidence, and I shook my head at the strangeness of hearing it from him. "Philip has no idea of their uniqueness. But I do."

I was not sure what he meant, or meant to imply. I was glad when, after another moment, he opened the door and jerked his head at Hal, and they left. I could see, finally, why he'd been sent to Vere.

★★★

Weary of pacing the library, I returned to my chamber and paced the erstwhile storeroom, the smell of last year's apples lingering in the air. The poem mentioned not one, but two unknown countries. Were they allies? Did the threat from Saradena imply a threat from Carlomond as well? Or might Saradena and Carlomond be enemies? If so, could Carlomond be enlisted as *our* ally against Saradena?

I walked as if I were trying to wear a groove in the floor, questions pelting through my mind.

I should search for Carlomond as well as Saradena. Had I seen anything in what I'd already read that referred to Carlomond? What was Martin de Kolone the Founder *of?* The speaker considered Martin a famous enough person to use as a metaphor, and that his audience would be familiar with Carlomond, Sera Serdent, and Martin de Kolone. But that need not mean a connection existed amongst them. The parts of the Three Lands also mentioned certainly didn't have any.

I swore until I ran out of breath, if not invective, and only the sounds of my footsteps accompanied me. *Martin de Kolone.* I'd seen that name before. The memory had flown through my mind like an arrow. I could recall its position on the page, the look of the script, but not the book.

He must be Ragoni, having been born in or living in the region Orlo now governed. 'Kolone' was clearly a variant of 'Kolon'. He need not be noble. Anyone could and did identify themselves by where they lived. Martin might have been a fish-monger, called 'of Kolon' to differentiate him from another fish-monger named Martin who lived in Tiland.

I turned and stalked the length of the room again. For me to have seen his name in the Ragoni books, he would have been noble. But the poem called Martin 'the Founder'. If he were founder of something, wouldn't he be important enough to have a *vita?* I had not seen or read a *vita* for Martin de Kolone.

The vitae...*of course.*

I stopped, rocking slightly with the force of arrested move-ment. The *vitae.* The memory clicked into place. *That* was where I'd seen his name. I saw the book, clear as if it were in my hands. Martin de Kolone had been named in passing as the disinherited younger brother of the man who was the subject of the biog-raphy.

I ran to the door, and, unbolting it, burst through and back to the library.

CHAPTER XVII

I stood before the *vitae* shelves, glaring as if the book could be intimidated into showing itself.

The memory was fleshing out. The manuscript I sought was about two fingers thick, written in the same tidy script as many of the *vitae*. Indeed, *so* many were in that hand it seemed indicative of something. But what? Had the commissioning of *vitae* been a fashion for a time? Had *vitae* been recopied for unknown reasons?

After long minutes staring, it was clear I was not going to recall anything more about the book. I couldn't remember the name of the person whose *vita* it was, nor how long ago I'd read it. A systematic search would be necessary. Not wanting to waste time carrying books to and from the table, I sat on the floor and began with the ones I'd finished most recently. Book by book, row by row.

Well into the second shelf, I found it. My shout echoed through the library. It was the *vita* of one Davin de Oris:

> *In addition to his estates in Oris, which came to him by right as the eldest son, Lord Davin also unexpectedly inherited holdings near Kolone after the lengthy disappearance, strange return, and ultimate disinheritance of his brother Martin, called 'de Kolone' from his anticipated demesne, whose shameful behavior and final disgrace are set forth in his own* vita. *At the death of Lord Davin, the estates of Oris passed to his eldest son, Daren, with Kolone going to the younger, Irgon...*

I read the passage again, frowning. The song spoke of Martin de Kolone as 'the Founder'—a reverential title, as Cynan Maccus was honored as the Founder of Vere. But Davin's *vita* spoke of Martin disapprovingly. *Shameful behavior and final disgrace.* Was it the same man? Or two different men with coincidental names? I leaned back, no longer looking at the book, puzzling.

Shaking my head, I read the passage again. This time something else caught my eye. *Whose shameful behavior and final disgrace are set forth in his own* vita.

What *vita?*

I hadn't read a *vita* for Martin de Kolone. If Hal had, he would have mentioned it when we found his name in Domon's song.

I scooted over to the shelf containing the few remaining unread *vitae*, and began searching, scanning initial leaves until I found the name of the subject, then moving on. It didn't take long.

Martin's *vita* was not there.

***

I must have missed it. I was tired. Careful as I'd been, it would have been easy not to recognize it. Or so I told myself and tried to believe it. I searched again, more slowly. But there was still no *vita* for Martin de Kolone.

Unwilling to allow the first thread I'd found to lead to nothing, I checked a third time.

Finally I stood, a bit clumsily, numb from the awkward position and the damp hardness of the floor. Quashed hope, like a palpable lump, stuck in my throat. There was nothing to do but go to bed.

Martin's *vita* had not survived.

***

I went to the library much later than usual the next morning, unable to force myself to come early after so bitter a disappointment.

At length I coerced myself back to the remaining *vitae*, my determined concentration so intense it was nearly evening before I realized Domon and Hal had never come. I worked late, ready to finish the Ragoni books and go back to Elbany. Come what may.

***

When I finally returned to my room, I slept instantly and soundly. I was surprised, then, to jerk awake only an hour or two later, heart pounding.

I rolled over, knife in hand, listening, thinking immediately of Domon. If he tried again, I would kill him, Philip's displeasure be damned.

It was quiet, the same deep quiet as every night, the stillness of stone deep in the ground.

The disturbance had come from within, I realized, grimacing as I sheathed my knife. I had been dreaming. Of what? I lay back, trying to remember. The images were fractured and fading. There were books. Stacks of books...

I smiled humorlessly in the dark. *That* seemed understandable. I'd spent enough time searching and reading these past weeks. But that did not seem right. In the dream, it seemed to me, I hadn't been doing either. I tried to recall more but the fragments slipped away.

★★★

I woke again with a start. At first it seemed only a few moments had passed but my body told me it was actually several hours later, just before dawn. I'd been dreaming again. This time, more of the images passed into my waking mind. There were books, piles of them, but I wasn't searching them. I wasn't even present. There was a scribe, copying book after book, quickly as he could. His haste quickened my pulse.

I fumbled in my belt-pouch for flint and steel. Striking a spark, I lit the candle at my bedside, then rose and dressed. Pondering the dream, I didn't go to the library. I stayed in my room, throwing my knives at the door, enjoying both the satisfying *thunk* as they struck and the childish thrill of damaging Philip's palace. I hadn't practiced recently, and my aim was, to my mind, sloppy. I worked for more than an hour until my control was honed again.

I cleaned and put away my knives. It was time to return to the library. I was much later than normal. Domon and Hal might even get there first. My eyes narrowed at the thought. But soon, I'd never be going there again.

I halted, my hand on the door. A sudden burst of insight, the strike of inspiration scholars cherished but could not explain, flared into being behind my eyes.

The scribe in my dream. My sleeping mind had been working out what I'd seen but not understood. I had noticed many *vitae* written in the same careful script, and wondered what it meant. What I had *not* realized was how old they must be. *Very old.* They described the lives of people who lived so long ago it was nearly impossible to find direct lineage connections between them and living Ragoni nobles.

My breath caught as comprehension pressed on. The people described in those *vitae* must have lived and died hundreds of years ago. *But the books themselves could not be so old.* The script, although archaic, was readable, as was the language. Unlike the ancient books Domon had found. These must be *copies* of earlier books. A later but still long-ago Ragoni lord or more likely his clerk must have realized the older materials had become difficult to use and had the books copied.

Or—perhaps not *all*. Perhaps only those deemed worth keeping.

I tapped the door with my fingertips, thinking too hard even to pace. It was a guess. But...

It would explain why the *vita* of Martin, the disinherited and disgraced, was not preserved in a readable copy, while his brother's, carefully transcribed, survived, complete with its reference to Martin's now-lost *vita*. My hand flattened on the door, palm pricked by fresh splinters my knives had raised. *Was* it lost?

Maybe. But I doubted it. Martin de Kolone might have been disgraced and perhaps his family preferred to forget him. I could not help a surge of sympathy. But a good librarian would never throw away a book—and whoever organized this massive archival copying project was an excellent librarian. The shelf of unreadable books. The originals of the *vitae* had to be there. Martin's might be among them.

It was possible. It was tenuous. *If* the Martin of the song, and this Martin were the same. *If* there were a connection between Martin and Saradena. *If* his *vita* had anything to say about it. *If* all that proved true, Martin's *vita* might be worth pursuing.

I had no other prospects. But it would take time. If I continued with the *vitae*, I could finish in a few days. *This* would take longer. There was no way to know until after I'd done it whether the time had been worth it.

I had to. It was the only trace I had.

I rested my forehead against the door. Could I trust my judgment? I had itched to dig into the unreadable books as soon as I'd seen them. The new work would mean more weeks before I returned to Elbany, to be sent to Ferrant. I could not imagine returning to Elbany and explaining the waste of several weeks.

But neither could I imagine telling the Roth and Lady Elsbeth this chance had presented itself but I'd not followed the thread.

***

I returned to the *vitae* shelves and sorted out those in the tidy recurring script. If they showed signs of being copies, my guess was probably right. It took all morning. But at last I leaned back in my chair, manuscripts lying in an arc around me.

They were undoubtedly copies.

This scribe was more careful than most but even he made occasional errors. Errors of the sort one was prone to when copying an existing work. Repetition of words. Sometimes an entire repeated line. With the books lying before me I could see their bindings were identical. Browned with age and cracked by mistreatment, it had once have been supple leather. Sitting as a group, the books let me see beyond their current appearance to how they would have been: a uniform collection, copied because the Valenian language was changing.

I leaned further back, tipping the chair, rocking as I considered.

The unreadable books were the next step. I needed to confirm that originals of the copied *vitae* were among them. If so—

The outer door opened. I leaned to peer through the doorway. Domon would *never* sneak up on me again. It was not Hal and Domon. It was Torrell. Seeing me, he bowed before placing a basket on the table, and left. Hungry, and not minding a respite before tackling the unreadable books, I went out. I ate at the outer room's table, expecting them to arrive any moment, my presence in his place certain to nettle Domon.

The door opened again. I turned, expecting Hal and Domon, but it was Torrell again. He blinked at my unexpected nearness, then bowed.

"Pardon my intrusion, lady. This..." he held out a rolled parchment in his fingertips, as if it might do something untoward, "came for you."

Chapter XVIII

I took the scroll with shaking hands. Saradena? Again? And to me *personally?*

My first shocked, frightened thoughts, which the next instant I dismissed as foolishness. The Roth, perhaps. Or, more likely, Magistre Poll. Perhaps he had found something in Vere's library.

But the seal was not Elbany's or Vere's. Nor Saradena's, for that matter. I'd never seen it before. I ran my fingers over the wax. What...? I broke it and unrolled the parchment. It was not a long missive:

To Doctora Bann—Maudlin, Princess of Bruster; Tedora, Queen of Ferrant; and clerk to Douglas, Roth of Elbany—

Greetings.
You thought I was not in earnest when I told you I had wished to offer for your hand when your father began your marriage negotiations. I was.
I am.
To show the strength of my purpose I have prevailed upon my clerk to teach me to read and write. For this letter I had him write my words. Next time, I will have learned enough to write without his help. I will speak more fully then.

Your servant,
Orlo, Lord of Kolon

Mercy. What was he thinking? Surely he had ears listening on his behalf in Peran. They must have heard Domon's suspicions. He had written to me anyway? This wouldn't calm those rumors.

But—what a letter. Only a rock would be unmoved. Learning letters to woo a lady. Had it ever happened in the history of the Three Lands? Or any of our stories?

But—what terrible timing. In the face of the Saradenian

threat and all it would entail, I had no part of my mind left to fret about this, about him, about what he was asking and what I might think about it.

But—I would have to write back. It was rude to leave a letter unanswered.

But not yet. I had no idea what to say. And I had work to do. Rolling the parchment as tightly as I could, I tucked it into my belt pouch.

The unreadable books were waiting.

Hurrying as quickly as I dared without risking damage to the books, I returned the *vitae* to their shelves. When the table was clear I ran my hand over its surface, brushing away dust, readying myself along with my workspace for the next step. I'd never studied books this old.

Inhaling, I gingerly lifted the first from the shelf. Despite my care, bits of the binding flaked away.

I squeaked, and was instantly flooded with shame at the sound, grateful no one was present to have heard it. Except Liath, who had apparently followed Torrell in during his second visit, and chose that moment to sidle up. I lowered the book to the table.

"Shoo." I waved a hand at her as she padded over to inspect the scattered pieces. Putting her nose in the air as if to say she hadn't wanted to see them anyway, she jumped up onto the table and sprawled. She was not touching the manuscript, so I let her be.

As I picked up the fragments, I saw writing on the reverse side. Brown-black ink-etched letters, strangely shaped but recognizable. The pieces were too small to tell if the language was readable. The binding had been made from an even older manuscript. Indignation flared, wrath evenly divided among those who would cut up a manuscript to use as another book's binding and generations of flagrant idiots who allowed these books to rot.

I cradled the pieces in one hand, the other hovering over them without quite touching. These broken bits were almost certainly the oldest writing I had ever held. I breathed deep, tamping down my appalled irritation. Everything indicated the competence of the ancient Ragoni clerks. Surely they had good reason to use the manuscript for binding. Perhaps the book had been damaged beyond repair.

But there was no excuse for the Ragoni lords' neglect.

That was not quite true. There was none I would accept.

I understood why they abandoned their books to the whims of time and damp. They could not read, and did not think their clerks would learn anything worth knowing from them. Forgotten, these books had not been thrown away, or reused piecemeal in the jakes or the kitchen. Neglect may have ensured their survival. As I stood with the parchment bits in my hand like the bones of the dead, knowing this did little to make me feel less murderous towards the lords, who held the precious gift of literacy of less worth than the slaves who dug their latrines.

I crossed to Hal's cupboard and put the pieces inside, in a small pile on one of the shelves. Returning to the table, I settled into my chair. I raised the front cover, wincing as the binding crackled. I didn't let the cover fall flat but held it up, not opening the book fully, trying to avoid further damage. Touching the book was a wonder, a heady rush greater than well-kept wine. My fingers reveled in the feel of the parchment, damaged as it was. If I could coax comprehension from the old words...unimaginable.

The first leaves were too warped and rotted to discern words, but by the seventh, I could identify groups of letters, some of which I recognized.

And—success!

As I'd hoped, I could, albeit slowly, locate names although I wasn't able—yet—to read the work. In this volume the name 'Arlon de Calin' repeated frequently. I couldn't be certain it was his *vita*, but it seemed probable. Which bolstered my theory that the unreadable books were the originals of copied *vitae*, but didn't prove it. To prove it, I needed to find an unreadable book with the same repeating name as a *vita*.

Proceed? Or stop, return to reading the remaining books, and go back to Elbany in a few days?

The internal debate was brief. So far, the evidence suggested I was right. And having gotten my hands on the ancient books, I wasn't leaving them. Not until I followed this strand of reasoning or came to its raveled end.

***

Liath stretched and rolled to her other side. I obligingly scratched her stomach before taking the unreadable book back to the shelf and returning with a second.

I wasn't so lucky this time. The book was heavily damaged. No matter how long I stared I could not distinguish one word from the next. The ink was too far faded. Here, indeed, I was forced to admit, was a candidate for reuse. I put it back, making sure it was well away from the others to keep its virulent rot from spreading.

The next didn't look much better. Pieces of its binding curled like tumblers at a fair. The leaves were so warped the strap could no longer be pulled closed. But its appearance was misleading. After the first quire, the damage became minimal. The script was small and a bit odd in the blockiness of its letters, but the ink remained a deep black. I found I could identify names easily. This scribe placed a small dot above each personal name. It was not, I concluded, a *vita*. No name repeated enough. What *was* it then? I wished I could read it and know what it said.

I worked steadily, although my frustration at being unable to read the old books grew with each manuscript.

"You! *Got* you!"

Liath jumped up, startled by my shout, then sat down to lick her tail and pretend she hadn't been.

Osric of Boltar. That name appeared again and again in the ancient book I held, which meant it was the original of his *vita*. I'd read his *vita*. I remembered. Another half-mad noble. Convinced dragons slept beneath the largest sea-mountain off Boltar.

I had a match.

From the pair, I *should* be able to learn to read the old form of Valenian.

***

One hand on each manuscript, I moved my fingers slowly from line to line as I mouthed words in a soundless whisper.

I had supposed correctly; the newer book was definitely a copy of the older. But the ancient language was *very* different, much more than it had seemed in my earlier, cursory glances. With effort and time, I could work it out. But how much effort? And how much time?

I closed both books. My next step was plain. Find Martin's *vita*. There was no point in chewing on the problem of the language further until I had Martin's *vita*.

***

Much later, Liath growled when I set a book too close for her liking, so I decided I'd better stop long enough to clean my work-table. I began returning the unreadable books for which I'd found copies to a shelf together, the others to their original places. I carried one at a time, not wanting to make their damage worse by letting one rub against another.

At the fourth I paused, running my fingertips over the binding. It must have been a handsome volume. A design whorled in the leather, coiling across the front to the spine and around to the back. It had been inlaid with gold, once; I saw flecks quiver and wink in the dark channels. Only a very fine book, now, would be given such a splendid binding, if anyone could be found who knew how to make it. I turned the manu-script in my hands, imagining it as it must have been, new and unmarred. The surface had been scored so deep it obscured the design in places. Regretfully I moved to put it back on the shelf.

I stopped, turning the book in my hands, trying to work out why my gut said to look again, that there was more here than I'd consciously seen. I touched the cover, the binding, the spine. Something felt strange. I lifted the book, spine upward, searching with touch and sight.

There. A short, narrow scar in the leather, but thin and clean-edged. It looked like a small knife-score. Intriguing. The time-born wear I could understand, but this seemed intentional. Why would someone damage the book on purpose?

I placed it on the shelf and picked up another manuscript I knew had a copy. Here, too, on the spine, I found a nick.

Moments earlier I had been weary, wondering whether I could continue working. Now I was awake and quick-breathed, rushing to the shelf holding the ancient manuscripts I knew had been copied.

All. All their spines had the nick. Mark. It was a *mark.*

I turned to the unreadable books I'd identified as *vitae* but which did not have a copy, and inspected their spines. It took me longer to find, but these were also marked, an indented dot in the binding. Both dots and nicks had probably been made by a knife. Scribes often hold a small knife in their left hands as they copy, to scratch off any mistakes from the quills in their right.

The scribe had coded the ancient books, a small vertical cut for those to be copied, a dot for those not. This discovery would save considerable time. Instead of having to look through each unreadable manuscript, I could use the marks to sort out those that had not been copied. Martin's should be among them.

It was late, but I had no intention of going to bed. Not with Martin's *vita* so close. I wouldn't be able to read it tonight, I knew. That work would take days. More likely, weeks. But I could find it and touch it.

I gathered the uncopied ancient *vitae* and settled myself at the table. Liath leapt down to prowl the rooms, then returned, curling herself on one corner of the table.

It went faster than my earlier work. I'd become more accustomed to the script of the old Valenian books, a small hand with blocky letters written so close together that discerning individual words was challenging.

The number decreased steadily, if not rapidly. I found myself listening for the outer door. If Domon had gone back to searching the library during the times he believed I would not be there, he would be arriving soon. Even with Hal's presence, I did not want to be caught unawares by Domon again.

But the door did not open, and I worked on, uninterrupted. Finally, closing a manuscript, I reached for the next.

None remained.

I blinked, feeling slow and stupid. How could there be none left? I hadn't found Martin's yet.

Realization trickled in like a slow spring filling a basin. Martin's *vita* was not there. It had not been copied, and the original had not survived. It was all for naught. I leaned back, too weary even to vent the luminous Brusterian erupting in my mind.

After a long while I straightened, steepling my hands. It was time to let this folly go. If I had not pursued it, I'd have finished the *vitae* by now and be on my way back to Elbany. There had always been little chance Martin's *vita* contained information about Saradena. It did not matter now. The *vita* was lost. As was the time I'd spent looking for it. Mortification spread heat across my face. One would think that, having faced renunciation before, I would have learned to do so with a steadier gaze. I swallowed a tremulous sigh, thinking of Martin, disgraced, disinherited, and now completely forgotten.

I knew what I needed to do. And—what I needed to write to Orlo.

CHAPTER XIX

Despite the late night, I came to the library the next morning at the usual time. I just wanted to finish the remaining *vitae* and return to Elbany.

One, maybe two days more.

***

The next day I found it more difficult to concentrate. My gaze kept straying to the shelf of unreadable books. I still longed to tackle them, to try to work out how to read the older language. Hundreds of years had passed since anyone tapped their meaning. I might be able to.

That, however, was not my task.

I turned my gaze back to the book, but it was one of the most dull of the *vitae*, and my attention strayed again.

Elbany. Soon I'd be back. How had my students progressed in my absence? Would I be allowed a day to check their work before the Roth sent me away again? I'd left them many tasks, more than they could possibly have completed, but they didn't know that. Returning before they finished their work would be good for them. They'd work harder during my next absence. I smiled. My young scribes didn't yet know that many times what scribes planned to copy was only tenuously connected to what they finished. Books always took longer than their copyists hoped—

I stood so fast I bumped the table, dislodging Liath. She yowled. I ignored her.

Of course...

I had assumed Martin's *vita* would be among those marked as not to be copied, because no copy survived and because Davin's *vita* said Martin was disinherited. That was a shaky assumption. Martin might have been too important, or too high a noble, to erase from history.

What if Martin's *vita* had been marked to be copied, but either no copy had actually been made, for whatever reason, or the copy itself was lost? It might still be here.

I pressed both hands against the sides of my head. *No.* I should not waste time with this.

But I knew I would not be able to let it go. Not without looking. Better to get it over quickly.

I brought the nick-marked books to the table, almost grudgingly. It was indulgence of my curiosity and scholarly hunger, not to mention Brusterian stubbornness. I scanned the manuscripts more quickly than I ought, and with less concerted attention. Liath finished devouring a mouse she had caught under Hal's cupboard and returned, purring self-satisfactorily.

Which was why I was well into the eighth book before I realized I'd seen Martin's name. More than once.

I flattened my fingers on the leaves. *It couldn't be.* But there it was. *Martin de Kolone.* Twice on this leaf alone. Inhaling shakily, I turned back to the first legible leaf. Running my fingers down the page, I found the name and touched it like a talisman. I turned the leaf. It appeared again. I turned another, and another, brushing my fingertips over his name, hands trembling.

"I found it." I kept one hand on the book, unwilling to lose contact with it, and reached with the other to stroke Liath's chin. "I found Martin's *vita.*"

***

Exultation at last gave way to fear. What if I couldn't unravel the language? Worse, what if I spent the time to learn to read it and it contained nothing about Saradena? Failing would be worse than not attempting it at all. I tugged at my braid fretfully.

So I would not fail. But how to begin?

I rose to pace, drawing my belt-knife and flipping it as I walked. I had planned to start with one of the pairs of copied and original *vitae* I had already found. But what if the original of Davin's *vita* were here? The brothers' *vitae* must have been written about the same time, most likely by the same scribe. The script and language would be the closest to Martin's I could hope for.

I returned to the shelf of unreadable—perhaps for not much longer—books and began searching the *vitae* marked to be copied that I hadn't looked through yet. My luck held. The third manuscript I picked up was Davin's. It took me longer to find its copy on the *vitae* shelves than it had the original.

By noon I was at the table with both versions open before

me.

When I finally stumbled out that evening, I found two baskets in the outer room. Despite my determination never to be caught unawares again in the library, I hadn't heard the door open when the servant brought either noon-tide or supper. Cursing my carelessness, despite the scholarly focus that had caused it, and wondering why Domon and Hal had not come, I salvaged something still edible before heading to bed.

★★★

I had expected difficulty. Even so, the second day's work was discouraging. The older form of Valenian shared many words with its descendant but I couldn't get a handhold on how it made meaning. Was *isc* a word or someone's name? Was *arbore* a variation of *arbos* or were they different words?

For the next three days I drowned growing anxiety in the thrill of the work. Once steeped in the language, I found I could identify more modern words' ancient counterparts. There were two letters in the older language that did not exist in the modern, but their roles were played by others. Once I figured this out I could find the parallel of words in the Old Valenian which had seemed incomprehensible. But I still couldn't work out how the ancient language conveyed meaning. Common linking words like 'of' and 'on' eluded me, and without them, it was impossible to figure out how the other words related to each other.

The soft scratch of wood on stone told me the outer door had opened. I cocked my head, listening, but heard neither Hal and Domon nor the scrape of a basket on the table. More intrigued than concerned, I was on my feet as Mistress Baynor stepped through the doorway.

"Good evening." My voice, unused for days, sounded strange in my ears.

Small tight lines stood at the corners of her mouth, as if she were worried. Or angry. "I have news."

"What has happened?"

"Laon returned from Elbany a week ago."

I skittered about in my mind, Old Valenian cluttering and slowing my thoughts. "Philip's son. Yes?"

"My feebleminded nephew." Her lip curled. "If he continues as he did at dinner three nights ago, the secret of Saradena will be known beyond any concealing."

"What?" The clouds of Old Valenian fled.

"He asked his father—" she stopped, pinching the bridge of her nose. "Openly—at dinner—in front of *guests*—and *servants* —about your search, wondering if you had found anything."

I bit back a Brusterian vulgarity.

"Philip shut him up as quickly and unobtrusively as he could manage, but subtlety is not his strength. Half a dozen servants heard everything that was said."

"That..." I switched languages.

Her eyebrows climbed. "I expect I agree." She rubbed her temple. "Are *all* my kinsmen fools?"

Why did Orlo's name leap into my head in rebuttal?

"The guests were Laon's friends," she went on. "My guess is they had so much wine they will not remember what was said. But my people do. I am in control of my staff, but this gossip is too exciting to suppress." A corner of her mouth twitched. "I did dilute it."

I turned from where I'd begun to pace. "What did you do?"

"My children are grown, all but the youngest," she replied. I nodded, although I hadn't known until that moment she had any children. Nor had it occurred to me to ask. "Her tutor, Arvetta, is friendly with many of the women on my staff. And, as I have long suspected, a gossip. I told my husband, in her hearing, that Laon had found another Ragoni royal bastard on his latest trip, a woman named Saradena."

"That," I exhaled, "is brilliant."

Her lips pressed thin, but she was clearly pleased. "It seems to have deflected the real story. For now. Too many people heard what Laon truly said. But it confuses the issue. And it has spread quickly. Of course I told my husband later it wasn't true but I needed to cover up a slip of Laon's. Don't worry," she added. "I didn't need to tell Daron anything more." Her eyes shone with affection, and pride in his unmitigated trust. I looked away.

"Arvetta must have told everyone she met for the last two days," Mistress Baynor continued. "This afternoon I overheard Ina telling it to the rest of the kitchen staff. I had not thought her quite so keen to carry stories." Her eyes narrowed.

I doubted this boded well for Ina.

"This evening Daron told me our oldest son came by to ask about his new aunt." She smiled. It was the look of a well-hidden fox scoping out the chickens.

Philip could have no notion of how fortunate he was that Mistress Baynor had not married a rival lord.

"Have you found anything?" she asked abruptly, lips settling back into tense lines.

"Perhaps," I said. "I've found a book that may be useful but I can't read it. Yet."

She followed me to the table. I showed her Martin's *vita*, and the two versions of Davin's. "Reading modern Valenian copies in parallel with their Old Valenian originals should allow me to reconstruct Old Valenian enough to read uncopied texts."

"Like Martin's *vita*."

"Exactly." Frustration burned my throat. "But it's not working."

"Why not?"

"There are fewer words in the old language. I can't figure out how it signals the relationship of words to each other."

Her eyebrows drew together.

I tapped Davin's modern Valenian *vita*. "The copy might say 'he sat in the chair.'" I touched the older book. "I can identify the words for 'he', 'sat', and 'chair' in the Old Valenian. But not 'in'. And it's crucial. The little words tell us how the big ones go together."

"This book...will what it has to say be worth this effort?"

"That's the problem, isn't it? I can't be sure until I read it. I don't know," I said wearily.

Her face relaxed minutely. "You've been busy."

"It's been quiet." I drummed the table, letting my fingers fall heavily to vent my frustration. "That's a help. But also a worry. Where's Domon? What's he doing? He had been coming here in the night, trying to forestall my search." I wanted to pace again but forced myself not to. "I don't think they've been here. Nothing seems to be touched while I'm gone. I'm worried about Hal."

"So you did notice they were gone." Her voice was pleased, but with an undertone of irritation. "I wondered."

"What?"

"Gone." Mistress Baynor repeated. "Domon finally embarrassed Philip past endurance or pardon."

I dropped into my chair. "What happened?"

"Have you heard the rumors Philip means to arrange a marriage of his eldest daughter to the King of Marlon?"

I shook my head, gesturing to the other chair, and she sat.

"The rumors are true. Just over a week ago Marlon's representative and his wife arrived. He was escorted away to be entertained before the negotiations began the next day. She was left alone briefly as the household staff completed final preparations of their room before sending a servant to bring her there. Ten minutes—maybe—" Mistress Baynor's voice broke. It was anger, I realized, and shame.

"Domon did not know who the Marlone woman was, or, for once, was actually too drunk to care." She sighed. "Philip has had his hands full, shielding Domon as much as possible and trying to preserve the marriage agreement."

I shuddered, remembering my encounter with Domon. "Did he...succeed?"

"No." Her smile was bitter. "Domon barely got his hands on her. But it was enough." Her hand wavered in a measuring gesture. "Domon is not dead. Philip was able to spare him the worst. The Marlone representation would have been within his rights to demand it. But he agreed to settle for Domon's banishment. The marriage will go forward, but Philip had to increase Micela's dowry. Substantially."

I was surprised to feel tension ease from my shoulders. I thought myself willing to be rid of Domon by whatever means presented themselves. But I'd seen the scholar's gleam in his eyes, however briefly, and that was something. I was glad he was leaving, though. "Where did he go?"

"Verdun. Another natural sister, Berlain, is married to a minor Verduni lord. Domon will be confined to her household."

"There hasn't been time to send a messenger to Verdun and back."

"My sister does not know Domon is coming."

"Ah. What if Lady Berlain and her husband refuse him?"

A slight smile flickered across her face. "There, too, Philip will have to pay to ease Domon's path."

At least the library—and corridors—of the *palais* would be safe now. But I hoped Hal would find someone in Lady Berlain's household to bind the injuries his master would surely continue to inflict. I was sorry I'd not bid him farewell.

"Hal will be returning in a week or so."

"Oh. I assumed…"

She interrupted with a shake of her head. "He's a good servant. Philip wants him back. Our sister will not be pleased at having to assign one of her own people to Domon. Even less so when she discovers his heavy-handedness." She yawned. "Pardon. It's been a long week."

"I expect so." I waved off the look of apology as she covered another yawn. "I'm glad he's coming back before I leave. I would regret not telling him goodbye."

Her expression softened. "I was irked with you for not having the courtesy to inquire about Hal's health, when he had been absent so many days and with Domon's history."

"I'm sorry, I—"

"No, I apologize," she said. "I had not thought about what it must be like, searching for what we need and may not find, all the while watching our year slip past."

"It does tend to dominate other concerns," I whispered, looking down at the pair of open books, one comprehensible, the other still locked against me.

She leaned closer. "Let it."

CHAPTER XX

I spent the next four days diligently—and with increasing desperation—studying both versions of Davin's *vita*. I made progress. But too little, and too slow.

Scribes always spelled however they thought best, but they typically did not use more than two or three variants for the same word. Old Valenian employed many forms. Davin's *vita* had eight spellings for 'horse': *esteidu, esteidun, esteida, esteidan, estadio, estadis, esteidand,* and *esteidant.* Nearly every word had as many variations. Did it mean anything more than that the learned fore-bears of Ragonne had delighted in variety, the way a person enjoys a garden, all flowers, and yet none the same?

The afternoon of the fifth day I opened Martin's *vita* to see how much I'd learned. I found I could identify a rough meaning for just over half the words. But I still couldn't work out how the words related to one another. There was a sentence with Martin's name, his brother's name, one of the versions of 'horse,' and a form of 'hit.' Did Martin hit his brother, who was sitting on a horse? Had Martin hit his brother's horse? Or did the brother do the hitting, of either Martin or the horse? I rubbed my temples and stared, but the page remained maddeningly half readable.

The blazing weather did not dent my concentration, but neither did it improve my mood. Still, Domon was gone. I worked with greater ease, not starting every time the door opened. But after two more days' work yielded no improvement in my ability to read Martin's *vita*, fear began to well up like water from a covered spring.

Thinking perhaps I was trying too hard, I took a break to compose a response to Orlo. That, however, went even worse. I knew what I needed to tell him, but the words refused to convey to the parchment. After three ruined sheets I felt guilty about wasting parchment and got out my wax tablet, but in spite of the ability to start over without cost, I found no acceptable words.

Not ready to attack the Old Valenian again, I returned to the book in which Domon had found the song. Perhaps another part contained more information about Saradena.

At first it was a welcome change. It was a relief to turn pages, comprehending what the words said. Soon, however, understanding was more curse than blessing; the song was by far the most innocuous material the book contained. I read it all, quickly, shuddering at its depravity, but the *compilatio* provided no other references, however oblique.

★★★

I wiped sweat from my brow and dried my hand on my skirt. I had gone back to the beginning of Davin's *vita*, working line by line, but still could not make the older words into ordered sense without the copy.

Stymied on that front, I forced myself to sit with parchment and ink until I'd written a few lines to Orlo which would simply have to do:

To Orlo, Lord of Kolon:

The effort you have undertaken is admirable but better to do so for your own sake. You know I have a task at which I dare not fail. Pray do not distract me again.

Doctora Bann

Barely waiting until the ink dried, I rolled the sheet and sealed it. I could ask Mistress Baynor to arrange a messenger to take it to Kolon.

That finished, there was nothing more to do than return to Davin's *vita*. For all the good I was doing.

★★★

I carefully moved both versions of Davin's *vita* aside. Elbows on the table, I closed my eyes and let my head fall into my hands. I pressed my thumbs against the bridge of my nose, willing thought to arise within, something, *something* that would make the Old Valenian comprehensible.

It was a measure of my desperation that for a moment I wished Domon were there. He *was* a clerk. Maybe if I showed him what I'd learned...I knew Valenian well but perhaps not as well as a native speaker...perhaps there was something I didn't understand enough to tease meaning from its older form. Even as the thought bloomed, I recoiled from it. The less frantic parts of my mind did not want Domon back for any reason.

At last I rose. After pacing for a while, I began throwing my knives at the door to the unused room. *Hal.* My instincts were right, calling to mind Domon, but it wasn't him I needed. I was stuck. I needed to talk with someone, preferably someone who could read.

But Hal wasn't here.

I sheathed my knives and headed for the kitchen.

***

The kitchen, always abuzz, was louder and busier than I'd ever seen it.

"What's going on?" I asked as Mistress Baynor came towards me.

"Betrothal dinner." She spoke loudly to be heard over the din. "Our household *will* show its excellence." She lowered her voice. "Particularly after our embarrassment." She glanced around at her bustling staff. "It's a small price to pay to be rid of Domon." Her head jerked towards the servants. "The flurry is as much excitement as effort."

I looked again. The women were nearly dancing as they worked. The men held their shoulders more loosely. They smiled at each other as they passed. Cups stood upon the tables.

Mistress Baynor laughed. "They opened a barrel of Philip's brownest. No, he doesn't know. Yes, I let them do it." She lowered her voice again. "These women were Domon's favorite targets, close to his territory and often alone. Several of the men caught bruises when they intervened. They're not all as big as Torrell."

"It's been days since Domon left!"

"I know. I expect it will run its course in a few days more. I won't stop it as long as it doesn't get in the way of giving Micela an exquisite betrothal. She deserves it." Her lips thinned. "I'm sure you can appreciate how difficult it would have been to make another match."

"Yes." That Marlon had *not* broken the engagement was telling. The kingdom was large, wealthy, and had been powerful before its previous king set out to restore Otto's empire. Which meant attacking and attempting to conquer his neighbors, many of whom did fall to him before he was finally defeated. The new king of Marlon was trying to ease his country back to respectability.

Philip's daughter would marry the nephew of the man who killed her cousin, and both sides deem it a good match. Politics.

"Come, sit." Mistress Baynor touched my shoulder. "Philip feasts tonight in honor of his guests, so the evening meal is later than usual. We have not begun serving yet, and when we do, it will be prolonged. There will be entertainment between the courses. As you would know."

Yes. I had endured many such spectacles. They had been merely annoying in Bruster. The food was superb, the verse and music beautiful, but the company an arrow storm. In Bruster you weighed each word as if handing gold—or steel—to the person you spoke with. In Ferrant, feast days had been agonizing. Every eye I passed flicked to my belly. At first the looks were jovial and indulgent, enjoying their imagined notion of their king's newly-wedded delights and anticipated heir. After a year, the gazes held concern. After two, anger. After three, betrayal, as if I had chosen to deny Francis a legitimate son. After four, the glances became surreptitious but the lines between their eyebrows more pronounced. One of the few benefits of my reduced status was no longer having to attend feasts. A library, even with a thorny problem, was preferable to dining room diplomacy.

The servants' happiness seemed to enhance their efficiency rather than detract from it. Mistress Baynor supervised their efforts, but her direction was rarely needed. Presently the first course, a dizzying array of fish dishes, was steaming and ready for the hall.

"When do you expect Hal?" I asked in the quiet after the kitchen staff had carried the dishes to the adjoining room, where the hall staff—and, for the highest lords, their own retainers—waited to take the food to the hall.

She pursed her lips. "I'm not sure. Why?" Before I could respond, she added, "He won't be returning to the library."

I hadn't realized until that moment that I'd been assuming he would. "You advised me to have him help search." It sounded like a complaint and an accusation.

"I know," she said. "But Philip will not assign him merely to books, now Domon is gone."

"But—"

"I already asked Philip." Her gaze sharpened but the return of her staff interrupted her. She left to oversee the final preparation of the second course.

I began to feel awkward that I was the only one idle. When Mistress Baynor returned, I asked if there was something simple I could do. Perhaps working with my hands would help calm the waves in my mind. She looked sharply at me again but gave me a bowl of nuts to crack.

"What is the entertainment?" I asked after Mistress Baynor sent up the second course.

"Verse about the heroes of Valenna during the Ottonian war. Between later courses will be poems about Valenna's role in the Ricardian war." She snorted. "What nonsense *that* will be I can scarcely imagine. Ragonne had no part in opposing Richard." She paused. "No official part, anyway. Orlo and Oliver—" she broke off. "I take it the search isn't going well? I thought you had found something."

I stifled the desire to ask what she'd meant to say. None of my business. *None.* "I thought I'd be able to figure out how to read it. I haven't." I paused. "I'm not sure I can."

Her mouth twisted sympathetically. "Is there no one else who would know? At Vere?"

"No. We have old books at Vere, but they're in Brusterian, not Valenian, and they can still be read without much difficulty." *But not by me.* No one but the *magistres* were allowed to touch the frail oldest manuscripts, although the students and *doctores* were permitted to read copies. "Either Brusterian has changed less than Valenian, or Vere's oldest books are not as ancient as these."

"There's nothing else here that might help?"

I cracked nuts with frustrated vigor. "Not that I can find."

"What will you do next?"

"I don't know." I turned my attention to the bowl, picking nutmeat from the shells with more force than was effective.

As the dinner dragged on, Mistress Baynor's staff became tired and the work of the kitchen occupied the cook's attention. I was guiltily relieved. I'd come there hoping talking might help me sort the chaff and wheat of my flailing thoughts.

It had. I just didn't like the answer.

If I could not work out Old Valenian, all that remained in Ragonne was to finish the few remaining *vitae*, and leave.

If I could not work out Old Valenian...this point was the sorest. I did not like to give up, and I did not like to fail. But I couldn't afford to waste time on a fool's errand.

At last the weary kitchen workers sat down to their own meal. When her staff was settled, Mistress Baynor returned with a tray.

"Before you leave, talk to Oliver."

"Who?" I floundered, trying to bring to mind anyone in Ragonne I'd met by that name. It didn't sound Ragoni. But the name tickled. I hadn't *met* him. I'd *heard* it. Where? Why? And why should I talk to him?

"He washed up on our eastern shore...oh, more than twenty years ago. He was about four, we think."

Of course! The Roth and Lady Elsbeth had mentioned him, as had Orlo. And Mistress Baynor herself, not two hours before. The millstones of my wits were turning slowly.

"He's not Ragoni. Maybe..." She tapped her spoon on her plate. "Maybe he's from...elsewhere."

I froze, mortification spreading like spilled water. I should have remembered him, have thought of talking to him myself. "What does he recall about where he came from?"

"I have always heard he remembers nothing but his name. But—" she went on over my annoyed exhalation, "he may remember more. If we ask him...differently."

I narrowed my eyes. "What do you mean?"

"I don't want to explain here." Her eyes flicked towards her staff. "Are you willing?"

I hesitated.

"Talking to him is no more desperate or unlikely than anything else."

I bit my lip, telling myself not to compound my stupidity by refusing. But I knew better than to open my mouth. Mistress Baynor did not deserve my vitriol. But it was a struggle. *Fool!* my mind howled, Brusterian equivalents following. *Trained by the scholars of Vere so thoroughly you forgot what a Brusterian princess should know from birth? Books can tell tales. But so can people.*

Mistress Baynor seemed content to attend to our meal in

silence. After a while, I had my self-directed fury in hand enough to eat, and later, speak.

"Yes."

She broke the loaf and handed me half. "I'll arrange it."

CHAPTER XXI

I arrived in the library as usual the next morning before sunrise. Mistress Baynor would contact me when she had our meeting arranged with Oliver. The night had brought little coolness. It was already hot, the air heavy with moisture. I wriggled my shoulders, feeling my smock stick to my skin.

After two hours, I was having no more success than before. Grasping at straws, I began speaking Old Valenian aloud, as scholars did when they read or copied difficult passages. Reading silently, I'd focused on the elements most similar to modern Valenian, but hearing the words drew my attention to the parts unmistakably different. The older language used more g's, but fewer s's, and almost no f's. Vowels often appeared at the end of words. Old Valenian would have sounded very different from its descendent. Interesting. But it did not help me understand it better. I stretched, splaying my fingers.

It was, of course, time.

Time to abandon the attempt to read Old Valenian. It had never been likely to succeed. All I had accomplished was wasting too many precious days of the year Saradena had allowed us. I had tried. Now I needed to finish the remainder of Ragonne's books, meet with Oliver—and go back to Elbany.

I returned the Old Valenian books to their shelf.

The temptation to bring them back to the table hit immediately. If I worked harder...

I shook my head. The books would remain unread.

No. I couldn't bear that bleak assessment. Not unread, ever. Just not *now.* After Saradena, if there was an Elbany to leave or a Ragonne to come to, I could return.

A more honest corner of my mind doubted Philip would permit it. But it was less painful than leaving them, damp and dying, and bluntly knowing no eyes would look upon them again before they rotted away.

I realized I'd been hearing, and could not say for how long, a

Brusterian dirge in my thoughts. A wry smile quirked. Slowly I turned away.

Sudden anger flooded me. Brusterian curses, equally vile and fantastical, sprang through my mind, all directed towards *Saradena*. To give a year's warning, the hope of preventing the storm if certain demands were met—but demands no one could understand, let alone fulfill...

A new thought surfaced, icy and dreadful. We—me, the Roth, Lady Elsbeth, Orlo, all of us—assumed the Saradenians did not know the Three Lands had forgotten them. The coldness slid into my stomach, chilling me to shivers despite the summer heat. *Perhaps there had been no offense.* Maybe Saradena knew of our ignorance and had feigned their complaint. Perhaps the letter was part of their attack, meant to unnerve and distract, taunting, holding out false hope.

I pulled my belt knife and threw it into the door of the third room before I knew my hand was on the hilt. Maybe I'd found nothing because *there was nothing to find.*

I strode across the room, and, wrenching my knife free, stood leaning against the doorway, breathing hard.

It was not a waste of time, and it was *not* hopeless. It could *not* be.

Saradena might know we'd forgotten them. But even if their grievance was a pretense, it didn't mean there was nothing to find. Saradena and the Three Lands had contact before. Knowledge of and from that relationship must be preserved somewhere.

***

I finished the remaining *vitae* late that evening. But I went to the library early the next morning anyway. What else was there to do?

It was foolish, perhaps. With Domon gone, when I left the door would close on Ragonne's library and who knew when it might open again, but I wanted to leave the space tidy. I cleared the table of the *vitae* I'd left there when I'd finally come to the end of the last one and stumbled to bed, then dusted the table top with my sleeve. I walked through the library, straightening books, clucking my tongue over pages warping further as the summer air thickened, leaves and covers straining against the clasp like the belt of a well-to-do merchant.

I hardly dared look at the shelf of unreadable books as I passed. I was glad I'd be leaving soon. It would be terrible, having touched those books and *almost* read them, to sit beside them day after day, and never open them again.

I turned and found myself facing the shelves of lewd books.

Oh, no.

The only snippet of information I'd found about Saradena had been among them. The path had dead-ended in the unreadable books, true, but a clue had been found...here.

I had to read them.

Cowardice masquerading as caution spoke up. Did I really? It was unlikely I'd find anything and the search would be unpleasant.

I imagined trying to explain that to Lady Elsbeth. I picked up the first manuscript and carried it to the table.

★★★

The best that could be said was that they skimmed easily.

Most of them contained only one narrow column of writing per leaf, with the ruled lines for the script spaced widely. Was this because their scribes were also their authors, and were too debauched to write smaller? Or were the wide lines and margins to leave room for illustrations? There certainly were *many.*

The foulness of the pictures, somehow more shocking than the equally vile text, made my lip curl. They were impossible to ignore, whereas I could skim the words without having to entirely comprehend their meaning. But I was grateful for the copious illuminations. They made the reading faster.

Domon had read them. Voluntarily. For days. I touched the books as little as possible, as if their foulness might rub off.

A different thought struck: were such books among the collection at Ferrant? Had Francis read them? Not 'read', of course; like all nobles, Francis could not read, but the pictures would suffice. Had he come to my bed, his head crammed with such images? My stomach pitched. That would...explain a great deal.

★★★

I heard Torrell bring a basket, but decided to keep on. After a day of reading filth, I wasn't hungry. At least I was getting through them quickly.

The next one, though, slowed my pace. I understood why it'd

been placed in that section; it was frank in its descriptions. But its perspective was utterly different. A woman, describing her enjoyment of her husband, seeming to genuinely love him and revel in his attentions.

I didn't know what to make of it. Was it real? Women had been painted as sexually voracious in other books. But here the woman spoke for herself, of her experiences, of a deep and genuine passion in marriage. That was another difference between it and the others—marriage. Was it as much of a fantasy as the others, albeit of a different type? My marriage had been nothing like this.

But royal marriages were not concerned with love. For anyone with property worth protecting, marriages were for advantage, alliance, and control. How strange if it were otherwise. I tried to imagine the political chaos that would erupt if kings married where their loins led rather than as diplomacy dictated.

But sometimes love did follow, or so I'd been told. My parents had seemed pleased with one another, as much as I could recall, but my mother died young and my memories of her were few and unclear.

I thought of Mistress Baynor's face as she spoke of her husband. But her match had not been political; indeed, having the ability to choose had been a chief reason she refused acknowledgement of her royal blood.

What of a truly political match? Did it ever work out well? I tried to imagine asking Lady Elsbeth, then shook myself. It was a measure of how much I did *not* want to work on these books, to be distracted easily into useless speculation.

I completed the manuscript, then rose to put it away. I stretched, considering whether to begin another. I should have, but I couldn't. I just couldn't face another one that day. I left, walking past the tray, feeling guilty about Torrell's wasted effort, not to mention the waste of food, but the bile churning in my gut left no room for anything else.

***

I found it difficult to settle to work the next morning. The book was no worse than the rest, but my mind kept slipping from it, wondering when I'd hear from Mistress Baynor, whether I'd learn anything from Oliver, whether Hal would return before I left, whether Magistre Poll had found anything in Vere's books...anything other than the manuscript. I wasn't even half-way through when the door opened.

It was too early for noon-tide. I leaned in my chair to look through the doorway.

"Doctora?"

Torrell jerked back as I met his gaze. What stories were circulating the *palais*? Apparently leaving a meal was utterly unlike speaking to the dread beast.

"Mistress Baynor has asked to see you, lady, if it is conve-nient."

I stood. "Certainly, Torrell." His eyes widened as he realized I knew his name. "I'll come now."

Chapter XXII

The kitchen was busy as ever, cleaning up after the palace's breakfast and beginning preparations for noon-tide. With a bow, Torrell escaped to his place at the hearth.

Mistress Baynor approached. "Can you go now?" she whispered.

I felt my pulse quicken. "Of course," I whispered back.

"You mentioned wanting to see more of Peran before you leave." She tipped her head a fraction towards her staff so I'd know for whose benefit she spoke.

"Yes," I played along.

"I have errands in the city this morning. Would you like to accompany me?"

"I'd appreciate that. Thank you."

At the top of the stairs we turned right instead of left. Rather than to the main entrance, we came to a smaller back door, functional not grand, clearly used by tradesmen and servants. Another point of access! The clever, defensive but understated design of the *palais'* small windows and decorated yet stout walls would keep out a moderate assault or mob rabble-rousing, but multiple doors meant it would take dozens of men to defend the *palais* against a well-manned and formulated attack. I followed Mistress Baynor along a dirt path around the side of the *palais* to the paved courtyard out front, somewhat mollified to find that the indifferent attention to controlling entry did not extend to having multiple openings in the wall.

Only once we'd passed through the gate did she speak. "I apologize for that bit of deception. Oliver does not want it known he spoke with you."

I stiffened. "I see."

"Not because of *you*." Her hand flicked impatiently. "He is concerned for his safety and his wife's. Everyone has heard something, however garbled, about a large ship at Boltar. Oliver thinks, and I agree, this is not a good time to remind folk of his odd origin. Especially when the boat pieces that washed up with him were unusually large."

Interesting. I hadn't heard that part of Oliver's story before. No wonder she thought he might be from Saradena. But if he remembered nothing, what good would it be if he were?

She was still speaking. "His worry is reasonable. You know what could happen, especially if Saradena does strike."

I did. People distrusted strangers, more so when they were frightened. Despite the years Oliver had lived in Ragonne, the Perani could turn on him if they were afraid enough.

Her lips thinned. "This makes it harder to learn anything from him. It's in his best interest to remember nothing."

"So we will ask 'differently,'" I said encouragingly.

"Yes." She did not take the hint.

What *was* she planning? "How well do you know Oliver?" I asked, wondering with a sudden chill if her political instincts told her he was expendable.

Her quick stride slowed as she considered. "His wife, of course, knows him best. But I've known him for many years and count him a friend. I can remember, barely, when he arrived. He was often with us. The king's natural children, I mean. It was a good place to put him. He was too clearly noble to be fostered with a merchant's family but not important enough to be reared with Philip. He's usually at the Fields when I come to check the stores."

I felt relieved. It was unlikely we were going to torture someone she considered a friend.

"We can't go directly to him," she said. "I said I was running errands. I have to make purchases or my staff will notice. I'm sorry to waste your time, dragging you around while I market."

"I don't mind," I said. "It's a good story, and I *am* glad to see more of Peran than the *palais*. Or its basements."

A purr of amusement rumbled from her. We walked on.

***

The street narrowed, becoming more crowded. I kept close watch on my guide. The bustle was fascinating, but overwhelming. My eyes ached, trying to look everywhere at once. When a princess or queen needed a new gown or gloves, the household staff would make it. If something *must* be purchased, the merchant came to the castle to show his goods. I'd never seen anything like this.

"Most of what I use in the kitchen," Mistress Baynor spoke louder in the increasing hubbub, "comes from Philip's stores. But it is good policy to buy from the city's merchants as well." Her eyes went slitted. "George promised me lemons for Micela's cake. He'd *better* have them."

Lemons. I hadn't tasted lemons, or oranges, since leaving Ferrant. The trees didn't grow in Bruster or Elbany, only in more northerly but warmer Valenna. I'd never eaten either before my time in Ferrant. I recalled the tartness on my tongue, the smell in my nostrils.

Their scent had permeated the air in the castle garden in Ferrant, the only place I was allowed to be alone. I stayed there as much as possible, from the earliest days of spring, coolness in the air and the sun's warmth on my face, through late autumn, the crisp promise of winter belying the last heat, and shivered through as much of early winter as I could bear, re-reading in my mind every book my father owned.

Mistress Baynor stopped periodically, inspecting wares and placing orders. Her purchases would be delivered to the *palais*; the king's head cook did not tote parcels like an errand boy. It took well over an hour, but at last we stepped from the final shop, the fruitmonger's. Fortunately for him, he had managed to procure lemons.

"Now," she angled a glance at me, "the Fields."

The pieces clicked together at last. "Philip's storehouses are outside the city walls?"

"The old walls, yes." The streets had tapered farther, and she turned to let a man carrying two buckets get past. "Our grandfather built new walls, farther out. Before that, the Fields were outside—literally, a group of wheat fields just beyond the city walls. Our grandfather chose the site for his storehouses. Philip added the stables. Did I mention Oliver is his Horsemaster?"

I didn't think so but before I could say anything she went on.

"Rogirn oversees Philip's storehouses. He answers to the Steward." She nodded a polite greeting as a passing woman swung her basket out of our way. "It's a big job. He makes sure the crops are gathered and stored at harvest time, and manages the distribution of the grain throughout the year, while keeping enough seed for next year's planting. Right now, of course, stores are low, with summer almost over but the fall crop not yet ready.

In addition to the wheat, barley, oats, and beans from Philip's fields, there's salted fish, beef, and mutton from the fishponds and herds to account for, as well as the fruits and vegetables from his orchards and gardens. Ragoni apples are particularly fine," she said, pride in her voice.

Having eaten them raw as well as in a tart, I had to agree.

We turned a corner, and I saw the street ended in a gated wall, fifty feet or so ahead. It wasn't the city walls, I realized as I looked again, but an enclosure within the city. These walls were not quite as tall as those of the city. But they were stout, thick, and crenellated, more like a proper castle than anything I'd yet seen in Ragonne.

I followed her through the gate, the guard nodding at her as we passed. "I would rather face a siege here than the *palais*."

She gave me a sidelong glance. "So would I."

Besides being defensible, the Fields was well-designed in other ways. The walls enclosed a wide paved courtyard flanked on both sides by long buildings. Beyond the courtyard was a grassy meadow, clearly for the horses. From the sounds and smells, the left-hand buildings were the stables, which I supposed meant the buildings on the right were storehouses. Philip's horses lived better than his books.

Just inside the gate, pressed against the wall, were three smaller buildings. Of these, the largest, Mistress Baynor explained, was the lodging for Philip's guardsmen assigned to this section of the city, while the two smaller housed the storehouse overseer and the Horsemaster. Oliver.

I followed Mistress Baynor to the Horsemaster's house. I didn't begrudge the horses their fine treatment. But it pained to see money lavished here when so little would have been required to keep Ragonne's books from damp and mold.

She touched my arm, and I turned towards the now-open door.

My distraction, perhaps, intensified the shock of him. Or perhaps not. Oliver—I realized after a long moment it must be the man himself—was the most striking man I'd ever seen.

Not handsome. Or not merely so. Certainly he was comely. Tall—a full head taller than myself, and I was not a small woman. Black hair, close-cropped, but not so close as to remove its wavi-ness. Longer and it might curl outright. Blue eyes, startlingly bright blue, blue as Saradenian ink. Francis had been handsome, but nothing like this man. The steady gaze, the intelligence in his eyes, the strength both in arms and brow bespoke more, and deeper, than simply a man pleasing to look upon. He reminded me of my father.

I realized with a guilty start that he held out his hand to me. Mistress Baynor was already inside.

"Doctora Bann. I've heard of you, of course. I'm pleased to meet you." His voice, too, recalled the High King's, rich as dark wine and velvet.

He couldn't have missed my rude staring, but he made no mention of it. His eyes betrayed no glint of amusement. Had *he* caught me gaping, I thought suddenly, Orlo's eyes would have had been dancing, listing towards mockery but not fully there.

"Welcome to my home." He bowed, and I returned his courtesy.

The house was oddly quiet. The home of a man of Oliver's station should have had two or three servants around. I supposed he'd arranged for his household staff to be out, that we might meet unobserved.

Through a doorway leading into a large room I could see Mistress Baynor talking to a tall blond woman. A table stood in the middle, surrounded by half a dozen chairs, and upon it a pitcher and cups. Oliver gestured me through the doorway. "My wife, Ruth."

She was not as stunning as Oliver but that was more his uniqueness than her beauty; she was an attractive woman, as tall as me but with straw-blond hair to my bark-brown. Her eyes were blue but the more typical blue-green rather than the brilliant sky-blue of her husband's.

"This is Doctora Bann," he said to his wife.

Ruth inclined her head. "Lady. You honor our home."

Except in Rothbury it had been years since those words had been spoken to me with their meaning intact; usually the tone implied the opposite. Ruth's voice held nothing below her words.

I bowed in return. "Thank you for agreeing to see me."

Oliver sat, inviting us to join him. Ruth took the chair across from him. Mistress Baynor settled herself at the end of the table nearest them. I took the opposite end, closest to the entryway.

"What brings the Roth's new clerk to see me?" Oliver said. "I've been in Ragonne more than twenty years. My story is old. I remember almost nothing of...before. What possible help can I give you?" He flashed a quick smile. "And in what cause?"

Mistress Baynor frowned reproachfully. "Do not play at being naïve, Oliver. You were raised in the king's household."

He frowned as well. He picked up a cup and turned it in his hands, his gaze upon it. Finally he set it down, reaching for the pitcher. He poured something into the cups and passed one to each of us, filling his own last.

I picked mine up but set it down again after a quick, surprised glance. It was water.

I looked around the table. The others were drinking. I hadn't drunk water since coming to Peran. In a city you drank ale, small beer, milk, cider—anything but water drawn from the same streams where people dumped their filth. I brought the cup to my face and inhaled the water's scent. It smelled fresh, like water from the mountains of Bruster. I sipped. It was good—cold and clean, tasting of rocks and earth.

I met Mistress Baynor's eyes, and understood. Here was another crucial, hidden strength of the Fields. The old king chose his location with care. There was a well here, a precious source of fresh water. The walls guarded the well as much as the horses and foodstocks.

If I were Philip, I would have a tunnel, if there isn't one already, dug between the palais *and the Fields, and if trouble comes, retreat here.* Then, as I held Mistress Baynor's gaze, I knew. A tunnel was being built, but *not* by Philip. I whistled soundlessly. Mistress Baynor tipped her cup, almost imperceptibly. *How could she have arranged it? The cost would be staggering...* My head began to swim as I thought it through but I didn't suppose for an instant I'd guessed wrong.

Oliver raised his eyes. "What I hear bandied in the streets made me hesitant about this meeting."

"I understand," Mistress Baynor said.

He shot her a dark look.

"Who was blamed if any of Philip's little treasures went missing?" she asked.

"Me." He paused. "Or you." He made an exasperated noise. "But a switching for a lost knife is hardly the same—"

"I know," she said. "Your concern is real. But if you've guessed the trouble Ragonne faces, you know we have no choice but to check everything that might tell us more."

He leaned back. "Tell me what has happened. What you think is going to happen." He looked between us. "I doubt I can help. But I will if I can. Even if I can't, I would like to know...what is coming."

"Fair enough." Mistress Baynor nodded at me.

I hesitated, wondering whether I should, and then wondering whether I had any choice. I sighed, and described the letters that had come to Elbany, Ragonne, and Logan.

He nodded from time to time, slow nods of recognition rather than quick nods of realization, and no surprise sparked in his bright blue eyes. "Yes," he said. "This is what I feared."

"Because of something you remember?" I asked.

He shook his head. "Because of what I've heard." He turned. "You know, Baynor, this cannot be kept quiet much longer."

I tried not to gape. He addressed her, head cook and natural sister of the king, by her name as an equal.

"Yes," she said grimly.

"The king is gathering his army and making weapons." He paused. "Tradesmen and farmers do not worry about other kingdoms. But when the king readies for battle, everyone notices, and worries, and wonders who they'll be fighting. When they realize the enemy is a country they do not know, across the ocean...that will be very unsettling." One fingernail scratched at the tabletop. "What do you want to know?"

"What do you remember?" Mistress Baynor asked.

"Very little." He closed his eyes. "There was a tall, blue-eyed woman. Her hair was usually coiled around her head. I remember seeing it down once, and being surprised." He was quiet. "Wind. I remember wind, stinging my face, so hard I had to close my eyes." Another pause. "Music. I remember just a few notes, but they sounded like nothing I have heard here."

He was silent, his eyes still closed. Then he jumped up, stalking across the room and putting me in mind of a cornered *leoyong*. "I don't remember. I've *tried*. For years. I wanted to know, long before now." He shook his head fiercely, as if he could jostle the memories loose. "I'm sorry. Believe me, if I am from Saradena, I want to *know*. I want Ragonne to know what we need to defend ourselves. I don't remember."

"You might remember more than you think," Mistress

Baynor said.

He swung towards her. "What do you mean?"

"I have an herb—"

"*Veritan?*" He cut her off. "You and I both know truth tea is a story that kings bandy about to keep ambitious lordlings on their toes. All it really does is upset the stomach." He waved a hand. "Even if it worked, what good would it do? I've willingly told you everything."

"Nausea can have its uses," she flashed a smile. "But no, not *veritan.*" She paused, and for the first time, seemed to hesitate. "I should not tell you this." She began again. "What do noble-women do beside embroider and sew?"

"Supervise the servants, if the household has no steward, and see to the child-rearing. Garden—"

She held up a hand. "What do they grow in their gardens?"

He shrugged, looking bewildered. "I don't know. I never thought about it. Fruits? Flowers? Herbs?"

Her lips pursed in satisfaction. "That, my foster-brother, has been the downfall, or at least the discomfort, of many a nobleman." Her fingers flexed, as if sprinkling something into her cup. "Does my lord subject you to...excessive attentions? Or perhaps his attentions are acceptable, but his fertility is unwanted?" She leaned forward, offering him the cup.

He eyed it. "You can't mean..."

She grimaced. "I do. I am breaking more than one vow, telling you. As an unacknowledged natural daughter, I was not really heir to the secrets noblewomen pass from mother to daughter, but Berlain was. That seemed unfair to her, so she told me." Her face twitched at his appalled expression. "It is a recourse used sparingly, I assure you."

Oliver's gaze turned towards his wife, suspicion blooming. Ruth laughed. "I am common-born, and not in Ragonne. As you well know. No one has shared these secrets with me."

"There are many herbs, for various purposes," Mistress Baynor went on. "One is *valern.*"

"What does it do?" His voice was still tinged with suspicion.

"It's a calming herb."

His mouth twisted.

"Truly. Like chamomile, but stronger. A large amount will put a man to sleep. An even larger amount can kill. A small dose relaxes."

His face remained doubtful. "How would that help?"

"I think," she said slowly, as if choosing her words with care, "you *want* to remember so much you hinder yourself from doing so."

I noticed she did not tell him she suspected at some level he did *not* want to remember. This choice made sense. Trying to explain that idea would probably just anger him. Indeed, both could be true. Oliver might believe he wanted to remember while at the same time and without knowing it, fear doing so.

"Trying too hard?" He looked thoughtful. "I suppose that could be..." His fingers tapped the table. "Very well, Baynor. What do you propose?"

She drew a small pouch from her pocket. "I need water, hot but not boiling."

"Wait." Ruth said. "Does the herb have any other effects?"

Mistress Baynor shook her head but her eyes flashed approval at Ruth's foresight in asking. "Good question. But no. Dried and powdered, *valern* will only calm. In small doses."

"But kill in large," Oliver said. "Has any nobleman been killed with it?"

She shook her head again. "Even if I knew, I would not tell you. As I said, these are recourses taken only at the most desperate need. That is part of what is promised when one is given the knowledge."

"Ruth?" Oliver asked.

She gave him a long look, then turned her gaze to Mistress Baynor. "If it could help," she said at last, "and will do nothing more than make you tired, I think you should." A smile flitted. "As long as Mistress Baynor is certain she can get the amount right."

The cook laughed. "A reasonable caution. Yes. I'm certain."

Ruth went to warm the water. Oliver's gaze followed his wife until she was gone, then shot back to Mistress Baynor. "Baynor, we were foster-siblings," he said urgently. "You would not poison me under the guise of this herb? Even if Saradena is coming?"

Mistress Baynor's eyebrows flew up but before she could speak I leapt to my feet, thinking of ships spilling into the bay below Rothbury. Elbany, Ragonne, Logan were threatened, and all he worried about was his own skin? "Let's go. This coward has nothing to tell us."

CHAPTER XXIII

"Doctora Bann!" Mistress Baynor barked. Oliver's face was white. She threw up a hand, warning him not to move, but it was unnecessary. He was rigid. "How can you? How do you not know..." Then, "Vere. Of course."

"What?" I spat.

"Oliver—and Orlo—defied Philip's orders and went to fight Richard. They were with Douglas and Edwy at the battle of the Conlo pass."

"Would we had been with Edwy three months later," he grated.

"It wouldn't have mattered," she said in a tired voice, as if they'd trod this path before. "You know that."

I tried to sift what I was hearing, reconcile it with Oliver's apparent cravenness. "Are you saying *this* man," I could not mask the disbelief in my voice, "fought alongside the Roth? Against Richard?"

"With Orlo. Alone of the might of Ragonne. Without leave. Defying their king." Her eyes sparked. "It's one of the reasons Philip suspects Orlo now. You need not sound so surprised."

"Enough," Oliver said.

"But—"

He held up his hand, restraining her in his turn. "Let me speak."

She was silent, but her lips were tight.

"Doctora Bann's accusation is not unjust—"

"*Not unjust?*" Mistress Baynor exploded. "It is *entirely* unjust —"

"Baynor!"

Her jaw worked, but she said nothing further, her glare snapping between us.

Obviously hearing raised voices, Ruth stepped back to the doorway. Oliver exchanged a look with his wife.

"Tell her," Ruth said.

"We are worried. Too worried, if it makes me recreant."

Mistress Baynor quivered with outrage.

"I was concerned with the Perani, what would happen when they remembered about me. Then we realized our greater concern might be within the palace."

The head cook froze. "What do you mean?"

He did not meet her eyes. "What if the king thought my presence might be connected to this threat, that I was sent here to learn about Ragonne, to be contacted when they arrive?"

She gasped. "Oliver, that's...that's..." she groped for a word horrible enough. "You were a *child*. Surely you cannot believe a child might be trained, and sent—that we could believe a child could be trained, and sent—"

"Children have been used for filthy deeds before now. We begin training our own warriors, here in Ragonne, when the boys are not much older than I was then. One of the first lessons is to go through a battlefield and slit the throats of enemy warriors too wounded to make good slaves."

"Do you really think Philip would not consider it should the idea reach his ears?" Ruth said.

Mistress Baynor said nothing, which was answer enough.

"I apologize." I said into the silence. "You have reason to worry."

"No. I am grateful to you. Caution is one thing, cowardice another." He gestured to my empty chair.

After a moment, I rejoined them at the table. Mistress Baynor was right. I had overreacted. I swiped a shaking hand over my face. My temper had never been even, but lately, the fire of my anger never went out, and little was required to stoke the coals into a blaze. It was foolish to lash out at friends. It was wrong. The problem was, it did not *feel* wrong. Not until after.

"I am no coward, and I will not behave like one." Oliver's eyes flicked to the head cook. "It is I who should apologize, Baynor, for thinking you would poison me if Philip demanded it."

She shook her head furiously, as if warding off his apology. "No need, Oliver. Never."

Discord smoothed from her household, Ruth left again to bring the warmed water. There was silence for a dozen heartbeats.

"These past months have been...very odd," Oliver said. "Waiting, worrying, wondering what's coming."

"It's different from a battle," I said. "Even from waiting for a battle. That's usually a few days at most."

"That's true. But that's not it, not entirely. What has been truly, *truly* strange is that it feels...familiar."

Mistress Baynor cocked her head.

"I feel as if I've done this before. Or that I've always been looking over my shoulder, watching for the knife." He looked between us. "I'm going mad, aren't I?"

"Interesting." She let out her breath slowly. "I think, Oliver, that you're already remembering more."

His eyebrows drew together.

"There may be other countries in the east, but would they all sail...?" Her fingers rapped the table. "In the Three Lands only Bruster builds boats..." She spoke rapidly, more to herself than to us. "Saradena's letter bespeaks a suspicious, hostile realm...a memory of danger and vigilance..." Her voice dropped off as her thoughts became fully inward.

"Baynor," Oliver hissed.

She remained silent, thinking so hard she was entirely still. His lips thinned as he summoned patience.

Finally she looked up, turning to me.

"Boats are costly, yes?"

"Yes. It takes at least sixty trees and—"

"Fine." Her hand flung up. "I don't need details. They'd be expensive in Saradena as well?"

"Hmm." I considered. "I'd think so. Probably more. Their ships are greater."

"That's what I thought." Her piercing gaze went to Oliver. "The old king was right. You are nobility. Just not *our* nobility."

***

Oliver stood, gazing out the window, his back to us. He had stood there, unmoving and unspeaking, for long minutes, the house so quiet around us I could hear the click of hooves of the horses outside on the stones of the courtyard.

"Baynor," he said finally. "Be serious."

"I'm guessing, I know." Mistress Baynor lifted a hand, waggling it palm down to indicate the uncertainty. "But it's plausible."

"No."

"Why not?"

"But you're saying..." He began again. "I'm a foundling. Your affection makes you see more than what there is."

"Your worry makes you ignore what *is* there," she snapped. "What's wrong, Oliver? Fretting isn't like you."

His eyes flicked, just for an instant, to the doorway where Ruth had gone.

"Oh," Mistress Baynor said in a low voice. "I understand."

He sat again, planting his elbows on the table, his head going into his hands. She patted his shoulder. "A gift, brother."

He gave her a bleak look.

She laughed. "Truly."

"What's going on?" I stared at one, then the other.

"The world is a more fearsome place when you are soon to have a child in it," Mistress Baynor said. "As Oliver has learned."

"Oh." I looked away.

Satisfied, and clearly amused, Mistress Baynor returned to her interrupted thoughts. "Saradenian lords would face the same dangers we do. Perhaps more." She crossed her arms, the fingers of one hand tapping against the other arm. "Saradenian ships have not come to our waters in living memory, nor in our fathers' or grandfathers' time. So what would bring one to the Three Lands thirty years ago, with a noble child on board, and few others?"

She touched Oliver's shoulder. "When the Saradenians come, you must stay away from them." She grimaced. "I should have realized as soon as I heard of the ship."

"What are you talking about now, Baynor?" He sounded tired.

"If you think he's a member of an important Saradenian family," I asked, "wouldn't they be pleased to find him? Or are you thinking of using him as a bargaining chip?"

Suspicion returned to his eyes.

"Of course not!" she said. "If he's recognized, they'll try to kill him. *Again.*"

"Baynor!"

"Nothing else fits." She matched his glare. "An accidental shipwreck—here? Why would a Saradenian ship even be here?"

"A message," he said. "That's why they're furious now. They

sent a letter before. It was lost but they think we ignored them."

Skepticism curled her features. "An embassy ship with a child aboard? The ship doesn't return, but they assume the message was received?"

"We don't *know* my ship was from Saradena," he said.

"That's true," she conceded. "It is probable there are other countries in the east, as there are here. But two sailing lands? That seems less likely. The wreckage was from a large ship. Like the Saradenian ship."

"But—"

Oliver was interrupted by the return of his wife, a steaming mug in her hand.

She looked from one to the other. "What is it?"

Neither spoke, tension in his face, defiance in hers.

"Mistress Baynor thinks Oliver is a lost prince of Saradena," I said, lightly as I could.

Ruth laughed, the sound fading as she glanced again from face to face, realizing it wasn't fully in jest.

Mistress Baynor glared. Then her face cleared and she sniffed. "Nobility. I said nobility, not prince."

"Oh?" Ruth looked at her husband. "What do you think?"

"I doubt it." He glanced sidelong at Mistress Baynor. "But Baynor's argument has some strength."

Mistress Baynor laughed, a release of tension. "You know I'm right. You just need time to accept it."

Ruth set the mug before him. "Perhaps you'll remember more, one way or another, after this."

"Yes." Mistress Baynor sprinkled a powder into the water, swirling the cup to stir it in.

Ruth moved around the table until she stood beside her husband's chair. He sipped, grimacing at the taste.

"It's worse cold," Mistress Baynor said testily.

Ruth laid her hand on his shoulder, easy comfort and companionship offered in a simple touch. I glanced down at my hands.

Oliver put his hand over hers. "*Is* it better to know more? If Baynor is right... perhaps not."

"You know it is," she replied. She leaned over, whispering into his ear. Then she raised her voice, still low, but we heard, as we were meant to. "Besides, I doubt it will work. Noble ladies' secret herbs!" She rolled her eyes. "Just drink it. It'll make her happy."

His eyes crinkled.

My breath caught, waiting for Mistress Baynor to explode. But the glint in her eyes was amusement.

Oliver lifted the cup to Mistress Baynor as if toasting her, and drank. "Now?"

"We wait."

He nodded. Silence lengthened. He crossed his arms, uncrossed them, shifted his feet, fidgeted in his chair.

"Ruth," Mistress Baynor said to distract Oliver, "what was *your* childhood like? Which province of Elbany are you from?"

My attention snapped to Ruth. She was Elbish?

Ruth returned to her seat. "Gwynt."

Gwynt...pieces clicked in my head. Something had been nagging at me about Ruth's speech, the hint of an accent I'd never heard before. Then I remembered something I'd read in Vere. "Is it true?"

"Is what true?" Ruth asked, clearly puzzled. "I *am* from Gwynt. The village of Wells. My father was a baker."

"No..." It was my turn to sound confused, as my words caught up with my galloping thoughts. "I read Gwynt had its own tongue. Is that true?"

She smiled. "Yes."

"Is it still spoken?"

"Yes." Her smile broadened. "But only in Gwynt." Her eyes narrowed with held-in laughter. "We've found the Elbs and Balards too stupid to learn Gwyntl."

"Balards?" I'd not heard this term before.

"People from the province of Garland."

"Why are they called Balards?"

"I don't know."

My lips pursed as I considered, trying to see a link between the two words. "Is your language difficult? Or your fellow Elbish just not as clever?"

One hand cupped her chin as she leaned an elbow on the table. "It is difficult. I've never heard of anyone learning it as an adult. Even Gwynts who do not hear it as a child can't get it. But it's more beautiful than Elbish."

"Valenian," Mistress Baynor said.

Ruth laughed. Her determined amusement, I decided, was

for Oliver's benefit. "Not in Elbany." Her eyes flicked to me. "Bruster?"

"We call it Valenian. I've never heard Gwyntl. Would you say something for me?"

She spoke, her voice shifting to accommodate a language more lyrical than Valenian and entirely unlike the guttural force of Brusterian.

"What did you say?" I asked.

"That I have never heard anyone speak Brusterian. Would you return the favor?"

I responded, always ready to speak the language of my thoughts.

"A strong tongue," she said. "It fits what I have heard about Bruster. What did you say?"

"That Vere had no books in Gwyntl. Do you know of any?"

She shook her head. "I doubt whether in all of Gwynt there is anyone who can read and write. Wells is our largest city, and compared to Peran, it is a village."

My mouth went dry. What if no books, *ever*, had been written in Gwyntl?

It would take years to learn the language, adapt an alphabet to suit its sounds, and begin to write down the stories and learning of the culture. She said Gwytl was too difficult for anyone who had not grown up with it but surely a Vere-trained clerk could learn enough...or perhaps one could work with a native speaker... Gwynt was part of Elbany. Once I had the Roth's library established, he might agree to let me spend part of my time in Gwynt. He might be pleased to have its language and history preserved. He might want me to go to Garland and Elbs beyond Rothbury as well, transcribing what could be learned of each province's history, of stories and poems no longer remembered in Rothbury, and create books about Elbany for his library. I saw myself, horseback, parchment and ink in a pack behind the saddle, crisscrossing Elbany to record its history.

Someone coughed. My attention returned to the room, and I found Mistress Baynor's gaze upon me, smiling knowingly.

"I'm sorry," I said, trying to clear my head. "Um—Ruth, what was Gwynt like?" Real curiosity edged out polite interest. "How did you meet Oliver?"

"It's different than Ragonne. Cooler," she fanned herself with a rueful smile, "and hilly. Mountainous, really. We raise sheep. Gwyntish wool is worn throughout Elbany. From what I've heard of Bruster, Gwynt is the part of Elbany most like it." She went quiet. "How I met Oliver...that's a long story. I ended up with Belenda and Douglas during the Ricardian war, and met Oliver when he came to Elbany to fight with them."

I was surprised to hear melancholy in her voice. "Why is this memory sad to you?"

She sighed. "Everyone remembers Edwy. And I am sorry for his death. But I think no one but me recalls that his wife was killed in the ambush as well. She was a friend. We grew up together."

"How—?" I began, but Ruth was looking at Oliver. I turned. He was leaning back in his chair, one arm hanging at his side. The other was on the table, one finger circling the rim of his cup. Ruth took his free hand. "Oliver?"

Slowly he turned his head to meet her gaze. "I feel very strange."

CHAPTER XXIV

"Are you all right?" Ruth asked.

"Yes," Oliver yawned. "I think so."

Mistress Baynor moved her chair closer. "Oliver, Ruth was just telling us about growing up in Gwynt. She said they raise sheep." She paused. "Were there sheep when you were a child?"

"No." He shook his head. "I'd never seen them before I came here. Strange creatures! Clouds with legs. The first time I saw a shearing...! That was *very* strange. They cut off the animal's *skin*, without killing it."

She laughed. "I suppose it might seem that way. There were many things here, I expect, that you had not seen before." She was quiet. "What was it like, seeing Ragonne for the first time?"

"We were—" His eyes closed. "We were," he began again, "coming here. Escaping. There was wind. So much wind, stinging my face, whipping water into my eyes. He told me to go below. The rocks..." His eyes flew open. "We hit the rocks."

"The Margantes." Mistress Baynor turned to me. "They must have been blown against the sea mountains." She looked back at Oliver. "Escaping? From what?"

"They came against us." His voice was flat. "My lord father had feared they would. There were screams. Outside. Then inside. Lady mother—" His voice caught. "Ran into my room. Her hair was down. I'd never seen her hair down. It is a mark of honor among the *Egol* that women wear their hair braided and coiled around their heads. I had certainly never seen her run. Our *persh* was with her. They moved my bed. There was a door under it. He picked me up and we ran downstairs into the darkness."

Ruth gripped his hand, staring into his face, but he seemed not to see her.

"Dark as it was, Skir ran hard, carrying me. We could smell burning. Then there was screaming again. He put me down. He stood still, listening, holding my hand so he wouldn't lose me in the darkness. I don't know where lady mother went. She wasn't with us anymore. *They're burning the boats*, he hissed. *All the tall ships of Saradena are going to the fire.*"

His mouth opened and closed soundlessly. All color had drained from his face. His breath came in quick, shallow gasps.

"I could barely hear him," he finally spoke again. "He sounded as if someone had died. He picked me up and ran a different way. We came at last to the small harbor, the one north of the city. The crowds were not there yet. He chose a ship. We sailed west. No one had been west for many years, but we knew there were other lands across the wide water. He thought it safer to try our luck there than in Celedor or Carlomond."

His gaze darted sightlessly around the room. Ruth clutched his hand in both of hers, her brow wrinkling as she watched him. He turned to her, his eyes finding and settling upon her, and slowly recognition and thought returned to them. No one spoke. Oliver's eyes held his wife's, and gradually his chest stopped heaving.

"Could I have water, please?" he asked, barely above a whisper.

Mistress Baynor filled his cup and handed it to him. He raised it left-handed, his right still held tight in his wife's, and gulped.

"Well done, Baynor," he said, somewhat later.

"Is there any more?"

He shrugged. "I didn't know *that* was rattling around in my head." He drew breath, almost steadily. "But no, I don't think so." He was quiet again. "So I *am* from Saradena."

Mistress Baynor lifted one shoulder. "As we guessed. But it is good to know for certain."

"Perhaps," he said. "But I don't think we learned much helpful to Ragonne."

"No." I said. "We did."

They looked at me as if they'd forgotten I was there. "It confirms several suspicions," I went on. "You remember at least two harbors and many ships, which means Saradena is indeed a formidable sea-faring power." I held up one finger. "We suspected there are other countries in the east, not just Saradena. Now we *know.* You named two of them. Carlomond and Celedor. 'Carlomond' was also mentioned in a book." I raised a second finger. "We learned other things, things we hadn't suspected yet.

Saradena has its own language. You spoke two of the words: '*persh*' and '*Egol*'." I ticked off a third finger.

"Given the situation," Mistress Baynor said, "I would guess '*persh*' means something like 'steward' or 'head servant.'"

"I agree." I lifted another finger. "They've remembered Valenian. Their letter was in that language. We will be at a disadvantage there. They know our language but we do not know theirs."

Mistress Baynor scowled. "I wonder if Oliver...?"

He laughed unsteadily. "There might be a word or two more we could shake loose but not a whole language."

"But—"

"He's right," I said. "It's unlikely he'd remember enough. He hasn't heard it for twenty years." I let my thumb slide out. "The last and most important thing we learned is," I pulled my fingers into a fist, "Saradena has a weakness."

I let the moment draw out, pleased to at last have found something to grasp.

"Well?" Mistress Baynor demanded. "What is it?"

"Internal strife."

Ruth's brows drew together. "How do you get that?"

But Oliver and Mistress Baynor were nodding. She tapped his arm. "She's right. Your memory. That was an uprising. "

"A successful one, I'd say," he answered.

"All the better. The losing side will want revenge. I had guessed a household struggle but a wider conflict makes more sense." She gestured at me, a sort of ironic salute. "Trust a Brusterian to see it first." Her smile took any sting from the remark.

"Such things rarely happen once," I said. "One ambitious lordling succeeds, and the others take note."

"How does this help us?" Ruth asked.

I opened my mouth but Mistress Baynor spoke first. "It's likely they're not unified in their threat against us, or are only superficially so." She rose, going to the window, her fingers drumming the open shutters. "If we can learn more about the factions...perhaps make contact with the disgruntled nobility..."

"We weaken their hand, and strengthen ours," Ruth said.

"You realize, of course, Oliver's family most likely—" I halted at the bleak look on Ruth's face. Oliver's was gray. "...lost their holdings," I amended hastily, and pointlessly. My first thought was clearly in Oliver's mind already. "They surely would have come looking for you if they could."

"If they lived but were banished, they would have been too impoverished to send a ship." He looked into my eyes. "Is it your experience an overthrown lord or his supporters would be allowed to live?"

"No," I answered. "Not if they can be found."

Blue fire sparked, the first real hope since his fragment of memory had surfaced. "We were fleeing. I'm here. Some of us might have escaped."

Ruth squeezed his hand. "If they're alive, we'll find them."

***

"What did you give him?" I asked as we walked back to the *palais*.

Mistress Baynor turned her head. "*Valern.*"

"Not just *valern.*"

Her gait hitched. "No."

"My herb knowledge is limited," I said. "We know some things, but not as much as you Valenians. But I've seen *valern* used before."

She hesitated. "*Meroner.*"

"I've never heard of it."

"As far as I know it doesn't grow outside Ragonne, not even in the other Valenian kingdoms. It's helpful for improving memory. I haven't heard of it being used to recover forgotten experiences. But it was harmless to try." She nodded thoughtfully. "And worth it. I dared not hope he might remember so much."

"Why didn't you tell Oliver?"

"I can't. *Valern* is one thing." She raised a shoulder apologetically. "You know of it. You could recognize it growing?"

"Yes, of course."

"*Meroner* is another matter. It is one of the most closely guarded of the ladies' herbs."

"Why?"

"It has other effects."

"Such as?"

"I can't tell you."

"*What?*"

"I'm sorry." Her gaze stayed firmly forward. "I trust you. But I can't. Some vows are absolute."

I stopped dead. "I told you about the Saradenian letter."

She came back to me. "That's different. I'd already guessed most of it."

"I take my oaths as seriously as you do," I hissed.

"Of course!" she hissed back, her nose close to mine. "But there is no benefit to anyone to breaking this one."

"What about Oliver? You told them there would be no result except weariness."

"That's true. *Meroner*'s other effect does not work on men."

"What effect?"

She glanced down the road. I braced like a stubborn horse. She tapped one foot. "It's related to child-bearing," she said, making an exasperated noise. "I won't say anything more."

"Oh."

"Oliver will be fine. *Now* can we go back to the *palais?* I have been away longer than is advisable for a market trip."

I scowled but began walking again, wondering if she'd lied, knowing I'd shy from that topic. "Will he?"

One corner of her mouth rose. "Bodily, yes. I promise."

"I wasn't thinking of that."

"I know." Her hands spread. "I'm not sure."

"His family is probably dead."

"Yes."

We walked on. "If they're not..."

She sighed. "They may not have come for him because they've thrown in their lot with the victors. He may find his people only to have to fight them."

"Would he?"

Her eyes kindled. "You've already impugned his valor. Do not question his loyalty as well."

I pressed on. "I know you want to believe so. But *would* he?"

Flames roared. Then she blinked, and they were gone. "I hope so. But who can say what they would do in his place?" She gave me a long stare. "What would you do, if the alliance between Bruster and Elbany failed?"

I shuddered and did not answer.

Chapter XXV

Mistress Baynor caught my arm before we parted on the stairwell. "Come to the kitchen later. We need to consider what we've learned. And what to do."

"Very well."

"I'll cook something special."

I mopped my brow in mock relief. "That will be a mercy. I've choked down my meals thus far from mere courtesy."

Her fingers flashed a moderately rude Ragoni gesture, so fast I scarcely had time to recognize what I was seeing before it was gone, her smile letting me know how it was meant.

My lips were still curved in answer as I opened the library door.

***

I returned to the filthy books. Or tried to. As afternoon unwound I found it more and more difficult to keep my thoughts on the manuscript.

Why should I? I had searched for weeks, wasting precious time, and found almost nothing. Certainly nothing worth the time I had spent in Ragonne. I'd learned more about Saradena in one day from Oliver than I had in all my weeks of desperate reading, steeped in obscure Ragoni history and, worse, lurid imaginings. At least I *hoped* most of the lewd books were fancy rather than memory.

Wading through the muck would have been worth it if I'd found anything. I'd imagined myself saving Elbany. *Fool.* The lords were right to value swords above books. When an enemy came, you wanted a sword in your hand. Not a book. Certainly not a book about the energetic and improbable activities a man might perform if he found himself in the company of a woman, a goat, and a pot of honey.

I moved the book aside and let my head drop to the table. Not sleeping. Doing nothing. Which seemed consistent with my ability to help my new home in her need.

***

I heard the outer door open but didn't raise my head.

"You didn't come." Footsteps approached. "What's wrong?"

Mistress Baynor. I sat up, rubbing my cheek where it had pressed against the wood. "Why should I?"

Her brows shot up. "Why? We agreed to meet. To make plans. I cooked *beef.*"

"No. This." I waved a hand at the room. "These."

"The...books?" She sounded baffled.

I pulled the open manuscript closer. "Not just *any* books. Look. I'm reading...*this*...and what for?"

She leaned closer, her eyebrows climbing higher as she scanned the leaf. One finger tapped the picture. "Is that a goat?"

"I think so."

"What's that man...*oh.*" She closed the book. "Come along."

"What?"

She grabbed my elbow. "With me. To the kitchen. Now."

"But—"

She levered my arm up until I could either follow it or risk having my shoulder pulled out of joint.

***

"Now," Mistress Baynor dropped me into a chair in the empty kitchen, "what's the problem?"

"Me."

She stepped to the table. "What do you mean?"

"I thought it would matter. I thought I could help."

Her fingers drummed the wooden surface. "What have you done?"

"Done?" I laughed. "Nothing. Weeks gone. Nothing." My elbows pressed down on the table until they hurt. "What I've been doing. It's worthless. The Roth and Lady Elsbeth thought of Oliver. Orlo did. What did I do? Forgot him. So intent upon books. I should have visited him the day after I got here. And then left."

"If you had, you would have learned nothing from him." She lowered her head, her eyes level with mine. "Did you not hear me before? Oliver has been questioned. Many times. By the old king. By Philip. By me. With *valern.* Without it. He couldn't remember. I only thought of using *meroner* last week. That's not its usual service. Not even close. Nor am I persuaded *meroner* was the key." Her gaze flicked upward. "The ship, the rumors, the churning of his worry did as much to unearth those remembrances as my herbs, although the herbs gave him a way to accept their return."

"We learned more about Saradena from Oliver in two hours than I have found in two months. Two *months*." I pressed my eyes into my palms. "Foolishness."

"I completely agree." When I looked up, her hands slapped hard on the table. "Comport yourself. We have work that will not wait."

"You're right." I stood. "I need to leave."

She caught my arm. "And go where?"

"I need a boat." I tugged but she didn't let go.

"Why?"

"To sail east." The idea had come to me as we'd walked from library to kitchen. "I can't find Saradena in books. Maybe I can find it in person."

Her grip tightened as her head tipped back, a full-bodied laugh braying out. "Do you really believe the Roth, Logan—not Philip, I grant you, but Orlo—have not sent men to search?"

I stared. "Do you guess or do you know?"

"I know."

"How do you know?"

She waved an impatient hand. "Gathering information is part of my effort to advise Philip."

"But...how? Boats?" My shocked mind stumbled from despondent shadows towards real thought.

"Logan stole one." She ticked off one finger. "The Roth paid a Brusterian merchant to claim his boat had been damaged beyond repair. Orlo could not secure a Brusterian longboat but his man volunteered to set out in a coracle."

"No." My hands clapped to my ears and I barely resisted the urge to pull on them. "No. *No*. No one could be so foolhardily brave." Brusterians were the only inhabitants of the Three Lands who sailed properly, but some folk made small skin-covered craft for river fishing. Four feet wide and barely a foot deep, a coracle had no hope of crossing from Elbany to Bruster, let alone taking to the open sea in search of Saradena.

"All the men who went volunteered." She shook her head at my unspoken question. "None have returned."

She loosed her hold as I let myself fall back into the chair. "None?"

"No. Not yet. They may."

Not likely. But neither of us wanted to say it. A worry I'd pushed aside returned. If I discovered what Saradena wanted and we decided to comply, how would we tell them? "We have to inform my father," I said. "Bruster must build a longboat capable of crossing the sea, one larger than has ever been made."

She pursed her lips. "Perhaps. It's a good thought. But none of the three threatened countries are yet willing to share news of their danger with those not facing it." She held up a hand before I could speak again. "If you see him, tell him in confidence and ask for the boat. But there's no point in approaching Logan, the Roth, or Philip about the matter. They won't agree."

"Not yet," I said.

"Not yet," she agreed. She went to the hearth and returned with two bowls. She set one bowl before me, taking her own to the other side of the table.

I inhaled the scent of the stew. Beef, she'd said, and it was, but beef cooked with venison and bacon, along with carrots, peas, and small, round black beans I'd never seen before. Were they native to Ragonne, I wondered, or found throughout the former kingdoms of Valenna? They didn't grow in Bruster or Elbany. In any case she had, indeed, outdone herself. I'd feasted at the king of Ferrant's table and not smelled better. I sipped a spoonful, and could not keep back a low-voiced sigh.

"Good?" she asked, a trifle smugly.

"Oh, yes. As you already knew."

"Good," she repeated, now a statement. "So, tell me why you were reading *that* book."

I blinked at her. "Did I not tell you about the song? The song Domon found?"

"*Domon* found something?" She dipped her spoon into her bowl. "About Saradena?"

"He didn't realize it, but yes. That's how I found Martin de Kolone's connection with Saradena, and from there, his *vita*."

"Which you can't read," she said. "Yet. This part I do know."

"Domon found the song in a book of that sort."

"Here. Among Philip's books." She set her spoon down. "Are there many such?"

"Yes."

She picked it back up. "I see. You're reading them, supposing that since Domon found a bit of information there might be more."

"Just so."

"What did the song say?"

I recited it for her, watching her face twist in wry amusement at the dreadfulness both of the verse and its content. "'—But the eagle ladies let be, for all the ships in the sea, / Else her purse will take your stones in fee,'" I finished.

She laughed. "That seems clear enough."

"It does, doesn't it?" An answering chortle died in my throat. "No. Wait."

She looked around, startled. "What?"

"Something Oliver said..." I swore in Brusterian, a particularly colorful oath about drowning one's foe in a chamber pot. "I didn't pay these lines much attention before. Their meaning seemed obvious..."

"Isn't it?" She cupped her free hand meaningfully. "Don't look too closely at a noble woman or she'll lop off your hangers and keep them in her belt pouch?"

"That's the gist." I stared down at my hands, fitting pieces together in my mind. "But I think there's more. Remember what Oliver said about his mother? 'Her hair was down. I'd never seen her hair down. It is a mark of honor among the *Egol* that women wear their hair braided and coiled around their heads. I had certainly never seen her run. Our *persh* was with her.'"

She stared.

"*Egol*," I said. "Don't you hear it, in the song?"

"*Egol*," she breathed a moment later. "Not eagle. A Saradenian word for high rank."

"Yes, I think so. And not purse. *Persh*. Look at a noblewoman wrong, and her steward will do the chopping. As the song traveled, the Saradenian words, like the name of Saradena itself changed to sounds friendly to ears unfamiliar with their language."

She leaned back in her chair, quiet for a time. "You can do *that*, and you want to plop yourself in a boat and head east?" Admiration and incredulity wrestled in her tone. "*Anyone* can go looking for Saradena, and die of thirst and sunbake, lost at sea."

Suddenly her face was a hand's-breadth from mine. "Only *you* can do this. Read, search for shavings and parings about Saradena, and put them together."

I made a doubtful noise.

"No," she said. I could see her nostrils quaver in outblown breath. "You're needed here, doing this. All of us must do what we can. *This* is what you can do." She took up her spoon again. "I told you I didn't believe there was anything here to find. I was wrong."

"Precious little," I grumbled.

"A start," she said.

The stew was too good for me to remain irritable. I felt the knots loosen. "A start," I agreed. "Together with what we learned from Oliver, a good start." I sipped a savory spoonful. "I wish I could read Martin's *vita*."

She paused with her spoon lifted, inhaling the fragrance, letting the soup work its magic on its maker. "No warrior wins every battle."

We finished eating in silence. I resisted the temptation to lick the bowl, but it was a hard fight. I settled for running my finger along the bottom, slicking up the last drops.

"How many more of those wretched books are left?" Mistress Baynor asked.

"Five."

"How long will they take?"

I considered. "These are among the shortest, and they usually have a significant number of drawings."

"I saw." Her nose wrinkled in distaste.

"An hour each, I think."

She cleared the bowls away, returning with a bag. Knitting needles peeked from the top. "Let's go."

Her unblinking stare was irresistible. I stood. "Where are we going?"

She paused, her hand on the door handle. "The library. I'll sit with you while you finish them." She cut off my protests. "I know you could. But why should you? Not all burdens can be shared, but this one can. I'll knit while you read, and the unpleas-antness will be lessened."

I looked at her. How did she find such a pool of kindness in herself, to be concerned enough on my behalf to put aside her own weariness and give up her few hours free of the kitchen? "Very well," I said, agreeing only because the twin set of lines above the bridge of her nose told me she would accept no other response. "Tomorrow I go to Philip and make the arrangements to return to Elbany."

I did not relish that meeting. Once Philip had tired of proving his mastery by forcing me to do Domon's clerical work, he had left me alone, and I'd gratefully stayed out of his way. But before I could leave, I had to see him, report my findings, and formally request permission to go. We had agreed not to tell him what we'd learned from Oliver, but I had to report *something*. Scattered facts from the books seemed safe. He'd enjoy gloating over my failure to find anything substantial.

It would be another infuriating encounter that must not end in a skewered king.

I heard her sigh as we passed through the doorway. "Philip. Yes. That trouble will keep for tomorrow. We have enough for today already." Her sigh redoubled. "At least Philip won't be fondling a goat."

Chapter XXVI

Kings do not, as a rule, spend their days waiting for clerks to request an audience. So it might have been true Philip had no time to see me that day. But if he *had* a free moment, he would not have granted it upon such short notice. Underlings must be reminded of their place. I was told to return the next day.

Despite expecting it, I took the snub in the manner it was intended. Fuming at the loss of a whole day, I was too angry to trust myself around anyone I liked. I avoided the kitchen. Nor did I dare go to the library. Not with free time in which to be tempted to try once more to decipher Old Valcnian.

I went to my room and threw knives until I felt calmer.

The improvement lasted until the moment I passed through Philip's door the following morning.

***

The full-steeped satisfaction on Philip's face instantly flamed my painstakingly quelled temper. I looked around the room, trying to distract myself. When I'd been there before, I'd been too flustered by his insults to notice much. Now I was grateful to turn my gaze anywhere but his smirk. I *had* to keep control. Whatever his provocations, I could not allow my anger to rage unchecked. Not here.

Tall windows faced the enclosed courtyard. When I'd arrived, the trees had been in blossom; now apples ripened on the branches. Two massive cupboards stood along the side walls, their doors carved with the raven device of Ragonne. A tapestry hung beside each, breathtakingly well done, which was unsurprising. Ragonne was as known for the quality of its weaving as Bruster was for the hone of our knives. The one to my left showed a king, crowned and seated; to the right, another king, sword in hand and surrounded by his warriors.

Inevitably, I had to look back at Philip. He was seated in a high-backed chair, as richly carved as the cupboards. A rug, the blue and black of Ragonne, was at his feet. It was well woven but not as fine as the tapestries. Two other chairs, not so high or decorated as the king's, stood at either hand. He did not invite me to sit.

Why did that rankle? I had expected no different. I looked away, back at the tapestries.

He followed my gaze. "Superb, aren't they? I expect you have not seen their like before." He paused to let the strike hit.

I clenched both hands behind my back and kept silent.

"This," his eyes flicked to the fighting king, "is my grandfather, King Lotris. He defended Ragonne fiercely at any need."

Sometimes at *no* need, I had heard.

"The other is King Halden, first of my family's royal line. Ragonne has flourished under our hands." The arrogance in his voice was insufferable.

I could only hope my face did not convey my revulsion. Or at least not too much. Unable to both meet his gaze and hold my tongue, I risked offending him and glanced around the room again. I hadn't seen so much glass since leaving Ferrant. The windows were larger than I'd remembered, rising behind Philip in three sets, each taller than a man. The shutters were open, ushering in a breeze cooler than Ragonne had felt for weeks.

The room would have made a wonderful library. I did not think, did not dare to think, of the room below to which he consigned his books.

A small cough behind me made me turn. I hadn't heard the door open. A man stood there. I recognized him from the time I'd spent doing Domon's clerk duties. Philip's steward.

"Lord?" He stepped forward. "Pardon the interruption, but this really could not wait..."

Philip's smile broadened as he motioned him forward.

I waited a full twenty minutes while the steward reported his assessment of the coming harvest and the state of their stores. How much was left from last year, how the crops were looking this year, what could be expected from the fish ponds and herds. Summoning every ounce of my ragged patience I stood quietly. This was somewhat less painful than it might have been. Knowing I was being goaded made it easier to keep my temper. The business could easily have waited until after my interview; the interruption was another of Philip's attempts to put me in my place.

For the first several minutes, I ignored their murmurings, thinking of my library in Elbany. Would I have a day or two there before the Roth decided what to have me do next? How had my students done in my absence?

But a conversation in an otherwise silent room draws one's attention despite one's best efforts to ignore it. I began attending, and realized the discussion had moved beyond how well the king's household would eat until harvest. Other stores were being discussed: foodstuffs that traveled well, armor and weapons, the number of fighting men each of Philip's holdings could supply and still plant a crop in the spring.

Ah. So that was his aim. Philip wanted me to know he planned to sail east, whatever I'd found.

At last Philip steepled his fingers. "Very good. I want to hear from you again in a week's time."

The steward bowed. Philip watched me as he left, and did not speak until the door closed behind him.

"Doctora Bann." The smugness in his voice and bearing were unmistakable. My jaws ached from being held clamped. At his gesture, equally infuriating in its pomposity, I crossed to stand before him.

"King Philip." I bowed. Not as deeply as he would have liked but he would get nothing more.

He remained seated, unmoving and silent.

I recognized his stillness for what it was. A strategy to intimidate, as much as the luxurious surroundings and the wait had been. I waited, taking deep, regular breaths, and at last was able to meet his gaze.

It was he who looked away first, under the guise of shifting minutely in his chair. First hit to me.

Still he did not speak.

I realized with surprise his efforts were having the opposite effect from what he intended. Allowing me to stand silently, assessing him without distraction, was instructive. Philip was superficially similar to Francis, but a closer look revealed him to be less imposing. His black hair was beginning to shade to gray. His eyes were dark but without Francis' or Orlo's intensity of gaze. Standing, he seemed taller than he was. Sitting, he was diminished despite his high chair. Indeed, by the chair. An onlooker couldn't help but notice how much grander it was than he, despite his velvet and fur. His chair, like his maps, was an inheritance. He was a *scirgam*. I did not know the Valenian word, if there was one, for a man whose trappings were braver than himself. *Small wonder he feared Orlo.*

"Why have you come?" he said slowly, as if aware the ploy had failed but unsure how.

"I have finished my work, lord. I thank you again for allowing me to examine your books." I pointedly did not call his collection a 'library' but that swipe was for my sensibilities only; he would neither notice nor care. "I ask leave to return to Elbany."

His smile returned. "Of course. I can provide you an escort back to Rothbury." He reminded me of a cat feigning disinterest in a mouse's movements, waiting for the right moment. "It is too late to leave today. Would tomorrow suit?"

"As the king wills." I inclined my head.

"If I may ask," he said, voice oilier than ever, and I knew the paw was coming, "what did you learn during your time here?"

I was glad he put his question in those words and not others, such as 'what will you tell the Roth'? I could avoid outright lies. Direct falsehood, if discovered later, could cause trouble between Ragonne and Elbany. Concealment through omission, in the warped world of politics, would draw admiration. "Little," I said, "and fragmentary."

His eyes lit. "I knew you would find nothing."

I blinked, not at his words but at the emphasis he'd placed upon 'you'. Ah. His satisfaction was twofold. Nothing had been discovered to disrupt his intention to attack, and *I* had failed. Anger flared. I knew better. But trying to quell that surge was like trying to hold back the tide.

"There are other countries in the east besides Saradena," I snapped. "Two at least. Carlomond, and Celedor. I found references to them."

"So?" His hand turned in the air.

"But, lord," I couldn't stop myself, "now that we know this—*know,* not suspect—will you sail east?"

His lip curled. "Of course."

I stared, ignoring the frantic objections of my judgment. "How will you know whom to attack?"

"Whomever we find." He shrugged. "If it is not Saradena, word will reach them." Wild fire brightened his eyes, and, oddly, a flicker of fear.

Then I understood. His own emptiness made him misapprehend his lords. They feared his recklessness. He saw their reluctance as disloyalty. I felt a flicker of unbidden pity. I knew what it was to feel scorned. "Your men are bold, true warriors. They will follow their king wherever he leads."

He laughed. "Kings direct battles. They do not fight them."

My sympathy vanished. Not leading them himself? A Brusterian king who was not first in the battle line would be held a proven coward. Even in Valenna kings wore dinged armor and real weapons, and fought with their men. Francis had gone to battle three times in the years I was with him. I looked at Philip again. He was not even wearing a sword among his feast-day adornments.

***

I could not remember how I got out of the room. I hoped I'd begged Philip's leave with enough politeness to avoid notice. Given the lack of warriors at my elbow I must have been successful.

I made it to my room before I exploded.

In one part of my mind I knew I must look crazed, stomping and swearing like a foul-mouthed child. Fool! Insufferable idiot! Eager for battle as a boy with his first sword. With an unknown enemy. Of unknown strength. With unknown reasons for their hostility. He was planning to attack *them*. Whose location was also unknown. To prove his valor to his lords. By sending *them* into battle. Stupid *scirgam*!

Kings needed better sense, or to listen to people who did.

I threw my knives at the door with more vigor than accuracy. They hit the door anyway because of years of training: at that moment, my arms remembered more about proper aim than I did. I threw and threw, letting the worst Brusterian I knew course through my head. I knew, even as I let the knives and curses fly, that it was overmuch. Philip was foolish, certainly, but I was overreacting. Knowing that did not, however, bring my galloping rage back to a walk.

After some time I quieted enough to pace the room. At length, I was able to pack the few belongings I'd brought with me and the even fewer items I'd acquired during my stay. In the evening I went to the kitchen, and lingered while the servants finished their chores. Boys scrubbed pots with sand. Two bigger boys swept ashes from the hearths. Women kneaded bread for the next day. Men restocked the woodpile. Mistress Baynor wanted to hear what I had to say as much as I wanted to tell it, but both of us had to wait upon tasks that Philip, in his forebears' finery, scarcely thought of, but which his *palais* depended upon more than anything he did.

Mistress Baynor listened, sympathetic but unsurprised. "Philip has always fancied himself a military genius."

"Is he?" I asked snidely.

She looked at me reproachfully. "He has never handled so much as a border skirmish. He's waited for an opportunity since he came to the throne, but Ragonne's neighbors are wary and have stepped lightly."

"What about Richard? Ragonne did nothing during the Ricardian war. Surely *that* was excuse enough."

She shook her head. "Philip did not want to *help* in someone else's battle but to wage, and win, his own."

"Lunacy," I hissed.

She held up her hands. "I understand his actions. I do not excuse them." She hesitated. "There's something else I've learned."

I motioned for her to continue.

"I'm not sure I should tell you."

"Why?"

She drew a parchment roll from her belt pouch and passed it to me. It bore the seal of Kolon.

"He's sent letters to you twice. You've written back. I'd wager he's twisted his clerk's arm to teach him to write, not just dictated the letters."

I stared open-mouthed. "How did you...?"

One shoulder lifted. "Orlo is not a man to woo through another."

"Woo?"

"You know his aim. Don't pretend otherwise."

"But—"

One hand rose. "Don't."

I turned the letter in my hands. "What does...this...have to do with what you've learned?"

"When Philip sends his army east, it will be Orlo who leads them."

CHAPTER XXVII

I set down the parchment roll rather than let it shake with my hands.

"If it goes badly, Philip figures he will be rid of a rival." Mistress Baynor's voice was harsher than I'd yet heard it. She held up a hand before I could begin. "Peace! I know Orlo does not want the kingship. What matters is that Philip believes he does."

I picked up the letter again, one finger touching the seal.

"There's nothing you can do for him." Her hand turned, flattening, palm up, supplication and invitation both. "For yourself, perhaps."

"I see." I felt my jaw tighten stubbornly. She meant to spare me pain, and I was grateful. But she didn't understand. I did not know Orlo well enough to know if I would like to know him better. But after Francis, the pain of possible loss did not frighten me.

"Do you?" She lowered her hand.

I tucked the letter into my belt pouch. "I leave in the morning."

"I heard," she replied, letting the subject shift. "You *will* find what we need, in Ferrant, or wherever the Roth deems best to send you."

I wasn't sure if it was a command or a statement of confidence.

She stood. "Greet my nephew for me."

"I will," I said, wondering whether she meant the Roth—or Orlo.

***

I pivoted the roll of parchment between my fingers. Perhaps Mistress Baynor was right. With Philip convinced of Orlo's ambition, it would be wiser to avoid contact with him, let alone give ear to his enticements.

I looked at the candle on the bedside table and imagined holding the parchment over the flame, watching it writhe and crumble as it burned.

It might be the smarter path, but it felt like cowardice.

I slid my thumb along the edge, breaking the seal.

The page was full of wobbly letters, painstakingly and awkwardly formed. One line squeezed along the bottom: "I am learning. But I swear it is easier to kill a man than write his name!"

I laughed, my first full, real laugh since the Saradenian letter had arrived.

It was madness. Madness to heed him, madness to respond. Madness like drinking *metheglin* without bread, the spices prickling the inside of your nose while the mead strung a net between your ears. Sweet and savory, too strong but for festivals and feasts.

I took out parchment, ink, and quill and wrote:

It is.
But if you'd been practicing letters as long as you had fighting, a quill would feel as natural in your hand as a sword. Your skill will improve the more you exercise it.

I thought, then added:

Well done. I have seen new students at Vere do worse after half a year's study.

I blew on the page to dry the ink and began to roll the parchment. Then I flattened the sheet, dipping the quill again:

Mistress Baynor sends greetings.
★★★

Two of Philip's men were waiting for me just after dawn. I stroked the nose of the mare, making her acquaintance. I thought of Oliver, who as Horsemaster had probably chosen her for me. I hoped he would survive what was coming.

The mare nuzzled carrots from my palm. I'd brought them from the kitchen when I'd gone down to ask Mistress Baynor to send the letter. She'd sighed, but said nothing as she'd taken it. When the carrots were gone, I rubbed my hand on my skirt and slung my bag across the back of the saddle.

We hadn't gone far beyond the *palais'* gates when we heard

another group of riders approaching.

Philip's men reined their horses grudgingly to the right, allowing the other horsemen space to pass. My mare followed. The incoming group, however, was larger than ours, and all three of us were forced aside as the riders reached us. I squinted at the sky, trying to ignore the jostling. The morning was warm, not miserable yet, but the sky was cloudy. I hoped we would not have to ride in rain.

"Doctora Bann!"

I looked around, surprised, and spotted Hal among the arrivals, waving and turning his horse. I reined in. Exchanging annoyed looks, my escorts did likewise.

"You are leaving?"

"I've finished here." I nudged my horse closer. "There's nothing more for me to find. I've read every book I can." I sounded surly, and I felt odd, as if I'd been caught trying to sneak away. In fact, I realized guiltily, I hadn't thought about him in days, unconcerned I was departing without taking leave of him in any civil manner.

His eyes glittered. "There's still one book to consider."

I sighed, but before I could reply Hal leaned forward and took hold of my horse's bridle, pushing both animals further to the side.

"Hal!" I hissed.

He opened a parcel tied carefully to the saddle before him.

"Look!"

Surprise and annoyance vanished. I took the book as if cupping a butterfly. Perhaps there had been manuscripts like this in Vere. If so, I hadn't been allowed to see them, let alone touch them.

The cover was sumptuous. In the center the device of Vere was inlaid in white, of what substance I could not guess. The rest of the leather-covered wood was embossed with gold, a blue gem as large as my thumbnail at each corner. I stared, long after my escorts lost their initial interest in the gold object and began chatting in low voices.

"Where did this come from?" I asked.

"Lady Berlain sent it."

"To *Philip?*" My alarm was so great I spoke of Philip by his name, as I thought of him, rather than as I ought when speaking aloud and in public. Both soldiers looked round at me. "To the King?" I amended. But in my mind all I saw was this book in the palace's basement.

"No." A broad smile creased his face. "It's a gift for her nephew the Roth's library. I deliver it to you as his clerk."

"Oh," I breathed. My fingers stroked the cover. "We will cherish it."

My thoughts danced, moving beyond the book's beauty to wonder about its purpose. Why did it carry Vere's sign? Why was it so highly decorated? What was it *about?* It would be torture, carrying it to Elbany before reading it, but horseback was no place to examine a book. "Thank you."

"You have Domon to thank for it."

My head jerked up.

"It's true. He found it hidden in their castle, two days after we arrived." He shook his head. "He must be able to *smell* books."

He waved a hand, catching my gaze from where it'd strayed back to the book. "And it was Domon who suggested giving the manuscript to the Roth. I think," he paused, "even he did not want such a book moldering here. Lady Berlain grudges becoming Domon's keeper. It was not difficult for him to persuade her to send it to the Roth rather than King Philip."

I frowned. "I'm grateful to have it, of course, and I know the Roth will be as well. But why send it to anyone?" My fingers tightened on the gold cover. "If I'd found this, nothing would have induced me to let it out of my hands."

"Open it," he said.

"Hal..."

"You need to see."

The codex had no clasp to unbind. I settled the book securely on my legs and lifted the cover.

Purple. The leaves were *purple.*

Astonishment, then envy, shot through me. How had the makers of this book dyed the parchment purple? I wasn't as well trained a book maker as some, but even Vere's best hands could not have produced this book.

I held my breath as I looked more closely at the writing itself. The first leaf held two neat columns of script, written in a fine, true black ink, the initial letter illuminated in gold...and it was Brusterian. I drank in my birth language.

Then I gasped, and read the words again. "This..." I glanced back down, not quite believing what I'd seen. I read it again. "This is the *vita* of Cynan Maccus."

Wherever he'd been trained, he knew enough about Vere to give a low whistle.

"There's a *vita* for him at Vere—a very old one, and its copies. Some continue the history of Vere, after its founding by Cynan Maccus. This one..." my eyes flicked down again, "must be as old. If not older. And I have not heard Vere's is so rich." I hadn't seen it, of course. I breathed in slowly. "The device on the cover...this must have been made at Vere, long ago. The techniques are lost now." I smiled. "If they knew, they would *certainly* want it back."

I read the first lines again, reveling in the touch of the parchment, the richness of its color, and my own language.

I started and looked again. Above each line were Valenian words—small, lightly written, almost imperceptible. At some point the book had been translated into Valenian, interlineated with the original Brusterian.

My stomach turned over, and I swore in soft, almost reverent Brusterian. Not Valenian. I recognized many of the words, but could not read them. It was Old Valenian.

I sat unmoving, eyes fixed upon the page, too stunned now to even swear. My mind flew. If I studied Old Valenian in comparison to Brusterian, the language of my thought, might I get sense from it?

Hal's horse sidestepped nervously as a cart brushed past. He leaned forward, patting its withers.

I was ready to return to Elbany. I could pack the book up and take it with me. But what if I studied the book in Elbany and found that with its help, I could read Old Valenian? Even *if* Philip, and the Roth, allowed me to return—which was doubtful—more than a week of our year would have been lost.

My escorts waited with less patience than Hal. They glanced at me, growing more openly annoyed.

Should I stay—and spend more precious time on Old Valenian? My knowledge of Valenian was thorough, but it was a learned tongue. Working from Brusterian might change my capability to puzzle it out.

"There *was* discussion about the ornamentation," Hal said. "Several of Lady Berlain's people were in favor of removing the cover. Domon—" He looked squarely into my eyes. "He has his faults, but that book is in your hands and in one piece because he demanded it. Think better of him, if you can."

I was too preoccupied at that moment to spare thought, or thanks, for Domon. We were horseback, sitting in the street in Peran. I had to choose. Now. Return to Elbany, or ride back to the palace.

I glanced back the way we had come.

"Are you still leaving?" Hal asked.

"Not yet."

★★★

My escorts grumbled, but when I turned my gaze full upon them they quelled, and made no further complaint when I returned my horse to their care in the palace's courtyard.

Hal dismounted as well, dusting himself after his long journey. His first step, naturally, was to present himself to the king and report upon his errand. He promised to inform Philip of my postponed departure and why. I was shamefully relieved to avoid that task.

"You'll have to tell him about the book," I conceded. "Say I must stay a few days longer to compare it to a volume in his collection. But stress it is a gift for the Roth. And do *not* mention the ornamentation."

He dipped his head. It was unnecessary to say that Philip would have not scrupled to appropriate the richly decorated cover if he knew of it, no matter what Berlain had intended.

"With Domon gone you'll be removed from service in the library," I added. "The king has probably already decided where to use you instead. He may well give you your new post now."

"I expected as much." He untied his pack from the saddle. "But I will come to the library after my regular duties."

I was taken aback. There was no obligation for him to continue, and doing so would mean extra work for him. "Hal—"

"Unless you wish to be rid of me," he added, his tone light but the full meaning of his words intact.

I thought of working alone in the library. The quiet, the thrill of being by myself with so many, and such ancient, books. It was true I hadn't particularly mourned his absence. I'd been more than willing to do without his help if that meant being rid of Domon. But I remembered as well the days we had worked side by side, the companionable silence different from being alone, but still pleasant.

If I were successful in unraveling Old Valenian, I could teach him. My imagination leapt. If we worked quickly, we might be able to read them all. Not just Martin's *vita*. All the Old Valenian books. Who knew what might be among them?

"I would welcome that." I said. "Thank you."

Chapter XXVIII

It felt longer than the scant hours that had passed since I'd closed the door to the library. But the room was, of course, unchanged. Removing the wrappings I laid the manuscript gently on the table. Even in the gloom that hung perpetually in the dingy library, the book was magnificent. Gold glittered in the flickering candlelight, gems sparkling blue, seemingly brighter than the light itself. I could scarcely believe it was mine to touch, to open, to read.

Although I was expecting it this time, the purple still astounded. It was deeper than I remembered, the gold initial letter shining in a dark sea. Black script followed, like shadows burned on the dyed parchment. I had seen the highest finery of Ferrant, ladies lambent in jewels and silk, but nothing so beautiful as this book.

No one now living had the skills to have made it. Not in the Three Lands, at least. Who could say what the Saradenians might be capable of? But we had once. The book itself was proof of it. What had been known could perhaps be rediscovered. I ached to live long enough, and learn, that this glorious book would not be the only such in the Roth's library.

After long moments admiring and coveting the skill of the work, I was able to shift my gaze to the words. The thrill of my birth language returned in full measure. The Brusterian was old fashioned. Some words were now rare; others had a somewhat different meaning. But overall the text was accessible.

I read.

The heat and stifling air slipped away, the ever-present stench of mold fled, the room itself blurred into the background, as I drank words.

Where Cynan Maccus had been born, no one knew. He had been known as Cynan then, having adopted a second name later, according to and indeed most likely establishing the tradition of Vere's scholars choosing a new name when they became *doctore*.

Nor was anything known of his upbringing. He first came to

public notice when he approached the High King of Bruster and begged leave to create a city to preserve books. The High King was hesitant but at length Cynan Maccus persuaded him.

I read the passage again:

The High King finally agreed, and in the 23rd year of his reign, 503 years after the fall of Bruster, he granted the island of Lastland to the petitioner. Cynan Maccus gathered a small group of willing men and came to Lastland, exploring the island for many weeks until deciding upon the best place to build their city...

*503 years after the fall of Bruster...*that wasn't in Vere's version. The wisest scholars in Vere believed the city was so ancient no one could know how old it was.

This book knew. Or its author believed he did. But what did *503 years after the fall of Bruster* mean? Bruster had never fallen, not to an outside power. Our conquests came from within.

Ator? Could it mean Ator, the High King said to have brought all of the Three Lands under his control? No written record of him survived but most Brusterians believed him to have been real. Most in Elbany and Valenna held otherwise, deeming Ator a legend, the dream vengeance of a smaller country towards those who scorned it.

I frowned. That couldn't be what the book meant. Ator had conquered other countries. The book referred to a time Bruster had fallen.

A few months before, perhaps, I would have dismissed the passage as fabrication or error. Surely if Bruster had suffered the indignity of a conquest, it would have been remembered. But I'd seen too much evidence that those who had come before had known more than we did now. It seemed wisest to assume that here too, their knowledge was deeper.

So Bruster had once been conquered. By whom? When? And why had my forebears chosen to memorialize our humiliation? Strange—

No. It was brilliant. Our records were dated, if at all, by regnal year. As in the passage: *in the 23rd year of his reign.* Dates started over with each new king. But the book's additional marker, *503 years after the fall of Bruster*, provided a measure of time beyond kings.

I had to close my eyes against the surge of possibilities. Such a system would create a stable, continuing timeline, a way to track events consistently, making the recording of history more reliable. If I could find more about this defeat, I could use surviving records to determine when each king had reigned according to this external measure of time. I could reconstruct the history of Bruster. Our full history, in its proper order and place. Bruster could know its own story.

It would be work. Profound work. A lifetime's work. But worth the effort—

Bitter truth returned, dry in the back of my throat. This was not my task. Could not be mine. Even if the Saradenian threat was resolved and the Three Lands survived. Even if I taught my students and we filled the Roth's library with all the books we could borrow to copy. Even if I learned enough Gwyntl to ride throughout Elbany and collect unique stories and Elbish history. All of which were undertakings enough for more than one life span. But were I to finish them and be free to choose where next to turn my feet, it could not be to return to Bruster to work on its history. Bruster would not welcome my hand in anything.

My gaze returned at last to the words, dutifully at first. But at last I succumbed to the lure of my birth tongue, which I never heard now in any voice but my own, and read in earnest, in pleasure—and in haste.

***

Late in the evening I heard the door open. I looked up. I was in the midst of my second reading. The book was more intriguing, yet worrisome, the closer I studied it. The walls seemed strange, as if I had not seen them for years.

Mistress Baynor stepped through the doorway, carrying a basket. "Hal told me you would be staying a bit longer. You must be hungry."

I blinked, trying to shift my mind to Valenian. "Yes," I said. "Thank you."

She jerked her head towards the outer room. I stood, a bit stiffly, and followed her. She laid out the meal on Domon's empty table. It smelled wonderful, reminding me I hadn't eaten since that morning. Only that morning? It seemed strange, after spending the day steeped in the golden book.

She nibbled a roll while I ate, a smile playing over her lips. Like all good cooks, she was pleased to see the food she'd prepared enjoyed.

"Hal told me about the book he brought from Verdun," she said. "What is in it?"

"Nothing new, not in what it says," I said. "It's a copy of a book I read in Vere. The *vita* of Cynan Maccus."

"The Founder of Vere?"

I sighed. "Was there anything Domon didn't tell you?"

She ignored the question. "What have you learned?"

"Well..." I doubted she would be interested in the book's intriguing dating system, nor was I enthusiastic about telling anyone not Brusterian about our humiliation of having been conquered, no matter how ancient and forgotten. What I had just found might be intriguing to her, but it wasn't relevant to Saradena.

"What?" she demanded.

"I'll show you." She followed me back to the second room. This time, she came close enough to see the manuscript. Her lips made a surprised circle.

"Purple? How did they...?"

"I don't know. It's old."

She stared. "Even I could tell that."

"No. *Really* old. I think the version I read in Vere..." I paused before voicing the suspicion that had been growing in my mind all afternoon, "is copied from this one. This is *older* than Vere's."

Her hand crept forward to brush the parchment. "How could you possibly tell?"

"There are minor differences between this text and the Vere version. Information that isn't in the other. Then there's the scribal errors. Or more precisely, lack of errors." I took a deep breath, ready to explain, but she was nodding.

"Of course. That makes sense. The more a book is copied, the more little mistakes would slip in."

"Just so," I said, slightly miffed.

Marking my place with a finger, she closed the book to admire the cover. "Oh! It's even more beautiful than Hal described. And—Vere. The device of Vere." Her fingertips touched it. "The book must have been made there. That makes sense. How did it end up in Valenna?"

"I don't know." I tried to shake off my annoyance at having her guess everything I'd meant to tell her. "Some of the older scholars told me the city was sacked once, long ago, and many manuscripts stolen. I've never seen written evidence of it. It might be true. It might not. Sometimes we remember rightly—"

"Like the Cynric," she said.

"Yes." I did not shudder but I felt the inside of my nose contract. The very name smelled of blood and cold, like when the bull is slaughtered for the midwinter feast. "Sometimes we don't."

"Like Saradena," she said.

I touched the jeweled cover. "If we cherished books half as well as Philip does his horses, we would not have to rely upon memory."

Her hand brushed mine. "They did. Our forebears. You'll find the right one of theirs." She eased the book open again. "This is gorgeous. But why did Hal think it would help with Saradena?"

I leaned closer, perking up at a new chance to show her something she had not already caught herself. "There's—"

"I see it! Above the Brusterian writing. Is that...?"

"Yes," I said glumly. "Old Valenian."

"Hal thought you'd stand a better chance with the Old Valenian comparing it to Brusterian?"

"Yes." I heard the sulkiness in my voice.

Her fingers stroked the parchment. "Purple. Amazing." She swallowed. "I am content in the life I have. But...seeing this...I wish..." She paused. "Are all the books at Vere so fine?"

"No," I said shortly, uncomfortable with her heartfelt yearning when I was half-annoyed with her.

"Domon found it." Her voice was flat and heavy with the injustice. "At least his time at Vere was not entirely wasted." She drew back her hand. "Will it prove an aid, or merely a beautiful distraction, I wonder?"

The same worry had slithered in oily coils in my gut all day. "I don't know." My hands fisted. "I just started comparing the Old Valenian to Brusterian. But I see no answer to the problem I had before. The small words are not there."

Her brows angled. "What do you mean?"

"I can't find the Old Valenian versions of small but important words like 'on,' 'of,' and 'at'. It's as if they don't exist. But they must. It's impossible to determine how words relate to another without them."

"Yes, I can see that. They must be there." She rubbed one thumb. I noticed a short, half-healed nick, as if the knife had slipped while she was slicing something "Or *something* must be."

My irritation returned. "If not words, what? Words are how we give form to our thoughts."

She shook her head. "See? The gesture conveyed my meaning, without words."

I waved a hand impatiently. "In speech, yes, our bodies can be part of the message. In books all we have are words."

"And the books in which they are written," she persisted. "What about marks in the margin? Or above the word?"

"No. Not there. I would have noticed."

"I don't know." She flung out a hand, her arm stretched full length. "But they must be there, in some guise. Look, when I put onions in soup, I can see them but I also know they are there because I can taste them. If I put salt in, I can't see it, but I can taste it and know it is there. Perhaps," she folded one hand over the other in a gesture that mimicked patience more than demonstrated it, "in Old Valenian, these words are salt rather than onions."

Annoyance flared, stoked by weeks of frustration, the seeming hope offered by the new book, my dread of failing. Again. "They're not there. I looked. For days. For weeks. There's a secret in this language I cannot get my hands around." I closed the book. "I wouldn't expect you to understand. Go back to your pots."

Her eyes widened, then narrowed, surprise and rage crackling from her. Without a word she rose.

I heard the door shut. The cook's—and she was just *the cook* —analysis was far too simplistic to be useful. I had combed Old Valenian. It was easy to insist the small words *must* be there. They weren't. Had they been, I'd have found them long ago. Books and languages were not soup. Onions and salt, indeed!

A snippet of Old Valenian flitted through my mind, like a bird startled from one thicket hastening towards another.

Salt...in the soup, unseen, but tasted...

Could that be it?

I began pacing the room, unable to stay still. Could it? *That?* How?

CHAPTER XXIX

Evening stretched into night, night passed, but I had no thought for anything beyond the book. I turned its leaves with solicitous fingers as I read for the fourth, then fifth, times. I slowed my reading, taking in each word, each letter. Only my quickened breathing betrayed growing excitement.

Just before dawn I finally looked up. There were no windows, of course, to tell the time. Since Mistress Baynor left, I'd marked its passage only when a candle guttered and I hurriedly replaced it. Now my body told me night had peeled away, leaving a raw new day.

As I'd studied the book, mulling my improbable thought of the night before, conviction had budded. Hesitant, afraid to believe too soon, I'd read, and read again. But the branch had grown, green and straight, and did not break when I leaned on it. It was time for the next test. I rose, ignoring the cramp in my left leg from sitting so long. I wasn't ready to try Davin's *vita*, so I took down two other Old Valenian *vitae* I knew had modern copies.

There I paused, wondering where to put the golden book while I consulted the other manuscripts. My fingers itched when I considered putting it out of sight, or even much beyond my immediate reach. But I didn't want it close to enough to risk bumping with an elbow. I shuddered at a vision of the golden book falling, falling, falling and the stone floor waiting below. Nor did I want it in open view should anyone unexpected come to the library. This had never happened, but it could. It was worrisome enough that two of Philip's men had seen it. Sooner or later, word would get back to him. But later was better.

At last I moved the golden book to my left and back, beyond reach of a wayward elbow but away from the damp wall. I fetched two of the ugliest *vitae* and placed one beside the golden book, the second atop. It wasn't an ideal arrangement; the air couldn't flow freely around the book, but for the moment keeping it concealed and near at hand was most important.

That problem solved, I settled back into my chair, turning my attention to the paired *vitae*. Moving one set aside I opened the other, the Old Valenian on the left and its modern copy on the right, and kept my attention on the Old Valenian.

If I were correct, I'd be able to read it.

Halfway through the first leaf, I thrust my hands into my hair, tugging more strands free from my unraveling braid, but my gaze stayed on the page.

It worked!

With considerable effort, maddeningly slowly, but *reading* nonetheless. My fingers tightened until I felt hair pulled loose not just from braid but scalp. It was too soon to be sure. Something might yet go wrong. But the book *was* speaking. Many years— probably *hundreds* of years—had passed since it was last read. Now its words trickled into my ear.

In the mountains of Bruster we had a saying: sometimes the slowest-running spring is the sweetest.

★★★

I had struggled through ten leaves when I heard the outer door open, dimly, as if from another land instead of another room. One corner of my mind recalled that with Domon gone, I need not fear him sneaking up on me. I doubted I could have looked up even if he'd still been in Peran. I was reading, reading *and understanding*, the Old Valenian *vita*. My mind was too full to be troubled by mundane worries such as whose knife might be gliding towards my back.

"Doctora Bann?" someone said. "Have you been here all night? Are you well?"

The words were faint, as the sound of the door had been. The voice was familiar but I could not place it, or focus enough to care that I couldn't.

"Doctora Bann?"

I blinked again. *Hal.* But forming and speaking modern Valenian required more effort than I could spare. "Later," I choked out.

There was a pause. "I'll come back this evening."

Only after he had gone did I realize I'd spoken in Brusterian.

★★★

That evening, a light rapping on the door startled me from

my work. Hal opened it a sliver. "Doctora Bann?" His voice was muffled, calling through the slight opening.

"Come in." My voice sounded odd, as if speaking aloud were ungainly.

He stepped gingerly to the doorway of the second room. "Are you all right?"

I forced my thoughts into the paths of modern Valenian. "Yes." Exultation steeped my voice but I would never have been able to keep it out.

His eyebrows flew up. "What has happened?"

"I can read them."

His gaze slid, following the shelves of books, confusion in his face.

"Not those." I turned my eyes to the shelf of Old Valenian books. "*Them.*"

"Truly? How?"

"I found them. At last."

His brows folded, like a hawk's wings as it dives at an unsuspecting rabbit. "What? Domon found—"

"Not the books. The little words." Then I remembered he had left with Domon before I had found Martin's Old Valenian *vita* and first attempted to read the older language. "Let me tell you what happened while you were gone."

He lifted his hands and I saw he carried a basket. "Would you like something to eat while you do?"

I needed no further coaxing. We settled ourselves at the table in the outer room and were soon buttering bread. Between bites, I explained how I'd found Martin's *vita* and the trouble I'd had with the small words.

"So where were they?" he leaned towards me.

"They're not there." I smiled at his blank look. "But the meaning they carry is, as it must be. I thought there were multiple spellings for words. There's always variation, even within a single scribe's work. But the meaning of the little words, showing the relationship among the other words, is there in the multiple spellings. Take the word for 'sword'—"

I brushed crumbs from my skirt and stood. "It'll be easier to show you."

He followed me into the second room. I opened the Old Valenian *vita* I'd been reading, turning the leaves carefully until I found the one I wanted. "An account of a battle," I said. He edged forward to see, so close my sleeve brushed his as I tapped the page. "'Sword' is spelled eight different ways: *swyrde, swyrdes, bronden, bronde, swurd, sweordas, brondes,* and *swurde.*" I pointed to each as I spoke. "Obviously *bronden, bronde,* and *brondes* are related. The others are clearly a group as well. I'd supposed the varied spelling was scribal preference. More than usual, certainly, but I thought perhaps the ancients enjoyed this variety and encouraged it in their books.

"But that's not what's here." I felt tiredness slipping away as the thrill of discovery ran across my shoulders again. "The last one or two letters is a marker of the word's role in the sentence." I tapped *swyrde* once more. "This form, for instance, is used when a sword belonging to someone is meant. Other forms indicate other possibilities."

"Fascinating," he breathed. "Well done."

"I've never seen anything like it." My fingers stroked the soft vellum. "No language now spoken, at least none I know, varies its words according to their role." I thought of Gwyntl, which I did not know and few did. What might it be like? Then another thought struck. *What of the language of Saradena?* How might it work? The handful of words we had learned gave no hint.

After a moment I blinked and my gaze focused again on the manuscript beneath my hand. "This certainly explains why the older manuscripts became incomprehensible. Many words remained recognizable. But the key to understanding how the words relate to one another disappeared." My gaze shifted upward as I thought. "I wonder why. Brusterian did not change so much."

He tsked. "King Philip will be disappointed."

I drew a sharp breath.

"He may not get his war after all." He released the smile he'd been holding in.

I let out the air. "We'll see. I still have to read Martin's *vita*. It may contain something of use. Or it may not." I yawned. "There's a great deal of work to do—and real information to find —before Philip's attack is in any danger." *But how exquisite it would be to present such evidence to him.*

"But not now." His eyes glinted. "Even Vere-trained scholars must sleep."

I didn't want to stop, but I knew he was right. I yawned again and turned to go. Then I wheeled back, gathered up the golden book from its concealment, and, hugging it to me, moved again towards the outer door.

He walked with me. "Shall I come again tomorrow? In the evening, of course."

I nodded, weariness settling upon me too solidly to reply, and opened the door to my room. I slept, the first deep, restful sleep I'd had in weeks.

***

After a respite the last two days, the heat returned the next morning but once I was at the table I didn't feel it.

I got out three pairs of *vitae* in ancient and modern versions, reading the first few leaves of the Old Valenian unaided, then comparing my understanding with the copy. When I was satisfied that I could really read Old Valenian, I returned to the golden book. Perhaps I was stalling, not ready to face the real test— Martin's *vita*. I told myself I needed to understand Old Valenian better first, as a tongue that had been spoken and sung as well as written, in which commands had been given, battles fought, love declared. It had to become, for me, a living language again.

Hours slid by. After frustrated and fearful weeks, productive reading was a relief and a reward. The time passed so swiftly that I was startled when a knock sounded on the outer door. It was surely too early for Hal.

But it wasn't. "Doctora Bann?" he called as he stepped through the doorway.

"*Vele.*" I replied without thinking, a rapid burst of further speech following.

His brows shot up. I blinked, astonished, the flood of words slowing as I heard them. They were not Valenian. Nor Brusterian.

"What...?" He stopped. "Was that...?"

"Old Valenian," I breathed after a moment, and with effort. Modern Valenian felt strange on my tongue, as it hadn't since I was a child, first learning the language of the mainland. My mind brimmed with the concise beauty of the ancient language. The descendant Valenian seemed scattered and wordy by comparison.

"That was wondrous." He bowed, his head nearly level with his knees. "I stand before a true scholar." He paused. "What did you say?"

I replayed the words in my head to find out. "'Welcome, friend. The books are speaking. They have secrets to share. Would you like to learn to hear them?',", I said, unable to keep the pleasure from my voice. His approbation was, of course, an agreeable change from public and widespread humiliation, but more savory still was the celerity with which the language had built a nest in my mind, a friendly bird settling to brood and hatch its young.

I had learned Valenian with relative ease, but like all Brusterian nobility I had been tutored in it since childhood. A language acquired when grown was different. Finding I had a dexterity for it was a thrill almost as electric as discovering the marked endings. "I wish I knew how the ancient words sounded," I said, rubbing at an elbow numbed from leaning on the table. "There's no way to recover that. Books speak silently." I cocked my head. "No, wait. If there's verse...if it uses rhyme or alliteration..."

He threw his head back and laughed.

I glared at him.

"Your pardon," he gasped, laughter still filling his voice. "The notion is sound." He shook a hand, as if urging himself back to seriousness. "Indeed, it shows what I said: you are a true scholar. But..." He paused, choosing his words. "Do we need to know how the language sounded, to learn what it can tell about Saradena?"

"I want to *know*. Because no one does."

"You do realize," he said, leaning forward and bouncing lightly on his toes, almost like he was preparing to flee if I reacted badly to what he meant to say, "that if nothing had been lost of what the ancients knew, you could not ken it all? It was the knowledge of many, gathered over generations, more than any pair of eyes could read, or one mind could compass."

I sat rigid for a long moment, then sighed. "Yes. But I *want* to."

He leaned back on his heels. "Scholars long to fill their minds the way most of us ache to fill our bellies."

I objected to the category in which he'd placed himself, but decided arguing would sound like soliciting praise, which he'd already lavished. "Are you ready to begin? Learn to read Old Valenian?"

"Certainly," he said. "But would you like supper first?" His eyes crinkled. "Even book-fed scholars need real food some time."

***

We did not talk of the ancient books as we ate. They had waited long years. They would wait a few moments more.

"Where have you been placed?" I dug my spoon into the flaky crust of a pork pie.

"The Fields." His own spoon was already busy. "I think Mistress Baynor had a hand there. She asked me to be alert for wary looks or suspicious glances."

I nodded, my thoughts skittering away from the cook. "What do you do there? Besides watch Oliver's back?"

"The first day, cleaning the stables. Then they found the horses liked me and I was given brushing and saddling to do. Today I brought horses to and from the palace for the king's household, and helped exercise others."

"You like horses?"

He raised one shoulder, jostling a drop of gravy from his spoon. "Who doesn't?"

I'd met many who didn't, among them the fancy ladies of Ferrant, but it was as inexplicable to me as it apparently was to him. Among Francis' petty cruelties had been denying me a regular mount. But I'd not forgotten the black mare that had been mine in Bruster, unimaginatively named Midnight, with butter-smooth gaits and silky mane, unusual in a mountain horse.

He chewed a bit of bread. "My lord Philip asked about your work today."

My thoughts were clouded with memory and work. "Who?"

"The king." His voice was amused. "Of Ragonne."

"Oh. What did he want?"

He wiped his knife. "To know how much longer you'll be staying."

I scowled. "He wants nothing to imperil his war."

"'Only a fool seeks war when peace is possible, but only a fool seeks peace when war is inevitable.'"

"That's nicely put." I scraped up the last of the superb pork pie.

"The one who taught me to read instructed me in other areas as well."

Which reminded me of how much I would have liked to

know more about *that*. My teaching had made liberal use of maxims as well. But I didn't ask. It wasn't my place, I was already itching to get back to the Old Valenian books, and I suspected Hal would not answer. Wiping my own knife, I returned it to the sheath. "Ready to learn a language no one has spoken or understood for years—centuries, maybe?"

"Except you." He slid his knife home. "I would be honored."

CHAPTER XXX

It was still night but not by much when Hal departed. I leaned back in my chair, hands clasped behind my head. I'd be tired soon, I knew, but right now exhilaration suppressed exhaustion.

He had learned quickly, proving deft beyond my expectations, sparking a hope I'd only dreamed of before. Between us, perhaps we could read *all* the Old Valenian books. Not just Martin's *vita*. All.

It had to be fast. I wanted to get the golden book away from Philip. But my gut said the Old Valenian books were our best chance of finding information about Saradena. I could not depart in good conscience, leaving them unread, if it was in my power to do otherwise. We would read them, and go.

Both of us. I stretched my legs, toes curling in my boots, waking muscles that had gone numb. Another realization I'd arrived at during the night was that Hal was too useful to my search to leave in Ragonne. I didn't yet know how I would persuade Philip to part with him, but when I left, I was taking Hal with me.

***

I returned later than I'd intended, having slept three hours past first light. My bag hung at my side, my left hand resting on it protectively. I'd decided that carrying the golden book with me everywhere was the simplest way to keep it safe from Philip, but concealing it was prudent. I'd dumped my belongings onto the floor, wrapped the book in my spare shift, and tucked it carefully into the bag. I set the bag on the table, beyond elbow reach, and fetched Martin's *vita*.

Martin's *vita*.

Time to find out if I had learned enough to sift meaning from an Old Valenian book for which I had no copy, and from which meaning was most needed.

My fingers hovered over the cover. I closed my eyes, reaching for Old Valenian, wanting to bathe my mind in it, to *think* in the lost language.

A sudden burst of Brusterian shot through my thoughts instead. *Sabidur gerva eng protege.* I blinked, wondering why the charge of Vere, the words that curved beneath the crest, had flashed into my mind. *Preserve and protect knowledge.*

Then I understood. Vere had taught me reluctantly, refused to keep me, and been relieved to be rid of me. Nonetheless it *had* taught me. Patterns learned there had etched themselves into the workings of my soul. *Preserve and protect knowledge.* That was, of course, the work of my life. How strange to recognize it, on the cusp of opening this critical codex. After baring my teeth at Vere for so long, denying kinship with the scholars because they denied me, I was, in essence, one of their number. A scholar. As Hal had said. But now I believed it as well.

I breathed in, deeply and slowly, and opened the cover, turning leaves until I found a legible page. The first half dozen were too damaged by moist and mold.

I couldn't read it.

Panic tightened my throat. After all this time, all I'd done...

I couldn't read it. I stared at the page, disbelief wrestling dismay for dominance.

The moment passed. Words resolved themselves from the muddle of script. It was simply coming to a manuscript for the first time, exacerbated by the Old Valenian and the sloppiness of the script, one of the worst I'd seen in the Ragoni library, quite unlike the tidy hand that had copied the *vitae* into modern Valenian.

I began parsing sentences in earnest. After several minutes I glanced up, feeling a smile spreading. I *could* read it. Not easily, as I would Brusterian or modern Valenian, or even one of the other, more neatly written, Old Valenian books. I read laboriously, like a *novicio*. But it was Martin's vita, and I was reading it. My skin shivered as I unraveled tangles of script and language, and wove sense from the straightened threads.

★★★

After several hours, meaning came more easily. Rivulets of thought in Old Valenian trickled through my mind, as they had the day before. I worked through about a tenth of the *vita* before Hal arrived. As before, he brought a basket.

"Where would you like me to begin?" he asked as we ate.

"You know enough to begin muscling through one of the other Old Valenian books. Which one...?" I shrugged, scooping one hand to catch the crumbs dislodged by the movement from the bread I held in the other. "It probably doesn't matter."

After piling the dishes back into the basket we headed into the second room. "There's only one book I have reason to believe might contain information about Saradena." I swirled a presentation gesture over Martin's *vita*. "Just pick another." I tapped the open leaf. "I'd recommend one with a clearer hand."

He leaned over. "That looks like someone inked a spider and let it crawl on the parchment." He frowned at the snarled script. "May I ask if you've found anything yet?"

I felt the tug of the book but resisted. For the moment. "Nothing about Saradena. The first leaves are too damaged to make out anything but a few isolated words. It picks up in his childhood, during which he exhibited unusual wits and courage. When he was twelve he saved a younger cousin from drowning."

"How does he go from hero to disgrace?"

"And what's his connection to Saradena? Why does Domon's song call him 'the Holy Founder'?" I realized the sound of my fingers rapping the tabletop dominated the room. I tried to still them and succeeded in drumming more softly. "I don't know. Yet."

He turned away to select a volume, and I let the book draw me in.

★★★

Someone touched my arm. I started.

It was Hal, I realized in the next heartbeat, and he'd said my name twice already. I shook my head. I was picking through a wickedly difficult passage, the sentences long and complex, filled with words I'd not seen before. Terms for weapons and armor, I suspected, given the context, but that seemed strange. I was familiar with many such words, in both Brusterian and Valenian, and these were unlike the nomenclature of battle in either language. Had I misunderstood the passage? Or could weapons have changed so much—

"Doctora Bann?"

I put both hands over the leaf, forcing my gaze up.

"It's very late. I'm sorry, but I need to go. I have to be at the stables at dawn."

"What?" I blinked as he came into focus. "Oh. Yes. Of course."

He closed a codex gently and returned it to the shelf.

"Did you find anything?"

"Not to the purpose. But the book was interesting. It—" A gigantic yawn stopped him.

I quelled the answering one that rose within me. My own weariness clung like the clay-infused mud of Ferrant. My boots had never been free of it, for five endless years. "Tomorrow."

He picked up the dinner basket on his way to the door. "No one will be there now but I'll return this to the kitchen." He stopped, his hand on the latch. "Mistress Baynor sends her regards. She hopes you are well, and that you have not visited the kitchen in recent days because of the demands of your work rather than that you have wearied of their company."

"Of course," I said, my thoughts shying away from Mistress Baynor like fingers pulling back from a bruise.

He did not yet open the door. "*Are* you well?"

His face held nothing but kindness, so I bit back my first, snappish response. Why was he asking? What had Mistress Baynor told him? It was possible I didn't look particularly well. When had I last combed and braided my hair? I couldn't remember. Not to mention how I might smell, with my spare smock swaddling the golden book. "I'm fine."

***

I went to bed soon after, and slept quickly but not restfully. For the first time I dreamt of what would come if I failed. Rothbury falling by fire and sword, the Roth overcome, Lady Elsbeth taken. Or more likely, killed at his side; she was a staunch warrior herself. Mistress Baynor, trapped in her kitchen as flames took the *palais*.

Still weary, I returned to the library the next morning. It was early but it felt as if it were already afternoon. The air was heavy, so thick I could taste the stale wetness. It had to rain soon, or the walls would drip outright.

***

That evening Hal brought a pear tart in addition to our supper basket. "From Mistress Ruth," he said, setting it on the table.

The basket produced a bean and kidney pie, a small loaf, and butter. I broke off a piece of bread. It was wheat, white and soft, still warm, melting the butter as I pulled a thin layer over the slice. Hal spooned pasty into two bowls and handed me one. It'd been a long time since breakfast, apparently, for both of us. A bowl of lentil stew had been left for me at noon-tide but I hadn't noticed until I joined Hal and found it cold and congealed on the outer table. We did not speak until we turned to the pear tart.

"The Horsemaster and his wife send their greetings." Hal's spoon dug into the tart. "They hope your search is going well and they are grateful you allow me to help during my free hours. The Horsemaster says also he is sorry he cannot send me during the day but he does not desire to attract the attention, or incur the anger, of the king."

"Of course. Please tell Oliver I understand, and give my thanks to Ruth for the tart." I took a bite. "Oh! That's exquisite. If Ruth and Mistress Baynor are to judge from, Ragoni cookery must be the envy of the world. Including Saradena."

"I'll tell her you said so," Hal smiled. He pulled a parchment roll from his belt-pouch. "Mistress Baynor asked me to give this to you."

I stiffened at her name, then recognized Orlo's seal, which merely changed the source of my anxiety. Hal, wisely, said nothing as he handed me the letter, his face blank as the best tutored prince's. I tucked it into my belt pouch. Hal's attention turned to his bowl as if a map to Saradena were inscribed on the bottom.

***

I waited to open the letter until Hal had gone.

You asked me not to write again. If that is what you truly wish, ask it again and I will cease. But I beg leave to be heard. Do you not wonder why I wanted to offer for you, and why I renew the offer now?

I set the parchment down, cursing both Orlo's foolhardiness at continuing to write and mine in answering. But my annoyance was halfhearted. If in truth I wanted him to cease, I could simply not respond, or I could request once more that he leave off. But I knew I wouldn't be able to make that request twice. Which must mean I didn't want him to cease. More fool I than he, then. Had I learned nothing from Francis?

And yet more the fool, for I took a clean piece of parchment, sharpened my quill, and wrote:

I confess the question has been in my thoughts.
***

The next day was perhaps the hottest since I'd arrived. My shift clung to my back like a second skin, and reading Martin's *vita* was like trying to sort seed from sand. And something in the library had begun to stink. When Hal arrived, his presence, usually agreeable, was an irritant. Every scrape as he turned a leaf, every sound as he shifted in his chair, grated my sensibility. I was shamefully grateful when he left.

But I did not forget to send my letter for Orlo with him.

Chapter XXXI

My mastery of Old Valenian grew. But I read more than half of Martin's *vita* and found nothing about Saradena. Worry as much as heat made the sweat drip between my shoulder blades.

So far it had been a standard *vita*. I'd read about Martin's life as young man. His efforts on behalf of his brother the king, Ragonne being beset with border skirmishes with Avice and the occasional raid from Logan. His willingness to work for his brother despite having to leave Kolon governed by his brother's nephew Halden in his absence.

The *vita*'s tone was judicious, praising Martin's victories but emphasizing that his deeds were in the king's service, that Martin was to be remembered only for his connection to the king. The writer commented that it was just as well Halden had experience governing Kolon since after Martin's disgrace, Halden, the son of the sister of Davin's queen, was chosen by the king to rule Kolon.

All of which was moderately interesting but told me nothing about Saradena.

***

All the next day my anxiety continued to deepen. I was only a few dozen leaves from the end of the *vita*. Nothing about Saradena. Not even an indication of the cause of Martin's disgrace.

I heard the outer door open, and realized with a guilty start that I'd been staring at the same page for long minutes, seeing nothing. Wasting time, of which I had too little. But I didn't push my attention back to the words. I welcomed Hal's arrival and the interruption it provided. Maybe I'd be able to think more clearly after supper.

***

"How's Martin's *vita* coming along?" Hal pitted a cherry neatly with his belt knife.

I cut a sliver of cheese and wrapped bread around it. "How about your reading?"

"Ah. That well?" His wrist twisted and another pit dropped. "Yesterday I began the *vita* of a King Grindor."

"A king?" I shaved another morsel of cheese. "Strange. Why would a king's *vita* go uncopied when Old Valenian became unreadable?"

"Maybe something later in the *vita* will explain. I began late last night so I haven't gotten much past his lineage." His gaze unfocused as he consulted memory. "'Here begins an account of the life of Grindor, King of Ragonne, the son of Halron, son of Halden, first king of their house.'"

"Halden?" I reached for a cherry. "There's a Halden mentioned in Martin's *vita*. His brother's nephew. He was given Kolon after Martin was disowned. I wonder if it's the same man."

He hesitated, clearly choosing his words with care. "If he is...would that...matter?"

"I doubt it." I pitted another cherry. "All the same...if he is, I'd be curious to know how he went from lord of Kolon to king." I sighed. "I expect this will be another of those things I'd like to know but won't find out." I'd calmed enough to answer his wry smile, though it felt tight on my lips.

***

Sometime after Hal left, a savage thunderstorm burst upon the palace.

I could hear the rain only intermittently but could tell from it and from the cracks of lightning, the following thunder sounding like rocks rolling in a barrel, that the downpour was fierce. But whatever mayhem the storm might be hurling outside, I turned my face upward; the mere sounds of summer rain were refreshing in the stifling library.

Better still was to come. As the rain slowed, every window and door in the *palais* must have been opened to welcome the cooler air. Fresh breezes gusted even to the lower passages. I propped open the outer door and drank it in, then removed the golden book from my pack, unwrapping it to expose it to cleaner air also.

Newly cheered, I turned the leaf.

The page was blank.

I blinked, fearing my sight had been pushed too hard for one day, then turned the leaf. The back was also blank. The script resumed on the following leaf, but only for another half dozen pages, after which the book was too damaged to read.

I rubbed my eyes with the heels of my hands. Merely a scribal error, and not an uncommon one. It was not difficult to miss a leaf when you were writing—the parchment stuck together, you turned the leaves too quickly—and not notice until you were too far along to go back. That I'd been thrown off by a simple scribal mistake was worrisome. The refreshment of the rain-washed air was gone. I was tired—too tired—and weary scholars think through wool. It was late, only a few hours before dawn, but this close to finishing the *vita*, I kept on.

The final pages went by all too soon. I leaned back, both hands braced on the table. I might fall over otherwise.

Martin's *vita* had nothing to say about Saradena. Not a mention. Not a hint. Not a marginal notation. Nothing.

Nothing.

I stood, still gripping the table but now as much in enveloping, erupting rage as for support.

I had gambled, and I had lost.

Nothing.

Weeks spent untangling Old Valenian, then reading Martin's *vita.* Wasted.

Nothing.

I'd pushed away the closest thing I'd had to a friend in years out of anger and frustration but I'd kept at my task.

Nothing.

I'd worked myself—and Hal—past endurance and good sense.

Nothing.

I had spent almost two months of our precious year in Ragonne, but had little to show for it. Oliver's fragmentary memories. A bawdy song. A second name of an unknown country. Three words of Saradenian.

In other words—nothing.

I spun, grasping, seeking something to throw, to vent thwarted struggle or the rising steam of it would split my skin like a roasted piglet, hissing as juices splattered into the flames. My knives were *meant* for throwing. Not enough. Not nearly enough. Fingers raked the table, found something, closed. Hurled.

Something crashed into the cupboard with a sound like a

man's head splitting beneath an axe stroke. It dropped. Covers splayed, leaves crumpled.

I stared, all thought frozen. Except one.

A book. I had thrown *a book.*

Not just a book. The golden book.

Then I was on the floor, cradling the codex in my lap. The wood in the back binding had snapped, dangling loosely within the gold-wrapped leather like a lightning-blasted treetop. The gold plating was dented and scuffed. Two of the jewels were gone. A third was loose. The beautiful purple pages were bent, twisted like an old woman's hand. I heard something between moaning and keening, an animal noise that it was long moments before I realized was coming from me.

I ran my hands over the end binding. But this, and not just this, could not be healed by remorse or shame. I had known that my temper was becoming ungovernable. I had regretted lashing out at Oliver. I had struck out in frustration-born fury and derided Mistress Baynor when she made a suggestion—a suggestion that had proven key to unlocking Old Valenian at last. I knew I'd reacted too strongly to Philip's provocations. But I'd done nothing. Indulging my wrath when it flared was too pleasant. Now I had struck in unchecked fury and harmed the oldest, most precious book to ever rest between my hands. I opened the cover, meaning to see how the binding was made, if it might be possible to cut the stitches in the leather and replace the damaged wood.

A leaf bowed up from the force of the misshapen cover. A leaf I'd not seen before. It had been glued down against the inside of the end binding. To strengthen the binding, perhaps?

Perhaps. But there was something on it. Despite the shadows lurking beneath the curve of the page like a mountain cave, I could see the golden glint of an illumination. I eased my fore-finger around the edges between loosened leaf and back cover, slowly coaxing them apart.

It was an illumination of Cynan Maccus, seated in the Pedag-no's chair, the same still used in Vere. A harp nestled into the crook of his left arm. His right hand rested upon a book on his knee. Interlacing framed the page and crept into the portrait. One tan ribbon curled against his foot like a friendly dog. Another bent from the upper border to lap onto his hair.

And—

Again all thought stumbled. Not now in horror and shock, but disbelief.

He looked like Hal.

No. He did not merely resemble Hal. He *was* Hal. The portrait was stylized, of course, like all illuminated representations of people. But that did not obscure the fact that the figure in the picture bore Hal's image. The same bark-brown hair. Brown eyes. The same straight nose.

My thumb skimmed the soft surface of the parchment, as if I needed to touch to believe what I saw. How? Why?

Then I understood. *Of course.* No wonder Hal could read, and did not say who had taught him.

When Cynan Maccus founded the city of scholars, among the rules he set down was that *magistre* were neither to marry nor have children, that they might devote their mind and life to their work. It was clear enough—clear as Cynan Maccus' nose on Hal's face—he had directed his followers upon a course he himself did not follow. I wondered where his secret family had dwelt, and continued to dwell, how many generations had passed, and whether Hal knew he was descended from Cynan Maccus or whether the family continued to teach their children to read from tradition but no longer knew whence that tradition derived.

Of this I was certain: if Vere had known of this *vita*, it had forgotten it long ago. It was commonly accepted wisdom in Vere that no images of Cynan Maccus had survived. How strange, to think I alone now knew what he had looked like. Stranger still, to think of *how* he looked. Not marked by appearance as great, but a slender young man with slightly shaggy hair whom you would more expect to see saddling your horse than sharpening a quill.

I gathered up the maimed book, wincing as the end binding dangled. I returned it to the table, then took up a candle to search the floor until I found the missing gemstones. Then I set the jewels on the front cover, near their bent settings. The distraction of the Cynan Maccus illumination had drained away, leaving bottomless shame. I had done this. To this marvelous book.

I would repair the golden book as best I could, but I could not bear to touch it again tonight. It would be like trying to comfort the dog you struck in anger. The thought made bile rise in my throat.

Weariness hit, dropping in a heap on my shoulders. I stumbled to my room, asleep nearly before I pulled the blanket up.

★★★

I slept so long that Hal was in the library before I returned.

"Bad day yesterday, I gather." He stepped from the second room. "Come. Let's eat. You can tell me after." He moved to Domon's table, where he'd put our supper basket as usual. But he hadn't opened it. Waiting for me? So it seemed.

A small gesture, but I was touched. Grim shadows lightened, if not dispersed. The food helped a bit as well. It was mid-August, still summer with the heat to prove it, but crops were ripening. We had roast beets and onions, none larger than a cat's paw, sweet as honey and soft as warm cheese. There was a small loaf so delicately scented and fresh-tasting it had to have been new-cut wheat, recently milled. A bunch of small purple grapes, tart but not bitter, rounded out the meal.

I leaned back, idly picking seeds from a grape. I thought of the Cynan Maccus portrait and tried not to stare.

"What has happened?" His voice was shrewd.

"I finished Martin's *vita*."

"Oh." He rolled a grape on the table with his forefinger. "Nothing?"

"Nothing."

"That's odd." He set the grape aside, the fingers of his other hand tapping with unusual agitation. "The song...Sera Serdent... discovering Martin's *vita*...working out Old Valenian...I thought for certain you'd found it. Found something."

I pushed down on a grape seed with a fingernail until it jumped away. I *had* found something. But not in Martin's *vita*, and not something about Saradena. Should I tell him?

"There was *nothing?* Not at all? Not even marginalia?"

His family might know, and wish to keep their secret. If the knowledge had been lost to them, would they want it? One fingernail scraped at the knuckles of my other hand. Impossible to know what was best to do, so perhaps not doing anything was best. But the illuminated portrait changed nothing about what I had to do about Saradena. "I need to see Philip, ask again for leave and an escort, and go back to Elbany."

He shook his head. "Not yet. Let's check again. It has to be there."

I bit back an immediate denial. I wouldn't have missed it. *Probably.* I'd been tired, and scholars were careful, not perfect. A second look was prudent. If I were honest with myself, I knew I'd never have left without combing the *vita* again. More than once. "Very well."

Martin's *vita* lay where I'd left it, on the work table in the second room. It was a measure of how soul-sore I'd been, that I'd left it there, out and open.

Beside it sat the golden book. Whole.

I stopped short.

Hal turned, a puzzled look on his face. "What is it?"

"The book. How?" I rubbed one temple. "It was...I had...wasn't it?"

"Work has not jumbled your mind." He smiled. "At least not in this case." He ran a hand over the gilded cover, all jewels securely back in their settings. "I mended it."

"How...?" I stepped closer, stretching out a hand towards the book but did not touch it. I did not deserve to.

He picked the book up and set it in my hands.

He could not have made it as if the damage had never happened. No one could. But he had done at least as well as I could. Perhaps better. Dimples and dings still shadowed the golden surface, but they'd been smoothed. The jewels were reset so cunningly that if I hadn't known with gut-churning clarity which I had knocked loose, I likely would not have been able to guess. I turned the book over.

The back cover did not dangle sickeningly like a broken arm. He had cut the stitches and replaced the snapped board, as I'd meant to last night before I discovered the glued-down page containing Cynan Maccus' portrait. I lifted the end binding.

The leaf was as it had been. Pressed flat against the back cover and glued down at the edges. I looked up, meeting Hal's eyes. "It's all right. I saw the illumination. But your secret is safe."

He went rigid. "Secret?"

I patted the leaf. Even knowing it was there, it was hard to detect, so cleverly had it been reattached to the end binding. "Cynan Maccus."

He swallowed audibly.

"You're descended from him. Clearly." I tapped the hidden portrait. "Whether you knew before you saw the illumination, I

don't know, but you must have worked it out when you saw it. As
I did. That's how you know how to read, isn't it? Passed down in
the family?"

His mouth, which had creaked open, snapped shut. "Yes. Yes.
Of course."

"Are you all right? I swear I will not disclose this to anyone, by
any oath you choose."

"Of course," he repeated. "I'm merely startled to have
my...lineage...known. It's been a carefully guarded secret. In the
family, I mean."

"I can imagine." I closed the cover. "Do not worry. I will keep
it as if it were my own."

He inclined his head. "I am in your debt."

"No." I stroked the restored front cover. "I am in yours.
Discretion is scant repayment that I will amend as I may."

"Lady–" he began. Then he shook his head. "Shall we read
Martin's *vita*?"

★★★

We sat and read, together. I thought again of sitting with my
brother Murrow, closest in age to me, sharing a book as we
studied our lessons. Hal and I had both improved our Old Valenian, it seemed. We moved briskly through the leaves. I was
impressed. It was one thing for me to hie through the manuscript. I'd read it the day before, slowly and carefully. It was
another matter for Hal, coming to it unknown. But he kept pace
with me.

When we got to the empty page, he paused. "Why is this
blank?"

"Scribal error."

"Are you sure?"

I spread my hands. "There's no way to be certain. But it's not
unusual."

"What if it's not?" He drew the candle closer, so close I
yelped.

"Don't let it drip on the book!"

"Of course not. But I want to see...there!"

I leaned closer, keeping a wary eye on the candle. "What?"

"It's ruled."

I forgot the candle. *"What?"*

"I can feel it more easily than see it. You try." He moved his fingers and I touched the same place with mine, and then I could feel it as well. The dots along the margins, the lines scored in the parchment. "You're right. The page is ruled. This was meant to be written on. The scribe intended to add something later. Something he didn't yet know but was working to discover."

"Like why Martin was disinherited. Why he left. The *vita* doesn't explain what happened."

"Maybe..." I tamped down my excitement. "But it doesn't matter. If the scribe had found what he sought, he'd have copied it in."

His eyebrows rose. "The scholars at Vere finish every project they begin? None die with notes for things they meant to do but never got to?"

I felt my lips twist in a smile. "I grant the point. So?"

"His notes may be here."

"You cannot be serious." I felt my eyes crossing, trying to imagine it. A scribe's unattached jottings, scrawled on a bit of scrap parchment, surviving—*here*—for who knew how many years? "Impossible. If it ever existed it went to the kitchen or the jakes long ago."

"Probably. But maybe not. There's the loose parchment sheets."

"I should go. To Philip. Back to Elbany. There's nothing here." I blew out my cheeks, heeding him despite my better judgment. "But—"

He pushed back his chair. "What's the harm in looking? You can't go to the king *now.*"

As it was the middle of the night he was undeniably correct. But a scribe's untranscribed notes, surviving? It was *possible.* Just profoundly unlikely. *I would have to have the luck of all scholars since Cynan Maccus.*

But as he said, what was the harm? I could spend an hour or two looking, then go to Philip in the morning. And—I suppressed a smile—perhaps the luck of all scholars since Cynan Maccus *would* favor us, with his far-son helping. "Very well."

He was at the cupboard before I'd gotten to my feet.

Chapter XXXII

We each took a stack and returned to the table.

Searching the piles for pages in Old Valenian was not as fast as I might have hoped. Unsurprisingly, many of the leaves were damaged. Several, but fewer than I would have supposed, had become utterly illegible. Their varying scripts slowed the process. Even so, it took us little more than two hours to sort out those in Old Valenian.

"How did you do?" I asked as Hal set aside the last leaf.

"Eight. You?"

"Half a dozen."

We returned the others to the cupboard and settled down for the more difficult task of reading. *Hopeless. Foolhardy.* But at least it kept my mind from fretting about going to Philip in the morning.

The first page was only a small step above unreadable. The parchment was warped, the writing faded where unrecognizable drips had not obscured it. The margins had been clipped to the words, most likely to provide binding material for other books. Damaged manuscripts were more difficult to read than complete ones, in which context could aid the understanding of an unknown or badly written word. The creeping work of piecing together what could be read revealed that this leaf had nothing to do with Martin de Kolon.

I stood to stretch before going on. A few moments later, Hal finished his first page and followed suit.

The second sheet was in marginally better condition and written in a similar hand, although not the work of the same scribe. I progressed more quickly, but not at the usual pace I'd developed in Old Valenian. It, too, revealed nothing relevant to Martin.

The third one, I suspected, had not originally been part of a codex. It was larger than any book in the Ragoni library. Even more tellingly, the page was unruled.

And—it was in the same hand as the copied *vitae*. All of which was enough to quicken my pulse.

But I soon found it was not about Martin. It was a page of the *vitae* master's records: which *vitae* had been copied, which had been undertaken but were not complete, which were being considered but were not yet a certainty. Excitement surged past disappointment. Holding it was like a brush of hands across the years with the master librarian who had shepherded this massive archival work. This was his hand, his thoughts, a place where *he* survived, not just his work.

Reluctantly, I put it aside.

The fourth page was as much tedium and time as the first had been, and, in the end, to as little result.

But my heart quickened again when I turned to the fifth.

Like the sheet of notes, this page was larger and unruled. The hand was similar. Possibly the same. I couldn't be certain. The leaf was barely readable, and illegible in parts. The parchment had been gnawed by mice. Some of the holes were as large as a fingernail. The script was smeared by damp or devoured by rot. I was *almost* certain a line of paw prints crossed from corner to corner, like one of Liath's forebears had stepped in spilled ink and traversed the page.

Martin's name was in the fourth line. I thought.

"Hal?"

"Have you found something?"

"Maybe. What does this word look like to you?"

He scooted his chair closer. "That?" He considered it, a forefinger rubbing at the opposite arm as if the concealed scars itched. "That's Martin's name. I think."

"Me too."

He crammed closer, brushing my side as we bent our heads over the leaf. I thought of my brother Murrow again. Mouthing words aloud, we wrenched meaning from the text, as much as remained:

After the [word lost] *of the first years of King Davin* [two words lost] *enjoyed peace and safety.* [Two words lost] *Kolon* [word lost] *no exception. After his wife's death,* [word lost] *Martin* [word lost] *rode alone through his lands.*

[entire line lost]

...dirty child with black hair and ragged clothes. [word lost]

October [word lost] *cold and windy.* [two words lost] *Martin stopped* [word lost] *and asked the child where* [three words lost]. *The child said he was alone. Lord Martin gave the boy food* [two words lost] *asked again where his family was. The boy* [four words lost] *died. He shivered* [word lost] *cold wind.*

[two words lost] *impulse Lord Martin cut his cloak in half,* [two words lost] *around the boy and pulled the child* [word lost] *horse. When Lord Martin learned* [two words lost] *child's name was Linas,* [two words lost] *that of his lost wife, he* [three words lost] *the child his ward.*

The boy thanked [two words lost] *for his kindness and asked if he* [word lost] *the Defender* [two words lost] *Charles Henry.*

Martin rebuked [whole line lost]. *Linas claimed his* [two words lost] *had seen* [four words lost]. *Martin resolved to go* [word lost] *to learn whether* [word lost] *was true.*

No one knows [two words lost] *where Martin went* [three words lost] *but soon after he and the child Linas*

[two entire lines lost]

[half a line lost]...*rumor reached Ragonne that Martin* [two words lost] *east to found a sanctuary* [word lost] *saradomus* [three words lost] *ancient tongue of* [five words lost].

A brief note followed, written smaller but in the same hand: *"This is all* [two words lost] *about Martin de Kolon's departure. I will record it* [word lost] *vita but it is of* [word lost] *use because* [entire line lost]."

Unvoiced Brusterian wisped across my lips. All the scholars since Cynan Maccus *had* smiled upon us.

"You found it," Hal breathed.

"We found it."

He stood, stretched, then froze mid-stretch. "It's morning. Isn't it morning now?"

I consulted my body's sense. "Yes. Just after dawn, I think." We listened. The low sounds of servants in the stairwell and passages heralded the palace's waking.

"Definitely morning," he said. "I have to go. The Horse-master—"

"No, Hal." I jumped up also. "We only just found it. We need to read it again—"

"You read it again. I have to go muck stables." He muffled a head-splitting yawn with the back of a hand.

"I knew it was late..."

"Not anymore. Now it's early."

"I'm sorry."

He paused, his hand on the latch of the outer door. "Don't be. I'm honored to have been here."

"Thank you."

He opened the door and was gone.

He was so much like Murrow. I blinked back a sudden flood of misery. I missed my brothers as I hadn't in years. Generous-hearted, duty-centered Murrow. Cedrick, the only one of us who resembled our mother, who like her had a wide and wicked sense of humor. Birnan, serious as only a youngest child trying to show his worth can be. Most of all, Utor. Our oldest brother, who had more or less raised me after our mother's death. I was too old to be left with the nursemaid assigned to Cedrick and Birnan but the wrong gender to join Utor and Murrow's official training, and in danger of our father's grief-wrought neglect. Utor kept me at his side, close as a belt-knife. I learned a great deal watching his training, and more, after hours, when Utor taught me the attacks and stances I'd watched him learn. When Anhud, our father's armsmaster, finally began my 'real' training, he was surprised to find how much I already knew.

Utor had not agreed with our father's decision to make a match for me with Francis. Nothing he had taught me could help in Ferrant. One could not physically resist the king to whom one had been given. Perhaps our mother could have advised me how to subtly evade his attentions. Perhaps she knew about Mistress Baynor's herbs. But I was only a child when she died, too young to have been taught whatever she might have shared about the handling of husbands.

Six years I had been away. I could have gone back. Vere allowed *novicios* one visit home each year. The Roth would have given me leave if I had asked it. I had not. I had pulled anger and pride tight around what remained of Maudlin of Bruster when Francis had cast her off under her own name rather than the Valenian name he'd made her take. *Tedora, Queen of Ferrant*, had gone like smoke in a stiff wind. I had hemmed the tatters of Maudlin, that she might not unravel further, and at Vere I stitched those fragments into Doctora Bann.

I had told myself that I did not wish to return. I hated my

father. But that was untrue. I did not. Not fully. I knew why he had sought the alliance with Francis, even if I had doubted, as Utor had, that it would succeed. We were shown to be right, but my father could not have known it would turn out so. Bruster did not reward cautious rule. Yet I could not go back. I had told myself I had seen disgust and rejection in Utor's eyes but that was not true either. It had been pity. A sea of unendurable pity which I had no steerboard to navigate, nor even a boat to keep my head above the waves. It was a lesson we learned early in Bruster. *Avoid ungovernable waters if you did not care to drown.*

★★★

When I could not keep my eyes on the book any longer, I left to sleep for a few hours. But I was back in the library by mid-afternoon, still so tired that idle thoughts danced through my head. If I kept working all night and sleeping in the day, would I eventually become an owl? Eating rabbit was fine but mice—

I shook my head. Weary foolishness.

As if the mere thought of mice had called her, Liath appeared, sliding through the door behind Torrell as he brought a late noontide basket. I spent an idle moment wondering how Mistress Baynor had known I wasn't here yet at the usual time, then shrugged. I doubted much took place in the palace she didn't know about.

I bent to scoop up Liath. "Where have you been? I haven't seen you for weeks. All libraries need a cat. Even rotting, dreadful excuses for a library—Ah." My hand moved from her back to her belly, and the reason for her absence was clear from her milk-filled teats. I gave her head a final scratch and set her down on the worktable. *Even the cat.* I scrubbed my cheekbone with the heel of one hand, refusing to think of Hilde's sons. Francis' sons. I reached for the leaf.

Liath curled into a neat circle in one corner. I read the fractured text again, then sharpened a quill and wrote a translation in modern Valenian so I could study the new information without having to use the battered original.

It wasn't much. And yet it was. More pieces. The shadowy outlines of a picture, if not the image itself, were emerging.

Martin's meeting with the child had sparked some process of thought which led to his disappearance and ultimately his disin-heritance. Some time later, rumors reached Ragonne that Martin had gone east to create a sanctuary, a *saradomus* in the old language. *Some* old language. I tried to imagine a language so old that the *vitae* clerk considered it old, when his tongue was ancient to us. Who spoke it? What might they have known?

My attention moved back to the text. *Saradomus*. The bawdy song called Martin "the Holy Founder." Founder of Sera Serdent? Put together with the new passage, it seemed likely. *Saradomus* could easily result in the variant forms Sera Serdent and Saradena.

Saradomus...Saradena...sanctuary...for what?

The passage didn't say but I supposed something to do with children. Martin's journey was caused by his encounter with a lost, most likely orphaned, child. It stood to reason he'd create a shelter for others like the boy he'd found.

Or perhaps I merely had children in my heart that day. I had to be wary of assumptions.

But the text did say something else. *Charles Henry.*

The Saradenian letter demanded we return to the "behaviors and expectations of Carolingian tradition" and restore neglected "Henrican observances." The coincidence was too great to be credible. Charles Henry had to be connected. 'Henrican' derived from the man's second name while 'Carolingian' came from a form of his first name. Not the Valenian 'Charles'. The Brusterian version of the same name, 'Carolus'.

Two names, one of them Brusterian. Was Charles Henry a scholar? If so, what did that mean?

And the boy Martin found, Linas, called Charles Henry 'the Defender'. Defender of what? I turned back to the original, checking the line again but the words remained stubbornly obliterated. *Children*, my mind whispered again, but I was chary of giving it too much credence.

I'd found the source of Saradena's grievance. I still didn't know what it meant. The passage gave no hint what the "behaviors and expectations of Carolingian tradition" and "Henrican observances" might be. But it did tell me where they came from. *Charles Henry.* I needed to find more about Charles Henry. How he had become the source of what now held sway in Saradena, and in which cause Saradena threatened us.

I pulled a deep breath, suffused with satisfaction and relief, welcome as a fire in winter. The hunt was no less intense, nor was the pleasure less gratifying, because the prey was on parchment not its heels.

I rose, took out Martin's Old Valenian *vita*, and, sharpening my quill once more, copied the passage into it. As the *vitae* clerk had meant it to be.

***

After Hal's sleepless night I wasn't expecting him that evening, but he arrived nonetheless, in a storm of clattering and banging that had me rushing into the outer room.

Arms laden, he staggered into the room as I caught the door and held it open. "What are you...?"

He set down a steaming pail covered with a cloth, then handed me a wrapped bundle that'd been tucked precariously under one elbow. "This is a loaf Mistress Ruth sent. This," he plucked the handle of a basket from the crook of his other arm, "is our supper."

I set both on the table and tapped the bucket with my foot. "And this?"

"Ah. Yes. That." He took out a small bundle. "Mistress Baynor sent these for you."

I could feel my forehead wrinkling.

"A change of clothes. And—" His eyes sought a corner of the room. "Hot water and a cake of soap. She thought...with the importance and urgency of your work...you may not have had...time...to ask one of the household staff to launder your things...or draw you a bath."

With growing mortification, I understood. So Hal and Mistress Baynor had put their heads together and decided I smelled a bit ripe? Ha. They should've been with me in Vere. Some of those men hadn't bathed in *years*.

They should've been with me in Vere...half-blown annoyance wilted. Mistress Baynor would have liked nothing more.

Something stung between my shoulders. Mistress Baynor's kindness had been unrelenting since I arrived. Meals. Advice. Assistance. The suggestion that led to my unlocking the Old Valenian at last. How I'd spoken to her... I felt my cheeks flame. I owed her thanks, and an apology.

I sniffed. *After* I bathed and changed. It was true. I reeked.

CHAPTER XXXIII

I wriggled, trying to become settled in the borrowed dress. I could feel a damp nimbus spreading across the back from my wet braid. My stomach rumbled and I thought of the basket, waiting in the library. It would keep. I had something I needed to do first.

***

The kitchen was empty but for Mistress Baynor, for which I was cravenly grateful.

She had turned when I opened the door. "Doctora Bann. Good evening. How may I help you?"

I knelt before her, the cloth of my shift and over-dress cushioning the stone floor only in part. Pressing both palms together I raised them to her, as a retainer swears fealty to his lord.

"Most humbly do I beg your pardon." I spoke formally, in the manner in which oaths were taken and court guests received. "I spoke you ill. Throughout the Three Lands it is held that I, the castoff queen, have no honor to call my own. I say otherwise. But at the least I am clerk to a worthy lord, and may draw from his deep well of honor. In wronging you, I have stained that honor. I am in your debt, lady, and I beg you to command me, when you find it convenient, how I might discharge my account."

"Doctora Bann." She spoke softly, laying her hands over mine as a liege lord would in accepting his vassal's homage. "I held no charge to you before. But since you ask my pardon, know I grant it, and willingly. I ask but one thing."

"Name it," I said.

She shifted her hands, taking mine into her own and drawing me to my feet. "I will not ask you to promise to find Saradena. That may not be in your power. I do ask you to keep looking."

"I never meant to do otherwise," I protested.

"I know." She squeezed my hands gently before releasing them. "Your thoughts are ever there. I knew you spoke in distraction and frustration, not true intention to wound."

I was not convinced this charitable interpretation was, in fact, accurate. I suspected that, goaded by my failure, I had given way to an impulse to inflict pain on the nearest person available. "But —"

"Enough of this," she interrupted. "What have you found?"

I told her about the loose page of Old Valenian, what it told us about Martin, his *saradomus*, and Charles Henry.

"Well done. *Very* well done. You found something. Something big."

"Thanks to you."

As her brows touched, I explained how I'd unraveled the secret of reading Old Valenian from her suggestion.

"How intriguing," she said. "I'm pleased to have been of assistance. And I'm glad you came by. I was going to stop at the library on my way home. Something has come for you. And I have news to share." She drew a roll of parchment from her belt pouch.

I was disappointed to see the seal was that of Vere, not Kolon; the next instant discomfited by that disappointment; the next, hastily breaking the seal and unrolling the parchment. *Magistre Poll! Had he found something about Saradena?*

Dear Alumna...

Magistre Poll's hand. But the words were lightly written, and shakily formed. What was wrong? What had happened? I turned my gaze back to the letter:

Dear Alumna,

I write with ill news and I will tell them straightaway. Prolonging will not make them easier to hear.

Vere has nothing to offer in regards to the question you posed in your last letter. I am sorry. I have searched our books, and have discretely questioned those of our colleagues whom I trust, but no one has heard or read of the land about which you expressed a desire to know more. I wish Vere could offer more aid in this matter.

My *maestro* had searched Vere and found nothing. My thumbnail worried the broken seal on the letter's other side. I was more troubled than I would have expected. I had hoped more than I had realized that Magistre Poll would be able to add to what I'd found.

I would have to write back and ask him to check for Charles Henry. There was still a chance Vere's vast collection might hold something useful to understanding the Saradenian letter.

I read the passage again. He did not write 'Saradena', I noted approvingly. It was risky enough, although unavoidable, to have written it in my letter. A lump rose in my throat when I noted his phrase *our colleagues*, his offhand acknowledgement that he considered me a scholar like the others.

I turned my attention back to the letter:

The other news I must relate is equally bitter: the Pedagno is dead.

I blinked, shock quelling for the moment the mourning that would follow. Pedagno Honre Olwen had been a relatively young man, for a scholar, and could have governed Vere many more years. What had happened?

But Magistre Poll did not explain what had ended the Pedagno's life so unexpectedly. Other matters pressed him more urgently:

When Honre became the Pedagno, he named his successor, as is the custom. Alumna, he chose me. I am now the Pedagno.

My gaze cast upwards as I sought to grapple this new information. I had not known how the Pedagno was chosen, nor that my *maestro* would succeed Pedagno Olwen. *Novicios* were not privy to the internal workings of Vere; even *doctores* were not given information of that sort. Only the *magistrum*, the permanent scholars of Vere, knew. It had been clear from the beginning I would not be invited to become *magistra*, and they had been unwilling, even Magistre Poll, to divulge much.

My heart thudded with a sudden, wild thought.

My *maestro* was the Pedagno.

He could invite me to become a scholar of Vere.

Magistra Bann.

The idea coursed through me, roaring and swift as a rain-swollen river. I saw myself returning. Taking my place among them. I was as good a scholar. My chin lifted. *Maybe better.* How many of them could have parsed Old Valenian? Images came, clear as if memory. Any book in the library, even the oldest, rarest volumes, would be open to my hand.

The vision faded. There was no reason to suppose Pedagno Poll would invite me to become *magistra*. Indeed, there was every reason to believe otherwise. The Pedagno was Vere's leader. He should not use his power to promote a former student the rest of the community would not accept. I knew him well enough to know he would not.

More strangely, I realized slowly, even if Pedagno Poll were to invite me, I could not go.

The recognition dried my throat like bread too hastily swallowed. Since leaving Vere, despite its hostility, I had believed if I were welcomed as *magistra*, I would accept. To show them.

Now...I shook my head, as if shedding the thought required bodily effort. The Roth was a good lord, his wife Elsbeth all I could want in a liege lady—clever, discrete, and subtly influential. I had meaningful work to do for them, both in their library and countering the Saradenian threat.

Moments passed in silence, which Mistress Baynor did not break, although she watched me with apparent concern, before I turned my attention to the letter once more:

But I fear I will be a poor one. My instruction in this role was not complete. Few but the elder scholars know this, but after Honre's predecessor taught him what he needed to know to become Pedagno, he drowned himself. I remain baffled, and saddened. He was my maestro. I have no idea what caused him to despair so thoroughly he preferred to die. But at least he made sure his successor was well prepared.

In that task Honre and I failed. Honre was the youngest Pedagno in many years. We thought he would have ample time. With the duties of his post, and my own work, we seemed to have few free moments for the training. One of the responsibilities of the Pedagno is to read and preserve a special collection of books, kept within his chambers. The existence of these books is known only to the Pedagno and the successor he is instructing.

I paused. How great must my *maestro*'s misery be, that he told me this secret. In writing. A cold mass settled in my stomach.

But it would not matter if the scholars knew. No one can read them. Not anymore.

The books are old. Very old, Alumna. I don't know how old with any certainty. But their antiquity is obvious. They were made so many years ago their very words are not ours. What we speak and write bears only a passing resemblance to what is preserved within these books, like a child might carry the shadow of a forebear in his features. Most are in a form of Valenian. A dozen or so are in what I think is Brusterian, but so different that I hesitate to call it that. A few are in a language I cannot identify at all.

Blood pounded in my ears. Vere had a secret collection of ancient books, older than the rare, protected volumes in their library. Some—no, *most*—were written in an ancient version of Valenian. *Old Valenian?*

I forced myself to read on:

Honre had barely begun teaching me to read the Pedagno's books. I bitterly regret his loss, but I regret my laxness more. I should have...but what good is it to lament what I should have done? My foolishness has caused the knowledge of these books to be lost. I shiver to think what might be in them, too secret to translate but too vital to lose.

Until me. I have lost it.

Perhaps something among them might have sped your quest, Alumna. I do not know. If it is there, it is as lost as if I had burned the books. I am sorry.

The writing grew shakier. My heart contracted at his desolation.

I send this letter in well-trusted hands. I expect you know to burn it. No help for your troubles will come from Vere. Trouble has come to Vere. Through me. Alas for the city of scholars. Our future will be lesser than our past because we can no longer learn what the past would tell us.

Your maestro,
Antoun Poll

"Ill tidings?" Mistress Baynor asked as I looked up.

I handed her the letter, and went to fetch a candle while she read it.

"Those books...they're Old Valenian?" She handed back the curling parchment.

"Maybe." I held the letter over the flame. The parchment burned with a stench that remembered the sheep whence it had come. "Probably. At least some."

"You mean to go to Vere."

"Yes."

"When?" She took the candle.

"Now. I have a better idea what to look for. Not just Saradena. Carlomond. Martin. Charles Henry." I began to pace, unable to keep still, thoughts churning like the wind-stirred sea. "The Pedagno's secret books. *Too secret to translate but too vital to lose.* It is not unreasonable to think information about the forgotten east could be among them." *And—I might be able to help the Pedagno. Magistre Poll. My* maestro, *who had taught me when no other scholar would.*

"I concur." She moved to the cupboard and took out half an apple pie. "You should go to Vere." Bringing two plates, she motioned for me to join her at the table. "But that's not why you're going, now, quickly, without returning to the Roth first. You're worried about him. The Pedagno." She held up a hand before I got a sound out. "There are no secrets with your face."

I paused in my stalking, then reluctantly sat on the bench across from her. "I am concerned."

She cut a slice for each of us. "Because of his unhappiness at not being prepared for his new role? You can help him, at least with the books in Old Valenian."

"In part." I picked up my spoon but twirled it through my fingers rather than using it, although the pie smelled delicious.

She dipped out a small bite as if to encourage me. "What more?"

"I'm Brusterian. When a powerful man dies before his time and not on a battlefield, we wonder."

She fixed me with a steady gaze until I lowered the spoon to the pie. "Better." She waited until I took a bite.

I barely held back a shameful moan. The pastry was exquisite. Thin slices of apple crowded beneath the buttery crust like men at a dice game. But it wasn't solely apple. There were bits of dried cherries as well, fragments of tart mingling with the apple-sweet in cookery perfection. I had to leave, but how would I *eat* again, away from Ragoni kitchen art?

"Better?" She said again, but as a question this time.

"Better." I took another bite. "But I'm still worried. Even if Pedagno Olwen's death was natural, Pedagno Poll could be in trouble."

"'When a crown passes, another hand often tries to seize it'," she said. We had a similar saying in Bruster. "What of Elbany? Will you forget Saradena to save your *maestro*?"

"No. I'm going to Vere to save both."

"But once you're there..."

"*No.*" I let the spoon dangle.

"Very well."

Silence held sway for a dozen heartbeats as we finished the pie. I felt calmer, as she'd intended, but my worry for the Pedagno had not abated, nor had the niggling concern she'd touched. What would I do, after I got to Vere, if helping the Pedagno and searching for Saradena were no longer aims I could pursue together?

"I should go," I said.

"Wait." She touched my arm. "I also have news." I braced, but a thin smile parted her lips. "Good news."

I let my breath out.

"Philip's war plans have met with difficulty."

I felt an answering smile, although my face felt stiff unto cracking, letting it out. "That *is* good news. What happened?"

"Boats." Satisfaction filled her voice. "The High King of Bruster refused to sell him any."

"Ah!" It burst out, propelled by the irritation of sudden and seemingly obvious insight. I'd been too infuriated by the stupidity of Philip's plan, as well as distracted by my search, to give thought to *how* he was planning to sail east. Else I'd have realized he must have assumed he could simply buy boats from Bruster. But he wouldn't have told the High King why he wanted them.

Brusterian politics engendered deep suspicion in its survivors. We guarded our vessels jealously, from, among other reasons, a pragmatic desire not to provide boats to those who might invade us. Even if Philip told the truth, the High King likely wouldn't have believed him. After all, no one, not even Philip, could be foolhardy enough to attempt the open sea an unknown distance in Brusterian coastal boats. "Well done, Father," I murmured.

"Yes." Her fingertips rapped the table. "This will slow Philip down. But *only* slow him down. He's determined. He'll get boats eventually, somehow."

Ice bloomed in my chest. "Would Philip try to take them by force?"

"How? You need boats to *get* to Bruster." But her eyes misted as she considered. "Hire two or three boats, leaving from different Ragoni cities, filled with as many men as they can hold...a pretext to explain the presence of so many men in Bruster at once...or steal the first boats outright, if it could be managed without word getting to Bruster...or, better yet," her voice quickened, "hire boats in another kingdom—Marlon perhaps, that would be a good bit of misdirection—and have the men dressed in the garb of a different kingdom—Ferrant would be a good choice, Marlon and Ferrant fervently distrust one another, which would both add to the confusion and make it less likely anyone would work out where the raiders really came from."

Her unseeing gaze sought the ceiling. "Once there, by whatever means, seize the boats and row away, east and north, well around the Margantes...sail separately into Ragonne to avoid notice...that would be the most difficult part...It could be made to work."

I watched in mixed alarm and admiration the speed and ease with which she devised a feasible plan of invading my homeland. Particularly unnerving was her assessment that the 'most difficult part' would be sailing the stolen boats back to Ragonne unnoticed. She was probably right. The rest *would* be frighteningly likely to succeed.

"But you asked a different question," she went on. "Whether Philip would do this thing, if it occurred to him it was possible." She paused. "I suspect so."

My mouth went dry. "Surely you would not—"

She scowled. "Of course not. Philip's plan is foolhardy. I'll not aid him in pursuing it. Nor do I think it wise to begin a war with an ally. Especially not now. The High King would have little difficulty working out who stole his ships, so soon after he declined to sell them."

She flashed a smile. "Philip's plans are scuttled for a time. He'll stew, then make a higher offer to the High King. It will be tempting. Philip's original bid was staggering. You would know better than I how high it will have to go before the High King might reconsider."

"I haven't seen my father for six years." I wondered if the sting I felt showed on my face. Probably.

"Ah." Her shoulders rose. "In any case, if Philip is refused again, my guess is he will then begin to consider...other options."

I felt my teeth set. "Let's hope by then we'll know enough about Saradena to convince him of his foolishness."

"That would take volumes." She sighed. "But we can hope."

CHAPTER XXXIV

Hal was in the second room when I returned, but rose as soon as I opened the door. "I've found something."

I hurried to him. "Saradena?"

"No. But important."

There were four volumes open on the worktable, three Old Valenian *vitae* and one modern. "This," he said, tapping a codex with his forefinger, "is the *vita* I mentioned." He looked sideways at me. "King Grindor. You remember?"

"Yes," I said slowly, tracking the memory. "Yes," I said again, more firmly. "We wondered why a king's *vita* had gone uncopied."

"I think we don't have to wonder any longer," he said grimly. "I began another Old Valenian *vita* while you were gone. Guess whose it turned out to be?"

I shrugged, but he continued too quickly to have expected an answer.

"Grindor's father's. Haldor." He touched another of the Old Valenian manuscripts. "Also uncopied. So I looked around and found his grandfather's."

"Uncopied." I said.

"Yes." His finger moved to the third Old Valenian book. "See his name?"

I leaned closer. "Halden. That was in Grindor's *vita*. I remember. 'Grindor, son of Haldor, son of Halden, first king of their line.' It's the same name as the nephew given Kolon after Martin's disinheritance. We wondered whether they were the same man, and if so, how he went from lord to king."

"They are."

I heard sorrow like a rising tide in his voice. "What is it?"

"Halden's route to the throne." He ran a hand through his hair. "Two years after King Davin named Halden lord of Kolon, the king and his four oldest sons died within two weeks of one another, in a wasting sickness that swept Ragonne that summer.

The surviving princes were only five and seven years old. Halden became their regent."

"Why?" I craned my neck to look at the *vita* more closely, as if the answer might leap at me from the page. "Halden was their mother's nephew, not Davin's. He's not royal. His aunt just married well."

He nodded. "Martin's *vita* said so, yes. Not Halden's. But Martin was gone, and Davin's only remaining brother also died from the sickness."

Dread began to tighten like a sea-soaked knot in my stomach. "What happened to the children, that Halden became king?"

"Halden sent them to his holdings in the country, claiming it would be safe, and more pleasant for them." He pressed the palm of his hand against his forehead for a moment. "They never arrived. No one saw them again. Halden ruled in their name for five years and then had himself crowned in his own right."

"Convenient. Where does it say this?"

"All three *vitae* mention the princes' disappearance."

Silence fell as I read the passages. Then I took a shaky breath. "Even in Bruster, seizing the throne over the bodies of children is held vile. Not that it hasn't been tried."

Memory twitched, a pebble of thought wriggling loose to reveal a bare spot beneath. My brothers and I had nearly been the victims of such an attack ourselves. Odd. I hadn't thought about that incident for years. One would think that foiling an assassination is the kind of memory that would remain foremost, but much had happened in the years since. Francis. Vere. Elbany. Nor was usurpation a rare sport in Bruster. "The kingdoms of Valenna do not have anything like Bruster's stomach for politics. I cannot imagine how shocking such an atrocity would be here."

"How can we be certain?" There was a note of desperate hope in his voice, painful to hear.

I glanced towards the shelves of modern *vitae*. "What's not here speaks as loudly as what is."

"They weren't copied," he sighed.

"Halden killed two children to seize the throne. His son and grandson knew." I pinched the bridge of my nose. "Whoever was king when the copying was done made sure no one learned of it. Monstrous."

"Horrible," he said.

"To let everything in the three *vitae* be lost to suppress knowledge of the crime—"

His face went white.

"I'm not saying that's worse than murder and usurpation," I said. *Just almost as bad.* But I did not say it.

"Not merely suppression," he said. "Worse."

"Worse?" The knot of dread twisted again.

He touched the modern *vita*. "This is for a later king Halden. A descendent. Here," he turned the book so I could see more easily.

King Halden was named for his most famous forefather, the first king of their line, who came to the throne after the untimely deaths of King Davin and his heirs. The first king Halden guided Ragonne through a time of great danger and turmoil—the reign of Otto Valennus. He was a great warrior, preserver of Ragonne during that difficult time. The current line of kings is proud to claim as its forebear...

"They made a usurping murderer into a hero." I didn't try to keep the loathing from my voice.

"And still revere him." He made no effort to keep scorn and revulsion from his voice either.

I felt a question form but knew the answer before I put it into words. I closed my eyes, seeing the tapestry in Philip's study, hearing again his preening description. *Halden, first king of our line.*

***

At dawn, I went to the kitchen.

The night before, I'd sat at the worktable long after Hal left, going over his discovery. It was certain Halden had removed his nephews to make room for himself on the throne. I was at first appalled, but then intrigued. Information could be a tool, as much as a spade or a hammer. Or a weapon. We had this knowledge. What might we do with it?

Then I knew. But I needed Mistress Baynor's help.

I was not as fortunate as I had been the evening before. Servants filled the space, moving in smooth efficiency, some about the household's breakfast, others in preparation for noontide. Ina, who was inclined to gossip, was kneading bread not six feet from the door.

Mistress Baynor approached, flicking me a warning glance towards Ina. "Doctora Bann. I know you don't normally take breakfast but since you're here am I to assume you'd like some this morning?"

"Yes, please," I said, grateful for her subterfuge.

"We're busy now. If you can wait a bit, I'll bring it myself once the *palais* has been fed."

"You're very kind. Thank you."

★★★

After half an hour I tired of pacing and switched to knife throwing. When my arm ached, I went back to the Old Valenian *vitae*.

I'd not been reading Martin's *vita* for ten minutes before a new thought struck with the force of a longship hitting rock. The heels of both hands pressed against my eyes until I saw flashes of light behind the lids. *Fool! Kolon!* Why had not I asked Orlo in my last letter to question his clerk about books? Martin had been lord of Kolon when he met the beggar child. Perhaps he'd left something written, something that would explain why he'd gone east to create his *saradomus*.

It was unlikely. But everything I'd found so far—Oliver's memories, Carlomond, Martin, Charles Henry—had been unlikely. It was no less probable that a book might have been commissioned by Martin and survived in Kolon.

What was *truly* unlikely, I thought as the first zeal of the idea gave way, was that Orlo had not already done so. He knew what we sought.

But, another part of my mind argued, he did not know I'd found a connection to Kolon. He didn't know about Martin.

It wouldn't hurt to ask.

I took out parchment and wrote quickly, before I had time to consider whether I thought the possibility really promising or was just grasping at a plausible reason to send him another letter before I left Ragonne.

★★★

Mistress Baynor arrived as I was sealing the letter. "What has happened?"

"Let me show you." I beckoned her into the second room, to where the *vitae* lay open, and explained what Hal had found.

She straightened. "What are you going to do?"

I stared. "Are you not surprised? Disgusted?"

She sighed. "I'm one of so many royal bastards it's difficult to keep count. Not all were the result of free relations. No, I am not surprised to learn of other, worse misdeeds in our past." Acrid shame filled her voice.

I let the matter go. "Use it," I said, answering her question.

She narrowed her eyes. "How?"

"I'll tell Philip I will give this information to his lords unless he abandons his plan to sail east." I raised a hand, like a conjurer revealing an empty palm where the polished stone had been.

She shook her head. "No."

I stepped closer. "We can prevent a war."

"You *already* have a war to stop."

"He means to attack whomever he finds. Saradena or not."

"I know." She clenched her hands. "But it won't work. You'll simply get yourself killed."

"But—"

"I know Philip. He does not have the right character to be threatened. He's confident. Arrogant. If *he* does a thing, it is the *right* thing. He suspects you already, because of Orlo. You wouldn't leave his chamber alive."

"Should we do nothing?" Irritation roughened my voice. "Hal handed us a weapon. It would be foolish not to use it."

"I agree. But how?" Both fists clenched now. "Philip will ignite like last winter's wood if you try." Her fists planted on her hips. "And *I* cannot allow this information to go to the great lords. They might see it as an excuse to move against him."

My eyebrows rose. "I meant to bluff only."

"Don't threaten what you're not willing to do. It's guaranteed to fail." One hand, but only one, left her hips. "We have to be careful. If this gets out...the great lords would move, I'm sure of it. Philip has always been a stench in their nostrils, but more so since the Saradenian letter and his wool-headed scheme. Ragonne cannot have internal dissension. Not now." Her mouth pursed. "They would rally around Orlo."

"He doesn't want the throne."

"I know. But they could easily get him killed trying to put him there." Her other hand left her hip to rub her temple. "Philip will manage that himself."

I pushed it away, refusing to think about this bleak assessment. "Very well. What is your counsel?"

"I doubt we can prevent Philip's attack, even with this." She spoke slowly, thinking aloud. "But perhaps I can persuade him...would having Hal with you be useful?"

"*Yes.*" I'd meant to figure to out a way to take him with me. Hope returned. We might use Halden to force something from Philip after all. "He's learned to read Old Valenian. But—"

Two fingers of one of Mistress Baynor's hands chafed the palm of the other, as if thought could be warmed by rubbing. "I'll tell Philip I learned of this by chance...Hal found it before Domon left and doesn't realize its importance...I want to help Philip keep it secret...by sending Hal away and getting rid of the books."

"What?" I shouted.

She smiled. "Not destroy. Get rid of. Doctora Bann leaves for Vere. Send them with her. A gift to Vere. The scholars will assume Philip's trying to get a better clerk. Once among Vere's vast library, the books will never be read again, certainly not by anyone able to understand their import. Ragonne's secret is safe. Make a gift of Hal to the Roth and send him with Doctora Bann."

I blinked as the torrent stopped. "You think that will work?"

Her smile broadened. "Be ready to leave in the morning. I'll get word to Hal." She turned.

"Wait." I held out the parchment roll. "Can you send this to Orlo?"

Her face fell into sober lines. "Of course." She hesitated. "You have not asked for my counsel in this matter, but I will give it. Receive it as you will. Orlo is a good man. He has loved you, or fancied he does, for years. It cost him, greatly, to accept Philip's refusal when he asked leave to present his suit to the High King." Her eyes flashed anger. "If Philip understood that, he would not question Orlo's loyalty so lightly." The fire vanished. "Unless you have grown to savor the taste of pain, do not consent when he offers again."

"He might not." But I knew better, as did she.

"He will." She closed her eyes, kept them closed for a long moment. "You know what Philip intends. Orlo will lead the eastern attack. My heart tells me that win or lose, Orlo will not survive. Death attends him like carrion birds follow armed men."

My mouth was dry. I had to swallow before I could speak. "Are we not all but one heartbeat from death?"

She met my gaze, her eyes somewhat narrowed, as if looking for something far off. "Very well."

"Send the letter." I held it out. This time, she took it.

BOOK II

CHAPTER I

I sat in the fore of the boat not far behind the bow, which narrowed to a point and rose, curving, nearly my full height above the gunnels. A scroll, like interlacing in a manuscript, topped the bow.

I glanced back at Hal, where he sat watching the slaves bend their backs to the oars, the late-morning sun glinting dully on the iron rings around their necks. To our right the Margantes stood like sentries in the water. The sea mountains studded the coasts of the Three Lands, thick as hazelnuts in autumn, making sailing difficult and dangerous. Only Brusterians, it was said, were mad enough to willingly take to the sea.

Odulan, the boat's captain, sat in the aft, his hand on the steerboard. Some boat masters preferred to leave the steerboard in another's control while they stood further forward, directing the ship's activities. Wary of the rocks that slipped and hid among the waves, Odulan permitted no man's touch on the steerboard but his own. I remembered him from my time in Vere. He was the master of Vere's ships and the ship slaves, and a useful man to listen to if you were a Brusterian princess wishing to expand her vocabulary.

My eyes narrowed as I looked out over the water, but it was against the brightness, not from displeasure. Most Brusterians liked sailing, for perversity if nothing else, doing a thing the rest of the Three Lands feared. I was no exception.

It was a spectacular day to be on the sea. But it'd been a long day before we'd embarked, a long week leading up to our departure, and more than three long months since the arrival of the Saradenian letter. I yawned in the enveloping calm of warmth and waves, and edged along the thwart until I could lean against the gunnel.

Mistress Baynor's plan had gone as smooth as warmed butter. She'd spread her snare before Philip, and he'd stepped into it, uncharacteristically expressing gratitude to his sister for bringing both the threat to his attention and the means of defusing it. I'd been summoned and prevailed upon to take the books to Vere. It was a measure of how unnerved Philip was that he was civil to me.

Mistress Baynor had helped me pack the books, giving me clean, soft cloths to wrap them and a larger bag to carry them. I kept the golden book separate, in my own pack, although I was grateful for the cloths, relieving my spare shift of that duty. She'd also given me a cloak to replace mine, which had unaccountably disappeared during my stay. Warm as it had been, I hadn't noticed the loss until it was time to leave. Even in August, traveling on the sea could be chilly.

Not today, though. I pushed the new cloak back from my shoulders.

Lassitude spread through me, a heady draught of exhaustion and satisfaction. I was shipboard, the scent of the sea filling my nostrils and the breeze touching my hair, and soon I would see Magistre Poll again. Pedagno Poll.

Strange to think of Vere without Pedagno Olwen. He had been tall and slim with blond hair fading to gray, and his strong hands and quick eyes made you remember he'd learned the sword and spear as a young man. But I'd seen him hold books in those same hands as gently as an egg, the scholar's intensity in his eyes. He'd accepted me as *novicia* only with my father's coercion, but he had never been personally unkind, unlike the other scholars. If Pedagno Olwen's death had been natural, why had Magistre Poll said nothing of its cause?

The slaves' oars slapped the waves. Sea spray misted my cheeks. I looked across the waves towards where Vere lay, not yet in view. Slowly my head returned to the side. My eyes flicked open once, twice, then slid closed and remained so.

★★★

I woke. It was hours later, I realized from the change in the sun. I stifled a yawn, stretching my shoulders, then glanced down to make sure the bags still lay safely between my feet. The leather was misted but I was not concerned; it was oiled to keep out the damp. Looking up, I saw the tip of Lastland beginning to grow before us while to the right the clustered islands of Bruster were coming into view beyond the shadowy edge of the Margantes.

The rowing paused as a new shift of slaves came on. I stared towards Solud and Bruster, the only ones of the clustered islands visible; from here Eban, Punlan, and Verten were screened by the larger, closer islands. If the boat were to turn towards Bruster, soon the Black Keep of Reud would rise shining from the water. My childhood home. It had been six years since I'd seen it last.

Most likely I never would again.

***

In late afternoon Odulan gave orders to slacken the rowing. We were approaching Lastland.

The first scholars had quickly learned that Lastland, although the largest of the islands of Bruster, had not been an unambiguous gift. It was presumed to be, as its name implied, the last land before endless sea. The eastern shores were bare rock cliffs, useless for living and deadly for sailing. Most of the rest was mountains. The only truly habitable part was the northwest.

We passed the ruins on the northernmost tip of the shore, then turned south and east, following the coast. Vere was not visible, nor would it be from the landing place. The city of scholars lay a mile or so inland, beyond the coastal hills. What they were ruins *of*, I didn't know. The scholars had been tight lipped on this subject. I'd once overheard two scholars discussing them and gathered that some believed them to be the remains of an earlier Vere. If there were records to support this claim I did not know of them. The ruins might well be the outpost the High King had maintained before giving Lastland to the scholars.

The coastline abruptly bent southwest but Odulan had already called the orders. The boat turned to follow.

Now the landing place was in sight, tucked at the end of the cove. As we drew close, Odulan halted the rowing. The boat drifted in on its residual motion. At his gesture, two slaves vaulted overboard and pulled the bow of the longship up on shore. I climbed out, holding my bags so high that the water lapping at my heels would have had to leap like a stag to douse them. Oiled leather kept out drips, not a soaking.

The landing place was little changed since I'd been there last. There was a round stone watchtower and beside it, three thatched houses where Odulan and his men lived, and one larger, rougher building for the ship slaves. Smoun, Odulan's chief retainer, stood waiting, the leads of two horses in his hand. Quick work, to have noticed us as the longboat drifted in and prepared for guests, but Smoun was famous in Vere for his aptness.

He handed me the reins of a sleek tan mare with pale hooves, and the bay's reins to Hal. I thanked him, and he helped us secure my bags behind the saddle. I led the mare to the mounting block. She nickered as I settled in the saddle, and I stroked her shoulder.

"Where now?" Hal asked, patting his own horse.

I turned the mare's head. "This way."

The road to Vere followed the Munlon river, winding beside it from its mouth near the landing place. Had the river been deeper the longship could have sailed inland, but only a coracle could take the shallow, fen-like Munlon, and not far.

Hal breathed deep. "Thank you for bringing me. I am grateful to be out of the palace. Those lower levels were like a dungeon."

"Don't thank me yet," I said. "Who knows what we're heading into." But I took a slow, full breath as well. It was good to be out.

It was warmer than usual for August in Vere. Like the rest of Bruster, the elevation and the winds off the mountains kept the weather cooler than in Valenna. But compared to Ragonne, the heat was easily endurable, although I was glad I'd tucked away my new cloak before setting out.

As we rode inland, the saltiness faded from the air, replaced by the scents of forest and water. Closer to Vere, we caught the scent of crops beginning to ripen as the fields of Vere's tenant farmers came into view. Oats, barley...I looked again, puzzled. *Wheat?* Since when did Vere grow so much wheat? High effort and low yield, wheat required a costly investment of land and labor, and returned less than any other grain. It was, in consequence, a luxury, and Cynan Maccus forbade luxury foods except for festival days.

I glanced at Hal. He was looking to the other side, at the trees growing thickly there. I was relieved he was content to ride silently. I could not tell him why we had come, at least not until after I'd seen the Pedagno, and I doubted my ability to construct sensible but harmless conversation about something else. And it was pleasant to ride quietly, hearing the leaves rustle as a light breeze caught them, the wisp and call of birds in the branches.

The road began to climb. As the slope sharpened, the river fell away into a ravine, deep enough that the water could not be seen. I could hear it, though, prattling like an old gossip.

The river curved right, and with it, the path. When both straightened, I saw the highest towers of Vere peeking between the trees, and beyond, the distant tips of the Reuth mountains like a ridge of clouds. *Almost there.* I tried to keep my breathing even but found myself holding it instead.

The road twisted again, following the winding course of the river, and the city was hidden once more amongst the trees. I let out my air. Perhaps it had been a mistake, coming back unbidden. I saw Hal watching, curious and concerned, and did not meet his eyes.

Suddenly the woods gave way.

Vere.

White stone walls flamed orange and red in the westering sun, the tower of the scriptorium gleaming like a beacon. I did not realize I had drawn rein to look in stillness upon the keep until the mare shook her head questioningly.

We started forward, moving with the path as it dodged left, ending in a bridge over the Munlon. The horses' hooves rang on the stones of the bridge, the same white rock as the castle. I'd been told once, but could not remember by whom, that the stones had been quarried from somewhere within the Reuth mountains. I glanced up, but the mountains were hidden now behind the castle.

The bridge ended in a courtyard, paved with the same gleaming white stone. At the far end stood the gates of Vere. Beyond them, the keep rose, beautiful and imposing as the mountains from which it had been formed.

I reined in. Hal let his horse advance a few steps until he was beside me. "Magnificent."

"Yes." I remembered waiting at these gates, my father beside me, his retainers at our backs. We had not waited long. But it had been enough. He was furious by the time they opened.

Heavy wood, like the gates of a true castle, but painted dark green, the same color as the robes of the *magistres.* The device of Vere was carved at the top. A hawk, his wings outstretched, a quill in his beak, showing the perseverance and pursuit necessary for the making of books. It was painted dark blue, the color of wisdom, the child of knowledge and reflection. The same color as the Pedagno's robes.

I had wanted to become a scholar long before I bowed to my birth and wed Francis. I had, finally, gone through these doors, but had not found Vere what I'd hoped it would be. Even so, the same thrill pulsed down my back that had run through me when I'd first looked upon them, coveting learning like a pinchthrift did silver.

I turned to Hal. "Welcome to the City of Scholars."

We waited. The gates did not open.

CHAPTER II

I pushed down anxiety that I had been recognized and deemed unwelcome. If the porter were still Doctore Unwin, the neglect was perhaps unsurprising. He tended not to notice visitors because he was in the porter's nook reading copies he'd been allowed to make for that purpose since Vere's books could not leave the library. Few visitors came to Vere, so his reading was seldom interrupted.

I rode forward and rapped the wicket gate without dismounting.

At last it opened. Doctore Unwin's shaggy gray head emerged, blue eyes bright amongst hair and beard like a jay in a thicket.

I braced. I'd had little contact with him during my time at Vere, and had never been sure if he disliked my presence as thoroughly as the other scholars, but he was a fresh reminder I'd soon enough be among those who had unambiguously despised it.

He stepped out, squinting as he left the shadows of the doorway. "Doctora Bann. It is you. I thought so." He smiled—or at least a wide gap appeared in his beard—and put his hand to my horse's bridle, holding the mare's head as I dismounted. "I did not expect to see you again. But here you are. Well met. And welcome." He extended his hand to me.

I was so astonished I blinked silently at him for a long moment.

"Was it a long trip?" His brow furrowed. "Are you well?"

I took his hand hastily. "Yes, thank you, sir."

He laughed. "None of that. You are *doctora*." He leaned closer, eyes glinting in the gray flurry of hair. "Do not speak as a *novicia*. They," his gaze flicked towards the gate, "must remember you are *doctora*, whom they must hear if not heed." He released my hand. "I worried about what you might portend, when the High King forced us to take you." He wagged his head slowly. "Your presence shook Vere. But for the better, I think.

Perhaps you can again." His voice went so low I could scarcely hear him. "Things are not well in Vere."

I'd suspected trouble, but finding it was another matter. "What...?"

He shook his head. "You should not hear from me. The Pedagno. Be cautious." He whistled.

A moment later a boy ran through the gate and took our reins.

"Jumon will see your horses to the stable," he said. "I will take you to the Pedagno."

★★★

Inside the gate stood a smaller inner courtyard, in the center of which stood a statue of Cynan Maccus. Half again as tall as a living man, it suggested determination and wisdom, a representation of his status as Vere's founder, not a portrait of the man himself. No image of Cynan Maccus survived. *None known by Vere, at least.* I patted my bag, where the golden book rested with its concealed illumination, and wondered what the scholars would say if they knew the man who walked at my side wore the face of our founder.

Two arched doorways led out from the courtyard. The one on the left led to the meeting hall, where the scholars convened each morning to discuss any business before beginning the day's work. Behind the wall directly in front of us lay Vere's library, but no door opened into it from the courtyard. The library, the keep's most valuable possession, was accessible only through passages at the very heart of the keep. I smiled, looking at the inner courtyard with different eyes than I had when I'd arrived with my father. I'd been too excited and nervous to notice that while Vere was not a true castle, its design *was* defense minded.

"The Pedagno is at supper with the scholars in the *comedor*," Doctore Unwin said, leading us through a doorway to our right, which opened onto a passage leading to the Pedagno's chambers. "Would you consent to wait in his sitting room? It will not be long until he returns."

"Of course," I inclined my head. "Thank you, Doctore Unwin."

He motioned us inside. "I must return to my post." His hand on the handle, he looked back. "Be cautious," he said again.

"What are we to be cautious of?" Hal asked after the door

closed.

I shook my head. "I'm not sure. But something is wrong." I turned, appraising the room, listening, testing the scent of the keep. "Vere was fraught when I was here, but that was *because* I was here. This feels different." I turned a second slow circle. "Like fear rather than anger."

"The castle feels tense," Hal said. "Like everyone is looking over his shoulder."

"You feel it too," I said, relieved.

"How could I not?" Following my lead, it seemed, he pivoted, considering each wall. "It's heavy in the air, like a coming thunderstorm."

On the wall opposite, a doorway led to another chamber. The inner room was where the Pedagno slept, if I'd been told true; I'd never seen it. This room, the sitting room, was where the Pedagno worked and received Vere's guests. Seven years ago I had been here with my father.

I studied the chamber as intently as I had Vere's gates. In outward seeming, it was little changed. A small fire against the evening chill that lingered in Bruster and Elbany on all but the hottest days of summer burned on the hearth, which was built into the wall between the two rooms. It was a clever design; a large fire could heat both rooms, or metal screens on either side could be closed to direct heat into one room. Both screens were open. I could see shadowy glimpses of the inner room through the flames.

The chimney extended to an identical set of rooms above, which I'd seen more than once. The King's Rooms. The High King who gifted Lastland to the scholars had required that they provide chambers for his visits. Most likely he had required the rooms because their existence reminded the scholars that they were bondmen of Bruster. Lastland was far from Reud. A Pedagno might forget. My father had come three times I could remember, for the same reason the rooms were demanded: to remind Vere of Bruster's overlordship. I had accompanied him, and never forgot my first glimpse of the walls of books that were the library of Vere.

My gaze returned to the hearth. When I'd come the last time with my father, there had been two chairs at the fireside, a low table between them, as there was now. The Pedagno had brought his work chair from his writing table for me. I looked at the empty chairs, seeing that night again.

Pedagno Olwen had sat to my left, a tapestry on the wall behind him the same blue as his robe, the device of Vere woven in white but glowing yellow and orange in the firelight. My father sat to my right. The two had argued in the cool, precise manner of civilized and powerful men. Quiet voices, but hard, accustomed to being obeyed. I sat listening, gut churning with the humiliation of the demand and the hunger that it be granted. Their eyes flitted to me rarely. I was the source of their debate, not its substance.

Later, they had turned to me in earnest, both heads swiveling to stare in unnerving simultaneity, and the Pedagno spoke. He questioned me for nearly three hours but I did not give him the easy path of being witless, untutored, or foolish.

After that, they sent me away. I did not know what the High King argued or offered to tip the balance. In the end, Pedagno Olwen had accepted me as *novicia*. He treated me graciously, if reservedly, and required the scholars also to do so. Which meant their mistreatment was coldly brooded and covert.

Now I looked at the empty chairs, feeling the loss of the Pedagno afresh, and perhaps fully for the first time. *Gone, and too soon.*

My gaze swept the room again. "The leader of Vere died recently, suddenly, and unexpectedly. Could the tension we feel be the shock of loss and mourning?"

Hal considered, walking, listening, as I had done. "I don't think so." He stopped, facing the tapestry. "Shock and sorrow are here, but there's more. A sharp, chilly thread of fear."

"I agree. But I have no idea why." I paced to the corner where the Pedagno's writing table stood, then, turning, to its opposite where a chair cradled a lap harp. "A time of change is a time of difficulty. But I see no cause for fear if the Pedagno's death was natural. Magistre Poll will be an excellent Pedagno." I looked back at the vacant chair. "Still, Pedagno Olwen's death is a great loss. He was young. He should have been Pedagno many more years."

"I agree," a voice said.

CHAPTER III

I whipped around. Behind us the door to the Pedagno's inner room had quietly opened.

"Doctora Bann."

I had known about his elevation. Nonetheless, I was stuck speechless at seeing Magistre Poll in the Pedagno's blue robes. I stared, incongruously registering the noteworthy fact the Pedagno's inner quarters must be accessible from elsewhere in the keep. The cloister garden, perhaps?

After half a dozen heartbeats, surprise faded, leaving a welt of fresh grief for Pedagno Olwen. In its place grew astonishment as I gazed at my mentor. I had last seen him in April. He had come to Elbany to assist in training my students, returning to Vere just two weeks before the Saradenian letter arrived.

He looked years, not months, older.

He was thin—no, *gaunt*—and pale approaching gray. He smiled, but there was no light in his eyes. It was the brave but fearful smile of those who know they have a mortal sickness.

"Welcome." He walked into the room more slowly than I recalled but his lightness of step was still evident. "Come. Sit by the fire." He moved to the Pedagno's chair. "It is perhaps more comfort than need." He stretched his feet towards the hearth. "But comfort is not unwelcome."

After a moment I gathered myself and went to the opposite chair, where my father had sat and disputed with Pedagno Olwen. I glanced at Hal. "Pedagno—"

He forestalled me. "Friend." He looked at Hal. "The Pedagno rarely receives more than one guest at a time." His gaze went to the corner, where the lap harp sat like a guest on its own fine chair, although not as fine as those that stood before the hearth. "You are welcome to Vere, and I look forward to greeting you properly. But could I first be so bold as to do you the double discourtesy of not only asking you to be satisfied with a lesser seat but fetching it as well?"

Hal bowed. "To be received by the Pedagno of Vere is a great honor. To sit with him, in any manner, a greater one still."

The Pedagno answered his bow with a courteous nod. "You are gracious, sir."

Setting the harp gently on the floor, Hal returned with the chair and gave a quick bow once more to the Pedagno before seating himself.

"Now, then," said the Pedagno. "Whom do I have the pleasure of greeting?"

Hal moved as if to stand again, but the Pedagno waved him down. "Your servant, Pedagno. I am Hal Carlson. I accompanied Doctora Bann from Ragonne."

The Pedagno's eyes narrowed at the second name. "I do not recall your time at Vere, Doctore Carlson."

"I am not *doctore*. Nor was I trained at Vere." He paused. "But I *can* read and write. I assisted Doctora Bann in Vere and was sent with her to continue doing so."

The Pedagno's gaze remained on Hal, assessing the younger man. "We will talk, later."

"As you wish, Pedagno." Hal inclined his head respectfully. "But I will not tell you."

"We will see," the Pedagno said. His gaze flicked to me. "Why have you come? Surely you do not suppose my new role means you could become *magistra*."

I guiltily recalled having considering just that possibility. But the coldness in his voice startled me more than his apt guess. "Pedagno—"

I was interrupted by a knock at the outer door.

"Enter," the Pedagno called.

The door opened and a boy appeared, bigger than the child who had taken our horses but so much like him I felt certain they must be related. He carried a polished wooden tray, a meal spread upon it.

The Pedagno noticed my glance. "This is Jurl, Jumon's brother. Their mother became Vere's cook last year. Their father oversees our stables, as he has done for several years."

I searched my memory but could not bring a face to mind for Vere's stableman. While I had ridden a great deal when I was *novicia*, neither the scholars nor the students were encouraged to go to the stables; when horses were wanted, they were brought to the keep.

Jurl placed the tray on the low table and left, closing the door quietly behind him.

"What happened to Mistress Kimber?" I asked.

"I am afraid her talent has taken her beyond us," the Pedagno replied. "When the High King's cook died, he remembered Mistress Kimber from his visits here and invited her to Reud. Perhaps you will have occasion to enjoy her cooking again there." His voice was crisply, painfully impersonal.

Had so much changed when he became Pedagno? Or did he truly believe I'd come to demand a place at Vere now he could give me one? "Pedagno—"

"Surely you must be hungry," he cut across my words. "You are a guest of Vere, Doctora. I must insist you allow me to treat you as one, with all the courtesy we can offer. Eat. Then you may tell me why you are here."

Doctora. Not *Alumna.* He *did* believe I'd returned to presume upon our bond as *maestro* and *novicia.*

"Pedagno—" I began urgently.

Suddenly, silent as a cat, he was on his feet. In an instant, his hand was on my arm, gripping more tightly than I would have thought possible in his wasted condition. His other hand rose, his forefinger on his lips. His eyes caught mine, then flicked towards the chimney.

In a quick flash, I understood. The Pedagno suspected someone was in the King's Rooms, listening. *Clever.* If fires were lit in the upper and lower hearths, the noise of the flames would drown sounds from the rooms. But if only one, or better, neither, hearth was lit, a sharp-eared listener on one floor could overhear what was said on the other. The design was assuredly meant to benefit the Pedagno, allowing him to listen to what the High King discussed during his visits. But if someone were bold enough to sneak into the King's Rooms, the arrangement could be used to hear the Pedagno's conversations. But who, and why? How could the Pedagno suspect this shameful treatment and be unable to halt it?

He squeezed my arm, the question still in his eyes. I nodded, letting him know I grasped his warning. His fingers uncurled and he returned to his chair, looking even more haggard than before. "May I serve you, Doctora? And you, Master Hal?"

"You are kind, Pedagno." I hoped I'd scrubbed the confusion and concern from my voice. "We thank you for your hospitality."

He poured wine, then began cutting the bread. I examined my goblet. It was very fine, delicate glass the deep green of the *magistres'* robes, with the device of Vere etched on the base. Exquisite Ferranti craftsmanship. When I was *novicia*, these goblets were used only on festival days. Surely, I thought dryly, my visit was not so momentous. What *was* going on?

The Pedagno handed me a plate—also the best—laden with food I would have expected for the feast of Cynan Maccus. Veal cutlets grilled to brown but not beyond, savory fish pie, creamed leeks, a soft Ragoni cheese, and white bread as fine as that which had graced Philip's table.

"I have just come from our evening meal," the Pedagno filled a third plate, "but of course it would be impolite not to keep my guests company."

"Of course." Drawing his belt knife, Hal began to eat.

I turned to the food as well but could not give the meal the attention it deserved. I did not suppose the extravagance was on my behalf any more than I'd believed Vere's best glasses had been brought out to honor my return. Was it a holiday, one new since I was *novicia*? Or did the scholars eat now as if every day were a feast day?

"Is the Roth pleased with your work on his library?" The Pedagno buttered a second slice of bread.

"Yes, Pedagno," Following his lead, I kept our conversation formal and innocuous. "If it would not be too bold to presume to know my lord's mind, I would hazard the Roth would have instructed me to convey his gratitude to Vere for answering his request."

"So you are not here at the bidding of the Roth?"

I frowned, realized I'd told more than I'd meant. Surely he didn't want me to explain why I'd come, not after warning me about the eavesdropper.

His eyebrows waggled a silent reminder. *Dangerous game,* maestro. I was not adept at the diplomatic dance of misdirection. It chilled me that he knew this and still deemed it necessary to engage me in it. "I am about the Roth's business," I said guardedly.

He raised his glass in silent approbation, although the roll of his eyes upward, all too clearly relieved that I'd managed to both answer and not answer, rather undermined the commendation. But it was affectionately done. His earlier rudeness, I realized, more relieved than I could have said, was for the eavesdropper. Not me.

"Business in which, I take it, Philip of Ragonne is also involved, since he has sent Master Hal to aid you?"

"Just so, Pedagno."

"That is interesting," he replied. "I would have supposed the lord of Ragonne preferred to work alone in most things."

"Have you met King Philip?" Hal asked.

"I have not had the pleasure," the Pedagno said. "But I have heard much of him, as with the other kings of the Three Lands."

"All leaders must know about their peers," Hal said. "Have you had the chance to visit Ragonne, Pedagno? It is a land of great beauty."

He chose another piece of bread. "I have, unfortunately, visited few places outside Bruster, and none since I came to Vere." He eyed Hal conspiratorially. I looked between them, wondering what understanding had passed there that I'd missed. "Perhaps, Master Hal, you could tell me somewhat about Ragonne?"

Hal dipped his head. "If it would please the Pedagno." He described the *palais*, the countryside he had seen on his trip north, the Fields and the city.

As Hal talked, the Pedagno ate. I had thought my curiosity full blown already but I was wrong. The Pedagno was eating as if his previous meal had been last week, not less than an hour before. He had very soon eaten all that remained upon the tray.

I looked again at his thin face and wasted form. He wasn't ill. He was starving. How came the Pedagno to be famished within his own walls, while splendid meals were set before the scholars?

CHAPTER IV

If I had any doubts about my conclusion, they fled when Hal passed his plate, nearly full, to the Pedagno. He quailed not an instant before plowing in. Hal continued to fill the room with polite drivel about the wonders of Ragonne. I handed over my plate, rather less full than Hal's. He had understood the Pedagno's trouble more quickly and saved most of his supper to share.

Hal moved to telling stories about his days in the stables, the humor in them mostly at his own expense, as if he were unskilled with horses and slow to learn. Untrue as I knew it to be, the tales were no less entertaining. The Pedagno laughed, a true burst of enjoyment but ragged, as though he had not done so for months.

He dusted crumbs from his robe. Again cat-like, he went to his worktable. He returned as quietly, something small and dark in his hand.

"Come now." The Pedagno placed the object on his knee. A wax tablet. A stylus was in his hand, and he wrote as he spoke. "Surely you do yourself an injustice, Master Hal. You seem a man apt for any task to which he put his hands."

"Perhaps my prior work addled my mind," Hal said, his tone light as the Pedagno's had been. "Before the stables, I was assigned to aid King Philip's clerk. You may remember him. Domon?" One fingertip circled on the polished arm of his chair. "Domon has been...unwell...for several years. It was my task to keep him out of trouble, as much as possible."

"I recall him," the Pedagno said, the stylus silently etching the surface of the wax. "By 'unwell' I gather you mean he remains overly fond of wine?" His tone sounded as if he looked up, meeting Hal's gaze in wry understanding, but in fact his attention remained on the tablet. "That one would be difficult to keep clear of calamity, I expect." He passed the wax tablet to me. *Why have you come? I looked. I told you. If we ever knew of Saradena, it is lost.*

"You're quite right," Hal said as I wrote. *Maybe I can help you.*

"Oh?" the Pedagno said. He read my words, then smoothed the wax.

"Indeed. One time..." Hal spun a tale about Domon shaking his oversight only to become lost in Peran. In his drunken confusion he'd pounded at a door he thought was his favorite brothel but which was really the house of the best goldsmith in the city.

The Pedagno slid the tablet back. *You must go. They killed Honre and are trying to kill me. My food tastes strange and makes me sick. I eat as little as I can.*

I had expected something fearful but this atrocity threatened to drown me in its depth. Such treachery, within the very walls of Vere. Unthinkable. But he would not believe so without good reason. *Who? Why?* I wrote.

Hal, his gaze shifting between us, following the tablet, began another account of Domon's exploits.

Six months ago Honre found a book about Vere, older than any we had seen before, bound in a compilatio *of dreadful ballads and assorted bestiaries.*

When I looked up the Pedagno gestured for me to hand the tablet back. "I shouldn't speak badly of a Vere-trained clerk, I suppose," he said as Hal finished his story. "But I can't say I'm surprised Domon found himself in trouble when he returned to Ragonne. He certainly made enough mischief here."

"Vere must know, of course, Domon's relationship to the Ragoni ruling family," Hal said as the Pedagno passed me the tablet.

"Oh yes," he said. "We would not have accepted him otherwise. We suspected he would be a nuisance. Once he proved our suspicion correct, he would not have been allowed to stay without the insistence of the Ragoni king." He nodded towards me. "Doctora Bann's case, while unusual, was not as unprecedented as some scholars wanted to argue."

The rediscovered volume was in the same language as many of the Pedagno's reserved books. Honre could read it. He suspected it had been taken from that collection and hidden deliberately.

"Hmmff," I huffed as I returned the wax tablet, on which I'd written: *If that were true, why hide it? Why not burn it?* "For those scholars, as you well know, that I am a woman made the request wholly unlike any other, and unthinkable."

"You must try not to be angry with them. It was a difficult path to ask them to tread." *That's princess thinking. You know a scholar would never destroy a book, no matter how much he hated or feared what it said.*

I returned the tablet and he hurriedly wrote again. *The book told how Vere used to be. Our history is incomplete. Perhaps altered. Cynan Maccus founded Vere to preserve knowledge— but also to gather it. Scholars used to go throughout the Three Lands and record what they learned, not remain at Vere and copy.*

"Which brings us back to my first question." He looked hard at me as he reached for the tablet. "Why have you come? You know the scholars would never accept you as *magistra*, no matter that your *maestro* is now the Pedagno."

I did not need his stare to know I should speak an incomplete truth, and I'd had time to consider what to say. "No, Pedagno, of course not. I would not dream of presuming to make such a request." *Not for more than a moment anyway.* "I am returning to Elbany. King Philip asked me to travel by boat and bring the scholars a gift. It is not a much longer journey to sail to Vere, and then to Elbany, than it would have been to ride overland directly. Moreover, the king asked it of me, so naturally I agreed."

I took the books from my bag and gave them to him, taking the wax tablet in exchange. "I present these volumes to Vere, Pedagno, from Philip of Ragonne."

Honre wanted to return Vere to Cynan Maccus' design. The scholars did not.

"I will send my thanks to the king." The Pedagno set the books on the table, taking back the tablet. "Vere extends its thanks to you as well. Shall I arrange for a boat to take you to Elbany?"

"I was hoping..." I hesitated, needing to sound plausibly humble but not too humble. "Since I am here, may I ask the favor of borrowing books to take back to Elbany, that my scribes might copy for the Roth's library?"

He put the tablet into my hands. "That is a weighty request. Vere rarely allows a book to leave the library. Let alone our keep." *They were implacable but Honre persisted.*

"Just a few. I will bring them back personally," I argued, becoming engaged with my pretended purpose. It *would* be good. My scribes should be ready—and, if that rot-brain carpenter had finally done his work properly, the shelves too. The Roth's library could truly begin.

"I did not deny your request." There was dry amusement in his voice. "But it is a serious one. I need to consider. I will give you my answer in the morning."

"I will await your pleasure, Pedagno." I inclined my head.

"These Ragoni books," the Pedagno said as he wrote. "Did they come from King Philip's 'library'? I have heard of his boasting that his collection outstrips anything his cousin of Elbany could hope to possess. I confess I questioned the veracity of the claim."

He passed the tablet. *They did not defy the Pedagno openly, but they stalled and schemed. Since only Honre could read the book, they claimed it was a forgery; that the Three Lands were too dangerous for travel; that all the important knowledge had been collected. But Honre knew they simply did not want to go. We had grown complacent.*

"They did indeed." I returned the tablet. "Philip's boast is partially true." I paused, readying myself to describe the Ragoni collection with as much detachment as I could muster, as if it did not matter that the second largest gathering of books in the known world was rotting. "He has a sizable number. Many are quite old. But more than a few are badly deteriorated, and the conditions in which they are kept do not improve their prospects." Detachment shattered. "It's shameful. It's a disgrace. It's—"

Hal waved a hand. I caught myself. The Pedagno, bent over the tablet and writing furiously, nonetheless saw our exchange. One corner of his mouth lifted, more knowing grimace than smile.

"I apologize," I said. "The Pedagno has more pressing concerns than Philip of Ragonne's neglect of his forebears' books."

"All news is welcome," he hinted with a hard look at the tablet.

Very well. We were to keep discussing harmless subjects while he wrote. "Um..." I said.

"The Roth has not yet been provided with a son," Hal said.

"A pity. What of the King of Logan?" The Pedagno passed the

tablet. *Honre said that as Pedagno he was charged with ensuring Vere followed the Founder's precepts. Cynan Maccus had sent out scholars, and commanded Vere to continue the practice. Honre gave orders and would not listen to objections.*

"No babe for him yet either," Hal said.

"Ah, well. He's but newly wed." The Pedagno leaned to receive the tablet.

"Not *so* newly," Hal said. "The Lady Belenda wed the King of Logan when the Roth married Elsbeth of Garland, two years since."

"I have an old man's memory," the Pedagno said. "Two years *is* recent."

"If you heed rumors, both ladies have been pregnant for eighteen months now."

The Pedagno laughed, less creakily than before. "It is always wise to remember that saying a thing does not make it so. Still," he put the tablet in my hands, "it will be better when Logan and Elbany have a clear succession. Better still when the heir is not a child."

"For Logan, certainly," Hal said. "But in Elbany, the heir need not be the Roth's son." He began to explain more details of Elbish succession than I knew, who had lived in Elbany for a year with the heir-prospects of the recently married Roth on everyone's lips. I stared before turning my attention to the Pedagno's writing. *Magistre Ulton was among those scheduled to go out first. Then Honre was hurt, and of course the Pedagno's own clerk couldn't possibly leave. It seemed like an accident. He fell and broke his arm. But I wonder.*

"Were he older," Hal was saying, "lord Edwy's son would be favored. But given his nephew's age, it is rumored the Roth has named his cousin Edmund. I've also heard some lords lean instead towards Lady Elsbeth's brother Lionel, who is of course the son of Lord Garland, the most powerful lord in Elbany after the Roth..."

Hal continued but I heard only the buzz of his voice. *Magistre Ulton. Perhaps the murkiness is beginning to clear.*

CHAPTER V

Magistre Ulton. I recalled him vividly. Tall, broad-shouldered, with the long, sharp nose characteristic of his family, he looked every whit the warrior king so many men of his blood had been. He was the youngest half-brother of the sitting under-king of Verun. The island of Verun and its rulers were wealthy; almost half of our shipbuilding took place on their shores, and their farms had some of the best land in Bruster. The kings of Verun had ruled under the High King for longer than men could remember, but no one could say they had ever done so willingly. The Verune under-kings had always, more or less openly, held that Verten, not Reud, should be the city of the High King. To this end, they cultivated ties with Vere. Three generations ago, they gave the City of Scholars a generous gift towards the expansion of its fields, with the agreement that in each generation a member of the Verund royal family would come to Vere to be trained and serve as the Pedagno's own clerk, a position of power and trust. Magistre Ulton had come to Vere under this arrangement.

As I handed the tablet back, Hal adeptly drew his discussion of Elbish succession politics to a close. "I weary the Pedagno with my long-windedness. Pardon me."

"No pardon is needed," said the Pedagno, his attention on the wax. "Do continue, if you have more to say."

"If you like, Pedagno," Hal said. "I find Elbish politics fascinating, with its workings so unlike the rest of the Three Lands. But the evening is wearing on, and I could not help but notice you have a lap harp. If it pleases, I can play for you before we take our leave. A guest-gift, if you like, albeit inadequate to your hospitality."

The Pedagno grasped the point immediately. If Hal were playing the harp, we could 'listen' in silence while 'talking' in writing, much easier than juggling two different layers of conversation. His gaze weighed Hal again, longer this time. "I confess I would welcome music. I play, but not well, and have had little time of late to hone the skill. But be gentle with the harp," he said, unfeigned disquiet in his voice. "It is held to have belonged to Cynan Maccus."

Hal went to the harp. The Pedagno slipped into the chair he'd vacated, which was closer to mine and hence more convenient for passing the wax tablet. The Pedagno waved Hal to his own seat when he returned. Hal grimaced, objecting, but the Pedagno waved more emphatically. Hal sat, settling the harp carefully into his lap, and began to tune the strings. His evident skill in handling the instrument relaxed the Pedagno, who returned to writing, the stylus making no noise as it scored the wax.

Finishing his tuning, Hal paused, apparently choosing a song, then began to play, eyes almost closed as he bent to the harp. I noticed his bark-brown hair was longer than when I'd met him, beginning to curl onto his neck. I recognized the sweet, soft music of a Brusterian sea song, and the next instant, the depth of his skill. He rendered it as fair as my father's own *filun* could have.

Pedagno Poll slipped the tablet back to me. *Even after Honre was hurt, he refused to postpone sending out the first scholars, Magistre Ulton among them. Then Honre became ill. Not his arm. He was weak, and his stomach bothered him. The others supposed his fall must have injured more than his arm. But I became troubled.*

Having nothing to say, I smoothed the wax and passed it back. Hal finished the song and began another. I recognized this one as well, the "Lament for Edwy." I had heard it played, as the Roth had decreed, on his brother's birthday. I thought of Pedagno Olwen, whose death Pedagno Poll believed to have been brought upon him unnaturally. I had not known Edwy but did not think he would mind sharing his music with Honre Olwen; like him, the Roth's brother had been struck down before his time.

The tablet returned to my hands. *I am from Eban. We have a plant,* luton, *that only grows on our island. Roasted, it is safe and rather tasty, somewhat like parsnips, but dried raw, powdered, and mixed with milk, it is poisonous. Honre's illness looked like* luton *sickness.*

I felt my forehead crinkle. I'd never heard of *luton*. Perhaps the Eband kept it secret, like the Ragoni ladies and their herbs. It would be a powerful weapon, and when did Brusterians let a weapon slip through their hands? I passed the wax back and waited while the Pedagno wielded the stylus. Hal's music, rising to a crescendo of loss, filled the room, sorrow distilled into sound.

The song descended into quiet sadness before the Pedagno handed me the tablet. *Ulton used his power as the Pedagno's own clerk to keep the rest of us from seeing him. Even me, his designated successor. He gave commands in the Pedagno's name but allowed no one into his rooms, claiming the Pedagno needed to rest undisturbed. New orders countermanded Honre's.*

There was another music-filled pause as the Pedagno wrote. Hal finished Edwy's dirge and started a new song. This one, I did not know. It sounded Ragoni. From its liveliness, I guessed it to be a dance tune.

Soon the wax, crammed with the Pedagno's tidy script, came back to me. *So the scholars were not sent out. But Honre did not mend. He worsened, and then he died. I don't know if Ulton meant to kill him. Keeping him alive but unwell, and running Vere as he wished in his name would have made more sense. Now I am sick, and I know it's luton. I've experienced it before. I know ways to mitigate its effects, but not enough. Everything I eat is tainted with it. Ulton is pressing me to name him my successor. Having killed one Pedagno, even if by accident, seems to have emboldened him. Resisting, I suspect, is all that's keeping me alive. For now. Sooner or later, Ulton will decide he is strong enough to seize control of Vere without the formality of having been officially named the next Pedagno.*

Proof? I scored the wax with a hand I could not keep from shaking. I had expected trouble but this was worse than I'd feared. Corruption and murder within Vere. Cynan Maccus meant the City of Scholars to be above the power struggles of the kingdoms, dedicated to learning. *Sabidur gerva eng protege.*

He shook his head, his inscribed response answering more fully. *Not that I could take to the High King. Nor can I search for it, if there's any to be found. As the Pedagno's own clerk, Ulton is often with me. When he's not, someone listens upstairs. If I leave my chambers, one of Ulton's followers appears and accompanies me.*

I held the tablet, considering before I wrote. *As Pedagno, what do you want for Vere?*

His response was quick and emphatic, the wax scored through to the wood beneath. *To reform Vere as Honre wanted. To be the City of Scholars the Founder intended.*

I had come to Vere to help him but also to pursue my task. *You are going to find Saradena for me,* the Roth had said. I would. *I had to.* I had found scattered clues in Ragonne. The Pedagno's books might give the next piece. But I could not leave until Vere had returned to being the Pedagno's charge rather than his prison. What could be done? Many scholars supported Ulton. Others, like Magistre Unwin, did not but were too frightened to resist him openly. Without the scholars behind him, the Pedagno's power was negligible. Vere was part of Bruster, subject to the High King, but he would not intervene without proof.

I will help, I wrote. *I'm not sure what we can do, yet, but I will help.*

The Pedagno smoothed the wax to write again. *My thanks, Alumna, but make no promises until you know all. The letter you told me about, the Saradenian threat against Elbany, when you asked me to search Vere's library—I found a copy amongst Honre's papers. Addressed to Bruster.*

CHAPTER VI

Bruster! Bruster under the Saradenian threat! Not bothering to smooth away his words, I scrawled below. *Does the High King know?*

The Pedagno shook his head.

Both my hands lifted in a gesture that said as clearly as if I'd spoken—or written: *What? How could you be so foolish?*

With one hand he pressed downward in a placating move, while with the other he reached for a fresh wax tablet since this one had been scraped to its limit. The remaining wax would need to be dug out, then fresh molten wax poured in, ready to be of service again once it cooled.

Still playing, Hal watched us. It must have been clear something had changed about our silent discussion although of course he'd have no way of knowing what. Uncannily, though, when he finished he began another Brusterian song, the tale of Ator—undaunted, triumphant, and possibly nonexistent. If you believed the story, Ator was a Brusterian High King said to have conquered all of the Three Lands, who would return to us at our greatest need.

We might yet learn if the legend were true.

Pedagno Poll passed me the tablet. *I found the letter four days ago, in a pushed-aside pile of Honre's papers. He did not believe it, I think. I'm not sure I would have, had I not learned of the others from you. Vere is the last land before the endless sea. Everyone knows that. If there were other lands beyond, surely we would know of them. Do not judge him too harshly, Alumna. His thoughts were filled with his plans for Vere.*

I wasn't angry with Pedagno Olwen. I might, later, have thought to spare for anger. Now I had no room for anything but the growing horrified drumbeat of my pulse. *When they come, they come against Bruster as well.* I had believed myself frightened before, when the threat lay upon my adopted country. Elbany had given me a place and the Roth had given me meaningful work. But my skin had not quivered, not like this, at the thought of Saradenian ships in Rothbury Bay. Bruster...the blood pounded in my ears until I could no longer hear Hal's music. It took all my will to remain seated, although my fingers twitched with the effort, resisting the impulse to jump up, to demand a ship for Reud immediately. Bruster was threatened, and my father did not know.

Home, apparently, did not cease to be home because you left with no intention of returning.

I breathed deeply, trying to clear, or at least begin to calm, my mind. Closing my eyes, I listened for the sound of the harp, and at last heard it, as if from far away. The music had changed. Another lament by the sound, although I did not know the song. The slow ache of the music cooled my flaring anxiety. I knew—*I knew*—even if my yearning did not, I could not leave straightway for Reud. I was in Vere, and must do what was needful here, for the Pedagno but also towards my assigned purpose. Which was more crucial now.

Then I would go to Reud, see my father, and make sure he understood the danger. I smoothed the wax and wrote. *I will tell the High King.*

He considered me, then nodded. After a short pause, the tablet returned to my hands. *But why are you here, Alumna? I spoke truth when I said there was nothing here about Saradena. I appreciate your willingness to help but I do not see what you can possibly do. You have a task. You should go.*

Not yet, I wrote back. *Your letter mentioned the Pedagno's books. I can read them. Or at least some of them. I want to search them for references to Saradena. And I can teach you.*

His incredulous look needed no words.

I smoothed the wax and continued, realizing suddenly how this slow communication christened each word with greater meaning. *In Ragonne I learned to read an old form of Valenian. It was difficult but I worked it out. Eventually. Let me stay. I may be able to help us both.*

The Pedagno sat, his head bowed, the wax tablet in his lap, for several long moments. Finally, he wrote again. *I should not agree. Vere is not safe. He has killed one Pedagno and is sickening another. Why would he hesitate at you?*

I took the tablet. *I can take care of myself.*

He smiled sadly. *Not here, Alumna. Not now.*

I'm not leaving, I wrote. *Not without trying. What I need may be in those books. And Ulton...I do not promise I can stop him. But we'll try.*

The Pedagno smoothed the surface. *Mercy of the earth, but I should like to learn to read the Pedagno's books, even if we can think of nothing to thwart Ulton. And even if the skill dies with me.*

My fingers tightened on the wax tablet. Of course. I'd want the same. I read the rest of his words. *We must be very careful. The makeshift story you gave before has merit. I will agree to your request to borrow books to copy. That will give us a few days.*

Hal knows Old Valenian too, I responded. *Whichever of us can manage to be in your presence can teach you.*

Very well, he pursed his lips as he wrote. *Sooner or later Ulton will abandon his effort to be named my successor, arrange my plausibly natural demise, and seize power. Alumna, I would rather have spent the time before then with you.*

I blinked, surprised by the depth of affection in his eyes. It was, perhaps, merely a man grasping hands outstretched in kindness when others sought to push him under. But perhaps not. Magistre Poll had been the only scholar in Vere who had welcomed me, like a father when my own had cast me adrift.

The Pedagno smoothed the wax once more. *It is late. Vere's steward will be coming to take you to a room.* With that, he cleared the tablet a final time. He tipped his head back, eyes closed, enjoying what was probably, like the food, his first time of safety in months.

Hal's music changed. After a moment, startled by hearing it out of context, I recognized it. The "Calling of the Scholars," Cynan Maccus' musical evocation of Vere's purpose, *Sabidur gerva eng protege,* played every year on the anniversary of the founding of Vere and at the commissioning of a new *doctore.*

It was only later that I thought to wonder how Hal knew it. I was instantly furious. It was a poor choice to inflict upon the Pedagno. Surely Cynan Maccus' call would only increase his anxiety, unable as he was to fulfill his role. I glared at Hal but playing with his eyes nearly closed, he took no heed.

But as I watched, it seemed not to be so. Rather, the Pedagno appeared to gather strength and serenity from the music. His face grew less gray, the lines smoothing as he listened.

My gaze went back to Hal as I listened, recalling the first time I heard the call as *novicia*. Then as now, I had been at my *maestro's* side, but we had been in the *comedor*, watching the ceremony before the feast began. As the harper tuned his strings, Magistre Poll told me in a low voice that it was believed among the oldest scholars that Cynan Maccus used to play the call himself for the scholars on—

My very bones chilled. The portrait of Cynan Maccus in the golden book sat living before me. It was not merely that Hal wore bore our Founder's face, sat in the same chair and played upon Cynan Maccus' harp. It was *how* he graced the seat, *how* he cradled the harp, *how* his fingers touched the strings. The illuminator might have stood at my back and sketched.

A good omen, I decided. Having the descendant of Cynan Maccus with me had brought good luck to our search in Ragonne. Surely he would in Vere as well.

As the last sounds of the strings faded, there was a knock upon the door. The Pedagno thanked Hal both graciously and sincerely for his playing, and Doctore Orsenius escorted us out.

***

Twenty-eight chambers for the scholars filled the space above the *comedor*. I had heard they were comfortably but sparsely furnished—given their size, they could hardly be luxurious—but I'd never been in one. Pedagno Olwen had made a condition of my acceptance that I never set foot within the scholars' dormitory, but I hadn't needed that prohibition to know it was in my best interest to stay away from the scholars' bedrooms. I'd been given quarters in the corridor above the cloister garden, in one of the rooms set aside for the rare guests of Vere. I now suspected I'd been given the smallest and darkest one. The room at whose door Doctore Orsenius inclined his head to me with stiff civility was noticeably larger than the one in which I'd spent so much of my time. He directed Hal to the next chamber. Following Doctore Orsenius' lead, we did not speak, exchanging shallow nods goodnight.

I thought sleep might prove a shy companion that night, my mind teeming with Vere's troubles and the new terror of learning that Bruster, too, faced the unknown peril of Saradena. But I'd barely stretched out on the bed, more comfortable than the one I recalled, before my eyes closed, the churning thoughts behind them lurching and sputtering, a veil of seeming quietude settling over the muddle.

***

Doctore Orsenius returned in the morning to escort us to the *comedor* to breakfast with the scholars and students. I thanked the steward politely enough, but his action was intriguing. I knew my way to the *comedor*. Nor had I forgotten the schedule of Vere. The steward's walking us the short distance to the *comedor* was clearly meant to convey a message: we were not to wander alone. Behind Doctore Orsenius' back, Hal cocked an eyebrow at me, suggesting the meaning of the steward's presence had not been lost on him.

The *comedor*, vibrant with the hum of conversation when the door opened, fell silent as we stepped inside. I felt my chin lift. I'd had a week to envision, and dread, this moment, standing once more before their gazes. It was no better than I had imagined.

Hal and I went to the unoccupied end of one of the tables. Once we were settled, backs gradually turned upon us, although long glances—curious, indignant, angry—were stolen over more than one shoulder.

We talked quietly as we ate, but only about our overt reasons for being in Vere: delivering Ragonne's gift and requesting the loan of books to be copied in Elbany.

As surreptitiously as our notoriety would allow, I scanned the scholars' faces for any sign of what they thought about what was taking place in Vere. Anxiety deepened the lines of many foreheads and fear quickened many glances, but I could gather little about their views of the conflict between the Pedagno and his clerk. Magistre Ulton was not present. It would have been interesting to see who was most in his company. Fully a third of the scholars were not there, but that was no different than it had been during my time. Some scholars did not care to breakfast, or preferred not to rise early enough to do so before the morning's work. It would be unwise to assume that anyone not at breakfast was a proponent of Magistre Ulton.

Scholars began to drift away from the tables, singly or in small clusters, back to their rooms to seize a few more minutes' sleep before the morning meeting or to other small tasks in the intervening time. After the gathering the scholars would go to the library or scriptorium. Both always buzzed with soft whispers as the scholars read or copied; they tended to talk quietly to themselves during such tasks. If a scholar were assigned to the education of a *novicio*, student and scholar would meet for part of a morning session twice a week.

After the noon meal, the scholars would rest or walk in the cloister gardens before returning to work. Some days, a scholar might forego the afternoon session in favor of riding out through Vere's holdings. Nearly all the students and scholars were noble born so they were competent horsemen. Pedagno Olwen had encouraged this activity both for the scholars' exercise and because riding through their lands reminded Vere's tenant farmers of their landlord's interest in their husbandry. I had often ridden. The solitary time on horseback was when I carded the tangled wool of my never-abundant patience and spun perseverance enough to return to Vere.

The scheduled life of Vere, each day alike and predictable as the tides, pulled to me more than I'd remembered or expected. It seemed an unbelievable blessing to know what successive days would bring. But I knew better. At this moment Vere's regulated harmony was illusory.

The *comedor* was becoming decidedly empty. "Did I misunderstand?" Hal asked. "I supposed Doctore Orsenius preferred to escort us through the keep, and would return."

I looked sidelong at him. "That was my understanding as well. I—"

The door opened before I could say I suspected we were being kept waiting to demonstrate we could be. Doctore Orsenius gestured for us to follow him. "The Pedagno can give you a short audience this morning." Disapproval was evident in his tone.

Once more we followed the steward through passages I knew so well I could have walked them in full darkness without bumping an elbow. What was Magistre Ulton so anxious that we not see? Or was there someone he was determined we not speak to? How could we help the Pedagno if we were always under guard?

CHAPTER VII

Pedagno Poll was in his front room, sitting before the tapestry of Vere as he had the previous night. At his wave, Doctore Orsenius stopped, waiting just inside the door; it would clearly be a brief audience, one meant for the steward's eyes.

I bowed. Beside me, Hal did the same. The Pedagno did not invite us to sit.

"I have considered your request," he said, cool detachment in his voice. "It is unprecedented. Our manuscripts, collected and copied with such labor, do not leave Vere."

"But—" I objected, as I would, hoping my skills at feigning had improved.

"But—" the Pedagno echoed, raising a hand. "I remember Vere is a fiefdom of Bruster. If I deny your request the High King your father might be displeased."

I heard a grunt from Doctore Orsenius. Because the Pedagno seemed amenable to my 'request' or the reminder of Vere's client status? Or, perhaps, that my estranged father would take offense if I were refused? If he questioned *that*, he did not know the High King. My father might have no affection remaining for me, but an insult to me within his demesne was an insult to him, and my father would defend his rights.

"Nor have I forgotten your new lord," the Pedagno went on. "Elbany has been an ally of Bruster for many years. Moreover the current Roth has shown favor to Vere." He let his gaze linger on me, reminding everyone present of the Roth's most pressing aid —giving Vere an honorable way to be rid of me. "We are in his debt. I will allow you to choose six books to take to Elbany to be copied."

"Pedagno—" Doctore Orsenius ventured.

"Steward?" His tone would have chilled ice.

"It this...wise?"

"In my judgment, yes. And my judgment is what matters." His hands folded in his lap. "Vere will lend you these books. With this condition: you swear personal responsibility for them. You carry them in your own pack, you see to their care and safety, you yourself return them to us. No more than three years from now."

"I understand the value of books," I said. "As well as the generosity of this gift. Thank you, Pedagno."

He acknowledged my thanks with a shallow nod. "While you choose which volumes to borrow, your companion may visit with me."

Doctore Orsenius gave a strangled cry.

"Steward? You have some concern?"

"You're not well, Pedagno. Should you task your strength, entertaining a visitor?"

"Ah." He smiled. "You force me to show my discourtesy openly. I rather hoped Hal would entertain *me*." His gaze went to him. "You played the harp so beautifully last evening." He raised one shoulder as if in apology. "I hoped you might again."

Hal bowed. "I would be honored, Pedagno."

Doctore Orsenius gave another unhappy grunt but held his peace.

"May I begin today?" I asked.

"The sooner you finish, the sooner you can resume your travel," the Pedagno said. Doctore Orsenius made another low noise but this time it sounded like approval.

"Thank you, Pedagno." I bowed.

"Doctore Orsenius, would you take Doctora Bann to the library?" The Pedagno gestured for Hal to come forward. "Now, young man, before you begin, I want to ask you about one of the songs you played last night..."

Doctore Orsenius scowled as he closed the door, leaving Hal with the Pedagno.

One small victory.

★★★

I sat in the library, surrounded by manuscripts, pretending to search for books to borrow although I'd already made my choices. In reality I was dredging my brain for a way to put caltrops in Magistre Ulton's path. Or to get myself back into the Pedagno's chambers to search the secret books.

Our ruse would keep me in Vere a few days. The Pedagno had been brilliant, arranging for Hal to be in his company. I was the Pedagno's former student. Magistre Ulton would assume I meant to help him if I could. Hal had no past here. Even if Magistre Ulton joined them, and I had to assume he would, I was confident that between the two of them, they could devise a way for Hal to search the secret books and teach the Pedagno Old Valenian despite the Clerk's presence.

Which was, largely, what we'd come for. But my fingers twitched as I fought the urge to tug my braid until it hurt, from the frustration of being here and not there. *I* wanted those books in my hands. *I* wanted to be the one reading them, scanning for Saradena's name, for Carlomond, for Charles Henry. Hal knew to look for all this, and he knew Old Valenian as well as I did. But it itched like a half-healed wound, trusting my work to someone else's hands.

***

Doctore Orsenius returned at noon to escort me to the *comedor*, and again at supper time. I didn't see Hal during the midday meal, and wondered if he was eating with the Pedagno. It was early yet; only half a dozen scholars were there. Nonetheless I went to the end of a far table. Old habits died hard. Particularly when they were still useful.

I had not been seated long when Doctore Orsenius returned with Hal. More scholars trickled in. The *comedor* was now halfway full. Bustling sounds behind the serving door suggested the kitchen servants would begin bringing the dishes shortly.

"Evening, lady." Hal settled onto the bench beside me. "Did your work in the library go well?"

"A good start." I let a quick glance around the room warn him of the listening ears around us, a warning he certainly did not need. "You?"

"I was honored to spend the day with the Pedagno and his Clerk."

"Ah. You were indeed fortunate to have such exalted company," I said drily.

The serving door opened, ushering in the scents of beef and white bread. More feast-day food.

"Nonetheless, a productive day." Hal pitched his voice low, to go unheard beneath the servants' clatter. "Not revelatory, but productive."

If I translated this veiled report correctly, he had managed despite the presence of Magistre Ulton to begin reading the secret books and teach Old Valenian to the Pedagno, but had not found anything about Saradena. I quashed resurging frustration. There was no reason to believe I'd have done any better.

The *comedor* became crowded, the unique scents of Vere mingling with the aroma of the meal. The parchment and dust scent of books, the acrid twangs of ink and sweaty scholar. I caught an undercurrent of leather and horse. Someone had gone riding during the afternoon session.

Hal cut a generous slice from a loaf and spooned up tender beef, cooked with leeks and parsnips. "Wheat bread and beef," he echoed my thoughts. "It seems I've been misled about house-keeping in Vere."

"New since my time," I whispered.

"'S very good," he said around a mouthful.

The stares and whispers that had begun at breakfast had only increased. I caught my name amongst inaudible conversation. After the servants had cleared the plates and brought cheese and fruit, Magistre Hulthon, at the next table, poked Magistre Thurl. "Why do *you* think she's back?"

Magistre Thurl seemed taken aback by his assigned role in the show Magistre Hulthon had begun. He gave us a quick glance over his shoulder. "I don't know. Who's that she's brought with her?"

Magistre Hulthon waved an impatient hand. "Some servant. Doesn't matter." He planted both elbows on the table, glaring past Magistre Thurl at me. "Know what I think?"

"Uh...no?" Magistre Thurl said.

"Now he's Pedagno, the old man figured he could bring back his tearsheet."

Silence fell like a dropped stone. Eyes turned, staring.

Hal's hand clamped around mine. Reassurance or a reminder to behave properly? Or both? "We brought a gift from Ragonne to Vere and to ask Vere to send a new clerk to King Philip."

"So Domon finally came to a sticky end?" Magistre Hulthon said. "Knew he would."

"Domon is not dead," Hal said. "But my lord does find himself in need of a new clerk."

"Why?" Magistre Thurl asked, honest puzzlement on his face.

Magistre Rouk, sitting to his left, looked at him incredulously.

"Domon? You don't remember him? I thought we'd have to start locking up the wine casks."

"Oooh." Magistre Thurl's open face clouded. "Him."

"What happened?" Magistre Rouk half-turned on the bench and looked at Hal, more curious than malignant.

Hal hesitated. Or seemed to. The swift glance in my direction let me know his intent. Distraction. I felt impatience and gratitude well up together. It was kindly meant but I doubted it would work. Magistre Hulthon looked like a dog licking his chops over a particularly meaty bone.

"Well," Hal said. "It *started* with a Verduni stallion." He launched into what was decidedly the long version of Domon's banishment. More funny than the reality had been, too, with himself the butt of the jokes. I couldn't help but stare at him sidelong. This trip had already proven instructive, at least as far as learning new sides to my companion. Even Murrow, the most self-effacingly charming of my brothers, couldn't have done better.

But, as I expected, to no avail.

"That's what *you're* doing here," Magistre Hulthon said as Hal finished. "I want to know what *she* is." One corner of his mouth lifted in a sneer. "Returning to her role as the Pedagno's doxy, that's my guess."

"I was *never*—"

Hal's hand caught mine again, this time a tight grip with a clear warning. "She's here for the same reason she was in Ragonne," he interrupted. "To borrow books to copy for the Roth's library."

"Borrow books? From Vere?" Magistre Hulthon brayed a laugh. "That's the worst lie I ever heard."

"It's true," Magistre Rouk said. "I heard it from Magistre Ulton."

Interesting. I'd have pegged the blustering Hulthon as an adherent of Ulton's, but instead it was the more controlled Rouk. Ah, well, it was too much too hope, I supposed, that Magistre Ulton would be careless in his choice of followers.

Magistre Hulthon caught sight of Hal's hand clasping mine. His eyes narrowed. "That's how it is? I understand now."

"I doubt it," Hal said.

Magistre Hulthon snorted, but Magistre Rouk looked

between us, frowning thoughtfully. *Let them think what they want.* I squeezed Hal's hand back in sheer perversity. *Once I leave, I'm never coming back here again.*

Of course, that was what I had thought about Reud. But there I must go, and soon.

Chapter VIII

Two days passed in the same way: Hal with the Pedagno and Magistre Ulton, surreptitiously teaching the Pedagno Old Valenian and searching the secret books. I in Vere's library, purportedly deciding which books to borrow but really trying to think of some way to thwart Magistre Ulton.

Meal times brought more stares and whispers, but not another confrontation. Perhaps Magistre Ulton had ordered his followers to be less overtly hostile. Perhaps the scholars were biding their time. But their silence translated to greater scrutiny, making it impossible to talk to Hal about either his progress or mine. Or, in my case, lack thereof.

By the end of the second day, I was frantic to hear how he was getting along.

"After three days in the library, I could stand to stretch my legs," I said to Hal. I had finished supper. He was sipping the last of his wine. "Would you care to walk in the cloister garden?"

"Certainly." A smile crinkled the corners of his eyes. He understood perfectly well what I was up to. He emptied his cup.

***

We had hardly set foot in the cloister garden before Doctore Orsenius appeared as if sprung from the stones. "Is there anything I can help with, Doctora?"

I smiled over the Brusterian words I was thinking. "Not at all, thank you. I need a bit of air after being in the library all day and Hal agreed to accompany me."

"Excellent idea! I'll join you."

There was nothing to do but begin walking again. Doctore Orsenius fell into step with us. So our nowhere-unaccompanied status reached to the cloister garden? Interesting. Not only did they want to make sure we went to no part of Vere unescorted, but also that we could not talk together unheard.

"Does Vere expect a good harvest?" Hal asked, showing his diplomatic skills.

"It's early yet," Doctore Orsenius said, "but yes. The wheat alone...." He launched into a description of Vere's wheat crop.

I had to speak to Hal...*how?* It was a measure of my desperation I considered sneaking into his room. Which would be truly foolhardy. Watched as we were, such a move would surely be noticed. It was not difficult to imagine the result. Well-stoked outrage followed by demands we leave. Which left me with my problem. How to speak to Hal without being overheard?

Doctore Orsenius was still describing the state of Vere's crops and expectations for the harvest. "—not just the steward's job, of course," he was saying. "All the scholars are encouraged to look over the tenant farms when they ride."

Of course.

"Is Starn still here?" I said.

"Who?" Doctore Orsenius frowned, halting.

"The horse I usually rode. I would like to go out tomorrow afternoon. That *is* still the custom, isn't it?"

He hesitated, as if wanting to deny the request but unable to think of a plausible reason. "Few scholars ride out these days," he said finally, "but some do." He waited, seemingly for the disapproval in his tone to make me change my mind.

"Could you have her brought tomorrow? And another, if you would," I said. "I am sure my traveling companion would like to join me."

"I would welcome the chance to see more of Vere's holdings," Hal said. "I am seldom away from Ragonne."

"If you wish," Doctore Orsenius said with obvious reluctance.

Behold the power of tradition. According to custom, scholars and guests were allowed to ride out for afternoon exercise. Doctore Orsenius' orders from his true master to not allow us a moment alone had come into conflict with Vere's ways. Without having been given a reason to subvert custom, Doctore Orsenius could not bring himself to do so. That told me something about both of them. Doctore Orsenius was cautious but not clever. Magistre Ulton was clever, but perhaps not as clever as he thought. He had not anticipated a request to ride out, as he clearly had that we might try to talk in a quiet corner in the cloister garden.

We began to walk again, Hal continuing his dexterous small

talk. As we rounded the corner and Doctore Orsenius' face turned away from him, Hal quirked one eyebrow up, which I needed no words to understand.

***

I did not breathe easily the following afternoon until we were away. It would have been a grave breech of custom for Doctore Orsenius to invite himself to come along but it was possible he had been instructed to since yesterday. Did it worry me more or less that he handed over the reins unhappily but let us go?

I was delighted that the horse brought for me was indeed the sturdy red-brown mare Starn, and more so when she nickered a friendly greeting. Hal's roan gelding was not a stranger either; I had often ridden him during Starn's foaling times.

We turned the horses to the river road, heading inland. I breathed deep, letting the warm scents of forest and field calm nerves tightened by surveillance. "How is the Pedagno?"

"No worse," Hal said. "Perhaps a bit better. We put the food brought for him down the jakes and he shares mine."

"That's good," I said. "Thank you."

"The implications are less pleasant," he said. "It proves someone is tampering with his food."

"The Pedagno suspects Magistre Ulton," I said.

"Suspicion is not enough," he said. "Would the High King act on suspicion alone?"

I scowled but he was right. My father would not intervene in Vere's doings without incontrovertible proof. Perhaps not even then, if it were not clear how the High King's power was imperiled by Vere's internal strife.

"If Magistre Ulton is to blame," he said, catching the grasping fingers of a branch before it could scratch his face, "proving it will be difficult."

Ah, well, it would have been too much to hope for. "What have you seen?"

"Magistre Ulton has been present most, but not all, of the time I have been there," Hal said. "I have watched him. As, I am sure, he has watched me. I'm willing to wager that even in his boldest plotting he ensures that if anyone is found guilty, it will not be him. He gives commands. Other hands dirty themselves with the deeds." He looked at me. "Does that fit what you know of him?"

I shook my head slowly. "I'm not sure. I knew *of* him. I inter-acted with him very little. It would not surprise me, given his family. But I can't say he was so." I shrugged. "Perhaps he wasn't. People, like circumstances, alter."

"I doubt it." His voice was uncharacteristically harsh. "These traits seem dyed in the wool in him." He shivered slightly despite the comfortable warmth of the afternoon. "He puts me in mind of a vulture, patiently circling, knowing eventually he will get what he wants."

His description made my own skin shiver. Worse, Magistre Ulton's patience *would* most likely be rewarded.

"The Clerk might meet with an…accident," Hal mused.

I fingered the hilt of my belt knife, considering our odds of success. "I doubt it," I said at last. "Men in the midst of a coup do not grow careless about whom they let in arm's reach."

"Surely there are scholars that remain loyal to the Pedagno," he said. "We could rally them. Lead them against Magistre Ulton and his followers."

It was a tempting thought. Too tempting, perhaps. My head filled at once with images: Myself persuading, demanding, inspiring the reluctant, timid scholars. Taking Magistre Ulton by surprise. Binding his hands personally. Taking him in chains to Reud. Redeemed in one bold move in the eyes of the scholars *and* my father.

Definitely too tempting. What I wanted to do, certainly, but just as certainly, for entirely the wrong reason. It would indulge every rough desire of my blazing anger. I'd promised myself in Ragonne to learn better. I shook my head. "Such a stroke might be a good idea. But only if we knew we would win. A disaster, otherwise. And the Pedagno's immediate death warrant. I don't know that there are enough scholars that are still firmly the Pedagno's men. And I doubt how many of the others that are remember enough fighting to be useful. It is too big a risk to take with another's life as the price of failure."

"Very well." His voice was frustrated but he patted the geld-ing's neck gently. "What of stealth? Can we steal away with the Pedagno to Reud? Perhaps the High King will be more likely to act if the Pedagno pleads his case himself."

Even more tempting. Because it was possible. Evade or tie up whoever watched the Pedagno while he slept and slip away in the middle of the night. The porter would let us out…the portman would certainly help us with a ship…

There was just one problem. "He will not go," I said.

"What?" Hal sounded incredulous. "Why?"

"I've known men like him all my life. This is his duty. He will not leave it."

"Even to do his duty better by regaining control of his charge?"

"I think," I said slowly, putting an understanding into words that was so deeply carven on my soul I had never had to look closely at it before, "that the Pedagno believes that if he needs help to keep control of Vere, he does not deserve to *have* that position of authority. My father believes the same. He would rather die fighting a rebellion on his own than accept the Roth's aid and win."

Hal frowned, unconvinced, but made no further suggestions.

"If we're to help, it has to be now. Before we leave." And we couldn't stay in Vere much longer. I left that unspoken. We both knew it already.

In my inattention Starn had slowed. Tugging at the reins, she dropped her nose into a clump of tender new grass by the road-side. I let her stay. The gelding followed her lead.

"What about the Old Valenian?" I said. "The secret books?"

"He's learning quickly," he said.

"With Magistre Ulton there…how?" I adjusted my seat as Starn suddenly lurched forward to another, apparently tastier, grass patch.

"With the best sort of lie. One very close to the truth. I told the Pedagno, in Magistre Ulton's hearing, that Domon had discovered books in a local dialect of Valenian and offered to teach it to him."

"Very nice," I said with unfeigned admiration. Of course, I lied badly, so people who lied well impressed me. "But doesn't Magistre Ulton want to learn also?"

"He's a busy man, Magistre Ulton. When he's there, he's not watching us closely. He's thinking, making notations on a wax tablet, consulting with other scholars from time to time."

"Acting as Pedagno," I said.

"In all but name, yes." He flipped the ends of his reins idly against his leg. "He's there, I think, to make sure we do not have unmediated access to the Pedagno again. We caught him off guard that first night. Though his man was listening, he's suspicious. Poring over old books? He's not concerned about that."

Despite everything, Magistre Ulton's scholarly heresy—his disbelief that what might be learned in old books could be important—shocked me. He did not want control of Vere because it was Vere, the city of scholars, preserver of knowledge. He wanted control to have control, the same cause for which under--kings gambled life and heirs to seize the High Kingship.

"Do you know what happens if a Pedagno dies without a named successor?" he asked.

"Something bad, I expect. Someone seizes power."

"No," he said. "Or, not so openly. The scholars choose the new Pedagno. So when Magistre Ulton tires of trying to persuade the Pedagno to name him his heir..."

"Or he has enough supporters to know he will be chosen..." I brushed away a fly that had become too interested in my ear.

"He will wait until we leave," he said, earning a savage glance from me. But it was true. Magistre Ulton would not take such action with outsiders present, no matter how unimpeachably 'natural' the mode of death he chose to employ.

The gelding tried to thrust his nose into Starn's bunch of grass. She pushed him away with her muzzle.

"I may have an idea," Hal said. "It's not much. But it may be worth a look."

"Tell me," I said.

CHAPTER IX

We requested and were granted an interview with the Pedagno after we returned. I knew from the crackle of the air when the steward opened the door that Magistre Ulton was with him. *Good.*

The Pedagno sat in his chair beside the hearth. Magistre Ulton was in the second, where I'd sat, where my father had. He turned as we approached. I froze, staring.

He looked more like my brother Utor than any of our blood brothers did. How had I lived in Vere so long and not seen it? But I'd spent little time in his company. He had never been assigned to instruct me, and I could recall passing him in the *comedor* or the corridors only a handful of times.

Then his face shifted. The resemblance fled. The affinity was surface and form. What lay within, and gave life and light to those features, was altogether different. Pride and contempt etched his face. Unconcealed because he lacked skill in dissembling, as I did, or because he was too arrogant to bother?

I blinked, suddenly realizing Utor had never turned such a look upon me. Not in the worst days after my return from Ferrant, nor in the dreadful weeks that followed, as they pondered what to do with their discarded princess. The knowledge that had crept towards me in Ragonne arrived in a tidal wash. I had believed I'd seen disdain and loathing in my father, revulsion and hatred in my brothers, but it had been my hurt that put it there. I should have known better. I had seen real contempt in Francis's eyes. I had been too marred to see rightly, and I had fled.

Now I had to return. Thanks be no one had died before I could come home and make peace. If they would have me. They had to, at least long enough to hear the news I brought. Nothing of peace there. Again I would return unlooked for, and bring trouble.

"Doctora Bann?" The Pedagno said in a tone of gentle but

genuine puzzlement. "You wished to see me?"

"Yes, Pedagno." I bowed, Hal following suit, his deeper than mine as was proper. "Pardon me. I'd not recalled that Magistre Ulton resembled Utor so strongly. It surprised me."

Magistre Ulton's nose rose at the perceived compliment. "It could be argued the blood of kings flows more purely in Verun than anywhere else in Bruster."

I let that insult go. "Thank you, Pedagno, for seeing us so promptly."

"We receive few guests but Vere prides itself on being hospitable to them," the Pedagno said.

A sly smile touched Magistre Ulton's lips, quickly smoothed away. At the reminder, I guessed, that I was a mere guest in Vere, never to be a scholar in residence.

"I wish to thank the Pedagno and Vere for agreeing to lend books to be copied for the Roth's library. My lord will not forget your generosity," I said. "I have selected the ones I would like to borrow."

"Pedagno?" Magistre Ulton said. "Surely you want to see and approve the volumes. There are books that must not leave Vere, even for so noble a purpose as starting a library." His tone belied his words. He clearly believed, like most of the scholars, that the Roth had no business making books.

"A reasonable suggestion," the Pedagno allowed. "One we can dispatch quickly enough." He began to lever himself to his feet.

"Wait, Pedagno," I said. Hal had said he seemed stronger, but that was before. Now his face was gray, lined with exhaustion. Making his way up the steps to the library...I shuddered at the thought of the strain on him. *Too late. The* luton *sickness was too far gone before we got here.* Untainted food was keeping him from getting worse, but not helping him get better.

"Doctora Bann—" Magistre Ulton said coldly. The Pedagno allowed himself to sink back into his seat while he waited for me to continue.

"Surely the Pedagno needn't come to the library himself," I said. "I can tell him the books I've chosen. He can approve or disallow as he deems fit. Someone else—yourself, or perhaps Doctore Orsenius—can return to the library with me to ensure I pack only those volumes the Pedagno agreed to lend."

My heart wrung at the relief on the Pedagno's face. "That will do," he said. Magistre Ulton scowled but said nothing. The Pedagno scrolled a hand weakly. "Which books have you selected?"

"Magistre Bulton's *vita* of Otto..." I listed the books I'd chosen. I had suspected Magistre Ulton would want to know which volumes I meant to borrow, to raise concerns if he could. But he was forced to nod agreement after each; all were books useful to seed Elbany's library, and existed in more than one copy in Vere. At the worst, from Magistre Ulton's point of view, if I refused to return them after he seized control of Vere, nothing was lost. His face told me the calculation had indeed gone through his mind, and I wondered once more whether he lacked the noble's skill of dissembling or was simply not bothering to use it, supposing Hal and I so powerless that concealing his intents was not worth the effort. *Not necessarily an incorrect conclusion*, I had to admit.

"Very well," the Pedagno said. "Magistre Ulton, check the volumes yourself before our guest packs them."

"I'll have Doctore Orsenius see to it," he said.

I was irked at his blatant refusal to do as his lord commanded, but clamped it down. There was nothing I could do. Or nothing more than what we were about to try.

Magistre Ulton looked at me smugly. Most likely my anger was as clear on my face as the insolence was on his. He decided to take it further. "If that is all, Doctora Bann...?" His gaze flicked towards the door.

He was trying to seize the Pedagno's prerogative and dismiss me. I looked pointedly at the Pedagno. "If we could beg the Pedagno's hearing for one moment more." I gestured to Hal.

He stepped forward. "Pedagno, you've already been so generous towards the Roth. Might I beg a favor for my lord as well?"

Genuine surprise crossed the Pedagno's face for a half-breath. "Philip of Ragonne desires a favor? Beyond a new clerk? I did not forget that request." One hand fluttered from the arm of his chair towards Magistre Ulton. "My Clerk has been compiling a list of prospects. We will send Philip his new clerk within the month."

But, I thought unwillingly, *it might not be your hand that signs the letter introducing him.*

"Thank you, Pedagno. Let me convey my lord's thanks as well for your prompt attention to his request." Hal paused. "If I may, I have another to put before you."

"Pedagno—" Magistre Ulton said impatiently. "You have shown these guests the depth of Vere's generosity already."

"Peace," the Pedagno said, his voice low and windy. "There's no harm in hearing what is asked."

"I'm afraid it will seem a trifle, after such discussion." Hal bowed his head. "King Philip has created a library, like Elbany. Given his newfound interest in books, he might in time become willing to sponsor a scholar at Vere." He looked at Magistre Ulton in surprise, as if a thought had just occurred to him. "Something like Verun's endowment of the Pedagno's own clerk. If I could bring back a copy of the charter that founded that position, the example of how such an agreement should be handled would be instructive if King Philip set his mind to do so."

"Pedagno!" Magistre Ulton exploded. "Philip of Ragonne? Sponsor a scholar?" Words failed him. He made a noise of disgust and disbelief, followed by a narrow-eyed examination of Hal. Hal blinked blandly, the picture of an earnest servant.

The Pedagno coughed into a handkerchief. "You are to be commended for your diligence," he said when he recovered himself. "I admit I concur with Magistre Ulton. From what I know of the king of Ragonne, it seems unlikely he would endow a scholar. But," he said, and lifted one shaking hand, "people, even kings, may change. Perhaps you are right. Whatever led him to create a library may in time lead to more."

Magistre Ulton snapped a furious glare at the Pedagno, who gave it no notice.

"Regardless of the depth of Philip of Ragonne's interest in books," the Pedagno continued, "he may find he has other reasons to seek the favor of Vere." The Pedagno steepled his fingers, pressing the tips together as if to still them. "I wonder how much like his father he will prove. Vere will not accept another like Domon without a demonstration of Ragonne's gratitude."

My admiration soared. Weak and ill, he made a better case for the plan we laid before him than we had, and on the instant. Insinuating that Philip might have bastards of his own to place, and be looking to garner Vere's good wishes, was a more credible stance than Philip becoming interested in books. One Hal and I should have come up with on our own.

"You may see the Verun charter," the Pedagno said. "There are others that would be useful examples as well. The charter in which the High King sponsored the renovation of our port house, for instance, or the King of Eban's provision of new tapestries for the *scriptorium*..." His eyes hazed as he listed charters, so earnestly I wondered if in his scholarly engagement of the question, he had forgotten the request was a ruse.

"Is it advisable," Magistre Ulton's voice frayed with irritation, "to allow this..." his disdainful gaze raked Hal, "person to examine Vere's private, legal documents?"

The Pedagno's eyebrows rose. "These charters are not sensitive or secret, or especially old. Vere's inner workings are our own, but these documents do not touch upon such matters."

Magistre Ulton's eyes flared. "Shall I accompany our guest to the library to...assist him?" By which he surely meant ensure Hal did not steal any of the charters, which, as his haughty glance conveyed, he believed him likely to try.

"A generous offer." The Pedagno inclined his head. "Since Doctora Bann has completed her task—"

If only, I thought.

"—she can undertake the more tedious demands of a good guest," he smiled, real affection and amusement shining through his weariness, "and keep her host company while you do so. As her companion has been so good to do while she selected her books."

Magistre Ulton's head swiveled so quickly my neck hurt. "But..." Looking like a bee-stung bull, he swallowed the rest of his words.

This, too, was as Hal had intended. Or part of it. 'I do not think the Pedagno believes it is possible to regain his authority,' he had said as we rode. 'He sees his death coming down a straight path.' He had waited while I blinked away wetness. 'So he craves what he believes *is* possible: a few hours in friendly company.' Maneuvering Magistre Ulton into watching Hal read and copy charters, leaving the Pedagno and me alone, was an unlooked-for blessing. At least by us. The Pedagno had seized the opportunity with both hands. And had suggested the other charters, to give us more time. *Oh, my* maestro.

"We can provide you ink and parchment but you will have to make the copies yourself. Unless Magistre Ulton means to help you."

The Clerk's nostrils flared.

"No?" The Pedagno lifted one shoulder. "How long will it take, then?"

"Unless they are unusually long charters," Hal said, "a few days. Four at most."

"It is late to begin such work today," the Pedagno said. "Is tomorrow acceptable?"

"I could ask no better," Hal said, truthfully enough. The Pedagno's quick thinking meant his plan was progressing better than we had hoped. The charter would list the formal require-ments of the arrangement, what would be expected of the Clerk, what Vere would receive in return. If we were lucky, it would list how the contract could be invalidated. I did not feel especially blessed by fortune at that moment, but nothing was lost by looking. We might yet find a way to help the Pedagno. If not...a few hours in friendly company was more than many men had as death approached.

"Thank you. I have been honored to meet you, Pedagno." Hal went on, spinning more complimentary phrases, all the more skillful for sounding sincere. Some were directed towards Magistre Ulton as well. His depth of tact was far beyond mine.

I slanted a look at him, pleased to have a moment to study him unremarked. How had he known the way a new Pedagno was chosen in the absence of a designated heir? The Pedagno would not have told him. Had Cynan Maccus' illicit family been privy to the secrets of Vere, and passed the knowledge down? He had seemed young when I met him, but he had to be older than he looked. He rode as well as any nobleman but was not thick muscled like a warrior. He was scarred like one, though. Not just his arms. As we rode back to Vere, he had tipped his head to watch a bird's flight. A faded line of silver had come into view, where a man would cut another man's throat. The blow must not have been deep or he would not have lived. But it had been enough to leave that mark.

Whatever he had been before, minding Domon had been an improvement, despite its dangers.

I wondered suddenly what he thought of being dragged away

from Ragonne, and the concomitant troubles gathering like flies at the jakes. I had been sent by my lord to search for information to help Elbany, and had come to Vere under that same aegis, as well as a desire to aid the Pedagno if I could. Hal was here because Mistress Baynor and I had decided his hands were competent and appropriated them. I had no idea whether leaving Ragonne had been a hardship for him, whether he had family or friends who would mourn his absence.

I shrugged down a creeping feeling of guilt. Our situations were, perhaps, not so different. The Roth had commanded me and I had gone. Hal's king had sent him, and he had gone. What either of us might have chosen did not matter.

That was not fully true. If the Roth had requested rather than directed, I would have gone. I didn't know whether Hal would say the same. Perhaps it still did not matter. It might have been civil to request his company. But if he had refused, would either Mistress Baynor or I have let him be? He and I were the only ones who could read Old Valenian. At least he did not have the aggravation of having had his view asked and then ignored.

But the reproachful itch between my shoulder blades did not go away.

CHAPTER X

I pushed my spoon around the bowl, heedlessly mangling the few remaining blackberries. Not that I hadn't enjoyed the berries; I had, very much. In Ragonne, berry season had passed but in cooler Vere, as well as Elbany and Bruster proper, their ripening came later. My thoughts had turned to the work of the morning, and I'd begun—or, more accurately, resumed—fretting about what Hal and I would encounter when we put our hands to our tasks. It had been gratifying to see Magistre Ulton startled and enraged, but it was rarely wise to tweak, let alone thwart, bad-tempered and powerful men. I had little doubt that Magistre Ulton, despite his outward acquiescence to the Pedagno's commands, could have devised a plan by this morning to keep the Pedagno observed and the charters unexamined if he decided both were crucial to his aims.

So when Doctore Orsenius left me at the Pedagno's door to escort Hal to the library, I was not surprised it was Magistre Ulton who answered my knock.

"The Doctora has returned." He opened the door but did not move. His tone was patronizing, as one would speak to a child or a pet, and he said 'doctora' with a slight emphasis, as if to imply he thought the title unmerited.

His gaze caught mine, fiercely predatory, and I fought to hold his eyes without flaring into anger. His verbal arrows were too subtle to allow open protest. He could easily deny any offense had been meant. But it had. His hard gaze and aggressive stance underscored his message. *Do not oppose me.* I let my eyes drop, thinking it best to allow him to believe he had cowed me.

A thin smile creased his face. He stepped back. I walked towards the hearth but the Pedagno was not in his chair.

"The Pedagno is finishing his breakfast," Magistre Ulton said. "Do sit down while we wait for him." He seated himself in the Pedagno's chair.

I understood the purpose of his brash action, but nonetheless

I stood in shocked silence for a moment. *He dared...* I took the chair from near the harp, the one Hal had used our first night in Vere, and joined him beside the hearth, leaving the second chair free. The one he *should* have occupied. I knew my posture was stiff, betraying my discomfiture.

"He hardly eats these days," he said somewhat later, as if he had savored his small victory long enough. "You were his... student." The implication I was more was clear. But that tired accusation did not stoke my indignation, and he moved on. His face went clear of all but solicitude. "Perhaps you could persuade him to eat more. He needs to build up his strength."

"The Pedagno is not a child, to be chided with his vegetables," I said.

He clicked his tongue, sounding like nothing so much as someone's anxious grandmother. *One who poisons the gingerbread,* I thought, even as I acknowledged the man's skills. He had clearly been surprised the evening before and had shown more than he would have liked. This morning he was prepared. His demeanor betrayed nothing but helpful worry. "I am concerned for him," he said primly.

"Why?" Even Reynard the fox, who would not break cover for a hunter subtly tracking his path could sometimes be started by a headlong rush. Magistre Ulton had likewise shown himself susceptible to surprise.

He blinked but recovered in a heartbeat, unctuous apprehension filling his face like molten wax poured into a wooden tablet frame. "You may not have noticed, being so recently arrived, but the Pedagno is not well." His tone implied if I had not noticed I was either a dolt or uncaring. "I hope his health is not failing."

"The Pedagno does seem more fragile than when I knew him as *novicia*," I allowed. "But his health may improve."

"We were untimely robbed of our last Pedagno." He lowered his voice. "We can only hope circumstances will allow our new Pedagno to prosper." His tone roughened. The threat was not as submerged as he probably meant it to be.

"Hal spent the last two days with him," I said. "He thought the Pedagno was getting no worse."

"Ah. Yes." His eyes flashed, looking as I imagined a *leoyong* would just before it pounced. "Hal. Do tell me about him."

This was treacherous terrain. I didn't want to admit how little

I knew about Hal. Neither did I care to tell him what I did know. "He is a servant of the king of Ragonne," I said, telling him only what he already knew.

He was undeterred. "Have you...known...him long?"

The insinuation was obvious. I was surprised he would try that gambit again, having found no success with it only moments before.

"Hal was sent to Vere to deliver a gift, as well as to convey Philip's formal request for a new clerk." I again told him no more than what he already knew.

"But surely you—" Impatience crept into his voice.

The door to the inner room opened. The Pedagno entered, unsteadily balancing a tray. I leaped up to take it from him. Turning back, I saw Magistre Ulton now occupied the other chair. Clearly the moment the door opened he had slid from the Pedagno's seat to the second, quiet as a water snake.

"Good morning, *alumna,*" the Pedagno said. "Magistre Ulton."

I placed the tray on the small table between the chairs.

"Pedagno," Magistre Ulton said, all unctuous concern once more, "you've scarcely eaten."

The Pedagno shook his head. "I'm not hungry. Perhaps when the harvest comes in. New apples..." his voice trailed off. "Fresh fruits and vegetables."

Magistre Ulton scowled, thinking, I felt certain, how much more difficult it would be to taint newly-picked food. "Of course, Pedagno. It may indeed."

The Pedagno looked expectantly at Magistre Ulton, who gazed back, his face bland and brazen at the same time. After a moment his eyes flicked to me. "Master Carlson has gone to the library?"

"Magistre Orsenius left with him after he escorted me here."

He nodded, his attention returning to Magistre Ulton. "You offered to help him locate the charters."

"Of course," Magistre Ulton said again, both hands slapping down onto his knees, too heartily. He stood. "I do hope we will be able to provide him the assistance you have promised." He turned, his hand on the door latch. "We have so many books in our collection. It can be difficult to find a particular manuscript. Small items, like charters, are especially easy to misplace."

I waited until the sounds of his footsteps, muffled by the heavy door, died away. "That sounded…"

"I know." The Pedagno leaned his head back against his chair. When he spoke again, his voice was strained but the gaze that met mine was glowing with satisfaction. "Good."

I made a puzzled sound, gesturing to the fireplace.

"No one's there," he said. "Now that I know to, I listen. It's difficult to sit perfectly still. The chair creaks. The robe shifts. I can hear when someone is above."

"Ah."

"I expected he would do this." His eyes closed. "He doesn't know why Hal, and therefore you, want to search that charter, but just in case, he wants to examine it closely himself first. So the charter will be 'lost' for a bit." His eyes opened a crack. "The longer he delays producing the charter, the longer you and Hal remain in Vere."

"What if he never 'finds' it?"

He shook his head, his eyes remaining shuttered. "If ours were lost, the current beneficiary of the charter would be sent to Verun to copy theirs. Him. And the last thing Magistre Ulton wants at present is to be away from Vere."

I gasped. "Why have you not burnt the charter already? In his absence you might be able to regain control."

His eyes opened, sadness and fatigue sea deep within them. "Would it were so easy to be rid of him. How would I get the charter to burn it? Magistre Ulton is with me nearly all the time. The head librarian, Magistre Borland, is one of his adherents." The fingers of one hand twitched, as if he had meant to drum them on his chair but lacked the energy.

I sighed.

"Even if I managed to destroy the charter, I would have to be certain I could have Vere in hand before Magistre Ulton returned. I am not sure I could do so. Many scholars oppose the changes Honre wanted to make and which I would make, were I able, and they take Magistre Ulton's part."

His head lolled back once more. "Do not be frustrated if I do not seem to fight him as fiercely as you think I should. I have fought. I am tired. And hungry." He laughed bitterly. "I had forgotten how the mind can be driven to wild distraction, unable to concentrate on anything but the roaring of the belly." His eyes went to the tray, and the untouched food. "The *luton*-sickness is worse than the hunger, when I weaken and eat." He sighed. "I...did you think to tuck away any bits from your breakfast?" His words were whisper quiet, but the mortification beneath was loud as summer thunder.

I brought out two boiled eggs, saved from my meal and Hal's. "*Maestro...*" I touched his hand as I gave him them to him, and he cupped mine with shaking fingers for the span of a dozen heartbeats.

He ate one of the eggs, putting the other into his belt pouch. "I expect you are bursting to see my books," he said as soon as his mouth was clear. His voice seemed stronger, but I suspected that was more feigned than real. "I am impatient to let you." He rose and walked back towards the second door, the one that led to his sleeping quarters. "If luck is with us, Magistre Ulton will delay the charter long enough for us to finish searching them for Saradena."

I strained to hear him as he moved away. His words seemed smothered by the thick walls, as if the keep sought to devour him. I went to the door. "May I assist you, Pedagno?"

"Thank you, but no," the muffled reply came back. "No one but the Pedagno is supposed to know where they are kept." I heard a dry chuckle. "A source of much annoyance to Magistre Ulton." His voice dipped into a surprisingly good imitation of Magistre Ulton's. "'Merely a tradition, Pedagno. Surely it should be set aside, in your condition.'"

"So he knows of the books, but not how to get to them," I said.

"He knows about the books, and that they require special training to read," the Pedagno said. "I am not certain how he came to possess this information." I heard footfalls. He must have begun moving back towards the door. "I believe he has searched for, but not yet found, where they are kept."

I stepped aside as he came through the doorway, arms filled. I scooped the pile from him, shaking my head at his protests, carrying the volumes to his worktable.

"If he *has* discovered their hiding place, that's worrisome. I cannot move them elsewhere."

Why? I instantly thought but held my tongue. I doubted he would answer.

He clicked his tongue in frustration. "It is difficult to know what is really in his mind. When he has time to prepare himself, he lies as easily, if not more so, as he speaks truth."

The last of his words came to me through a fog. I set the books carefully on the table and my attention was drawn inescapably to them. There were eight, so thick I felt certain several, if not all, would prove *compilatios*. "Is this all of them? The ones you and Hal haven't searched?"

He laughed, the first sound of genuine amusement I'd heard from him since my arrival.

"No. There are twenty seven more."

My breathing quickened. *Thirty five.* I wanted to see them, to touch their covers and open their leaves, and choose which seemed most likely to yield information about Saradena.

But the Pedagno's breath was also unnaturally quick, and not from excitement. I could not ask him to bring out the others. There was no reason to suppose picking which books to examine by instinct and impressions would result in a more promising selection than those the Pedagno had already brought. It hadn't in Ragonne. Indeed, the first clue there had come from the least likely source.

I stacked the books into smaller piles along the back of the table, leaving room for us to work. It was an ordinary flat table, not an angled surface for easier writing and reading. Perhaps he had a proper study table in his inner chamber. That seemed likely. He would need to write letters, among other things, most of which were for no eyes but his own.

Waving the Pedagno into the chair that already sat before the table, I brought over the one I'd appropriated earlier from its place beside the harp. "Shall we begin?"

He took the uppermost book from the pile before him. His eyes were shining with the scholar's fervor of seeking and learning. For the first time since my return, he looked like the *maestro* I remembered, the man who had left Rothbury only a few months before. I picked up a book and dove in.

CHAPTER XI

It could have been minutes or hours before a knock sounded on the outer door. Either way it was too soon.

The door opened without the Pedagno's giving permission. Another slight on his authority. Doctore Orsenius entered, carrying a noon meal upon a tray. The Pedagno's face settled back into gray lines of strain and dread.

"Oh," Doctore Orsenius said, setting the tray down and taking up the old one. "I did not realize Doctora Bann would be here so long. I'm afraid I brought only the Pedagno's mid-day meal."

The Pedagno looked as though he were wondering whether he could muster the strength to be angry. I understood. It was disingenuous for Doctore Orsenius to pretend he did not know I was to spend my days with the Pedagno until Hal completed his business with the charters. Indeed, it was his duty as steward to know such things. Moreover, Doctore Orsenius did not have Magistre Ulton's skill in subterfuge. His words claimed regret but his tone reveled in the slight.

I saw an opportunity. "Think nothing of it," I said. "I don't expect you to wait upon me with your many responsibilities. I'm happy to fetch my own dinner from the *comedor*. In fact," I resisted the urge to shoot the Pedagno a triumphant glance, "tomorrow, and however long I remain in Vere, I'm willing to spare you the trouble of bringing the Pedagno's meal. It would be no bother to collect his noon-tide while getting mine."

Doctore Orsenius' eyebrows rose. "That's...a generous offer..." His eyes darted as he sought a way to refuse. Magistre Ulton would be annoyed. The arrangement would make it that much more difficult to taint the Pedagno's food, at least the noon meal.

"You are a kind guest," the Pedagno said, "to provide a service rather than receive one. Doctore Orsenius certainly has other duties to attend to."

Doctore Orsenius scowled, surely realizing there was no

reasonable way for him to reject the offer. "Very well. But you will need to go to the kitchen. There are no trays in the *comedor.*"

"I will," I said. "Thank you." He was flustered, and I was glad of it. If he'd been thinking clearly, he could have insisted I collect a meal already prepared—that is, corrupted—for the Pedagno. Or I be accompanied by a *novicio* or servant. Or a *novicio* or servant would be delighted to bring a meal for both of us. He would realize soon enough he had agreed not only to allow me to fetch the Pedagno's dinner from the general meal but to walk alone to do so.

"Thank you," Doctore Orsenius said unconvincingly. "By your leave, Pedagno?" He glanced toward the door, and the Pedagno waved him out.

"He did not wait for my leave to *enter,*" the Pedagno said once the door had closed.

"That seems to happen regularly," I said. "Flouting your authority."

"Yes," he eyed the tray with mingled hunger and distrust. "They show their contempt through their actions. I think they also hope to catch me off guard, and glean what they can from observing me before I expect to be seen. Such as where the books are stored." His gaze returned to me. "Dinner from the general stock? A guest alone in the keep? Magistre Ulton will not be pleased."

He looked as if he would say more, then merely nodded. His gaze went back to the tray. "As always. Pottage. Applesauce." He blew out his breath. "They claim to be thinking of my health. I am ill, I need soft, easily eaten meals. Such food is also easy to add *luton* to." He grimaced. "I will maul it, to make it look as if I've eaten some. But you're going now to get other provisions...?"

I stood. "I'm feeling *very* hungry."

"Do not bring too much," he said. "They will suspect, of course, you will share with me. Let's not be blatant about it."

★★★

When I returned, the Pedagno was at the table, bent over his book, mouthing words as he worked through the Old Valenian. He walked slowly across the room to join me before the hearth. The tray Doctore Orsenius had brought was pushed to the side, the food upon it not only mangled but mostly gone. I looked the question at him.

"I put it down the jakes." His gaze flicked towards the second room.

"Ah. Hal mentioned that tactic."

"I doubt they'll be fooled but..." His eyes went meaningfully to the tray, and we did not speak again until after we'd eaten. I insisted he take most of it. His protests were perfunctory, their vigor sapped by need. He ate the stew and tucked the bread away for later, as he had the second boiled egg at breakfast. Enough for a meager supper tonight.

"Hal is a good teacher," the Pedagno said, later. "But I struggle with the language. It is more difficult to sort the words into meaning than I would have supposed." He turned a last piece of cheese in his fingers, as if now his thoughts craved the nourishment of activity, however small, more than his body needed food. I smiled to see his hunger slaked so far.

"I understand that the words build meaning independent of the order in which they come. But it is challenging to apply that knowledge to actual reading."

I nodded, remembering my first sluggish efforts to strain sense from the ancient language.

"I suppose," he said, breaking off a corner of the cheese, "that should not be surprising. We are taught from the first that order determines how words are understood. The letters of a word must be read as they are written, the words of a sentence must likewise be understood in sequence. Each leaf in a codex unwinds in their order like thread from a spool." He glanced across the room with heat and amusement at the book he had been studying. "Meaning marches in a set pattern. It does not flit about like a bee in clover."

"Meaning through sequence holds for Old Valenian, mostly. Letters in words. Sentences on the page. Leaves in the book. Just not *within* each sentence."

"Yes." He chewed the bit of cheese. "But when I read it, I cannot do as the book's writer and original audience must have, understanding as I go. I have to parse the words' relationships to one another, then in my mind put them into the order in which they would appear in modern Valenian."

"But you *can* read it," I said. "Two weeks ago, you could not."

"Yes," he said again, more cheerfully, and stood. "That opens most of the secret books to me. And we will find Saradena among them."

"*Maestro...*" I knew that conviction. It was the faith of Vere. Anything you needed to know could be found in a book, if you had enough of them. And if they were old enough. "I want that to be true. But wanting will not make it so."

"My death is coming. No," he held up a hand. "Do not protest and do not look away from it."

"Hal—the charter—the food—"

"I feel it," he said. "The world is thinning to me, like fog as the morning warms. And I can see...more." He met my eyes. "It's here. We'll find it."

"Very well," I managed.

"Maudlin," he said firmly. "Do not think about me. Think about your task. Bruster needs you. Elbany needs you. Not to mention Logan and Ragonne." He went to the worktable. "*This* is where your mind must be."

***

I finished the first book and set it aside. Beside me, the Pedagno glanced up. I shook my head, and he went back to his book. I turned my gaze to the remaining manuscripts. Except for the golden book Hal had brought back from Verdun, these were the oldest books I'd ever held, and I'd had no time yet to simply savor them.

There was no way to guess from their appearance which might be most likely to contain information about Saradena. Nonetheless I studied the manuscripts as if searching for such a sign. Two had bindings embossed with Elbish interlacing, their strands wider than in Brusterian designs. One had a clasp holding its bulging pages shut. Two had covers once inlayed with precious metal, but it was gone, the leather so damaged it was torn away in parts. One was no longer in its original binding. Its current cover looked to be a hasty work, overlapping the leaves by two fingers' width on all sides, the unsupported edges sagging. The last was plainly but carefully bound in leather dyed a deep walnut, adorned with a device I did not recognize.

The walnut-dyed book was on top of the pile closest to me, so at last I gave a half-shrug and lifted it.

***

Awareness returned slowly, and guiltily. I'd forgotten what I was supposed to be searching for. I'd forgotten the Pedagno. I'd forgotten where I was. I traced the device etched in the leather binding, my fingertips skimming the leather's surface. *This book...*

"Pedagno." My voice seemed strange in my ears, as if I'd not spoken for days, but I knew it was the lure of the book.

The Pedagno sat bowed over his reading, his concentration written in fissures on his forehead. He hadn't heard me.

I touched his arm. His head rose, and turned, his face coming into view slowly, as if reluctant to move away from the page. I waited while his eyes regained focus and found me, puzzled at first by my presence. Then comprehension returned to them.

"Maudlin?" His gaze darted downward towards the book before him.

Understanding lifted the corners of my mouth. "Your reading is progressing well?"

"Haltingly," he said. "But yes." His eyes flicked to the manuscript. But his attention was shifting to me, and his gaze moved up. "I *can* read it. I *am* reading it. You have given me this. Thank you."

"No." I shook my head. "Your own has returned to you." Now it was my eyes that flashed downward, towards the book that had held me captive. "But if requital were warranted, this would be guerdon more than generous."

"Is it...Saradena?" His voice slipped so low I saw rather than heard his words.

"Saradena?" I had not forgotten, not entirely. I was supposed to be searching for information about that land, but it had not seemed crucial as I'd delved this book. "No."

He looked mildly annoyed. "Then what?"

My fingers splayed on the binding. "If the volumes in the Pedagno's collection are all like this book, they are the greatest treasure in the Three Lands."

His brows rose. Amusement, tinged with curiosity that had been both stoked and stymied, settled over all. "What *is* it, Maudlin?"

"A history of Elbany." I pressed my fingers down, firmly now, on the volume. "Largely how Elbany came to be united, but it refers to earlier events as well. There is vastly more here than what is known in Elbany." My eyes held his. "You said I could choose books to copy for the Roth's library. This book," I gripped it with both hands, "*must* be among them."

"It is one of the secret books." His face pulled taut with distress. "Kept hidden even within Vere. It *cannot* leave."

"The Roth's sword," I went on ruthlessly. "Its forging is described. No one in Elbany remembers it was made from the remnants of an earlier sword, one supposed to have been carried by the greatest Elbish hero who ever lived—"

"Maudlin—"

"And the *shield*. Alfred of Roth had a shield made as well, the device of the newly-united Elbany upon it. The shield is lost and forgotten in Elbany. But not here. You must let me take this book to copy."

"I can't." Anguish steeped his voice, like oatmeal soaked overnight in milk. "They are secret."

"Why?" I leaned towards him, trying to ignore my guilt at the anxiety I was causing him. I needed this book. Elbany needed this book. "Why is it secret? Why should the knowledge in this book be kept from Elbany? This is their past."

He spread his hands. "I do not know why these books are kept hidden. But this one is among them."

"The *collection* is secret," I argued. "Should the knowledge they contain be? For some, perhaps. We haven't read them all. We don't know what they say. Perhaps the group is secret because of the books themselves, not what they contain. Because of their great antiquity. Vere's library is large. Such books could be damaged or lost among the throng. Perhaps they are here to keep them safe, and to do so, kept secret."

He looked doubtful. I remembered what he had written in his letter. *I shiver to think what might be in them, information too secret to translate and copy into new manuscripts, but too vital to lose.* If the ancient books were hidden to keep them physically safe, there were likely copies of them in the library. If, on the other hand, their contents were being concealed, no copies would exist among Vere's books.

At his querying look, I explained my thoughts.

"Perhaps," he said. "But we do not have time to check the library for copies. Reading the books themselves might reveal why the collection was created, and why it has been kept secret.

But I doubt we'll finish that task before you have to leave."

Sensing he had more to say but needed a quiet moment to winnow his thoughts, I kept silent.

At last he spoke again. "I understand your desire to have a copy of this book in the Roth's library. But I fear the Pedagno's collection has been kept concealed on good grounds, reasons I do not know."

"You may be right," I said. "There may be something within them that your predecessors thought too volatile to be known widely." I kept my hands on the book, as if readying to snatch it up. "But *this* book...I have read it. In full. There is nothing dangerous. It is merely the history of Elbany. What right does Vere have to keep it from them?"

Misgiving still suffused his face. But he had come to Elbany. He had seen the Roth's library, met the scribes I was training, heard the Roth's plans. I waited, shame needling me for badgering him in his weakness, but not enough to make me stop. Vere owned the manuscript but the history it told belonged to us.

"Very well," he sighed. "Perhaps it was only ours to safeguard until Elbany was ready to receive the knowledge it bears. Take it. But—" He held up a hand before I could speak. "You must promise to copy the book as it is, in Old Valenian."

"But that will make it inaccessible to my scribes, unless I teach them the older language." I felt my eyes rolling up as I considered *that* daunting prospect.

"That will keep its secret, if there is one."

"But—"

"Enough." His voice had an edge I had seldom heard during my time at Vere but learned to heed.

I bowed my head. "As you command, Pedagno."

He snorted, unfooled by my roiled quiet. But grudging obedience is obedience nonetheless. He touched my hand. "Once it is copied...if you cannot return it to my hands, it might be best not to return it at all."

My throat dried. It was more than I'd asked—and less than I hoped for. I turned my hand palm upward, clutching his. Not letting go, he turned his attention back to his book.

CHAPTER XII

I put the Elbish history into my bag beside the golden book. Since it had come to me, I carried my bag everywhere, with even greater anxiousness for its safety since my inexcusable furystorm and the damage I had done to it. In Vere, and perhaps in Ragonne, my room was undoubtedly searched in my absence. Magistre Ulton would have seized the splendid manuscript as readily as Philip if he learned of it. More. He would believe Vere had been the creator of the manuscript and as such, had claim to it that superseded all others. Indeed, I was not entirely certain that the Pedagno would not believe so, and thus had not shown him the book. I placed the bag back beneath my chair, thinking rather giddily I now had *two* unimaginably precious books in my possession, and resolved to step widely around puddles. And keep clear of hearths. And—

Suppressing a shiver of terror-laced glee, I set the next manuscript on the table before me. It proved tedious, containing nothing relevant to either Saradena or Magistre Ulton. Its chief virtue was being short. The next was interesting, at least in parts, although no more useful for my purposes. It contained a section about the Ottonian war. I slowed to read it, gaping at the description of Otto's open-eyed cruelty in pursuit of his ambition. As a Brusterian, I thought nothing warlike could shock me, but I hadn't known as much as this book did about Otto Tyrannus.

When Doctore Orsenius returned, there were two books left in the pile and I'd read six leaves of the third. As before, he knocked then entered unbidden. "It is time for our evening meal," he said before the door was fully open. "Allow me to escort you to the *comedor*, Doctora Bann. Magistre Ulton will come presently to accompany the Pedagno."

"It *is* late." The Pedagno shared a glance of annoyance with me before rising, but his tone was even. "I had not noticed. I thank you for your engaging company, Doctora Bann." His voice was formal, his words for his steward's benefit. "And for allowing me to lay this question before you." He gestured, encompassing the books. "It is an issue I have mulled for some time. I appreciated the chance to hear your thoughts on the matter."

I knew he was laying a false scent for Magistre Ulton. "It was an honor, Pedagno. But the problem is complex. If my companion has not finished his copying of the charters, perhaps we could continue our conversation tomorrow?"

He looked at Doctore Orsenius. "Has Master Carlson completed his work?"

"He was able to examine several charters, but the Veruni agreement..." He swallowed. "Magistre Borland is looking for it."

"I'm sure he will find it soon," the Pedagno said with apparent disinterest. My estimation of his dissembling skills ticked up a notch further. "Since it seems you must remain in Vere for another day at least, Doctora Bann, I will welcome your company again tomorrow."

"As you say, Pedagno," I said.

"Now," his attention went back to the manuscripts, "I will return these books to their homes."

Doctore Orsenius jumped as if a mouse had nipped his ankle. "Let me help, Pedagno."

I saw the Pedagno restrain a sigh. "Thank you, but you know I may not." He began to stack the books. "Go with Doctore Orsenius to supper, Doctora Bann. I will await your return in the morning."

***

Doctore Orsenius insisted on eating supper and the next morning's breakfast with Hal and me, with the result we had no opportunity for even a whispered conversation. An exchange of terse head shakes sufficed. He hadn't found anything either.

The Pedagno had another set of the secret books out by the time I arrived. His breakfast tray, its contents untouched, sat on the low table near the hearth. He was at the work table, bending over a manuscript.

"No time to waste," he said once the door closed behind Doctore Orsenius. "Magistre Borland will surely 'find' the charter today. Tomorrow at the latest."

"Breakfast first." I took my handkerchief from my belt pouch and handed it to him.

He moved his chair away from the table before opening it.

"Should I worry what you're planning for me? You're clearly fattening me up for something." Finishing, he dusted crumbs from his hands and clothes before moving back. "No Founder's Feast ever tasted so good."

★★★

We had read for only an hour or so before Magistre Orsenius returned.

I saw the Pedagno brace himself as the steward entered. "Has something happened?"

Master Orsenius' gaze, filled with unmasked curiosity, went to me. "The boat from Boltar has come. It brought a letter...for the Doctora."

"Give it to her, then," the Pedagno said implacably. But when he turned his head away, he raised a questioning eyebrow at me.

I took the scroll, not entirely surprised to see the seal of Kolon.

At the Pedagno's gesture, Magistre Orsenius left with badly-concealed disappointment.

I held the letter but made no move to open it. *'Do you not wonder why I wanted to offer for you, and why I renew the offer now?' 'I confess the question has been in my thoughts'.*

"Maudlin?" The Pedagno touched my arm. "Is this likely to be ill news?"

I shook my head.

"Then...?" he went on invitingly. "But do not answer if you don't wish."

"It's...courtship, I suppose." I scowled at his upshot brows. "That surprises you?" Then I sighed. "It should. It surprises me."

He took the letter long enough to see the seal. "Orlo of Kolon. I hear nothing but good of him. Better than of Philip, truth be told."

"That's part of the problem." I turned the letter in my hands. "Philip fears him. Too much, Mistress Baynor thinks."

He nodded. "I know who Mistress Baynor is."

"Then you know her shrewdness."

He wrapped one of my hands in his. His palms were dry, scratchy. An old man's hands. "You fear for him. And fear letting yourself become...attached to him."

"I suppose so." I fingered the seal with my free hand.

"There's more." He squeezed my hand. "Is there not?"

"I—" I could not possibly tell him about life with Francis.

I should have known better, to think I could keep any sort of secret from him. Whatever was on my face told enough.

"Hear me." He shook my hand gently until I met his gaze. "Not all men are Francis of Ferrant."

"I have found many to be so."

"But not all," he said.

"But enough."

He smiled sadly. "I expect that is true." His grip tightened. "But *this* man. What cause for concern has he given?"

"None," I said. "He has been charming. Charming beyond any reasonable expectation. He badgered his clerk to teach him to read and write, that he might woo in letters."

"I knew that already." He glanced at the parchment roll. "That is not Doctore Osgar's script."

"Francis was charming. Before we wed." I'd loved him, loved him after we married, despite all, until the moment he set me aside. Possibly even afterward, sometimes. I had wrapped outrage around the fragments of my shattered soul. Otherwise, it had seemed, the whirl and shock would have scattered them beyond reach. I had hated them all—Francis, my father, my brothers, the scholars of Vere—when, perhaps, only Francis had truly wronged me. As wrath ebbed, I was left with fear, cold and small, echoing in the void.

"Would it be safer to reject his suit or consider it?" he said.

I shuddered. But I understood. I must have already understood. I'd not encouraged Orlo, but neither had I pushed him away.

I put the scroll into my belt pouch. "I'll read it later."

He smiled. "As it should be."

CHAPTER XIII

The morning's reading proceeded in silence disturbed only by the rustle as the Pedagno or I turned a page, the occasional soft murmuring as one of us sorted through a knotted passage of Old Valenian and the low noises of an engaged reader responding to a work. I fetched our noon-meal, which we ate more quickly and with less attention than the stew deserved, and we returned to the books. I noted with one part of my mind that the Pedagno's skills with the older language were rapidly progressing. While it continued to require a great deal of effort for him to understand, the ancient words were nonetheless moving from being a barrier to the manuscript's content to providing a bridge to it.

Not long after, our study was troubled by a hurried knock followed immediately by the door opening.

Doctore Orsenius, I knew before I looked up.

"By your leave, Pedagno," the steward said in a rush. "I have come to offer whatever aid I may in keeping our guest company."

The Pedagno's eyes lifted slowly, conveying without speaking his displeasure at having his reading interrupted. One of Doctore Orsenius' feet tapped nervously. Not turning to me, the Pedagno asked, "Do you find yourself in need of further entertainment, Doctora Bann?"

"'In the company of books, one is never lonely,'" I said.

He smiled. The maxim was one of the first lessons *novicios* were set.

"The presence of the Pedagno is, of course, a privilege for any scholar," I added.

"Of course," he said dryly. "Your offer is gracious, Doctore Orsenius, but unnecessary. Doctora Bann is well occupied with our books and tolerates my presence as required to see them."

"Pedagno," I protested, knowing full well he was teasing me.

"Pedagno," said the steward at the same moment. He hesitated, glancing at me. I waved for him to proceed. "As steward, I wish to provide hospitable service to our guests."

"Indeed," said the Pedagno, glancing at the tray on the low table. Doctore Orsenius colored, surely remembering how he had objected to bringing meals for me. "Your desire is commen-d-able."

I wrestled a snort of disbelief into a grunt. What was *commendable* was the Pedagno's ability to say such things and sound sincere. I could not have.

"But, as you see, your services are unnecessary."

"Pedagno...Magistre Ulton..." Doctore Orsenius wriggled like a puppy. "Magistre Ulton thought it best if I remain here this afternoon, to be near-hand if needed."

"Magistre Ulton is thoughtful," the Pedagno said.

Of his own interests, I thought. *Doctore Orsenius is set to spy, of course. In person, rather than listening upstairs, to see what we do as well as hear what we say.*

"Very well," the Pedagno said. "You may stay. But do not disturb our study."

***

The Pedagno pointedly did not offer that Doctore Orsenius could move the harp and use that chair, so he stepped out, returning with another chair so quickly it must have been waiting in the passage. He settled himself in it, near enough to the table to watch but not so near as to be a distraction. The Pedagno and I returned to our reading.

I finished one manuscript and moved on to another. Opening the cover I recognized its type at once. An herbal, a book describing plants and their medicinal uses. It was an especially fine example, with drawings beside the descriptions so one might recognize each plant.

A scraping, shuffling noise that had been scouring my concentration for several moments finally shattered it. I looked up. Doctore Orsenius' feet stilled. But I'd barely read another leaf before the sound began again. This time, it was the Pedagno who turned to stare sternly, and the young scholar duly remained quiet longer. But inevitably, the noise began again.

I hunched over the herb book, knowing I must not reprimand him. Indeed, that I'd forgotten myself enough to glare could be understood as an insult if he chose. The Pedagno would have to decide whether, and when, to chastise his steward.

Finally he turned again. "Doctore Orsenius," he said grimly.

"I instructed you not disturb our study."

He slowed his feet did not fully still himself. "Pedagno, I am sorry." He sounded as if he truly were. "We are not allowed to bring books from the library, as you know."

I listened without turning, feeling more sympathetic. His disturbance was the result of boredom rather than an intentional irritant. I'd wondered if he were behaving badly because Magistre Ulton bid him not merely to observe but to obstruct.

"Ah," the Pedagno said, his tone less comminatory. He too had apparently considered whether Doctore Orsenius was being deliberately disruptive.

Hearing the difference, Doctore Orsenius' eyes scanned the table hopefully. "Pedagno," he hesitated, "may I read one?"

The Pedagno shook his head. "You would not be able. They are so ancient their language is no longer open to us."

His mouth twisted, as if he did not believe the Pedagno but did not dare say so.

"Come," the Pedagno said to my surprise. As well as Doctore Orsenius', from his wide-eyed response. He eagerly stepped closer as the Pedagno circled his fingers in invitation.

"See?" the Pedagno said, after Doctore Orsenius had stared for long moments at the Old Valenian, mouth circling in his astonishment.

"It is a difficult language," the Pedagno said as Doctore Orsenius returned to his chair. "A Pedagno trains his successor. Even so, the old books are slow reading."

I felt Doctore Orsenius' glower like a rock between my shoulders.

"Doctora Bann was not taught to read it here," the Pedagno said. "She worked it out on her own, while pursuing a charge given by the Roth of Elbany—Doctora Bann," he interrupted himself, "are you permitted to say what that task is?"

"No," I said shortly. Why was he telling him so much? I tried to quash my concern. The Pedagno surely knew what he was about.

Doctore Orsenius nodded thoughtfully, his face dark, and then I understood. Another scent to confuse Magistre Ulton. This time, entirely true. What was my task? How had I taught myself the ancient language? Questions to worry the Clerk.

The steward cast his gaze around the room. "You have no

books in modern Valenian or Brusterian, Pedagno?" He sounded so much like a bored child I nearly laughed. "I can't sit here and do *nothing*."

The Pedagno considered. "There are letters to copy."

Copying letters, those not so secret as to require the Pedagno alone to handle, was *novicios'* work, but Doctore Orsenius readily agreed. He helped the Pedagno fetch the letters, as well as parchment, ink, quill, and pen-knife, and seated himself at the table with us. Busied, he was able to sit without fidgeting, and I closed my eyes for a moment in the balm of quiet. That he now shared our workspace was an annoyance, but one worth enduring to be rid of his noise. The sounds of his quill upon the parchment and of the Pedagno's fingers gliding across a leaf troubled the silence not at all. They were, if anything, a comfort, the music of study and thought.

The book of herbs did indeed prove distressing to search as quickly as I had to. I pushed myself to go faster, as I was unlikely to find anything connected to Saradena or Magistre Ulton in such a source. Even in a rapid perusal, the book was delightful. The descriptions were precise and detailed, the drawings exquisite. I found myself watching for entries for the herbs Mistress Baynor gave Oliver, wondering if the Valenian ladies' secrets were secret from Vere. But what I found was of more immediate interest:

Luton is a fascinating, versatile plant, but it can be very dangerous. Found only on the Brusterian island of Eban, luton roots are safe to eat if prepared correctly. Turnip-like in appearance, the full-grown root can be boiled or roasted, and is similar in taste to the turnip, although blander. Dried and powdered, however, uncooked luton root becomes potent, and potentially lethal. Mixed with oil, it makes a powerful medicine, which, rubbed on the skin, dulls pain. Only a small amount is necessary for this purpose, and indeed too heavy-handed an application may deaden the area more and longer than is desirable. This mixture should never be eaten as it can sicken and even kill. It is unlikely anyone would want to, or do so accidentally, due to its bitter taste. Much more dangerous, however, is the combination of powdered luton root and milk. The milk masks the bitterness, allowing the mixture to be ingested. In minute quantities, milked luton can relieve inward pain, but it should only be used with the greatest care. Even a drop too much can sicken the patient rather than relieve him, and a clumsily large dose can prove deadly.

I found myself nodding and quelled the movement, not wanting to draw Doctore Orsenius' eyes.

The book's description of *luton* agreed with what the Pedagno had told me. I had no reason to doubt him, but like all scholars, I felt better about statements confirmed by a book. If we found nothing else, would the *luton* passage be enough to move the High King to act? It added weight to the Pedagno's suspicions about how he was being sickened, possibly how Pedagno Olwen was killed.

But I knew better. The High Kingship was a position of as much precariousness as power. Not only was Vere guaranteed a free hand over its own affairs by the Founder's agreement with Bruster, Magistre Ulton was a member of the second-most powerful family in Bruster. My father would not intervene without undeniable proof of the Clerk's duplicity. Which the *luton* passage was not.

Reluctantly I turned the leaf. I needed to finish the herb book. It was astonishing to have found anything pertinent at all. Surely nothing more remained. Suddenly it seemed as if I'd spent hours rather than minutes reading the *luton* description and considering what, if any, help it might provide. More of the Pedagno's books waited. I pressed forward.

Three leaves later, I discovered I was wrong. The little book was not finished yielding surprises:

Bloodweed is a plant of extraordinary properties, more useful than any other in the treatment of wounds. Placed between flesh and dressing, it is more effective in stopping bleeding than merely binding a wound, seeming to encourage the natural tendency of blood to dry, preventing more from leaving the body. Even more important, injuries dressed with bloodweed *fester much less often than other wounds. Since putrefaction kills as many warriors as outright battle,* bloodweed *gave Gwynt a marked advantage in its struggles with Elbs and Garland. It is said the king's chirgeon, Charles Henry, was the first to discover the properties of* bloodweed. Bloodweed *grows only in Gwynt and for many years it was the small kingdom's most guarded secret. Although its uses are now more widely known, the Gwyntish retain considerable benefit by it, able to use the herb themselves or sell portions of the prized plant to others, for unsurprisingly large sums.*

I stared at the page, trying to apprehend what I'd read. A reference to Charles Henry. That alone was superb. But *blood-weed...* the boon it would be to any kingdom was obvious. I'd never heard of it, either in Bruster or Elbany. It seemed unlikely a princess of a people as warlike as mine would not have been taught about the properties of *bloodweed* if that knowledge remained to us. The passage said the uses of the plant had come to be widely known. Clearly, since that time the knowledge had been lost. Perhaps it was remembered in Gwynt. Perhaps not.

If the knowledge was lost, the plant might not be. It might yet be growing, unremarked, in Gwynt. I steadied my hands against the page. I'd found something. At last I'd found something to help us against Saradena.

If *bloodweed* still grew in Gwynt. My fear-quickened fancy had little trouble imagining it gone. Its properties were so precious the herb could have been plucked more quickly than it could replenish itself. My hands curled, cupping the passage between them, as if the words themselves might flee. It would be bitter news to bring to the Roth, that a plant had once grown within Elbany that would improve our chances against a Saradenian assault, only to find the herb, too greedily grasped by past hands, no longer grew.

Or, its uses forgotten, it might flourish on every hillside. Or the Gwynts might remember when everyone else had forgotten, and reverted to keeping the plant a provincial secret.

I needed the herb book.

I winced, thinking about trying to persuade the Pedagno to let me take a second of Vere's Old Valenian manuscripts. But I had to. If no one living knew *bloodweed* by sight, the herb book was our only chance of finding it. If the Gwynts knew but were concealing it, the Roth could use the evidence of the book to force them to share with the rest of Elbany. Waiting for the Saradenians to convince them would be too late.

"Pedagno..." I said.

He took one look at my face. "No."

"But—Pedagno." I handed him the book. "Read. Then you'll understand."

"I see," he said later. "But no. I simply cannot." He held my gaze. There was no flicker in his eyes, nothing to suggest weakening or reconsidering. I'd pushed his sense of duty as far as it would go, and he would bend no further. "Copy the section. That is as much as I will allow."

"But Pedagno," I said. "The words without the sketch are worthless. This image, to be of use, must be rendered precisely, so one cannot tell which is the original and which the copy. You know my skills as an illustrator. I can't hope to do that."

"I can," Doctore Orsenius' voice sounded, too close to my ear.

CHAPTER XIV

My head whipped up, almost cracking into his. I had been so absorbed in the passage I'd not heard him come to stand behind me, looking over my shoulder. I caught the Pedagno's eye. He gave a half shrug. Apparently he'd noticed and decided Doctore Orsenius' interest was more harmless to let alone than attempt to thwart.

"What does the plant do?" It was a different tone than I'd heard from the steward before.

He could not read Old Valenian. I could tell him anything. But his voice...it was the first time I had heard him speak as a scholar, interested for the sake of the knowledge itself.

"I'll translate," I said. Running my finger beneath the lines of script, I did. He leaned closer, listening intently. I could feel the warmth of his breath on my cheek.

"Is it true?" he asked as I finished.

"The rest of the book has been impeccable," I said.

He straightened, stalked across the room, returned. "Do you understand what this means?"

"Yes," I said. "That's why I need a copy of the passage. More importantly, the drawing. We need to find this plant."

Cerebration rippled his face like a breeze-blown stream. I was taken aback at how different he looked as thought displaced suspicion and anxiety. "Are you *certain*," he stepped to my shoulder again to look down at the page, "the passage says what you think it does?"

His tone excused the question. He was not impugning my skills but thinking like a scholar, weighing possibilities.

"I—"

"It does," the Pedagno interrupted what was going to be, truthfully, an unnecessarily long explanation of why I was convinced of the passage's meaning.

"Could it be a fabrication?" Doctore Orsenius asked. "Books have been known before now, however regrettably, to contain misinformation and outright lies."

"Perhaps," I said. "But I have no reason to think so. From the book's descriptions of more widely-known plants, I judge it accurate."

"The *bloodweed* passage could still be false," he said. "Or erroneous. The author could have heard an untrue report which he dutifully but misleadingly included."

"It is possible," I conceded, struck by the enormity of the change in him. He seemed both younger and, oddly, older; younger in the emergence of his better nature, but older in his bearing, grappling with a problem, unfettered by distrust and misplaced loyalty.

"Doctore Orsenius is right," the Pedagno said. "This section could be false and yet its author correct in other matters." He shook his head. "But I do not think so."

"Why?" Doctore Orsenius asked. "It seems unlikely. Such an important herb, forgotten? I've never heard a whisper of anything like it."

"Neither have I," I said.

"There is the drawing," the Pedagno said. "It seems improbable a fabrication would have such a detailed picture. But also..." He paused. "You have never heard of the plant. I think...I may have." His voice softened, the words coming lingeringly. "I had forgotten..."

He paused again, as if the memory were rising within him, like bubbles in a steaming pot. "My *maestro* was from Garland. When I was *novicio*, not long after he agreed to be my *maestro*, I was reading an account of King Coel of Eban's attempt to supplant the High King. We began speaking of methods of warfare in Bruster and how they compare with those of Elbany. He mentioned his grandfather telling him that before Elbany united and Garland used to meet Gwynt regularly in battle, Gwyntl warriors came with linen to bind their wounds, like anyone else, but also a plant, sometimes freshly picked, sometimes dried. He said Gwyntl warriors believed the herb gave them protection in battle and helped heal their injuries afterward. But his grandfather said he'd heard these stories as a boy and did not know if they were true."

"The healing property correlates with what the book says," I said. "The warriors' belief that the plant offered protection seems understandable. Given the herb's properties in treating wounds, it is a small step to come to believe it might also ward against them."

"Might it still grow in Gwynt?" Doctore Orsenius said. Even without him knowing about the Saradenian threat, it was clear what a benefit the herb would be. To Elbany. And her allies. Of which Bruster was one. Doctore Orsenius, like most scholars, was Brusterian.

"The Roth could send men to seek it," I said. "If we had the drawing."

Doctore Orsenius stepped back to his end of the work table. I heard the scratch of his pen as he sketched. He paused to sharpen his quill, and continued.

"Will this do?" He shook sand over the page to dry it, then gently blew it away.

"That is...astonishing," I managed.

It was not merely a copy. He had faithfully reproduced the picture, but larger. Rather than a drawing the size of my palm, it filled the page. This image would be *more* helpful than the original in looking for the plant. I studied the picture, bringing the book to compare. I'd thought I had looked closely but Doctore Orsenius had seen and recorded details I'd missed.

"It is good enough?" he asked, some of his anxiety returning.

"Oh, yes. Thank you," I said with unfeigned sincerity, tamping down the strangeness of being aided by him, one of Magistre Ulton's adherents.

"Very well done," the Pedagno said. "You did not learn that skill at Vere."

"I did not learn it at all," Doctore Orsenius said. "I've always been able to draw what I see. But at Vere," he smiled, almost shyly, "I have parchment and ink rather than a stick and dirt."

A knock sounded. All three of us turned sharply, but Doctore Orsenius nearly jumped. "Enter," the Pedagno called.

The door opened, and a small head poked around it. "Pedagno?"

I recognized the child. He'd taken our horses to the stables when we arrived.

"Magistre Ulton has sent me to fetch Doctore Orsenius," the boy said.

The steward twitched. He glanced down at his drawing, confusion wafting across his face before it settled once more into hard lines. I wondered how much of his uneasiness was directed towards Magistre Ulton rather than on his behalf. The Clerk was unlikely to allow a follower to change his mind. Doctore Orsenius scuttled through the door.

The Pedagno sighed. "High among Magistre Ulton's ill deeds is misusing that young man."

I said nothing. Doctore Orsenius, perhaps, was being swept along by a river when he'd thought to wade in a stream.

"What else is in the *bloodweed* passage?" the Pedagno said, moving back to his chair.

I blinked at him, wondering how he had known, and whether Doctore Orsenius also suspected the passage was important for more than the plant.

He smiled. "He was not your *maestro*. What is there?"

But before I could say anything he made a sharp, sudden gesture, cocking an ear towards the hearth like a bird considering a grasshopper. I heard the soft shuffling, like robes slipping as someone settled into a chair. Doctore Orsenius—or someone— had returned, but not to the Pedagno's chambers.

"I do not require your help with this matter, Doctora Bann," the Pedagno said. He returned to the table, holding out a wax tablet.

I joined him and wrote quickly. The name in the *bloodweed* passage. What I'd learned about Charles Henry before, and why I thought him connected to the Saradenian letter.

"I appreciate your thoughts about the problem I showed you yesterday, but do not assume I therefore desire your suggestions in all areas." His voice had gone frigid.

"I apologize, Pedagno," I said.

"You are welcome until your companion finishes his study of the charters," he went on. "So long as you keep your impertinence in check. Vere has managed its books for hundreds of years. We do not require your suggestions to continue to do so."

"Of course, Pedagno." I held out the tablet to him.

"I expect Master Carlson is wasting his time," he continued, his eyes on the wax. "I would be very surprised if Philip of Ragonne will ever require the service for which he is so diligently preparing. But he is young, and I hate to discourage a man intent on serving his lord as well as he can. Reading the charters will do him no harm."

He nodded and smoothed the wax, then applied the stylus to it. *Your thinking seems logical to me,* I read as he passed it back. *But I can add nothing. I've never seen that name before, except its variants in the Saradenian letter, of which you already know.*

I scraped the words away.

"He will finish soon, and you'll be able to continue your journey," the Pedagno said.

I bowed my head, needing a moment to silently rage against the truth he spoke. When I looked at him again, his head was bent over his book, fingers sliding beneath the line of Old Valenian as he worked through the words. That, at least, was well done. For as much time as remained, the secret books were open to him.

I could not stay much longer. I *knew* that. But how could I leave, abandoning him to Magistre Ulton? I touched the herb book, still open to the drawing of *bloodweed.* Even so splendid an herb was of no use against what ailed the Pedagno. His danger lay in the hidden snares of ambition and arrogance. Not his own, but he was nonetheless wounded by them. Nor would he be the first to drown in those dark waters. Hard, proud men pushed aside those in their path, and held what they grasped with both hands, for as long as strength remained to them.

I pulled a deep breath, inescapable knowledge bitter on my tongue.

Once I left, I would never see the Pedagno living again.

***

I did not see Hal in the *comedor* that evening. Doctore Orsenius stopped by my table long enough to tell me Hal had chosen to skip the evening meal to continue his work. The supper was excellent, as all Vere's meals had been during our visit. The finest tableware was now in general use, and the food itself was exquisite. For the third time since our arrival, beef was served. When I was *novicia,* beef had graced Vere's table twice a year.

As soon as I'd eaten, I retired to my room. Despite the excitement of *bloodweed* and Charles Henry, I'd not forgotten Orlo's letter. It lay in my belt pouch, warm as a living thing, heavy as a burden. But I no longer felt a fool for wanting to read it, fear chilling my fingers like a December wind. I had come to Vere both in pursuit of Saradena and hoping to give my *maestro* aid, but the Pedagno had helped me more than I had him.

CHAPTER XV

I broke the seal and unrolled the parchment.

Maudlin—
I have determined to see the favor of a second letter, despite
its practical nature, before I had responded to the first as a sign of
enough favor to use your name. Forgive me. Think of Ragoni
poems and hold me excused. From them we learn that hopeful
lovers live upon such faint encouragement.

I smiled. I knew the sort of poem he meant, of course. I'd
read enough of them during my time in Ragonne. But I was far
from certain they were meant to be taken seriously. Neither was
he, from his tone.

Another constraint of the hopeful lover is that he perform
tasks set by his lady. In such manner, I have undertaken what you
asked. I consulted with my clerk and am sorry to report we have
no books in our possession on the subject you inquired about.

Parsing his discretion, what he meant was Kolon had no
books with more information about Martin. Ah well. It had been
worth asking but I had not really expected him to find anything.

To the other matter...
Perhaps I should affect being hurt that you do not remember
the gape-faced Ragoni boy at your stirrup the day a certain Brus-
terian princess was ordered by her brothers to stay home while
they rode into the mountains for an adventure, but she disobeyed
and followed them—and ended up thwarting an attempt on their
lives?

I looked up, seeing the past rather than the room. It was the
attack I'd recalled in Ragonne when Hal found that Philip's

ancestor had killed his nephew to seize the throne. Orlo knew of it? He had *been* there?

My brothers had decided to go hunting alone in the mountains, boasting they'd show their princely mettle and bring down a *leoyong*, the four of them unaided. Their sister, of course, was not welcome. I'd argued as much as I thought necessary to allay their suspicion. Once they had gone, I saddled my horse and went after them.

It was a well-planned attack. Someone in our household had been paid to provide details of my brothers' trip. Our father found him, later. The body hung from the walls of the Black Keep, until whatever flesh remained after the birds ate their fill rotted and fell away in chunks. I was the unknown, unplanned-for element, and I was enough. Barely. If they'd sent a dozen men rather than half a dozen, all the High King's heirs would have died that day beneath the hush of a glowering sky, brooding a storm that did not burst until the next morning.

And there was—*there was*—a Ragoni boy who caught my stirrup as we rode back into Reud to the shouts of a gathering crowd, who stared up at me with black fire in his eyes.

You were a child, and so was I—

Ten. I was ten. He would have been a year older. Why was he in Reud? Not fostering in my father's household. I'd have seen him before. This was the only time, I was certain. An embassage trip with his father, perhaps?

—but not so much a child I might not vow within my heart: 'this one, when I am grown, this one and no other. And if not this one, no other.'

I have kept this promise. What appeal had the pale ladies of Valenna after I had seen the fierce princess of Bruster?

I was clumsy in Rothbury. I knew you thought I spoke in ill-spirited jest. I had given up hope of laying my suit before you. I had denied my wishes at my king's command. When I saw my moment all unlooked-for, I ran hard and sprawled like a month-old pup.

I ask now, in all solemnity, and if you tell me no I will not trouble you again. Grant me leave to court the princess of

Bruster, whom the years have shown more magnificent than my child's mind guessed, or tell me in kindly honesty you have no room in your heart to hear me.

I sat, letting the scroll curl in my hands.

Francis had never spoken like this.

But how to answer...that would require more than a moment's thought. How different my life might have been, if Philip had allowed Orlo's suit and my father accepted it. It was bitter to think that those terrible years with Francis might never have been. There was no promise that we would have been happy, Orlo and I. He could have made a princess in his mind that I never was and could not be. But we might have fit well enough. We might yet, perhaps, learn a little about what had been lost, and find what could be still found.

At last I rolled the sheet, tucking the letter gently back into my belt pouch.

★★★

I saw Hal at breakfast the next morning but only in passing. He was up early and was scraping up the last of his oatmeal when I entered the *comedor.*

"Magistre Boland 'found' the charter last night," he whispered, rising from the bench. "Today is almost certainly our last day in Vere. Have you found anything?"

I gave him the shallowest of nods.

"Later, then," he said, more normally.

"At the evening meal, perhaps," I said. "'Have a good day among the books.'"

"'It is always a good day among books,'" he said, smiling. I saw more than one head turn to stare as he gave the correct response, and held in a chuckle, knowing he meant to divert their interest into wondering how he'd learned to read, let alone elements of Vere's workings.

★★★

Doctore Orsenius left me at the Pedagno's door. I knocked. When the Pedagno invited me to enter, I opened the door and stepped inside.

He sat at the work table, rivulets of tears etching both cheeks. I ran to his side. "What is it? Are you in pain?"

Both hands covered his face. I put my arms around his shoulders, rocking as he shook, asking no more questions. Not yet.

"I found it," he rasped, later.

"Found what?"

He shook his head, pushing a book towards me. "Read. Just read."

I sat, clutching one of his hands as I bent over the book:

Today we commemorate the one hundredth year since the destruction of Vere. To any eyes our new city exceeds the first so extravagantly an outsider might wonder why we yet mourn the elder. We delayed the completion of the final building that we might set the last stone today, and honor the lost while celebrating the new.

If it were only the city that had been lost, we would not mourn. The attack caused us to reconsider our site, and we determined to rebuild further inland, unseen from the shore, for greater safety. The powers of the earth forbid such a crime might be considered again. But it might. We decided we would do well to be wary.

But it was not the city alone. The marauding Farente stole books, all our library they could lay their hands on. For the books, or for their decorated covers? We pray the books were not thrown overboard as soon as the gold and jewels could be ripped free. Better the books be preserved somewhere, even if not in Vere, than destroyed.

The loss is bitter. Irreplaceably precious manuscripts, gone. Our oldest copy of the Founder's vita. Our only copy of a map of the lands to the east, as well as the adventurer Broun's account of his travels there. We have no other source of information about Sera Serdent, Carlomunde, or Celladorn now their ships no longer stop at Lastland. Our copy of the Rule of Vere, written in Cynan Maccus' own hand.

We have survived. We have rebuilt. We have begun again to create, as the Founder bid, the greatest collection of knowledge the world has ever seen. But we will never have our stolen books again. And so we place the final stone of our new home, and mourn the manuscripts that will never reside within it.

I swiped the heels of my hands across my cheeks. No wonder the most precious books in Vere were kept hidden. The ruins at the shore...they *were* the remnants of the first Vere, sacked and burned. By marauders —

I sucked air. My grip tightened on the Pedagno's hand. I saw again three chests. Francis opened them, making a mocking flourish. Each was full of books so old their white leather bindings had gone brown. "It was—it was Ferrant. They razed the city. They stole the books. Mostly likely whatever small treasures Vere had as well. They still have them. Or at least some of them."

His head whipped up. "Are you sure?"

"I've seen them."

Hope faded from his face. "Then the book the passage speaks of, a description of the countries of the east, a map...they are gone?"

"I don't know." Shame burned my cheeks so hot I felt the tears drying. "Francis forbade me to read them. I obeyed. I wanted to be a good wife to him, a good queen." I wrenched my hand away, turning in my chair. "We are unprepared for the Saradenian danger because I did as Francis commanded. Compliant. Weak. If I had defied him, we would already know what was in that book."

His hands grasped my shoulders and shook. "Think, Maudlin. How would you have read it? You did not know Old Valenian then."

"I—I might have—"

"We each have enough burdens in this world without seizing one that does not rightly belong to us." He shook me again. "This is not yours. Do you hear me? But...you have to return there. If there's a chance Ferrant has that book, you must go."

He was right. There was no evading that truth, unpleasant as it was. "Hal is working on the Clerk's Charter today. We should leave," I swallowed, "tomorrow. To Bruster, to deliver the letter. Then to Elbany, to apprise the Roth of what has happened. And then, if he concurs—"

"You know he will."

"—to Ferrant."

He touched my arm. "Francis can do no worse to you than he already has. You will survive him again, and be stronger for it."

I took a deep breath. "I am sorry to leave you."

"We can do no more than we are able, *Alumna*. Sometimes it is enough. Sometimes it isn't."

"Shall I see you in the morning, before I leave?"

He shook his head. "Say farewell this evening, and start anew tomorrow."

I did not like it but I bowed my head.

Our oldest copy of the Founder's vita...

"Pedagno," I said. "Ferrant has many books. Three chests, full to the brim. But some...they have lost or let go."

He looked at me, his head slowly shaking his question.

"I think I have one of them. One mentioned in the passage." I brought it from my pack. "This came to me while I was in Ragonne."

He unwrapped the cloak, sighing when the golden book came into view. "This is..."

"The *vita* of Cynan Maccus. It might be the stolen one. It's certainly very old."

His hand splayed on the cover. "It might be. Ferrant may have lost or sold some of the books. You still have to go."

"I know." I paused. "That book was given to me as a gift for the Roth. I have to take it when I leave."

He looked sad but unsurprised. "Someday, perhaps, it will return to Vere." He lifted the cover. "I have seen it. That is enough." At the sight of the purple parchment he gave a wispy exhalation. "Ah!" He bent over the book, then looked up. "Let us spend our day as we meant. Reading. I started early, and look how much I learned already." He aimed for a lighter tone, and nearly achieved it.

I set a book before me and opened it, but it was a long while before I could bring words into focus.

BOOK III

CHAPTER I

I sat in the boat, watching but not seeing the backs of the slaves as they rowed. Then I bent my neck, and read the Verune charter again.

"Anything?" Hal said when I looked up.

"No. As you thought."

"I would rather have been wrong."

During the ride from Vere to the port, we had at last had a chance to talk: the charters he had read and copied, without discovering anything to help the Pedagno. What I'd found. What the Pedagno had found. Nothing to help the Pedagno. Perhaps something to aid our own quest. Not something pleasant. But I had always known it would be Ferrant in the end.

"So we go to Ferrant next," Hal said.

"Soon," I said. "Bruster, then Rothbury. Then Ferrant."

He gave a sympathetic grunt but said nothing.

I rolled the charter, not looking at it, and passed it to him. I should not have hoped so fervently I'd find something he had not. He was as careful a reader and thoughtful a scholar as any Vere-trained clerk. I'd let my wishes cloud my thinking. I crossed my arms tightly across my chest. I could not afford to do so again. Not in Bruster. Not in Ferrant.

At last my eyes began to see what lay before me, and I turned my gaze to the sea.

"We're further than I would have supposed so soon," I said.

Hal scanned the water, his eyes narrowing. "We've caught the current. I would guess they'll be stowing the oars soon."

As if Odulan had heard him, the order boomed from stern to bow. The slaves pulled in their oars, shaven heads bobbing like apples in a water barrel. Some returned to their thwarts, while others raised the sail.

"They keep no slaves in Ragonne—" Hal began.

"No," I snapped. "Warriors captured in battle but not rich enough to pay ransom are simply killed. In Bruster, we offer such men a way to redeem their honor. Ten years' service is better than a slit throat." I shot him a fierce sidelong glance. "Our boat slaves are better placed than *some* Ragoni servants. Warriors do not mistreat slaves, lest fate be tempted to change their places."

He held up his hands. "I meant no offense. I was going to say, as you pointed out, that while Ragonne has no 'slaves', the difference from a servant's outlook is not as wide as might be supposed."

"I apologize. I should not have assumed the worst." I sighed. The practice of curbing one's temper, always trying to bolt like a high-strung horse, was weary work. It waited until you were tired, or anxious, or distracted, like a stubborn, cunning stallion feeling the reins slacken in your hands, and leaped. "We will be to Reud sooner than I thought."

"Ah," he said, and that small sound seemed to encompass all, as if he did indeed know what it was like to be coming home for the first time in six years, both hands spilling over with troubles to lay before my father. Saradena's threat. Upheaval in Vere. Philip's plan. Why Bruster's letter had been delayed. What I'd found about Saradena. What *little* I'd found. The need to return to Ferrant.

"I only ever bring him turmoil and disruption." I rubbed the ridge in the bone in the underside of my left forearm, the nearly-forgotten relic of a foiled attack that Orlo's letter had reminded me of. One of the assailants had caught me with the flat of his sword and broken my arm. Fortunately. If the edge had been turned, he'd have taken my arm off just below the elbow. At first the healing arm had itched, so I'd rubbed at it, and it became a habit. Until Francis objected that the gesture made me look as if I had lice. Now, on my way back to Reud, I found I could not help but chafe at the long-ignored scar. Fitting, perhaps. "Rejection and scorn from Francis. Upheaval in Vere. Rumor of war from elsewhere."

"I *had* heard that Bruster enjoyed naught but peace except for you," he said dryly.

I let one corner of my lip curl in mock grievance. "And I have a letter I want to send, but it will occasion questions."

"Ah," he said again, but now amusement filled the little word, and I gave him the exaggerated mock scowl he'd earned.

***

I had written a hasty response to Orlo, making no promises but giving him leave to press his suit. But I doubted a letter sent from Vere in its current situation could be relied upon to be sent promptly and safely. I did not care to have this one lost.

The burdens I was bringing home should have been enough to busy my thoughts, but as the waves slipped by I found my mind would not bide in the current tangles, dreadful as they were. The clustered islands of Bruster had begun to rise from the sea.

"What has caught your notice?" Hal asked.

I pointed. "Bruster."

He shaded his eyes. "The smudges on the horizon, scarcely distinguishable from the waves?"

"Watch," I said.

The boat pressed on, and the clustered islands grew like afternoon shadows. Bruster, the largest, sat before the ship, Solud to its right. Visible between them, further west, lay Eban. More westerly and south of Bruster, was Verun, obscured in part by the small spot that was Punlan, a holding of Verun but more curse than blessing—small, rocky even by Brusterian standards, barely habitable.

"I see them now," he said.

I sighed. Soon I would be able to discern the black mountain and Reud, chief city of Bruster, the hold of the High King, who sat the throne of Bruster like a skittish horse and coerced his under-kings to his lordship.

He looked at me. "Do you wish to return? Or dread it?"

"Both, I think." The Black Keep was not yet apparent even as a mote but I saw it clearly, remembering when I'd seen it last. I'd looked back, once, as the boat started for Vere. I'd left in bitter shame—and with bitter words—certain my father and brothers desired my departure, or, better, my death, to ease their humiliation. I no longer believed so. But I had left in anger, and stayed away and silent for long years. I pressed a tight fist against my lips. I might find cold welcome, and well-earned.

"Look." Hal's voice went reverent as the sun-splattered sides of the black mountain came into view.

I whispered its name in Brusterian. Valenian did not serve its dread beauty. Tallest in Bruster. In the known world, perhaps. From a distance, the jagged mass of the mountain gleamed solid black. Closer, it revealed itself to be speckled with gray flecks, and, rarely, white and brown. Perhaps my forebears were drawn by its strangeness to build their hold there, but the superb defensive position it offered was more likely.

"Look," he said again as the boat approached the inward curve of the island, and now his tone held surprise. "A city."

"*The* city," I said. "*Our* city. Reud." I waited, knowing what would come next.

"Such a large city...I never heard Reud was so—wait...how did they build houses there?"

I smiled. "Watch," I said again.

From afar it appeared as if buildings ringed the base of the mountain. But as we approached, it became clear that the city lay only to the right. The house-like shapes on the left were rocks, extending to and into the water, monstrous boulders of the same stone as the mountain.

At last his breath caught, and I knew he saw. The scattered black blocks like a shadow of the city made solid. "That is...very striking."

"Everything about the black mountain is striking." We were still too distant to see separate buildings but I knew what lay along the black sand shore and beyond. "If we're unlucky, we will see bodies rotting on the walls of the Black Keep. If we're lucky, we'll see the shipbuilders at work instead."

"Will we land near the shipyard?" He leaned forward, as if to see better. "I've always wondered why only Bruster builds ships."

"Don't you know?" I grinned. "We alone are mad enough to sail waters peppered with more rocks than acorns on a forest floor in autumn."

"Perhaps," he said, not turning towards me, "but where do you get enough wood?"

It was a fair question. Bruster was the largest of the clustered islands and the most forested, but trees did not grow as thickly as in Elbany or Valenna. Often we had to supplement with wood brought from Lastland or traded from Elbany. "With great care. In Bruster, peat is burned. Wood is fashioned," I said, guessing he most likely had not meant to ask a question that could only be answered with a lengthy description of Bruster's trading relationships and vassalage duties.

We left the current as the boat turned, moving into the bay.

At Odulan's orders the boat slaves lowered the sail and took up their oars. Muscles played beneath their sun-whitened shirts as they drew us in. Black sand glinted mutedly among the shipyard but lower, wave-wet, it shone. To enemy eyes, it must be an ominous sight: the craggy mountain, its teeth lying at its feet and spilling into the inrolling tide. The Black Keep crouched in a niche carved into the mountain's flank, the castle itself built of the removed stone.

"The Black Keep of Bruster," Hal said, "perched upon the black mountain of Bruster. Is there a more famous stronghold in the world?"

"It is a warrior's castle," I said, gratified by his recognition of its eminence. "Beauty or comfort came to it by accident or addition in later years." Thinking of attack, and defense, and loss, I glanced at my oiled leather bag, remembering the books within, and those stolen from the first Vere by Ferrant.

"It is beautiful," he protested, shooting an indignant look at me. "And must have been so from its making."

"I meant inside," I said. "Defense is its aim. The Black Keep could be defended at the last by two men."

"Could be?" he echoed curiously. "Has it?"

I lifted one shoulder. "As far we know, the keep has never been pushed to that extreme. But who could be sure with so much of our history lost?" I darted a sidelong glance at him. "In the time of my grandfather Bann, it was held by a mere eight men for two full months. The besiegers ran out of supplies before the defenders, and we won."

His lips pursed appreciatively.

"It is sparse as a warriors' barracks inside," I said. "That is, essentially, what it was built to be." I turned my gaze back, full upon the approaching scene. "Nonetheless, outside, it is beautiful. The blinding brilliance of the keep on a bright day. Its glowering darkness under a cloudy sky. More common than sunny ones." I felt a wry smile nudge the corner of my mouth upward. "These are appreciated but were not planned." How much of the High King's sway derived from the fearsome sovereignty of his stronghold?

"No one could look upon this castle and think to take it by force," Hal said.

Would the Saradenians? Would they look upon the Black

Keep and think themselves strong enough to storm it, a thing that had never been done in living memory or even memory become legend?

"*They* believe they can," I said. That was the simple truth underlying the letter. *They think they can take us. All of us. Elbany, Ragonne, Logan—and Bruster.* They made their demands and would come not as the enemy of any one but against us all, and deemed themselves sufficient to the fight.

Hal's stricken face looked as if he had the same thoughts, and was equally shaken by them. We stared at one another until my eyes burned and I had to blink. *All of us.*

At last my gaze went back to the Black Keep. I shook my head. Gloom and worry would not bide, not as I watched the castle grow. Its purpose was cold-eyed protection, but to my heart its black walls shone with warmth, and with a childhood as the cherished only daughter of the High King. Anxious as I was about how I would be received, about the ill tidings I brought by the bucketful—nevertheless, it said *home.*

Odulan signaled. The slaves raised their oars, swinging them into the boat. Momentum carried the ship forward, and as the water grew shallow Odulan raised his hand. Two slaves jumped over the side and tugged the boat the last few feet to where the black sand sloped down to the water. Another twitch of Odulan's fingers and the remaining boat slaves vaulted out, pulling the boat beyond the reach of the tide, pausing long enough to allow Hal and me to climb out.

Clutching my bag against my chest, well above the most ambitious spray, I nodded to Odulan, while Hal raised his hand, a gesture of thanks and farewell. Odulan, his careful gaze on his boat and crew, returned a brisk nod. We started across the sand to the road.

"A stone road," Hal said as we stepped from the yielding sand onto the hard surface.

"Yes," I said, unable to suppress a surge of pride. Even in Ferrant, where the ladies had sniffed about the 'barbaric south', not quite daring to say 'Bruster', I had seen none better. To be fair, it was the only paved road on the island, but ran all the way to the town, then beyond to the castle, and it was so wide that four men could ride abreast and not rub knees. It was paved with ordinary stone, the same as the stone buildings in the town. The black stone belonged to the mountain and the keep, nowhere else, not even Reud.

"Shall we?" Hal asked. His glance made clear he was asking about more than whether I was ready for the walk.

I shouldered my bag. "Let's go."

As we moved nearer, the solid mass of the town separated into houses. Some were turf with thatched roofs, pale as cloud against the black mountain. Others were dry stone, tapering in upon themselves at the top like an arrowhead, held together by the weight and placement of the rocks. A few were built of shaped and mortared stones, like the Black Keep—invariably the largest and tallest, the homes of the most well-to-do craftsmen.

Our approach was noted. Doors opened. People emerged. A wain came from between houses and stopped as its driver gawked, letting the reins slacken until his horse turned to see what had happened. The stares of the townspeople began to fall like cold heavy rain. Some hard. Some disbelieving. Some furtive, eyes widening as heads swiveled away, lips opening around whispers. I felt my chin lift.

"Don't let them," Hal said.

I looked at him sidelong. He was right. The stares could only sting if I allowed it. But it was not so simple to shrug away the gaping glances. The hostile glares. The not quite soft enough murmurs. The buzz of voices soon became loud enough to muffle the sounds of our feet against the stones. I thought of the triumphant farewell Reud had given when I left for Ferrant. Garlands of mistletoe boughs had draped every doorway, and even the children had donned shoes to wave their princess goodbye.

Perhaps that comparison was unfair. Perhaps it was more truthful to think of their subdued, shocked, curious stares when I had returned from Ferrant. Perhaps this was no worse.

I heaved my bag to a different place on my hip. Hal seized the moment to move to my other side, positioning himself between me and the gawking townsfolk. I would not have supposed that the slight screen of his body would make it easier to ignore them, but it did, and I felt some of the tightness leave my shoulders. Nonetheless I drew a grateful, deep breath when we passed the last house.

Only bare road, curving left as it followed the shoreline, lay between us and the keep. I tipped my head back, drinking in the mountain to its peak. Then, slowly, my gaze descended.

"Stunning," Hal breathed. His glance had followed mine. Up the mountain, down to the Black Keep.

"Oh, yes," I said.

"Parts of the parapet are weathered. Look." He pointed. I thought suddenly of my father inspecting the battlements for such places, weakened by wet and wind. He shook his head in apparent disbelief. "It is old."

"*Very* old." The Roth's castle had been built by his far-flung ancestor Alfred of Roth who had united Elbany, but compared to the Black Keep, the mortar was scarcely dry between its stones. The Black Keep was ancient beyond reliable knowledge. It was said the castle had been built by Ator, who conquered and held the entirety of the Three Lands. If he existed at all. Ator was also ancient beyond reliable knowledge.

The road narrowed as we approached the keep. Walking, we could go side by side, but horsemen would have been obliged to advance singly. This, too, served the castle's purpose. With the mountain to its back and the rock-scattered sea before it, there was no other entrance. It would have been foolish to provide a wide path to the door for attackers. The wall facing the water was smooth, with no window for twenty feet up. The entrance was to the right, where the road climbed a steep rise to a set of wooden stairs.

"Another defense," I said as we started up. "You burn them and leave the invaders to puzzle the problem of forcing entry into a castle whose door is now ten feet above their heads."

"Those that survived the rain of arrows as they struggled up the road," he said.

"Just so," I said.

Both the stairs and the gates that stood at their summit were wooden, but painted black as the castle and the mountain. Upon them, inlaid with gold, was graven the device of the High King.

After a moment, as if I'd been waiting for something without realizing it, I raised my hand. For the first time in my life I knocked upon the wicket gate.

CHAPTER II

My knocking was, of course, unnecessary.

Our approach had been observed. The small window in the wicket door slid open before the sound of my knock had died. "Who comes to the Black Keep, the hold of the High King of Bruster?"

The doorward spoke in Brusterian and I responded in the same language. "I am..." I found my voice shaking, and paused to steady it. "Doctora Maudlin Bann, Vere-trained scholar, librarian to the Roth of Elbany, and daughter of the High King of Bruster."

"Indeed," the voice said skeptically. "And the man?"

"Hal Carlson, in the service of King Philip of Ragonne," Hal said.

"Indeed," the doorward said again, but this time with respect and real interest. "Greetings, Master Carlson of Ragonne. And Princess Maudlin. If so you are. What is your purpose here?"

I tried to swallow growing irritation. "We bring messages for the High King."

"What messages? Where from?"

"Messages for the High King," I snapped. "Messages that are no man's business but his."

There was a long pause. "I never met the princess Maudlin," the doorward said. "But I have heard about her. Perhaps you are who you claim." He paused again. "In any case, if Master Carlson has come from Ragonne, the Steward will want to hear what he has to say."

Hal and I scarcely had a moment to exchange bewildered looks before the window slid shut and the wicket door opened. We stepped inside. The doorward shut it so quickly it brushed my skirt. He dropped the crossbar.

The guards were always vigilant, but this level of caution was unusual. Something was wrong.

A second door stood in the opposite wall, near the corner, a warrior on guard beside it. Given their wariness, it would be barred from inside. This room was another of the keep's defenses. The barred doors, cross-corner from one another, would create considerable difficulty for attackers having breached the outer door and attempting to break through the inner. Which they would be trying under a hail of arrows from slits in the walls and ceiling. Other defenses would rain down as well: scalding-hot water, mud, animal dung, the contents of the castle's privies. Whatever was at hand and might serve.

"Send for the Steward," the doorward said.

Nodding crisply, the guard of the inner door rapped upon it. After a moment, it opened minutely and he spoke to someone inside, too softly to hear. But I could hear that once the door closed, the bar was set in place again.

The High King's guards would not even leave the inner door unbarred long enough to fetch the Steward, with only two people waiting, one a woman, and neither armored? Cold fear twisted in my gut. Something was *very* wrong.

The moments stretched, long and taut. I found my foot tapping and quieted it. Surely I could recall some of the patient-seeming required of a princess of Bruster, even more so of a Queen of Ferrant. Hal tucked his hands behind his back and stood as unmoving as the stone walls.

At last I lowered my heavy bag, sliding it protectively between my feet. Both the guard and the doorward watched me closely as I did.

When Steward Bernuth came, all would be well. He knew me. He'd been with my father since before I was born. To the High King's children, the Steward had seemed a human manifestation of the castle itself, with his black eyes and black hair, and quiet but unyielding force. He ruled the household with efficient if laconic management. We, like his staff, feared his displeasure, which seared the more for the few words in which it came. We appreciated him more as we grew older and learned he had been one of our father's best warriors in the early struggles to keep his throne, who had agreed to forsake the field at the behest of the young High King, who needed a man of unbreakable loyalty to direct his household. It was easy to believe he had once been a formidable fighter. He moved with a warrior's stealth through the keep. Much to the trepidation of the servants.

It was at least half an hour before the scrape of the lifted bar touched my ears, and the inner door swung slowly open. *Finally!*

My relief died as the man stepped into view. It was not Steward Bernuth. I did not know him. Which meant he would not know me. Perhaps the Steward was occupied and had sent one of his men? Or—oily worry slid through me. Was *this* man now Steward?

He bowed politely, as to any unexpected and unknown guest, but not deeply, as to a member of the High King's family. "What is the cause of your coming to the Black Keep?"

Clearly, my identity remained under suspicion. Their skepticism was frustrating but not unreasonable. A proper visit would have been announced with messengers, weeks, even months beforehand. Arriving unlooked-for, unaccompanied but for one man...I could hardly fault their suspicion. My father or brothers would know me, naturally, but the High King's men would not let me near any of them until they were satisfied I was no threat. "We bring messages for the High King my father," I said.

He blinked slowly. "From?"

"That is the concern of the High King," I said. "But I assure you, the news we bring is grave. He will want to hear it, and quickly."

Again his eyelids lowered and rose. "You say you are the princess Maudlin."

"I *am* princess Maudlin." I pushed a note of panic from my voice. "Daughter of the High King. Vere-trained scholar and librarian to the Roth of Elbany."

He folded one hand over the other. "Strange that princess Maudlin should return from Elbany in a boat from Vere."

"The Roth sent me to Ragonne on a task. When it was finished, King Philip asked me to return to Elbany by way of Vere to deliver a gift to the Pedagno. We were asked to stop here on our way back to Elbany and deliver a message to the High King."

His eyes flashed, as if I'd given something away. "The message, then, is from the Pedagno?"

I felt my fingers trying to curl into a fist and forced them smooth. "As I said, the High King's messages are his own business."

His attention flicked to Hal. "And you are?"

"Hal Carlson of Ragonne," he said.

"Do you bring a message from Ragonne?"

"The High King's messages—" I interrupted.

He flung up a hand. "Ordinarily, yes. Not now."

The knot in my stomach tightened like a sail-cord in a storm. My father must be ill. Dying. *Dead.* What else could cause such caution? "What has happened?"

He shook his head, the look on his face reproachful.

"You do not know me, and so you bar my way?" I said. "It is equally true *I* do not know *you.* Who are you? Where is Steward Bernuth? He knows me." I met his eyes. "Our news is urgent. I need to see the High King. Or one of my brothers. *Now.*"

His eyes narrowed. I was reminded of a warrior, staring across the water at a mountain on the far side, trying to make out whether the shapes that moved were goats, deer, wild pigs—or men.

At last he jerked his head towards the guard at the inner door, who knocked for it to be opened. "Come."

***

The walls of the Black Keep were thick, even the inner ones, but that width was more noticeable walking from room to room within the castle than entering from the outside. One did not, in fact, merely go from one room into the next. Most often a cave-like passage led into the chamber beyond. A low-ceilinged passage that forced you to bend to avoid knocking your head. Like everything else about the design of the Black Keep, it was purposeful—and that purpose was defense. It slowed an attacker's progress, and obliged him to emerge with his head down. The more easily to have it struck from him with a blow to the back of the neck.

After a series of such passages and rooms, we came to the hall. I breathed out softly. Whatever was to hand, *the hall* was unchanged.

But cleaner. The plastered walls were newly whitewashed, the tapestries upon them standing out so brightly they must have been taken down recently to have the dust beaten off. Small fires burned on both hearths, and all the tables were in place, including the High King's on the dais. I frowned. The hall would normally be open and empty, the trestle tables apart and stacked against the wall. Perhaps the King held court soon, and preparing for that event had stoked the household's vigilance. Any event in which the High King appeared publicly was a source of concern to his retainers.

The man led us through the hall to a room beyond. It led in turn, I recalled, to a second, larger room. That was the reception chamber, where the High King's guests waited until formally entering the hall. Sometimes the High King would receive less important guests there rather than in the hall. Men of distinction met with him on the third floor, in his own work chamber. This small room was the Steward's, from which he managed the household. Unlike the hall, no fire burned here, but he gestured us to the chairs before the hearth.

I noted the ease with which he came into the room, his presence within it. I sat, placing my bag beside the chair. "You are now Steward?"

"Yes." He settled himself into the seat opposite.

Hal took the chair by mine, watching. I did not ask what had happened to Steward Bernuth. If he was no longer Steward, he was surely dead.

"I have been Steward nearly two years," the man said. "Steward Bernuth was my father. My name is—"

Old memories shifted into place. "Gustor," I said.

He gave a thoughtful nod. "Perhaps you are princess Maudlin."

Why did I know this man's name but not his face? I could see his father in him now, both in body and behavior—the dark hair and eyes, the sparse speech. But six years would not have been enough to blot him out if I had known him. "I don't remember you," I said. "Why would that be?"

He did not speak. I supposed that while he was inclining towards believing me, he was not yet willing to volunteer information.

I combed my memory. "I remember Steward Bernuth's son only as a child," I said. "A few years younger than me. He—you—were fostered in...Logan, I remember now, and had not come back before I left for Ferrant." I gave a half shrug. "If you were here when I returned, I'm sorry, I do not recall."

"I was in Eban during the few months princess Maudlin was home then." He steepled his fingers. "I suspect, lady, that you are who you claim to be." He lifted a finger as I moved to speak. "But I cannot permit you into the presence of the High King on suspicion." His voice was apologetic but firm. "You have been gone six years. In our current danger—"

"*What danger?*" I said.

He ignored this question. "You will have to give your messages to me, and I will deliver them to the High King."

"I may not," I said. "But I told you truly when I said they are urgent."

He frowned. "You bring more trouble to us."

Hal started to speak, but I waved him off. "Trouble was already coming. But I bring forewarning of it."

The Steward smiled grimly. "Perhaps your message is late. Perhaps it pertains to the danger already here."

"I doubt it," I said. "A great deal."

He tapped his fingertips together. "What—"

He was interrupted by a brisk rap on the door, followed by its opening. A higher-status person might enter the chamber of someone lesser, but it was polite to knock first. Pedagno Poll had been incensed by his Steward's behavior precisely because it implied he outranked his lord.

"Gustor, I—" a voice said. Then: "*Maudlin?*"

CHAPTER III

I knew that voice. "Utor!"

He crossed the room in long-legged strides. I jumped up as he approached. He'd obviously just arrived. His clothes were even more travel stained than ours.

His arms swept around me, pulling me to him. "Maudlin," he repeated, his breath in my hair. "Six *years*, Maudlin."

I found my eyes stinging. My arms went around him as I blinked hastily. "I am sorry, Utor."

He let me go. Surely he could not have grown taller. But his shoulders had broadened, ready to receive the burden of the High Kingship when he was needed.

"Why has the princess been kept from the High King?" He turned to the Steward. "He will want to see her."

"Your pardon, my lord." The Steward inclined his head to his Prince. "She arrived within the hour, and no one could immediately be found who had known Princess Maudlin well enough to confirm her identity." He hesitated. "I admit I was...concerned. In our present circumstances." His eyes met Utor's. "The princess arrived unannounced, unexpected, and unaccompanied except for this man," he gestured to Hal. Utor gave him a narrow-eyed look that showed more of an older brother's concern than political interest.

"This is Master Hal Carlson," I said. "A servant of the King of Ragonne. He was sent to help with a task that the Roth gave me."

This statement clearly handed Utor more questions than answers. I watched as he swallowed them. For now, I knew.

"She says she brings messages for the High King, but will not say who they are from," the Steward continued.

Utor's face stiffened. "You are not, I take it, simply come home."

I opened my mouth, then closed it. Nothing excused my stubborn absence, or that my return was compelled. Once compelled, I had been surprised to find that I was not entirely unwilling, that perhaps I was even grateful for the chance to mend bridges, if it might be; I had, after all, diligently tried to burn those connections to cinders. That did not change my uneasy knowledge that without the discovery of the Saradenian letter in Vere, I would not have come. It was too easy to let things go on as they had become. I let my eyes drop, evading the brittle disappointment in Utor's. "We bring news to the High King, too delicate to tell even his Steward."

"Maudlin," Utor said skeptically, "surely..."

I hesitated for an instant. Then, stooping, I brought out the Saradenian letter. "Read. The High King will inform his Prince before anyone."

His eyes widened as they scanned the page. All the High King's children had been taught to read as youngsters, and he did not struggle like the Roth or Lady Elsbeth, who had learned as adults and only recently. He glanced up, then shook his head disbelievingly, and returned his attention to the page, to read the letter once more.

At length he looked up again, thoughts veiled by a noble's impassive countenance. "You are right. The High King will want to see this immediately." He handed the letter back. I rolled it and put it into my belt pouch, ready to deliver to the High King.

Utor glanced at the Steward. "Thank you, Gustor. I will see to the princess now."

He bowed. If he desired to know more about the message that had come with Bruster's prodigal princess, and he assuredly did, he kept any hint from his face. *Everyone* had mastered that skill except me. "My lord."

"Wait." I drew out a second parchment roll. "Would you see this letter safely sent?"

Gustor took it. "Of course, lady."

"Who...?" Utor shook his head. "Later. Come." His hand touched my back, directing me towards the door. Turning to Hal, he asked in Valenian, "Will you join us, Master Carlson?"

"Thank you, my lord."

Utor caught my hand, tucking it against his arm, as if the hall was full and feasting, and he was escorting me to my place. One of his hands covered mine and squeezed gently. Again my eyes prickled. My fingers tightened on his arm, returning the small embrace, knowing what he meant as well as if he had spoken.

He led us across the hall to the spiral staircase. Bowing, he gestured for me to take the stairs first. I swung my bag around before me so it wouldn't bump against the walls.

Like the rest of the castle, the stairs were defense minded. They twisted tightly, curving left, providing a right-handed defender a wide space but impeding a right-handed attacker. The stairs themselves were uneven widths and heights, causing someone unfamiliar with them to stumble. But my feet had not forgotten these stones, and I moved steadily upward. I remembered tumbling down them more than once, though, skirt and braid cartwheeling, when haste overpowered judgment.

I passed the opening that led to the second floor and continued upward. The lowest two levels, the ground floor and one below, housed the kitchen, storerooms, the well, and the servants' quarters. The household's most important retainers, among them the Steward, occupied the second floor. The third floor was for the High King and his family. It had been a crowded, noisy, happy place before the deaths of our mother and newborn sister, both birth-mangled. The King's rooms, and the High King himself, had been quieter thereafter. But not wholly so. Four sons and a daughter remained to him. Few men, even among kings, could say as much.

I ducked as I stepped through the passage leading from the top of the staircase to the room beyond. A guard approached, drawing his sword.

"Easy, Ulf," Utor said as he came through, moving aside for Hal. "This is the princess Maudlin, and Master Hal Carlson of Ragonne."

Ulf dipped his head and moved back to his post.

We followed Utor into the first of the four rooms that had belonged to the royal children. It was the smallest, and my youngest brother Birnan had lived here. It looked as if he still did. At least, *someone* did. A tidy someone, like Birnan.

We walked through into the next room, which stood in a corner of the keep. This had been mine. It was unoccupied. And unchanged. The coverlet our mother had woven for me was on the bed. The raggedy, uneven tapestry I had embroidered when I still had my milk teeth hung on the wall. But Utor did not give me a moment to consider the strangeness of that, my room sitting unused in the crowded chaos of the Black Keep. He continued through the next passage, into the largest of the children's rooms.

It was also the warmest, containing the only hearth for the children's half of the third floor. Cedrick and Murrow had shared it. On cold nights, all of us ended up there, wrapped in our blankets before the fire. Here too, it seemed, my brothers resided where they had before I left.

Directly across from the hearth, two doors led into the next-largest room in the children's quarters. We had spent much of our waking time there when we were small, playing, eating, talking, and being taught around the large table. With the doors open, the hearth heated the inner room as well, and activities could spill over into the sleeping room. But the doors were closed now, and Utor led us past.

"The King asked Murrow and Cedrick if either of them would like to move..." Utor jerked his head towards the room that had been mine. "But they said this was a big room, they were used to sharing, and were just as happy to stay." He let his gaze slide to the hearth. "Personally I think neither of them wants to leave the warmth. Birnan must have ice in his guts. In January his room is so cold, water freezes in the basin."

"I remember," I said.

We followed him through the door on the far side, into a short passage that curved right then split. The leftward branch led to the second spiral staircase. Locating the stairwells in opposite corners was another strategy to make an attack difficult. The rightward passage led to what had been Utor's chamber, and, it seemed likely, still was. He went right, and we followed.

It was not a comfortable room. Warmth from the hearth barely wafted in. When we were old enough, Utor, Birnan, and I each had a brazier to burn peat, the smoke directed as much as might be out the small windows. In winter Utor's room *was* warmer than Birnan's, but only marginally.

One corner was taken up by the privy. In its own little room, of course, but it was the only privy in the children's quarters. To use it, we all had to traipse through Utor's room. If it were too cold to shiver down to Utor's room, or if one did not dare disturb him again, there was a chamberpot under each bed. More than water froze on January mornings in Birnan's room.

The cold, rather malodorous room might seem an odd

choice to house the Prince but I knew better. It was the safest place in the children's quarters. It also shared a wall with the King's bedchamber. There was no apparent door between them but I would have been very much surprised if a hidden one did not exist. The privy within the King's rooms used the same soil shaft, and I strongly suspected the castle's builders had designed the jakes to provide an escape route for the King and his heir in the last extreme.

"You can stow your bags here while we see the King," Utor said.

I shook my head. "I'd rather keep mine. There are items I should not allow out of my hands."

He looked hard at me, then at the bulging bag. "What *else* have you brought?"

"Precious, not dangerous," I said. "Books. Most are ones I borrowed from Vere to copy for the Roth's library."

"Very well. You, Master Carlson?"

Hal set his scrip beside a chair. "I have nothing irreplaceable."

"Anything you leave here will be safe," Utor said. "Would you like to wash before we see the King? There's fresh water in the bowl."

"I'm fine," I said.

"Maudlin..." He rubbed at his nose, his gaze dodging mine eloquently.

"Fine." Setting my bag well aside, I crossed to the basin. I washed my face and hands, and turned back to my brother. "Can we go?"

"But..." He touched my hair.

I stared at him for a long moment. Then I understood. The braid. I could not go before my father without our family's braid.

Utor's brown hair, a shade lighter than my own, hung halfway down his back, gathered in our distinctive braid, a mark of the High King and his family. That I'd forgotten, even among the worry and fluster I'd both found and brought, was a measure of how long I'd been away. I wrenched the leather tie from the end of my braid. What sort of Brusterian forgot her family mark? *No one can erase your blood*, Mistress Baynor had said. Except, perhaps, yourself. Reject, leave, deny—and you might, eventually, succeed. I pulled a deep breath, trying to calm my temper. Self-directed, but even so, it would not be wise to let it rage.

I found my comb and loosened my hair from the simple braid I normally wore. While I combed it through, Hal went to the basin. I separated my hair into nine strands along my forehead and temples, and began weaving them.

But the braid was intricate, and I fumbled the strands. I had not worn my family braid since leaving Bruster, and my fingers had forgotten the skill. I combed my hair and made the nine strands once more, but again it tangled in my hands.

"Here." Utor reached for the comb, hooking his toe around the leg of a stool. "Let me."

I sat. He began to draw the comb through my hair. For the third time that day I swallowed sudden tears. For I was seven again, and on the other side the wall, our mother was dying. No one had told me so. But then, like now, it was clear something was terribly wrong.

★★★

The screaming had finally stopped. I eased my hands away from my ears.

The shrieks were gone, but it was not quiet. Keening wails, interwoven with low sobs, swept through the castle like a rising wind.

I pushed myself further under the bed, the last few inches into the far corner, until I could not hear the sobbing and the wails were muffled. I clamped my hands over my ears again.

It *still* was not quiet. Only the most piercing howls made it through, but I heard my blood drumming and a rasp echoing between my ears and hands no matter how hard I pushed them together.

For two days, unceasing clamor—head-shattering screams, scurrying feet, deep-voiced bellows—had roiled the castle like a hurican. Even under the bed, palms flattened against my ears, I could hear it. Something was wrong. I didn't know what. But I hadn't seen our mother since the tumult began.

I must have fallen asleep at last. I stirred, and, finding my arms pillowing my head, I clapped them back over my ears, not yet noticing the silence. The room had darkened; night had come. The shadows under the bed were full black now, but I stayed where I was. I was not afraid of their darkness. I did fear what I would find beyond it.

Sometime later, the darkness beyond the bed lessened. I saw

feet, and a few inches of leg, in a pool of quivering light. After a moment, the light stopped flickering. Whoever it was must have set the candle down.

A knee appeared, then my oldest brother's face, right at the edge of the bed. Utor's braid spilled down and pooled on the floor beneath his ear. "There you are."

I heard, even through my cupped hands, the relief in his voice.

"I've been looking for you."

I tried to wriggle further back, but there was nowhere to go.

"It's okay—" He paused. "No. It's not okay. But it's over. Will you come out?"

I shook my head, arms waggling as my hands stayed over my ears, loosened just enough to hear his soft-spoken words.

The face left, but only for a moment as he shifted to lie on the floor, looking at me directly rather than sideways. "All right." He bit his lip. "Do you know what has happened?"

I shook my head again.

He sighed. "She is dead. And the babe."

I gave a jerky nod, blinking. The disaster I had dreaded, had heard howling like a hurican in the cries and chaos, and tried to hide from in the safest place I could find—under Utor's bed—it had come to me.

You are the High King's children. No one should read your thoughts from your face. Did the self-mastery they taught us—for me, with limited results—bind us even now? I looked closely at Utor. His face seemed calm. I saw no tears hanging in his eyelashes. But he was a big boy. Thirteen, and Prince. Surely more was expected of him.

I blinked faster, trying to keep the surging damp in my eyes. I had not thought I cried before, listening to the awful bustle, but my cheeks felt sticky and a little raw. I pressed my lips together, looking up to keep the tears from spilling, but without success. Drops teemed and ran down, spotting the stone floor.

"I'm sorry." He slid a hand under the bed to touch my arm but I twitched it away. His hand went up in a placating gesture and drew back.

"I'm sorry," he said again, but his tone had changed, and I knew he meant something else. "I shouldn't have left you alone. I should have thought about you. You're too little."

My chin came up.

He gave a small smile. "Yes, I know. You're a big girl. Only seven, and you can already write your letters, when Doctore Mustorn did not want to even begin teaching you until you were ten."

I watched as he blinked. "I was with Father...before, when we thought we were waiting for the babe...and then later, when we knew..." He sniffed. "Then...we were...waiting again." He paused. "But it wasn't...as long." He pulled a long breath. "The others are with Doctore Mustorn. I thought you were too."

I let my hands drop away from my ears but put them before me, fingers slightly bent, as if to ward him off should he reach for me again. But Utor remained on his belly on the floor, his forehead against the bedstead, and his hands stayed away.

I was surprised to see his sorrow twist suddenly into anger. "Mother should have agreed to have a nurse for you little ones. Father always says she can't watch you all the time. Remember when you fell down the stairs last year? We thought you'd cracked your head open. We thought you were dead."

He flinched as he heard his own words. His face turned away. I heard him sniff again.

I inched closer, stretching to touch the top of his head, my fingertips light in his hair.

His voice was wet. "Our mama is dead."

I scooted sideways and slid from under the bed. Utor sat up cross legged, flinging out his arms. I crawled into his lap, as I hadn't for years. He rocked us both. "I forgot you. I'm sorry. I won't again." His cheek was warm against my forehead. "Not ever."

After a while he moved me out of his lap and stood us both on our feet, still holding my hand. "Father wants us. He sent for all of us. That's how we realized you were missing."

I turned towards the door, but his hand stopped me.

"You can't go to Father like that. Your face is filthy, and your braid's loose."

I shrugged. I probably was a mess, but he couldn't look much better. A wispy cloud of hair, escaped from his braid, surrounded his head, but I was pretty sure that some of the gray mist hanging on one side was a cobweb, collected when he'd lain on the floor.

He caught a three-legged stool with his foot and dragged it

closer. "Sit."

I did. He went to the table by the privy door, where he'd left the candle, and poured water into the basin. Wetting a cloth, he handed it to me. "Shall I go first? I bet I'm a sight too."

I lifted the cloth tentatively to his cheek.

"Ow!" he yelped melodramatically.

Thus encouraged, I scrubbed harder.

"The dirt. Just the dirt. Leave the skin." His face contorted in exaggerated pain until I could not help but smile.

Finally he took the cloth, touching his nose as if to make sure it was still there, both shoulders sagging in seeming relief at finding it.

I giggled, then caught myself and waited in silence while he rinsed the cloth. Crouching beside me, he washed my face. Then putting the cloth aside, he handed me the comb, and settled on his knees, his back to me. "Do your worst."

Utor always braided his own hair. Despite myself, I was excited to have the chance to practice. Everyone in Bruster, man or woman, wore their hair long and braided; the noble families each had their own unique design. As the High King's family, ours was especially complicated—nine strands, beginning at the forehead and weaving in the rest of the hair as it moved back. Our mother, as she had promised, had begun teaching me when I turned seven, which meant I had been practicing for about four months, but only on myself and our mother.

I had to start over three times, and the result was unmistakably wobbly. Bits of hair were already staggering out in all directions. I thought he might do it over himself—it was a far sight from his own neat work. To be truthful, but for the combed-out cobwebs, it was not much of an improvement. But Utor merely tied a thin leather thong at the end. "Thank you."

He stood. "Your turn."

I looked up at him in sudden apprehension and awareness, and shook my head.

He waited, my comb in his hand.

My mama would not braid my hair today. She would not cut my bread at noon-tide, nor walk with me to the black sand shore after dinner, nor admire my care-cut letters in the wax tablet from my afternoon lessons. Utor had said it was over. But it was just beginning. A lifetime of losses, an absence every day.

He squeezed my shoulder. "I know."

He unraveled my braid. Slowly. It had been our mother's last touch upon me.

But our father was waiting. A moment later I felt the comb, drawn through from my scalp to my back.

His hands knew the braid well, and were quick. Before long the weight and warmth lifted as he tied the end. As it thumped back, I felt his hand brush the top of my head. "I'm not Mama. But I'll take care of you. Better than I did today."

I looked up at him, blinking against a new barrage against my eyelashes. "You promise? As Prince?"

If he noticed that it was the first time I had spoken, not just since he had found me but since the trouble began, he did not say so. "More. As the biggest brother."

I sniffed. This time, the drops did not come.

Huricans were uncommon. I had never seen one. But our mother had told us about them. The last hurican to strike Bruster in living memory had come to shore the night I was born. Our mother told us how the wind had whipped the sea like the cook beat eggs, and flung water at the castle like curtains, howling so loud that they knew the new baby cried only from my open mouth and crease-closed eyes. Our father would laugh when she told this tale, tugging my braid and saying it was a fitting entrance for his wild-willed girl. Our mother would push his hand away—playfully, but not merely so. Maybe, she would say. Maudlin can be unruly. But in the midst of every hurican, no matter how fearsome its winds and clamorous its rain, there is a pause, a time of still gray quiet. If she is a storm, the calm heart must be there too.

Maybe somewhere, our father would say. Or some time.

It was quiet. I heard nothing but my own breathing and, lower and slower, Utor's. The servants must have gone. People would return, as they must, in the morning, their voices and bodies filling the castle. But sunrise was a few hours away, and the High King was waiting.

I stood and threaded my fingers with his. "Let's go to Father."

***

Utor had declared me his personal charge. The newly-hired nursemaids were busy enough with our younger brothers. He probably thought he was easing my grief, and he was, but I could see now he'd been soothing his own as well. I became his shadow, and he taught me... everything. Knife throwing. Riding. How to fight someone larger. How to watch men's eyes to see if they spoke truth.

How to put our braid in my hair. Not an easy task. At seven, I could not even reliably comb out the tangles. He did that, his hands gentle, soothing. I cannot say truthfully that for a year or more, I put any substantive effort into learning. It was too much of a comfort to let him. Utor was the unbroken cord by which I finally found my way from darkness. It was almost as comforting to sit now, welcomed if perhaps not fully forgiven, and let him comb away snarls. But at last he handed me the comb and began to divide my hair.

Having finished his wash, Hal sat in the chair where he had left his scrip.

"Does Master Carlson bring a message from Ragonne?" Utor asked me softly in Brusterian.

"No, lord," Hal answered. *In the same language.*

Chapter IV

Utor's fingers stilled as both our heads swiveled.

Hal had spoken in Brusterian, with only the slightest Valenian accent tainting his words. Had *been* understanding and responding in Brusterian, I realized belatedly, since we entered the castle. How could he have spent nearly four months in my company and not mentioned knowing Brusterian?

I recalled profane outbursts, assuming no one who might hear could understand. Maybe Hal did not know *those* Brusterian words. I'd certainly had to search for them. He might, though. His accent was nearly perfect, and his diction lacked the typical awkwardness. It was a difficult language. The few outsiders who did master enough to converse sounded like half-witted Brusterian children with a split tongue.

I pressed my lips tight against questions that were not important at that moment. "You've kept that secret close."

He met my gaze unapologetically. "I have spent enough time around warriors to learn to never give up an advantage, however small."

Utor barked a laugh. "That's so." But he sobered quickly. "You truly have no message from King Philip?"

"Why?" I did not quite shriek but was no longer able to tolerate knowing something was amiss in Bruster but not what. "What is to hand?"

Utor pulled together the last strands of my braid. "The King of Ragonne means to invade Bruster."

"What?" I leapt from the stool, swinging around to face him.

"So it seems." His voice was calm. It had always been, no matter how I raged. "Ragonne approached the High King about buying boats. Many boats. Having his own men taught to control them. How to find their way through the sea. He offered a fortune but would not say why he wanted them. Naturally the High King refused. Now boats are missing from our port stops, and we have reliable information that Ragonne is gathering warriors and weapons." He spread his hands. "The under-kings have been called. We hold counsel tomorrow."

"Arrogant. Warmongering. Fool." I pressed the heels of both hands against my temples. Philip of Ragonne was a heedless idiot but Doctora Maudlin Bann was not far behind. I had known of Philip's intent to buy boats and sail east. I had known he would approach the High King. I had known my father would refuse unless he knew Philip's purpose. I had known Philip wouldn't say why he wanted boats. But since I knew where Philip's aggression was aimed, I hadn't considered how his actions would seem to Bruster. I let my utter disgust with myself forth in the vilest Brusterian I knew.

From Hal's raised eyebrows, he *did* know those words.

Even among allies, relations were often strained. Elbany and Bruster had the closest agreement, and that was dependent upon the good sense of the High King and the Roth. Little would be required, as was abundantly clear, to persuade Bruster that Ragonne, a supposed ally, would attempt conquest. Counsel had been called. My father needed to know about Saradena more urgently than I'd thought.

His task would be difficult: to persuade the under-kings, in whom suspicion and distrust ran as deep as their courage, that the letter and tidings brought by their long-absent princess were trustworthy. Or when the Saradenians arrived, they would find targets already weary and worn, easy prey for their warriors. All their targets. If Bruster and Ragonne warred, Logan and Elbany would not escape the conflict, although I could not say with certainty whose side they would step to.

I ran out of invective. Utor was quiet a moment. "Now I *know* you're home, Maudlin."

I glared at him, the distilled ire in a sidelong glance which younger siblings learn and never forget. "Ragonne is not invading. At least not Bruster."

"How do you know?" Bafflement, not suspicion, filled his voice.

I touched my belt pouch. "He's going against *them*."

At his look of utter confusion, I remembered I hadn't yet told him that more lands than Bruster had received a letter from Saradena. I began to explain but Utor held up a hand. "We should go to our King," he said. "Twice told is time lost, and I suspect we have little to spare."

★★★

The walk back to the entrance to the King's rooms seemed to take far longer than going to Utor's room had. Ulf nodded respectfully as he opened the door for us. The Prince and those he brought were not kept waiting—at least not by this High King, who trusted his Prince.

I had only a quick glance of him, sitting at his writing desk, before I, like Utor and Hal, bowed low before the High King of Bruster. It struck me again that my father should not have been surprised, and perhaps had not been, when I'd determined to study at Vere. He was the only literate king in the Three Lands. He could both read and figure, and had learned both fully, despite having received his instruction as a grown man. He had learned, and had his children taught, in defiance of the murmurings that such menial tasks were beneath the dignity of kings.

"Lord," said Utor, seeming to speak for us all, so I remained silent.

It was as well I hadn't tried to say anything. My father was before me in an instant. I didn't consider myself a small woman— I had loomed over the delicate court ladies of Ferrant—but for the second time that day I found myself pulled clean off my feet. "Maudlin. My girl."

I surged into his embrace. Yes, oh yes, I loved this man, my father. Despite all, I loved him. He had sent me to Ferrant, to Francis, whom I tried to love and whose hands I came to fear. But he treated me no differently than my brothers. We were all weapons in his store to defend Bruster. He loved us, no doubt, but he loved Bruster more. I could not say he was wrong. He was King.

When at last he set me down, still clasping my hands, and leaned back to look at me, I felt a twinge. The years had not sat as well upon him as on Utor. Still broad shouldered and lean waisted, he moved with the quickness and quiet of the warrior he'd always been, but his hair was more gray than brown now, and lines of care and weather had deepened in his cheeks.

"*Six years*, Maudlin." His voice was a touch deeper than Utor's, greeting me with the same remonstrance. He squeezed my hands once more and released them. "Should I worry more about why it has been so long or what has brought you back?"

I met his gaze. Utor was Prince, but our father was High King, and had been for many years. He had not supposed for a moment that I had returned, at this time and in this way, for no purpose but a homecoming.

"I bring news, my King," I said formally.

His brows rose slightly, acknowledgement of what he'd expected, not surprise. He did not return to his writing desk, but stepped to the high seat of his office, laying a hand on the carved arm nearest him. I could see the device of Bruster, a snarling *leoyong*, one paw outstretched to strike, inlayed on the back in the mountain's black stone, bright green stones for eyes. An identical chair, for the same purpose, stood in the hall beneath.

"Philip of Ragonne is a fool," I said.

The King's lips twitched. "That, alas, is not news." He paused. "But you never said so, and I certainly never agreed."

"Of course, lord," I said. "But he is not so great a fool as to think of attacking Bruster."

"Indeed." His face shuffled to the attentive, non-committal, concealing expression so needful to his duties, which I admired but could not emulate. "What makes you believe so?"

"Lord, I come most immediately from Vere but before that I was in Ragonne. I was there at the behest of the Roth." I gestured at Hal. A spark touched my father's eyes. He'd been wondering, apparently, when I would remember to introduce my companion. "This is Master Hal Carlson, a retainer of Philip's."

"Two names," my father said. "A Vere-trained clerk?"

"No," I said. "But he reads and writes like one."

"Interesting," he said.

"Lord," Hal said, bowing once more.

"Can you explain this puzzle? Two names like a scholar of Vere but not one?"

"I could, lord, but I won't." Hal bowed, softening his refusal.

My father smiled. "Later, perhaps. Ragonne, you say. Do you bring a message?"

"No, lord."

"Too bad. I regret this fight. I have enough other matters to concern me." His fingers tightened on the arm of the high chair. "But Philip will regret it *more*."

"He's not coming here, lord," I said.

He frowned minutely. "There can be no doubt Ragonne is

preparing for war. Philip gathers his forces. He's making armor and weapons. He tried to buy boats. When we refused, boats were stolen."

"He plans to sail and attack," I said. "But not Bruster." I took out the Saradenian letter. "You should have received this in May."

The King's gaze darted to Utor, as if wondering what the Prince already knew and thought, then went to the page his fingers had unrolled. His eyes swept the letter, eyebrows climbing, forgetting in the extremity of his surprise to keep his reactions from his face. His lips formed the unfamiliar name: *Saradena?*

"Maudlin," he said, very quietly, a moment later, "you are certain—*certain*—this is real?"

"Yes," I said. "I was in Elbany when the same letter came to the Roth. Logan and Ragonne received them also. Bruster's went to Vere."

"If this arrived months ago, why did Honre not sent it to me?"

"Vere has troubles of its own." I could not keep sorrow from my voice. "Pedagno Olwen is dead."

Both he and Utor gasped. Magistre Ulton had been successful in keeping that news from reaching Reud. I'd wondered.

"Magistre Poll is now Pedagno." A fresh wave of sadness crested and fell. "Probably not for much longer. His Clerk, Magistre Ulton, means to seize control. The Pedagno suspects him of poisoning his food and having a hand in Pedagno Olwen's death."

The High King lowered the letter. "You were in Vere. Is he correct?"

"I..." I paused to steady my words. "He is."

The shadows in his eyes deepened. "You were in Vere as well?" he asked Hal.

"Yes, lord."

"Does this charge seem credible to you?"

"Yes, lord," he said again. "The plot is subtle, and meant to go unnoticed, or at least unproved. But it is real."

The King rolled the letter and handed it to Utor, who set it on the writing table. "Wise High Kings hold their overlordship of Vere lightly." His face set. "But in this matter, there will be a reckoning. Keeping this letter from us endangered Bruster."

For one wild moment, I thought he meant he would send warriors to Vere. But that was not what he had said. "What will you do?"

"The Pedagno will know of my displeasure. Vere may quarrel among itself, but its struggles cannot be allowed to imperil Bruster."

"But, lord," I said. "Pedagno Poll is not at fault. Pedagno Olwen received the letter, in the midst of illness and strife, and died not long thereafter. Pedagno Poll found it among his predecessor's belongings—"

"Maudlin," he interrupted. I stiffened at the unmistakable reproach. "I am not unsympathetic to Pedagno Poll's situation. I know what it is to have enemies among underlings. But my foremost—nay, my *only* concern—is Bruster. And Bruster has been endangered by Vere's dereliction." His lips thinned, and a moment passed before he continued.

"It might be better if Magistre Ulton overthrew the Pedagno —" He raised a hand before I could speak. "If the new man proved more mindful of our defense. But—" His hand went higher, keeping me silent. "I do not wish it. A coup is dangerous. Rebellion spreads like pestilence. Like-minded others see, and water their hopes. But—" His voice rose as well, "my business with Vere will not be to bolster a Pedagno according to my preferences—or yours—but to rebuke, unmistakably and unforgettably, their error in not sending this letter the hour they received it."

"I was aware," I said, when I mastered myself enough to speak, "Reud would not meddle in Vere's concerns for any purposes but its own. But I had hoped, in this case, it might be otherwise."

"Maudlin..." My father's voice softened marginally. "Of course you are fond of the Pedagno, and wish to aid him. I like him myself. But I am High King."

"Lord..." Utor said.

The King turned, the end of his braid swinging out.

"The letter went to Vere. Not Reud. When they come, they will sail to Vere." Utor paused. "Or so it may be plausibly argued."

The King stroked his close-cropped beard, grayer yet than his hair. "Lastland's defenses must be strong."

"Much stronger than Vere alone can provide," Utor said.

"Vere cannot be expected to bear the sole burden of defense against such an enemy," the King said.

"Of course not," said Utor.

"Reud must send warriors," the King said.

"Alone, Lastland would surely fall," the Prince said.

"It may anyway," the King said.

"Many warriors," Utor said.

"And a prince," the King said, "to direct the preparations."

I looked between them, watching the idea form like a pot from clay beneath the hands of a master. "With the Pedagno."

Their heads turned, the light in both pairs of eyes one I recognized. Magistre Poll looked at me so when I mastered a lesson he considered basic, and been barely concealing his frustration I'd not done so more quickly.

"Just so," said Utor.

"After delivering our reproach in the sternest terms," the King said. "We will insinuate that after the Pedagno's failure to dispatch the letter to Reud immediately, Bruster does not trust his judgment in this matter, and we insist upon our prince remaining."

"Cedrick?" Utor asked.

The High King waved a hand. "We need not choose now."

The strategy was not unimpeachable. Magistre Ulton might act against Pedagno Poll before the King's party arrived. He might not feel as constrained as we hoped by a prince and his men. Magistre Ulton was determined and subtle. He would not be easily swayed from his path. But it was far more help than I'd dared hope might be forthcoming. "Thank you, lord."

My father took my hand. "I am glad your wishes and our need find common cause." He led me towards the chairs standing before the hearth, gesturing with his other hand for Utor and Hal to follow.

"Now," he said once we were seated. "Tell me what you've learned about this Saradena."

CHAPTER V

"Why should I know more than what can be gleaned from the letter itself?" I stretched my legs towards the fire, crossing them at the ankles.

Utor chuckled. "You told us you do, just now. Honestly, how can any Brusterian, let alone a noble, dissemble so badly? You say one thing but your body screams something else."

I scowled at him.

"Children," my father said, amusement and rebuke in his voice. He eyed me. "Come now. Why else would the Roth send you to Ragonne after the letter came, if not that he believed you might gather information there about it?"

Hal smiled at this, earning him a narrow-eyed stare from me. "I knew you reminded me of my brothers." I would tell my father what I knew. I knew this. But I hesitated. I felt like all I had done since I had made my vow to the Roth to keep secret the Saradenian threat was to break that vow. Always for good reason. Most likely, the Roth would approve. We faced an unknown threat. It might be that our old ways of doing things were not sufficient to address it. But in our lands, vows were meant to be kept, and the reasons you might have to do so did not matter. It stuck in my throat to break it again, although I knew that the Roth would have agreed to give the High King this information, had he known Bruster shared the Saradenian threat. But he did not, not yet.

"Maudlin," my father said.

I looked around the room. The King's room, if not the King himself, remained as I remembered. On the wall behind the high seat were three cupboards, walnut like the high seat, each door carved with a rampant *leoyong*. Concealed somewhere within them was the entrance to the King's sleeping chamber. I had only the vaguest memories of that room, having been in it seldom and only as a child. I could not recall having seen how the hidden door opened. And well hidden it was, given the number of times

I'd crept into the chamber to search for it. Perhaps the Black Keep with all its cleverness really had been built by Ator.

Part of that cleverness was that the room's most striking characteristic was understated beauty. As in the rest of the Black Keep, defense was primary, but here attention was not drawn to it. Here alone the builders had conceded tasteful wealth was as important to have at a king's side as thick walls and sharp knives. The carved stone mantle was as large as those in the hall below, and as many tapestries hung here. In the hall, the High King held court. Here he held counsel with his under-kings. More often, the greater danger lay here.

"You guess rightly, lord," I said. And I told him. Oliver. Sera Serdent. Old Valenian. Martin de Kolon. Carlomond. Charles Henry. Bloodweed. Ferrant.

When I finished, Utor looked at me with undisguised pity in his eyes. "Must you? Go back?"

Our father cast him a hard glance. "Don't be foolish." He leaned towards me. "Francis kept those books from you for no purpose but enjoyment of the pain it caused. To return, and read them..." He spread his hands as he sat back. "Not all vengeance need be bloody."

I swallowed hard. "Thank you, lord." Would it help, to think of returning in those terms? Perhaps.

"What will you tell Francis to gain access to the books?" Utor said. "Surely the Roth will not tell him about the letter."

"The library," Hal said. "He could offer to pay to copy books for his collection."

"That might—" I said.

"Bruster. Elbany. Logan. Ragonne." The High King's fore-finger tapped the arm of his chair as he spoke.

"Us, and our allies," Utor said.

"There's some reason for that," my father said. "As you search, watch for it. If we can determine why *we* were targeted, it might tell us how to avert it."

"Perhaps other Valenian kingdoms received them," Hal said, "and are keeping the threat to themselves."

"Perhaps," the King said, giving him an appraising look. "But I would guess not. There are sixteen kingdoms of Valenna. If fourteen more had received these letters...I think word would have begun to seep out."

"Our allies do not know Bruster also lies under this threat," Utor said.

"Messengers will be sent tomorrow," the High King said, sharing a look with his son. "I will write the letter to Ragonne myself."

"To Logan and Ragonne," I said. "I can take word to the Roth."

My father looked at me, distress shading his face for the first time. "To all three. Surely you will give us a few days before you leave again?"

I sat silent, arrested. To bring him such tidings—Saradena's animosity, its very existence, the trouble at Vere—and see his most uncontrolled response at the idea of my quick departure. I dipped my head, unable to speak.

"Just a few days," he said. "More would be unwise. You must return to your search."

Silence took the room. At last the King stood, and we followed. "Maudlin," he took my hand once more, "I may not do as I wish, or you and I would sit here hours longer."

I covered his hand with my other. "Of course, lord."

"The under-kings are coming. They may already have arrived. There will be a welcoming feast tonight, and tomorrow we hold counsel." A wry smile touched his lips. "Our discussion will be rather different than we thought."

"Will they believe me?" I asked.

"They need not believe you. They must obey *me*." His hand squeezed mine. "And there is the letter." He looked at Utor. "I must meet with the princes." His gaze returned to me. "You will come tonight?"

I nodded, dreading the public display but knowing I could not do otherwise. My presence would be known, and to stay away would be seen as an insult.

His gaze moved to Hal. "I expect you as well, Master Carlson."

He bowed. "Yours to command, lord."

The King embraced me, less tightly than before, but longer, as if reluctant to let go. At last his arms loosened. One hand touched my hair as he moved away. "I am glad to see you—and our braid in your hair."

★★★

Hal and I returned to the children's quarters to await the evening. Clean clothes and fresh water were waiting in Utor's room. For me, a fine wool dress of Brusterian black, *leoyongs* embroidered in gold at the hem and cuffs. My own, left when I departed for Vere. For Hal, the second best shirt and trousers of one of my brothers. Cedrick, if I had to guess. Hal waited outside while I changed and washed, careful not to disrupt the family braid, then I left so Hal could have his turn.

When I returned, I found he'd made himself ready, then stretched out on Utor's bed and gone to sleep. A warrior's habit, the discipline and ability to sleep when the opportunity arose. I wondered how he had acquired it. I did not grudge him the rest. He had had long nights, studying the charters. But watching someone else sleep is tediousness itself. I paced from room to room for a while, but it was irksome checking my stride to stoop through doorways, so I settled into walking the perimeter of the largest room. I felt strange and somewhat caged. The bag of books, which I'd carried so long, was not with me. I could not, of course, bring it to the feast. Before we'd left the King's Room, I had reluctantly agreed to leave them locked in the cupboard where the King kept his own books.

But this enforced change was not the sole cause of the unease I was trying to walk out. The King consulted his princes on a matter of dire importance, and I was not there. I felt a growing ache in my jaw from clenched teeth and called myself a fool. I'd left Bruster, had removed myself from its concerns without so much as a letter in six years. It was more than foolish; it was arrogant to be annoyed at my exclusion. But recognizing the absurdity did not remove the sting.

I went to my room and threw my knives at the door until my arm ached, as I'd done as a child. The gouges were still there, and soon fresh nicks joined the old. I pulled out the whetstone I wore on a cord around my neck and honed their edges before I returned them to their sheaths, remembering the time Utor and I were practicing together here and he nearly skewered Murrow, who should have realized what the thuds on the other side of the door meant. He had demonstrated his own training in a quick dodge when he opened the door. The unchecked knife had struck the back of a chair in Cedrick and Murrow's room. None of us ever confessed the source of the gouge, although our father had asked.

A knock sounded. "Enter," I called. A boy's head poked in. A fosterling in the household, most likely. "Lady, it is time to come down. I've woken your companion."

I brushed unseen dust from my skirt and followed him.

***

The Steward managed entrances and seating for formal occasions, and my sudden appearance was apparently a source of consternation to him. Since my disgrace, I could not be seated at the King's table but that would not be overt in this instance. Because of the Counsel, none of the under-kings' consorts or children would be there. He determined to seat me, and Hal, as my guest, with them and the princes, but bring us into the hall first to avoid insulting the under-kings, who would certainly hold their lawful consorts higher status than a cast-off princess.

A different, older fosterling escorted us into the hall when Gustor announced us. We were seated along the inner length of the side table at the dais' right hand, physical placement mirroring our processional one. Noble, but not as high as the consorts.

For a moment, there was a pause in which silence hung in the hall like mist, then a horn sounded, announcing the entrance of the queen consorts. A rustling followed as those already seated rose. Tradition, which prevented many quarrels in Bruster, dictated the queen consorts, then the under-kings, would enter the hall in order of the size of their islands. The king of Bruster, the largest of the clustered islands, who was by the same ancient understanding High King of all Bruster—a tradition not always honored—came into the hall last, in the position of greatest honor.

"Lady Wealdin, Queen Consort of Solud." I heard Gustor's announcement before I could catch a glimpse of the lady. But at last she came into view, escorted as we had been by one of the High King's fosterlings, but of a commensurately higher rank. He brought her to her place directly across the table from us, and she dismissed him with a gracious nod. She smiled pleasantly enough in greeting to me and looked at Hal with curiosity, which a moment later she remembered to conceal.

I'd met all of the queen consorts but had not seen any of them since before my marriage. Lady Wealdin was Elbish by birth, the sister of Lord Garland, who was Lady Elsbeth's father. If I'd not known they were relations, I could have guessed it. Gray had begun to touch Lady Wealdin's chestnut hair but the color itself was the same as Lady's Elsbeth's, the shape of their faces identical. Unusual among the nobility, Lady Wealdin was of an age with her husband. She seemed now past child-bearing but I remembered Solud had been provided with enough princes. Four, unless any had died during my absence.

"Lady Yvein, Queen Consort of Verun." The Steward's voice, rich and sonorous, flooded the hall once more. I pressed my lips together to keep from smiling. For a man, like his father, who spoke as little as possible, he did not lack ability.

Lady Yvein's ritually higher status was reflected in her place- ment at the table. She was brought to the second best seat, the honor of the dais end of the table but the lesser of the two end positions. To see the entertainment that would take place before the dais in the space between the side tables, she would have to turn in her chair. She would already have known her position and the traditional order that dictated it, but her face conveyed nothing but disdain. She was either as unskilled at a noble's impassivity as I was, or she simply did not bother to hide her scorn.

She dismissed her escort with a toss of her head, sending her braid, plaited in the fashion of the Verune royal family, arcing out. I was not sorry there was an empty seat between us, although I felt a moment of pity for whichever of my brothers was slated to sit in it. Murrow, unless Gustor knew something that I didn't about the precedence traditions.

"Lady Lida, Queen Consort of Eban."

This was not the name I expected, nor one I knew. King Petrus' wife must have died. I'd not heard this news, did not know whether it had occurred during my time at Vere, when the isolation of study had kept me ignorant of many happenings, or while I was in Elbany, when I could have chosen to inquire about Bruster but had not. I did recall hearing when I returned from Ferrant that King Petrus' only son had died. Had his remarriage yet provided him the partial consolation of an heir?

The new queen consort was escorted to the open seat at the top of the table. She nodded to Lady Yvein, directly across from her, and appeared unruffled by the slight dip of the head she received in return. It was nearly discourteous, and I wondered again at Lady Yvein's behavior.

Lady Lida turned to greet Lady Wealdin. My attention moved back to Lady Lida. She was young, perhaps as much as a decade younger than I, which would make her twenty years younger than her husband, but that was not uncommon among the nobles, particularly kings. If she were Brusterian, she was unusual, with her sunshine hair and pale blue eyes. More likely she was Valenian. She turned her head, catching my gaze, and nodded a greeting, which I returned with deliberately better grace than Lady Yvein. The new queen consort of Eban was lovely, I decided, but there was wit and comprehension there that cautioned against assuming she had been chosen for her decorative value alone.

There was a pause again, longer now. The trumpet sounded, more elaborately. The kings were coming.

CHAPTER VI

The under-kings came first, in the same order of precedence as their queen consorts, escorted by the High King's younger princes rather than fosterlings.

"King Otho of Solud," Gustor called.

The under-king stepped into the hall, escorted by a prince radiating such solemnity I was stunned to recognize, after a heartbeat, my brother Cedrick. He was usually...

I caught myself. *Had been*. My knowledge of my brothers was six years old. More honestly, twelve. I'd remained in Bruster only a few months after returning from Ferrant, and could hardly be said to have given them any thoughtful consideration during that time. Utor had not changed greatly but he'd been twenty-one, his ways and mind more fully grown than the younger princes. I was seventeen when I became Francis' bride. Now twenty nine, I scarcely resembled the princess who'd sailed from Reud. Cedrick's mischievousness might well have given way to adulthood, or at least been tempered by it.

"King Verun of Verun." Gustor's voice turned my attention once more to the hall. King Verun walked beside the High King's second son. Murrow bowed low to the under-king as he left him at his place on the dais, but like his wife, King Verun seemed to feel the honor accorded him was insufficient, and returned a slight nod. Murrow joined Cedrick, standing by the wall; after the kings were seated, the princes would be dismissed to their own places.

I tried not to stare, but the resemblance between King Verun and Magistre Ulton was arresting, as striking in its variation as its similarity. Both men bore the features of Verune nobility I'd noted in Magistre Ulton, but if they had been standing before me as strangers, I would have taken Magistre Ulton for the king and King Verun for the clerk. King Verun seemed dull compared to his cousin's keen-edged ambition.

Gustor announced King Petrus of Eban, whose traditional

position gave him the honor of being accompanied by the Prince. Utor bowed lower even than Murrow had. I recalled Utor had spent some of his fosterling time in Eban. The extra homage told me, and the hall, that he liked and respected King Petrus.

Instead of joining our brothers, Utor continued down the dais to stand before his own seat. The High King's place was in the center of the table, with Eban to his right and Verun to his left. Beside Eban was Solud, and to Verun's left, the Prince. Only the High King had the right of having his heir on the dais. I suspected this particular tradition had emerged simply to balance the table. But there was undeniable advantage in having the Prince on display, particularly when he was as obviously com-pe-tent as Utor for the role destined for him.

Quiet filled the room as Gustor waited, letting anticipation mount before signaling the horns, a sustained call that might as easily have been followed by the cries of warriors plunging towards their enemies as the step of the High King into his hall. All heads turned to the doorway, and bowed. Despite the mass of people, the hall was so still I could hear the sound of the High King's footfalls.

The High King came escorted by no man. His backguard, my youngest brother Birnan, followed at the customary distance. It was the High King's right that he went nowhere in public, not even within his own keep, without a sword of unquestionable loyalty at his back. In their own courts, the under-kings could decide whether to keep a man at their backs, demonstrating their importance and their caution, or dismiss him, showing their confidence in the security of their household. In the Black Keep, only the High King merited a backguard.

Birnan joined Murrow and Cedrick. The High King stepped onto the dais. He stood for a long moment behind the high table in his place, looking out and through the hall, seeing, I knew, who met his gaze, who glanced away, who seemed discomfited by his consideration.

My breath caught as I watched him. I could not have said how many years it had been since I'd seen him in the formal attire of the High King. I had forgotten how well it sat upon him. The snowy white linen shirt, embellished with gold and green braiding, belted over brown linen breeches. Noble, but not osten-tatious. Dark cloth was ten times as dear as undyed. The white shirt was yet more difficult and costly. The fabric had to be washed and laid out to bleach in the sun a dozen times. Only the most royal wore true white. His cloak was as black as his boots, clasped at the right shoulder. He was too far away for me to see it, but I knew the ancient bone pin that held his cloak, its triangular base carved with an image of the clustered islands, a small black-and-gray speckled stone, surely a fragment of the black mountain, inlayed in the place of the Keep.

Francis' raiment had been far costlier, gold thread used in much more than his braiding. Philip of Ragonne, too, boasted regalia as fine as his *palais*. The High King appeared in court as his father had, and further back. Well-cut garments of the finest cloth. But the elegant braiding at his cuffs and collar was the only showy part of his attire. The bone pin was brazenly modest; any farmer in his thatched hut could whittle a pin of bone. It bore a similarly common decoration. Not a costly Valenian gem, but a bit of the black mountain such as anyone might pick up from the shore. The court apparel of the High King bespoke age and tradition, and a lineage so secure in its authority that it need not flash the new fashion. It showed the difference between real power and mere wealth.

The King stood for a moment longer behind the high table, then with deliberate and slow dignity, sat.

***

Rustling filled the hall as the under-kings, then Utor, and finally those at the side tables, took their seats. Murrow came to the empty chair on my right.

"Maudlin!" His lips barely moved. Another of the noble's skills I'd never mastered. "We are glad you're home. Even so," by which, I knew, he meant the Saradenian letter.

Cedrick grinned like a lantern flash as he sat across from me. He had not lost his impishness, then, but had learned to conceal it. "Poor Birnan," he whispered in mock sympathy. "We get you, and he has to stand behind the King, watching Utor try to remember not to wipe his knife on the tablecloth."

Murrow squeezed my hand. Then he turned, his posture, the hold of his head, even the light in his eyes becoming guarded. "Ladies," he bowed his head to the queen consorts, "may I present my sister, Doctora Maudlin Bann, princess of Bruster, Vere-trained scholar, and clerk to the Roth of Elbany?"

Two heads dipped in polite greeting and one in a cursory nod, but I gave each a proper response. "Her companion," Murrow continued. "Master Hal Carlson of Ragonne."

Hal's bow went unnoticed. Three pairs of feminine eyes stayed, appraisingly, on me. Even for Lady Wealdin and Lady Yvein, who'd met me before, I surely was an object of interest. Before, I'd been the High King's daughter. Now I was his cast-off, barren, willful, long-absent daughter, returned but perhaps not fully received. All three must be wondering how my presence might affect the next day's counsel.

Lady Lida's gaze moved to Hal. I was right; there was calcula-tion within that beauty. *She thinks Hal brought a message and I accompany* him, *to cloak his doings and ease his access to the High King.*

Murrow interrupted further scrutiny. "You remember prince Cedrick," he said. "Especially you, Lady Wealdin, from his foster-ling years."

She smiled. "Certainly. Although he could not look over my head then."

"A tribute to the excellence of your household," Cedrick said. He returned her smile with his roguish grin, seeming years younger. "I'm nearly as tall as Utor."

Lady Wealdin let noble impassivity slip enough to laugh. "You may catch him yet."

He looked doubtful. She smothered a second laugh. His mouth opened, but his face froze as he realized he had let formality slip further than he ought in open court. He must have liked Lady Wealdin very much. Perhaps that was not surprising. Cedrick's fostering had begun early, only a year after our mother's death, and I had heard that Lady Wealdin had taken special care of the bereaved prince. Such connections were crucial if Bruster were to ever calm the crackling suspicion among its lords, a primary reason the High King had introduced the Elbish custom of fostering.

"Prince Utor is a fine heir," Lady Lida said, smoothing over Cedrick's embarrassment. "I am sure my lord of Eban hopes our son will prove as well."

So she had already given Petrus an heir. I wondered how old the child was.

"Height is no true measure of a man's stature," Lady Yvein

said.

Lady Wealdin's brow furrowed, clearly forgetting to conceal her thoughts in her astonishment at Lady Yvein's rude misapprehension.

"Certainly not." Lady Lida's composure remained unruffled. "The Prince has many merits."

Lady Yvein sniffed, but further response was forestalled by the first course.

"Did you speak to the cook, Cedrick?" Lady Wealdin spooned herself a portion. The dishes, like all else about the evening, honored the gathered rulers. The first was Soludin roasted fish. "I remember how much you liked this dish."

"The Steward did ask the princes' thoughts on the courses." Cedrick tasted the fish. "Kimbur did very well. But it is not quite the same."

Lady Wealdin took another bite. "No, indeed," she protested. "It is just as it should be."

Cedrick said Lady Wealdin was kind to say so but he was certain the fish was not as he recalled. As Lady Wealdin restated her conviction that the Soludin dish had been reproduced exactly, I turned my attention to Lady Yvein, intrigued by her undisguised disdain. Was she unable to conceal her thoughts, like me? If she could cloak her reactions, why didn't she? As I watched, she took one bite of the Soludin fish, then her mouth twisted and she laid down her knife and spoon. Not wanting to attract her notice, I moved my gaze to Lady Lida.

"My lord," Lady Lida said to Murrow, "you fostered in Elbany?"

"Yes, lady," he answered. "In the court of Lord Garland."

The father of Lady Elsbeth. My brother might have met her there, and perhaps the Roth himself when he was Douglas of Elbs and his marriage to Lord Garland's daughter was being arranged. It was strange to think of Murrow with my Elbish patrons. The Roth and Lady Elsbeth might know more of me than I'd hoped, coming to Elbany to begin anew.

Which was patently ludicrous. Of course they already knew all about me. The tangled web of relations among nations and nobles suddenly seemed a smothering weight, and I wished to be back in my Elbish library, teaching my copyists—no, the quill in my own hand, the exemplar text before me, inscribing old lines into a new book, the task both mindless and engaging, and sweet immersion in words.

"Did Lord Garland have Ragoni roses in his garden?" Lady Lida asked. "Mine are not thriving. If you saw them cared for, you might be able to advise me."

"Alas. I spent little time in the gardens, lady. Lord Garland's fostering focused upon weapon skills." Murrow let a smile flash. "I may still have bruises."

She returned his smile but amusement did not show in her eyes. Her attention slid to Hal. "Perhaps Master Carlson would have a suggestion."

Hal turned. "I'm sorry, lady, did you speak to me? Lady Wealdin was telling me about Soludin fishes, one of which becomes this excellent dish."

She repeated her question. She could now inspect him as he explained that while like Murrow, he spent few hours in his lord's garden, he had been in Ragonne for several years and had learned one or two things about their roses. She nodded encouragingly as he described Ragoni plants' preference for the longer Valenian days. Since she was seated at the end of the table nearest the dais while Hal was at my left, their voices were raised, but not so loudly as might be supposed. All other speech among us ceased. The other queen consorts also welcomed a chance to consider the Ragoni visitor.

"Is Ragonne really much warmer?" Lady Yvein's gaze flicked between Hal and Lady Lida. "Most of Valenna is, I know, but Ragonne is not far from Bruster."

"The mountains keep Bruster and Elbany cool, lady," Hal said.

"Elbany's northern mountains," Murrow said, "are as high as Bruster's." He paused. "Crossing outside the Conlo pass is...challenging."

"Impossible, most would say," Lady Wealdin said.

"I would not say they are wrong," Murrow said.

I wondered about Murrow's fostering, that he knew something of the terrors of Elbany's northern mountains. Even the Conlo pass was neither easy nor quick, I'd learned on my journey to Ragonne.

I'd not traveled the land route between Elbany and Ragonne before my journey with Orlo. The mud and chill of May, the river high and swift, its roar echoing among the surrounding mountains. The horses of Orlo and his men had clearly trodden the narrow trail that crawled between water and rock before. But the mount I'd been given obviously had not. I'd patted the skittish mare, crooning words instantly lost in the water's rush. As the horse's distress worsened, I decided I'd have to lead her. But the path was barely wider than the horse. If I dismounted I could easily be knocked into the river. Both the horse and I might fall in if her frightened dancing continued. As I appraised the inches between hooves and river, Orlo glanced over his shoulder.

Grasping the problem in an instant, he clicked his tongue and slipped his reins over his horse's head. When his man turned, not so deafened by the water's roar he did not hear his master's summons, Orlo tossed him the reins. Freeing his feet from his stirrups, he pushed himself back and off the saddle, patting his horse's rump as he slid over its tail. A warrior's horse, to tolerate such a strange and uncomfortable dismount, I thought, busy as I was with my own. Meeting my mare's eyes and speaking words I could not hear, Orlo eased his hands up to her bridle.

I was irked at the need for his assistance but before that slow walk ended, I was grateful for it. I doubted I could have guided the nervous mare alone. Once through, he begged pardon for not ensuring I'd been given an experienced horse. I told him I regretted not realizing the mare was in trouble sooner. The path widened as it sloped towards Ragonne. He rode beside me, talking of the challenge the mountains had been to Otto. Intrigued, I forgot his behavior in Rothbury for a time and spoke with him. Later, those moments confused me when I thought of them, before his letter had come. The glint in his black eyes had not felt like derision.

CHAPTER VII

Remembered black fire in Orlo's eyes and the road to Ragonne faded.

"I visited Rothbury once with Lord Garland," Murrow was saying. "But Maudlin would know better."

Lady Wealdin turned to me, smoothing her skirt. "Are the Roth and Lady Elsbeth well?"

"Very well."

She opened her mouth again.

"No children yet," I said. "Nor none expected, when I left."

"That was my question, I confess. I will hazard another." She covered one hand with the other. "It has been many years since I was in Elbany. I wondered—"

"Left? For Ragonne?" Lady Yvein interrupted. "What had Elbany's 'librarian' to do in Ragonne?"

Outrage at her tone was shouldered aside by astonishment not just at her rudeness but also that she knew I had been in Ragonne. I saw consternation shimmer on my brothers' faces for an instant before it was wiped away.

"Perhaps Ragonne moves with aid against Bruster," Lady Yvein said.

Lady Wealdin's composure crumbled. Face flushed, she seemed silent only because she had not yet found words dire enough to respond to Lady Yvein's insinuation that Elbany would join forces with Ragonne against Bruster. Then she caught herself. Watching her breathe deep, struggling for control, I found my irritation manageable, even as I was troubled by Lady Yvein's provocations.

"What had Elbany's librarian to do in Ragonne?" I repeated. "Books, of course. King Philip's clerk found some. I was sent to decide whether to copy any."

"King Philip has books?" Murrow said, helping steer the conversation to a safer path.

"I would not have supposed Philip of Ragonne interested in

books," Lady Wealdin said. Her voice quavered, indignation not quite suppressed.

"He may not be," Lady Lida said. "But Elbany will have a library, so most likely King Philip feels he must also."

There were definitely wits in Lady Lida as well as beauty, I thought.

"Did you find what you sought?" Lady Wealdin asked. Her face smoothed until it showed only earned lines of age, but she grasped the edge of the table one-handed, as if steadying herself.

I clamped my own hands together in my lap to keep them still as I studied her. *Did you find what you sought?* Not *Did you find books to copy?* Did Lady Wealdin suspect I sought something else? Or was I so taut with suspicion I saw meaning where none lay?

She blinked, and I let that break my scrutiny. Probably Lady Wealdin, like the rest of us, was grasping for topics that did not invite Lady Yvein's scorn. "Not in Ragonne," I said. "But I went next to Vere, where I borrowed several volumes."

"You return soon to Elbany?" Lady Lida asked.

"Yes," I said. "The Roth is anxious for his library to begin in earnest." My shoulder was jostled by a servant, slipping between myself and Murrow to set down the second course. I frowned, surprised Gustor would allow such a clumsy man to serve at court. Perhaps he was nervous, the fault uncommon. But he had not even asked pardon. I would speak to Gustor about him later.

"I have heard Ferrant has nearly as many books as Vere. More, some say." Lady Yvein's voice came clear and cold down the table. "Is that so, Doctora Bann?"

I wondered again how Lady Yvein knew such a thing. My consternation must have been evident. Her smile broadened.

Francis meant to keep Ferrant's collection secret, like so many kings before him. But Francis had forfeited my loyalty. "Ferrant does own books," I allowed. "But not more than Vere."

"If the Roth seeks books to copy, surely he will send you... *back*...to Ferrant?"

At least this jab was unmistakable, prodding a known bruise, perhaps for no other purpose than to see the wince. Perhaps. "He may."

"Why?" Lady Wealdin asked. "Surely you read them already. Send a message, if there are books suitable, asking to borrow them."

The question seemed honestly asked. I ate shame and answered it. "I have not. The King of Ferrant would not allow it."

Lady Yvein's smile returned.

"Ah." Lady Wealdin's impassivity wavered enough for me to see her real sympathy.

"King Petrus," Lady Lida began, glancing towards where her husband sat at the high table and the kings ate around a conversation clearly as stilted as ours, "has agreed to consider having our son instructed in letters."

Which suggested, I thought, that Lady Lida had urged it.

"Clerks' work," Lady Yvein said.

"It can be hard to let go of the...old...ways," Lady Lida said.

Lady Yvein's lip curled at the insinuation about her age. Point to Petrus' new queen, I thought. Lady Lida continued as if she had seen nothing amiss. "The High King finds merit in letters."

Lady Yvein's let her gaze slide to me in unmistakable contempt for the result of the King's experiment.

Murrow's hand squeezed mine under the table. "Have you tried the Verune soup?"

Watching my hand as if it would not move otherwise, I tasted the soup. I was surely hungry, although I did not feel it. I'd not eaten since Vere. But the Verune dish did not stoke my appetite. It was too salty for any but an acclimated tongue.

Lady Wealdin took her turn at conversational shepherding. Noting the hall's tapestries, she asked Lady Lida if she had made any. Lady Lida responded she was still weighing a subject. Lady Wealdin engaged the topic with enthusiasm, leaning slightly towards the other woman as she spoke. Then she nodded at me. "Are any of these tapestries your mother's?"

"Not the one of Ator," I said. "But those above the other hearth are."

"They're very well done," Lady Wealdin said. "Whom do they portray?"

"On the left is Magistre Feun. The other is High King Bluditor."

"Fitting men to grace the company of Ator." Lady Lida brushed a golden curl, escaped from her braid, back from her temple.

"Legends and quill minders," Lady Yvein sneered. "Have we

no real heroes?"

Murrow and Cedrick shared a glance, concern hovering below their trained impassivity like a fish in a pool.

"After Cynan Maccus, the founder of Vere, Magistre Feun was the most famous scholar to ever live," Lady Lida said.

Lady Yvein considered her nails. "A man wields a sword."

"Ator and Bluditor were warriors, lady," Murrow said.

"Stories. Fables." Lady Yvein bit the words like a crisp pickle.

"Mayhap they were real before they were stories, lady," Cedrick said.

"Ator is *said* to have conquered the known world. Bluditor is *supposed* to have died fighting an overwhelming invading force." Yvein twitched her shoulder dismissively, sending the end of her braid arcing out. "If such men lived and such deeds were done, why do we not know more of them?"

"Perhaps we would," my words leapt out unchecked, "if more nobles valued letters."

Her eyes narrowed. She could not have been more than half a dozen years older than Lady Lida, but the scornful lines at the corners of her mouth and eyes aged her. "Perhaps," her voice was smooth and cold as chilled wine, "we create kings of legend because our real ones are so uninspiring." She raised her goblet, shooting a glance towards the dais. "Bruster's High King should be the best ruler, not simply whoever is king of the largest island." She sipped her wine.

Murrow's hand was at his side, fingers on the hilt of his sword, his control not frayed enough to grasp it. Cedrick shot him a look half warning, half annoyance. "We are fortunate our High King is both."

Lady Yvein's eyebrows rose, slowly. Murrow's hand closed around the hilt.

"Our traditions prevent unnecessary bloodshed." Cedrick gave Murrow another quelling look.

"But surely you agree." Lady Lida smiled firmly at Murrow, as if demanding his return to court propriety. "King Bluditor probably *is* legend. After all," she laughed, the sound taut in the strained air, "his attackers were said to have come from beyond the Three Lands."

Lady Yvein's triumphant gaze remained upon Murrow for half a dozen heartbeats, then flicked to Lady Lida, speculation sparking in her eyes before impassivity returned. The queen consort of Verun was most likely wondering whether the queen consort of Eban was trying to calm nerves or was more sympathetic to her discontent than she had supposed.

With a deliberate movement, Murrow set his hand on the table, palm up. "Perhaps you are right, lady."

Lady Lida steered the talk back to safer ground, asking Lady Wealdin for suggestions of tapestry subjects. Her blonde head inclined as she listened to the older woman.

I heard this exchange distantly. My ears throbbed, as if Lady Lida's words had struck as fiercely in body as in thought.

Bluditor. I hadn't heard Bluditor's tale for years, not since before I left for Ferrant. The story hurtled back. I was seven—no, eight, and it was the first court held after my mother's death. I remembered the singer. Not my father's *filun.* Petrus', accompanying his lord to court. The conquerors had come, no one knew whence. The kingdoms of Valenna fell. Elbs, Gwynt, and Garland fell. Bruster, led by High King Bluditor, held out nearly two years —and fell. Attacks from an unknown land...of course it had seemed merely a tale. But if the tale were true...if that force had been Saradena...did that help us?

The High King's *filun,* carrying a stool as well as his harp, walked into the space between the tables. He bowed to the side tables, then to the high table, graceful despite his burdens. At the High King's gesture, he put down his stool and sat. Once settled, he played first, as was usual, a Reudian battle tune. Then he sang of High King Benult, who had joined Edward of Roth to oppose Otto Tyrannus. I let out my breath slowly. I knew this song— every Brusterian did. I was grateful for the time to consider, uninterrupted.

We already knew contact must have occurred before. But if Bluditor's enemy had been Saradena...if that previous contact had been unequal, not trade but conquest, Saradena's imperiousness was less strange. They commanded, because they had commanded before. Perhaps to them, the conquest had never ended. Perhaps Saradena considered itself our overlord, despite their long absence. Horrible speculation. But mere speculation. Perhaps I guessed rightly, but there was no way to know. Nor was I certain it was helpful even if it were true. Still, I resolved to watch for information about Bluditor as I continued to search. We yet knew so little, it was difficult to say what might prove useful.

The harper finished, tossing a final flurry of tune from his strings, the triumphant sound at odds with my thoughts. The last sounds had not died away before Cedrick had his mouth open, surely to lead the talk down a benign route, but Lady Yvein spoke first.

"He sang always ahead of his harp. This is the best Reud can offer?" Her hand made a dismissive flip. "At least the song was about a *real* king." Her gaze drifted to the dais. "One worthy of the rank."

Silence smothered our end of the table. I watched my brothers struggle to conceal anger and confusion, hoping that my face did not show either too strongly. Their training had included handling subtle insults and threats, but these blatant ones were beyond what they expected. How long should they tolerate such insults? Should they tolerate them at all? It might have been entertaining, seeing their jaws clench against whatever words boiled against their teeth, if the situation were not so perilous. My own outrage was accompanied by equally intense curiosity. What possible reason could Lady Yvein have for being persistently and unmistakably offensive?

Cedrick mastered himself first. "Indeed, lady," he said, apparently having decided to pretend not to have understood, "High King Benult was a farsighted king. Our friendship with Elbany has been an asset."

"That—" Lady Yvein said.

But Murrow, who had begun speaking at the same moment, pressed on. Eyes blazing, Lady Yvein subsided, and he discoursed about his longtime admiration for King Benult, a depth of interest I felt certain had been conceived moments earlier.

I studied her as surreptitiously as I was able as the servers began to bring the third course. The queen consort's statements were beyond offensive. They were provocative. Treasonous. Why make them, here and now? What benefit could appertain to Verun from open conflict at this counsel, with the supposed threat of Ragonne?

She smiled as she watched the servants moving through the hall. Verun had always been the most recalcitrant of the clustered islands, its kings chafing under Reud's overlordship. To judge from his queen consort, the current king of Verun followed his forebears with zeal. But surely their internal conflicts must quell in the shadow of a common fear? Would not stoking civil squabbles distract from that larger concern?

Distract...

I watched her eyes flick again to the servers. A prickle of suspicion tightened my shoulders. What if distraction *was* her aim? I glanced at my brothers, extolling in turn the merits of High King Benult. Lady Lida and Lady Wealdin listened raptly, most likely feigning interest but grateful for silencing Lady Yvein. But that lady, far from looking annoyed, shone with satisfaction through her noble's dispassionate expression. My unease deepened.

A serving man stepped between Hal and me to set down a dish. He'd jostled me before and this time leaned away from me, with the result he bumped Hal's shoulder. "Pardon," he murmured, straightening.

At least this time he acknowledged his rudeness.

I turned, watching him, wondering as I did what my instincts had noted that I'd not yet consciously seen.

Realization flashed. The man sounded nothing like a household servant of the Black Keep.

CHAPTER VIII

My attention full upon him now, I wondered why I had not noted his strangeness before. The deference in his voice was thin, and his accent, though Brusterian, was not Reud. The muscles in his lower arm, the calluses on his hands, spoke of sword and spear, not pots and spoons.

My gaze leapt around the hall. None of the men—and they were all men, although the Black Keep had both male and female servants—were known to me. Undoubtedly much had changed in six years, but it seemed unlikely the Black Keep's household staff would be entirely different. I watched as a man bent to place a platter upon the high table, and saw the grace and stealth of a warrior despite his servant's clothing.

The trickle of suspicion burst into a rush of cold fear. I saw the truth, too terrible to consider, too horrid to dismiss. The Black Keep had never been taken in an attack. But treachery might prevail.

I looked at the high table. How could I convey my concern to my father—discretely, in case I was wrong?

King Verun bent, his hand below the table. My breath caught. Had he dropped something? He was reaching for—what?

Boot knife. I was certain as if the under-king had shouted his intention. Each king wore his sword, but a close strike would be impossible with a full blade. But every Brusterian noble, man or woman, wore a boot knife, the reassuring presence of a weapon at hand, at need, and at the last. A boot knife, hidden until the last instant by the table...

Verun meant to kill the King.

I was on my feet in an instant. "Birnan! Ware the King!" One fragment of my thought wondered which I feared more. That I was right, that the next half moment Verun's arm would thrust upwards towards my father's heart. Or I was wrong, and would face his wrath for my unforgivable disruption of his court.

I was not wrong. But Birnan did not need my warning. He

did not stand at our father's back for mere ceremony. Verun struck, the flash of his knife swift and bright as lightning. But the point of Birnan's sword took him before his blow reached the High King.

The hall exploded in action and noise, pulling my attention from the dais. The 'servers' attacked, their efforts concentrated upon the princes, swarming our table like ants on a dropped apple. Lady Yvein drew her boot knife, her eyes on Murrow.

Cedrick and Murrow, swords in hand, shoved chairs aside as half a dozen men engaged them. I pulled my boot knife and scooped up my eating knife. Turning to help Murrow, I was surprised to see Hal, knife in hand, vault the table towards Cedrick and his attackers, keening something not unlike the Brusterian war cry my brothers were sending up. As was I.

Murrow was soon too busy to do more than grunt. He fought one, three more jostling to get near enough to strike. I saw his quick glance, which noted them but also me. He stepped sideways, forcing his man to turn his back to me. I thrust my belt knife in just below the Verun warrior's ribs. It was not a fatal blow but it caused him to leave himself open to Murrow's next, which was. I met my brother's gaze over the man's falling body. Confusion and surprise were gone. His eyes shone with unleashed Brusterian bloodthirst.

He turned. Understanding, I followed suit, and we awaited our enemies back to back. In the instant before the next attackers hit I saw Hal and Cedrick had one man down and each was fighting with another.

"Bruster! The High King!" Murrow roared.

"Reud! The Black Keep!" I called back.

Two came at Murrow, one at me. His arms were longer, and the sword gave him even greater reach. Under other circumstances, I would have dodged his strikes, then cut at the arm holding the sword before he could withdraw. But with Murrow at my back I could not step away from a blow which would then hit him.

I parried the sword thrusts with my eating knife, shorter and thicker than my boot knife and more likely to withstand the impact, watching for an opening. One came, an attack Utor had taught me, a seeming aim at the belly that arced downward at the last moment and caught the leg where it joined the body. The man fell, the large artery opened.

I looked around. Murrow had one of his men down but his left leg was bleeding above the knee. I joined his attack on the other. With Murrow parrying the sword, I waited. *There!* I thrust my boot knife towards the side of the man's neck, belt knife ready if I missed. I didn't. He crumbled onto his fellow.

Verune battle calls echoed from the walls, and were answered by the men of Reud.

"Where's Cedrick?" Murrow said.

"I don't know."

We scanned the hall. The men we'd seen attacking Cedrick and Hal were down, but where were they—

"There!" I pointed. They'd gone to hold the doors to keep the Verune from escaping. Murrow ran to help them. I turned to the fighting between the side tables. With the addition of Murrow's sword the small crowd of Verune at the doors thinned rapidly. I caught a Verune by the braid and jerked his head back, reaching around to slit his throat, stepping to engage another as he fell.

"Enough!"

The High King's voice thundered through the hall. His people turned, realizing in something close to disappointment that few remained standing but themselves. The sight of him, unharmed and in command, returned a measure of normalcy, despite the bodies on the floor and the blood on their knives. At his sides, King Petrus and King Otho turned, sheathing their swords. They had drawn, ready to defend themselves, but had not engaged the fighters. There had been no need. Once Verun's strike had failed, his attempted overthrow was doomed. *An uprising which fails to kill the King tends to be short lived.* That was the second maxim we had learned as children.

"Betrayal! Craven treachery!" His voice, if anything, grew louder. "But we are the heirs of Ator, and his Black Keep will not fall. Not to attack. Nor to those who bite from within."

Murrow appeared at my side, his mouth against my ear. "Where is Utor?"

I glanced to our father's left. Utor's chair was empty. "I haven't seen him since the fighting—"

"Verun—I will not call him 'king'—has bought his foolishness with his life," the High King continued.

Murrow had spoken softly but Cedrick heard. He stepped

closer. "Utor is dead." His words were a barely audible breath, wavering with sorrow.

"How do you—?" Murrow said.

"Look at Birnan."

We did. Our youngest brother stood in his place, guarding his King. But his face was moon white, his jaw clenched. His eyes kept darting to his left, and down. Dread quivered in my gut. Murrow caught my shoulder with his free hand and held. Cedrick reached for my hand.

"Yvein still lives," the High King gestured to where, I saw with surprise, Lady Lida held Yvein, one arm twisted behind her back, her knife at her throat. I'd forgotten her in the fight, I realized with consternation, and should not have. When I'd seen her last, she had a knife in her hand, advancing on Murrow. Lady Lida, clearly, had intercepted her. "I have no doubt," the King said, "that she aided her husband. She will be dealt with." King Petrus looked at his new queen consort with mingled surprise and pride, a look she returned levelly, as if asking him how he had expected her to behave, if not thus.

Surely Cedrick was wrong, despite Utor's empty chair and Birnan's agonized glances. Surely our father would not be calmly reasserting his authority if his oldest son lay dead at his feet. I searched the crowd.

I did not find him.

My heart lurched as I looked back to our father. If Utor were dead, he would and must act as he was. Bruster's aptness to civil conflict, as the evening had already shown, could be suppressed but not extinguished. If the Prince was dead in an attack meant to kill the High King and his heirs, the King *must* reestablish control immediately.

"You came here tonight for court, and tomorrow, counsel," the High King's voice rang dark and hard as the castle walls. "The Black Keep has seen battles before, but you did not expect one tonight. But you are Brusterian. If someone strikes, you return blow for blow. You fought well. Verun failed."

"Prince Birnan! Laud to Birnan!" someone called.

The King lifted his hand. "Prince Birnan's vigilance was Verun's undoing. His sword was faster than Verun's knife." He guided his youngest son forward. "Laud to Birnan!"

The hall echoed the shout. Birnan looked yet more miserable. Our father's hand clasped his shoulder.

"You may be thinking Prince Birnan does not look like a man who just saved his king and father's life," the High King said, full throated over the remnants of the crowd's acclamation. The hall quieted. "That is because," I heard the tremor of grief and anger in his voice, although I did not think the gathered nobles did, "Verun's defeat was not without cost."

The King stooped, hidden for a moment behind the table. Then he straightened, his arms full. Cedrick was right.

He laid his burden on the table. Cries and murmurs ran through the hall. Otho and Petrus bowed their heads.

Our father stooped again, and this time there was no gentleness. He flung Verun over the table and into the hall. The rage that he had kept under tight control burst forth, putting the strength of Ator in his arms. Verun flew like a rock from a sling. The crowd parted hastily as the body fell.

"He," the King said, "has killed my Prince." No amount of noble training could have kept the wrath and pain from his voice. "It is his great fortune he is already dead."

The hall was quiet as the gathered nobles' eyes flicked from Utor's body on the high table, to Verun's upon the floor, and back to the King.

"We will still hold counsel." He gestured towards King Otho and King Petrus. Like him, they had remained on the dais during the attack, ready to fight if need be but aware of what the outcome must be and letting the princes and nobles show their worth. "We had much to consider. Now we have more." He nodded to Cedrick, who went to open the doors. "If you will return tomorrow night, lords of Bruster, the kings will announce our decisions to you."

The nobles recognized their dismissal, and, it seemed, their blood now cooled, most were not unhappy to be allowed to leave. The kings were not the only ones with much to discuss.

CHAPTER IX

The King's gaze fell upon Hal. "Master Carlson, would you be so good as to search the keep and discover what Verun's men have done with my household staff and guards?"

He bowed. "Of course, lord."

"Let us hope they killed as few as possible." Once Hal had gone, the King gestured to Murrow and Cedrick, who barred the doors of the emptied hall, then relieved Lady Lida of her captive. Both glanced towards the spiral staircase, clearly wondering if any of Verun's men had slipped upstairs.

We stood in silence. The kings upon the dais. The rest of us —queen consorts, princes, and me—clustered before it. Verun's body crumpled on the floor. Utor's on the table. I kept my gaze desperately on the King's face. I could not think about my brother. Not yet.

At length King Petrus cleared his throat. "Lord, would you like me to go—"

"You will stay here, under-king of Eban," the High King said. "Until we learn what has passed, and what may remain to be done."

Realizing suddenly the depth of my father's stratagem, I could not suppress a shiver, with a touch of anger on Hal's behalf. The High King had sent out his guests, knowing that more of Verun's men might lurk in the keep but they *probably* would not strike the departing nobles. Verun had aimed to kill the King and princes, not mow entire swathes of Brusterian nobility. If Hal encountered any of Verun's men, he might not be so fortunate. The King had clearly chosen him as, from Bruster's perspective, the cheapest loss. I closed my teeth against a sigh. But the King calculated as he must, naturally as breathing.

But not easily. His hand lay on Utor's head, stroking his son's hair.

I strained to listen but the heavy doors admitted no sound, no hint of what might be transpiring beyond. The King's caution was warranted. Fighting was finished in the hall but the uprising might not be. Verun's men, unaware of their lord's death, could be readying a second strike, and might yet be successful. More fully successful. The King's hand moved slowly, as if soothing a fretful child.

"I should go look for him," I said, my words seeming loud after the long quiet.

"No," the King said. "They mean to slaughter the entire ruling family."

"Of which I am the least," I said. "I brought Hal here. I have a responsibility towards him."

"Master Carlson strikes me as a man capable of taking care of himself."

"He was the Ragoni clerk's keeper!" I spluttered.

Murrow frowned and came back from the door, brushing his hand soothingly down my arm.

"Even so." The King nodded slowly, as if glad to consider something else for a moment. "But he walks like a warrior. An intriguing problem, I admit."

The inactivity was maddening, at odds with the battle burst still coursing down my back. Murrow took two cloths from his belt pouch. Handing me one, he began to wipe his sword. I took my time with my knives, and did not put them away once they were clean.

"Lord," King Otho said. "Perhaps someone should go."

"No." The King's fingers smoothed Utor's hair but his eyes were elsewhere, fixed upon the tapestry of Bluditor.

"I'm willing," I said, swiveling my belt knife in my hand.

"And I," Cedrick said. Birnan opened his mouth, then closed it without a sound at our father's cold look. Murrow had not offered. He knew better. He was Prince now. If anyone were allowed to leave, it would be not him.

A muffled knocking sounded on the door. Murrow and Cedrick hurried over. An exchange of shouts followed. We could hear what my brothers said but not the speaker without.

"It's Master Carlson," Murrow said as he and Cedrick lifted the bar.

Hal entered, his arms full. Dismay bleached Cedrick's already pale countenance. "Gustor."

Hal walked with deliberation worthy of his burden to the

dais. Three other men followed, the first carrying another body, too bloodied for quick recognition, if indeed I would have known him. Yet I felt I should. The form seemed familiar. I recognized the man who bore him as a member of the Black Keep's household force. The two others I did not know, but from their attire I guessed them to be part of King Petrus' and King Otho's retinues. Before Cedrick and Murrow closed and barred the door once more, I saw men looking hesitantly into the hall. More of the Keep's guards. Some were wounded. I could hear their relieved murmurs as they saw the King.

Hal stepped over Verun's body and lay Gustor before the high table. There was considerably more blood on Gustor than Verun. "Your pardon, lord, for my delay." He bowed. "He...was not yet dead. I stayed with him."

The High King leaned forward, one hand on the table, the other still on Utor's head. "The father. Now the son." His gaze rested heavily upon his Steward. "Perhaps I should be glad you leave no son to die in my service." His eyes rose. "Thank you," he told Hal. "I feared this. The Steward directs court proceedings. He would have noticed the Verune at once."

His gaze flicked to the second body. "Anhud."

Anhud. I had thought myself brimful with sorrow, but new mourning welled up at that name. He had been captain of the Black Keep's force as long as I could remember. He had taught the King's children, including his daughter, the skills of a warrior. I remembered with glass-sharp clarity the scrape of his calloused fingers correcting my grip on a knife, his growl-like laugh at my follies, the rough music of his praise. Utor taught me how to throw knives, but Anhud taught me how to fight with them. He'd taught me knife tricks he'd not shown my brothers—"a lady might, at times, have greater need, princess." At the time I thought my father would not approve. Now I suspected he would commend anything that kept his children alive. I gripped the knives I still held tightly.

My father caught my gaze. His eyes flicked. Understanding his unspoken command, I sheathed both knives. The fighting was over. Most likely. If he were allowed to calm the situation, and no one ignited fresh trouble.

The man—Dunstan, that was his name—laid Anhud beside Gustor. "Lord Rummel, the leader of Verun's retainers, told

Anhud he was worried." He glanced, apprehensive and apologetic, at King Petrus. "He said he had heard whispers the King of Eban meant to try something at court."

"Rummel told me," King Petrus' man said, "that he had heard the High King had called counsel as a ruse to dispose of the other kings and put his sons on their thrones."

King Otho's man nodded. "I was told the same." Both, I realized, were not merely members of the under-kings' retinues, but their captains. The suspicion that had been poured into their ears would have been repeated to their kings—and had been deemed credible.

"He used our distrust to his gain." The High King's gaze flicked back to Dunstan. "What else passed outside the hall?"

"I can't be certain." He shrugged unhappily. "My guess is Rummel killed Anhud and Gustor, then the doorwards, and opened our gates to his men." He knelt. "They locked us in our own dungeons. We failed in our duty, lord." His head bowed, as if bitterness and shame were a palpable weight upon his shoulders.

"The servers they replaced?"

"I think they were locked in the storerooms."

Hal nodded. "I spoke to them, but told them to stay there. It seemed safest."

"Good man." The King was silent, looking out and over the bodies of his two most trusted retainers, his left hand still resting on the head of his son.

"Dunstan." His voice slid lower. Formal. "You were Anhud's second. You are now Captain. Secure the Keep."

His head came up. "Lord—I—"

"Secure my Keep. Captain."

I saw consternation in his face, pushed aside the next instant by duty, and the relief that *something* might be done. "Yes, lord."

At their kings' command, the Soludin and Ebane captains went with him, to gather their remaining men and provide assistance.

Silence returned as the door was barred once more. The King resumed stroking Utor's hair. I could not bear it any longer. I stepped onto the dais to his side, putting my hand on his shoulder. "Father—"

"Later, Maudlin."

I hesitated, then did as he bade, moving away. I kept my gaze on the bodies of Gustor and Anhud rather than my brother. I doubted I could look upon him, grasp and accept, and be as the King required.

King Otho and King Petrus exchanged glances as the quiet lengthened. "What will be done with Yvein?" King Petrus asked, as if his mute dialogue with King Otho had elected him to broach the High King.

"We shall take counsel, and decide."

"Lord—"

"*In counsel.*"

King Petrus and King Otho again shared a look. King Otho seemed as if he intended to speak—but did not.

A knock sounded, but this time upon the door leading to the main gate. Murrow went to it, unbarring it after determining it was Dunstan without. He entered, followed again by the under-kings' captains. The new master of the guards crossed to the dais and went formally to one knee.

"Lord. The Black Keep is yours."

"Thank you, Dunstan. Rise. Were any Verune taken or killed?"

"None taken. Eight killed. Five others found dead. More than a few, I suspect, escaped. Rummel among them. At least I have not found him among the dead." He paused. "I sent word to the shipyard, but the Verune boat was already gone."

I thought of Hal, searching the Black Keep with thirteen of Verun's best warriors wandering its chambers. Only later did I question how, with the Keep's guards imprisoned or killed, the five found dead had come to be so, and wonder about the deep pools he kept shadowed.

"Have your men search the town and the approach to the keep. Then release the servants." The High King looked at Hal. "Would you return to them and explain?"

"Your will, lord." Hal left once more.

The Soludin and Ebane retinue commanders knelt before the dais. King Otho's man spoke first. "Lord, I ask to be removed from my post. I was behindhand, not seeing this danger." King Petrus' captain expressed the same regret and request.

The High King looked sidelong at his under-kings. "What say you?"

"Rise," said King Otho. "I do not find you negligent, and I

will not lose my captain for the sake of his pride."

"Nor I," King Petrus gestured to his man to stand. "But I regret that our habitual suspicion made us vulnerable."

The High King looked back at his captain. "When you release the servants, send the cook to me." His eyes flicked sideways again, towards the under-kings. "When you can spare the men, have them take the bodies of Verun and his followers outside. Burn them and scatter their ashes in my pig-sty."

"Lord! A fellow king—" King Otho said.

"He will not be buried as a king."

"Tyrant!" Yvein's eyes blazed. "You show Verun was right! You are no true King!"

"Now you accuse me of heavy-handed rule?" His voice did not rise, and his hand did not move from Utor. "Verun moved against me because he thought me soft. I sought to prevent war within Bruster, strengthened our ties to our allies, and made wider alliances with the Valenian kingdoms, that our warriors might hone their skills but use them less. I learned letters, and had my children taught. In these things Verun saw weakness, and in weakness, opportunity."

He had asked no question, but her fierce stare confirmed what he had said. "Now tyranny. Your justifications shift readily." His free hand moved in a dismissive gesture. "Verun rebelled for his own ambition."

"How dare you burn him like a thief or an animal!"

"Be glad I do not hang his body from the walls." His voice was cold, and seemed more so in its quietness.

"We have proof!" Her gaze turned to the under-kings. "Bruster stands threatened and he does nothing."

King Petrus blinked. "We hold counsel to consider Philip of Ragonne's purpose."

"Not Ragonne." She was almost spitting. "We have the letter. Ulton sent us a copy. Sar—"

"Remove her. Now." The High King did not raise his voice but his command was a whip crack.

Dunstan leapt to obey.

"Take her to the King's rooms. Well guarded. Three men. Ones who know better than to listen to traitors."

He took her arms and began pushing her towards the stairs. She was still shouting. "He didn't *tell* you. Why do you follow this man? He—" Her words were lost as Dunstan forced her up the stairs.

The under-kings' captains forgot themselves enough to stare open-mouthed.

"Lord?" King Petrus said. The depth of uncertainty in his voice was all Yvein could have wished.

"In counsel, King Petrus," the King said wearily.

Half a dozen heartbeats later, the under-kings seemed to notice that their captains were looking from king to king in shocked curiosity, and dismissed them.

The wait was even longer this time. Dunstan had a great deal to do. The King would not remove until the Keep was set as right as could be. Nor would he discuss the Saradenian letter in the open hall. None were now present that should not hear of it, but the habits of secrecy that kept him alive were not easily put aside. If King Petrus and King Otho realized this, it did not soothe them. Their backs grew rigid as time dragged on. They were certainly wondering whether, as Yvein had claimed, the High King had concealed vital information. The Saradenian letter had come to Vere months before. When the High King told them he had first seen it that very morning, would they believe him? When they saw the letter, would they believe *it?*

Magistre Ulton had sent a copy of the Saradenian letter to Verun.

Which meant the Clerk—and Verun—had known of the danger, and neither brought it to the High King. To enable the accusation Yvein made? Magistre Ulton might even have encouraged Pedagno Olwen to assume the letter was a fraud, while planning to use that knowledge to his advantage, and Verun's.

For surely the cousins had colluded in their ambitions, Ulton to take Vere, Verun to seize all Bruster.

I opened my mouth, then shut it. The High King would not discuss *this* in court either. I would have to wait, as impatiently as the under-kings. Ulton and Verun. Vere. The Pedagno. Saradena. My thoughts circled and whined, like hounds off the scent, until Dunstan returned, accompanied by Hal and the cook.

Dunstan bowed. "The streets have been searched, lord. My —" his voice caught, "men are going to each house, but that will take hours. And," he paused, "a fire has been built."

"Well done." The High King dismissed him with a generous

nod that acknowledged how competently the hastily promoted captain had taken up the demands flung upon him. Dunstan bowed, very low. Taking up the body of Verun, he carried it from the hall.

The King turned his attention to the cook, who bowed. She was a short, broad-shouldered woman, her hair braided in a variant of the royal family's style, one of the privileges of senior retainers. I recognized her; she had been Vere's head cook.

"Lord." The cook looked at the disheveled hall, seeming to weigh what to say. "I trust the food was not the cause of this...disagreement."

He gave a strangled laugh, devoid of real mirth but appreciative of a moment's leavening. "Kimbur. The Steward of the Black Keep is dead."

She looked down at Gustor's body and sighed.

"Who should be my new Steward?"

The cook looked surprised, but considered. "Murton has promise."

"Too young."

"There's Almun," she said.

"Almun trusts too easily. The Steward must suspect everyone."

She was quiet for a moment. "Does the King have someone in mind? Trevur, perhaps?"

That name I recognized. Trevur was kin to my mother. For her sake, the King had given him a place in the household staff. It *was* a gift. He was lazy. Steward Bernuth always had Trevur work with another man; solitary tasks took him twice as long as they should. The King's generosity would certainly not extend to making him Steward, but Kimbur had not been with him long enough to understand.

"No," he said flatly. "Any others?"

"I am sorry, lord." She shook her head. "Almun is the most competent, but I agree, he is too trusting to make a good Steward. Gustor was training Murton but he is too young. Trevur —"

"Has nothing but his blood to recommend him."

"Yes, lord."

"Your assessment is just." He leaned forward, the fingers of his free hand brushing the table. "I hope you have trained your assistant well. You are now Steward."

Her eyes widened. Nor was she alone in her astonishment. The under-kings stared for several heartbeats before recalling themselves. My brothers were no less surprised but recovered more quickly. Even I, who through my father's doing was the first woman trained at Vere and knew his willingness to disregard how things were done if a better way presented itself, was taken aback.

"But—lord—"

"Head cook is nearly as demanding as Steward." He met his new Steward's gaze evenly. "No one is more ready to this task." His eyes flicked down. "It is not without danger."

I watched as the under-kings struggled to maintain an impassivity that did not conceal that they were nearly as appalled as if the King had chosen one of his boat slaves.

"I am pleased to serve, lord," Steward Kimbur said. "Until someone more suitable is found."

"As you will. But I suspect it will be years before you can return to your kitchen."

The Steward bowed her acquiescence.

"Steward," the High King said, formal once more, "return order to the Black Keep." He glanced around the hall. "In all haste."

She bowed again and left. Within minutes, household servants entered. The King waited until the bodies of Gustor and Anhud had been taken out, to be prepared for burial.

"Now," the High King gathered Utor into his arms, "we take counsel."

CHAPTER X

The guards held Yvein, wrists bound, just inside the door to the King's rooms. The High King nodded to Murrow and Cedrick, who dismissed them and took charge of her, each with a knife and a look that dared her to give him a reason to use it.

Before the evening had descended into madness, the room had been readied for the gathering of kings. The chairs that had stood before the hearth that morning were gone. The High King's high-backed seat was now encircled by three other chairs, identical to one another, ornate but not as large as the King's. I'd never seen them before. I supposed they were used only when the kings held counsel, and wondered where they were kept otherwise.

His face taut, the King stepped beyond the circled chairs to the hearth, where a low fire burned, and lay Utor's body on the rug before it. What would happen when his grief overpowered his control?

He went to his seat and stood in front of it. King Otho and King Petrus moved to what must have been their customary chairs and stood, again glancing at one another as if debating who should speak first.

I hovered near the door, Birnan beside me. The queen consorts had been granted leave to return to their rooms when the kings left the hall, but not before the High King thanked Lady Lida. He sent Hal to the Steward, to offer whatever aid he might give. The princes and I had been directed to follow the kings. Birnan's wretchedness had only deepened. I touched his arm. He gave me an ashen look.

The High King spoke before the under-kings had determined who should address him. "Under-kings of Bruster, shall we take counsel?"

Neither responded, their eyes flicking towards we others in the room.

"Only the kings hold counsel," the High King acknowledged

their reluctance. "But this is not a typical counsel. Any more than today was a typical court." His gaze moved as he spoke. "Yvein must be here to answer for her betrayal. She must be guarded by those whose ears may hear our discussion. Were your Prince here, Otho, I would welcome him."

King Otho's face darkened. Disgruntlement and dissent were not unique to the high nobility. He had lords who might be overly tempted if both he and his eldest son were gone from Solud.

"Birnan and Maudlin are here," the King continued, "because there are questions only they can answer. They will participate *solely* when asked." His gaze lingered on me for a meaningful moment. "Under-kings of Bruster, shall we take counsel?"

Both King Petrus and King Otho looked at us once more, clearly still troubled by our presence but assenting to the need. All three lowered themselves into their seats at the same moment, but how that coordination occurred I could not have said.

The High King steepled his fingers. "Raise your concerns, under-kings."

"What was Yvein talking about?" King Otho asked.

"Ah," the King nodded. I suspected he was considering the import of beginning there rather than with Verun's uprising, Yvein's sentencing, what to do about Verun's death, or even their outrage at Kimbur's appointment. In Bruster, suspicion trumped all.

The King went to one of the cabinets and removed a curling sheet of parchment. The Saradenian letter. He handed it to King Otho. The King of Solud looked at it, then passed it to King Petrus. Neither could read, but I supposed that the King thought handling the letter, feeling its weight and seeing its colors, would help the under-kings accept it. "This went to Vere."

"What does it say?" King Petrus passed the sheet back to the King. He read it aloud.

"This?" Disbelief thickened King Otho's voice. "Yvein frights us with this? It can't be real."

"So the Pedagno thought, and did not send it to us. Maudlin recognized its authenticity and brought it. She arrived this morning."

"What makes her believe it is real?" King Petrus demanded, one hand gripping his other elbow as if he wanted to cross his arms defiantly but managed to check the impulse. Mostly.

"Maudlin?"

I approached to stand before them, between the empty seat of Verun and King Otho's. "It is real," I said. "Logan, Elbany, and Ragonne received such letters also. Months ago." I described the coming of the ship to Rothbury, the arrival of the letter, the messengers from Logan and Ragonne.

"It can't be real," King Otho repeated, pulling fervently at his graying beard. "There is no 'Saradena'." His eyes narrowed, as if wondering whether I might be the cause of this fraud, and why.

"A ruse, surely," King Petrus rested his chin on his fisted fingers, his other hand still clutching his elbow. "Most likely Ragonne, to obscure their attack."

The under-kings looked at me with impatience, the High King with interest, and I realized my father meant me to argue the case to the under-kings. Cunning. They must be persuaded that the Saradenian threat was real. But much of my father's success as High King derived from his evenhandedness in adjudicating squabbles among the clustered islands. He would not force a grudging acceptance of the letter if persuasion could be made to work.

"That would be a stratagem both subtle and clever," I conceded. "Have you always considered Philip of Ragonne to be so?"

King Petrus' lips twitched in nearly-concealed amusement. "No. But his nephew is so reputed."

"Orlo of Kolon brought the letter to Elbany, as I said," I replied. "He saw the ship himself."

"Or so he claimed," King Petrus said, taking his hand from beneath his chin long enough to sweep his hand down in a negating gesture.

"There *was* a strange ship in Elbany," I said. "And in Logan. And Ragonne. Many people saw them. "

King Petrus' eyes rolled up impatiently. "Our own stolen boats, disguised."

"I do not think so," I said. "But I did not see the ship." I smothered irritation at the flash of triumph in his eyes. "The letter demonstrates its credibility on its own."

"I do not *read*," King Petrus' tone betrayed the typical noble disdain. "You can claim that letter says anything."

"Not the words themselves." I took the parchment sheet from my father and went to King Petrus. "The blue ink. Look."

He glanced at the letter, his hand tucked suspiciously under his chin once more. "Yes?" King Otho stroked his graying beard and leaned to look as well.

"There are nearly a thousand volumes in the library of Vere, and more than thirty scholars who tend them. Not one of those books contains that blue, and not a man of them could make it."

His hostility gave way to bafflement. "You expect me to ignore the known threat of Ragonne in favor of this... Saradena... because of...ink?"

"Ragonne prepares against Saradena. Not Bruster," I said. "King Philip told me he will not wait for a fleet of invading ships to appear on his horizon. In the spring, he sails east."

King Petrus's head wagged knowingly. "If Philip's aim is Bruster, using this ruse to cover his purpose, he would say just such a thing."

"Of course," I said. "But he allowed me to search his books. Grudgingly. But what I found confirms the truth of the letter." I told them, as I had told my father and Utor earlier that interminable day, what I found in Ragonne and in Vere.

"Enough." King Otho slapped both hands on the arms of his chair. "Petrus, I understand your reluctance. But you must see that to persist in it would be both unreasonable and unwise." The eyes he turned upon me were not friendly. "I wondered whether this might be a ruse coined rather in Reud than Ragonne." He left the rest unstated: a ploy of the High King's, to seize all Bruster, replacing the under-kings with his own sons, aided by his daughter. The whisper Verun had spread before them.

"Trust is a tender plant," the High King murmured, pressing the tips of his steepled fingers together. "Slow growing, and easily bruised."

The room was so quiet my own quickened breathing seemed a shout echoing from the walls.

"I do not renounce all suspicion," King Otho said finally. "But it would be more foolish to assume this letter is a fraud." Now his eyes, while not kindly, were at least not hostile. "Like Philip, I would not care to wait until there are ships in sight before making ready."

King Petrus let his breath out in a soundless sigh. "Neither do

I abandon my concerns. But Otho is correct. We must suppose this letter to be true, until we know, not merely suspect, that it is not."

The High King nodded, no hint in his face that his under-kings had just affirmed their belief that he would plot to murder them and their families. "Later, we will determine how to proceed in this matter." His eyes slid towards Yvein, and the under-kings' followed. "What shall we do with this traitor?"

"She has colluded against the High King—" King Otho began.

"Not just the High King," I interrupted. "Verun conspired with the Pedagno's Clerk, Magistre Ulton—"

"Lies!" Yvein shouted. "Everyone knows the dry-wombed are mad. My sister-son—"

"Be silent!" snapped King Petrus.

I stared. The relations of nobility were a tangled web, and I'd missed this strand. Magistre Ulton was Yvein's nephew as well as Verun's cousin? He must be the child of a much older sister. But if that were so...perhaps it was not Verun who had plotted with Magistre Ulton, but Yvein. She might even have persuaded her husband to rebel.

"You have admitted your collusion with Magistre Ulton." The King's composure did not hide the flash in his eyes. "He sent you a copy of Saradena's letter." His gaze returned to his under-kings. "Their complicity is undeniable. Ulton, Verun, and Yvein all knew of this danger. None spoke of it to any of us."

The under-kings nodded slowly, their clouded looks betraying a sense of watching a horse gallop past they thought they were to mount. The High King looked at me. "You suspect Ulton's final move against the Pedagno was coordinated with Verun's uprising?"

"Yes, my lord." I bowed my head. "We should assume Ulton now controls Vere. Pedagno Poll had no Birnan to watch his back." *Because I left.* But how could I have done otherwise? "We may be surprised. The Pedagno may yet live. But I doubt it."

I heard a gasp. Murrow's knife was at Yvein's throat. "What else?"

She arched her back, eyeing him, trying to push away from the knife. He tightened his grip, the blade glinting. She gasped again as he drew the edge across the side of her neck, making a shallow cut.

"Lord!" King Otho protested.

The High King did not move. "I doubt she will tell us will-ingly, Otho."

"But—" In his struggles with his fractious nobles, King Otho had undoubtedly had both men and women encouraged to tell what they knew, but probably not in his presence, and it was certainly not to his taste. Nor to that of any man in the room, from their drawn, unguarded faces. Which was well for Bruster. Only the cruel or the foolish relished the pain of others—worse, to inflict it himself—and woe to the kingdom led by such a man.

"What more need we know?" King Petrus said. "Her treachery is evident. Let us pronounce sentence."

"If there is more to be known," the High King said, "we would do well to have it." He looked at Murrow. He was weighing, I knew, the benefit of possessing what details—or perhaps more than details—might be learned against what could be lost. I was certain the King suspected Yvein had thread yet upon her spool. There were risks to Bruster in allowing her silence. But as Murrow held his knife at Yvein's neck, he had glanced no less than four times at Utor's still form. There was danger—to Murrow, to Bruster—in allowing the new Prince to put his foot upon this path, at this moment.

"As you say, Petrus, her guilt is abundant," the King said at last. He stood. "Bring her forward, Murrow."

"Hear me, Yvein of Verun," our father said formally. "You have betrayed your sworn lord, conspiring to overthrow the High King of Bruster. You will see the sun rise on the coming day but you will not see it set. One hour after dawn, an account of your treachery will be made, and you will be beheaded before the people of Reud." He paused. "I grant you the same mercy given Verun. Your body will be burned, not hung from the walls of the Black Keep." He turned. "Under-kings?"

"I assent," King Otho said.

King Petrus nodded curtly. "The sentence is just."

Fear and wrath filled Yvein's face, but she kept quiet.

"Remove her," the King said. "We have more to discuss."

CHAPTER XI

The door closed behind Murrow and Cedrick, each holding his knife and one of Yvein's arms, her wrists bound behind her. They would take her to the dungeons to await the morning. I wondered if I should leave too but Birnan was still present, and I did not ask. They might, after all, say yes.

The High King sat once more. King Petrus looked at the others. "What shall we do about Verun? Who should we name to rule?"

"Not Murrow," the High King said at once. "He is now Prince."

"Eldon must remain Prince of Solud," King Otho said. "My other sons are too young. Solud would be ungovernable without a Prince at hand." He grimaced. "Too many lords with grown sons of their own."

His son bore an Elbish name, I noted. It honored Lady Wealdin but something solidly Brusterian would have been better policy. The boy's otherland name would only deepen his lords' discontent.

"My only remaining son is a child," King Petrus said, old grief and newer cheer mingled in his voice. "What of Cedrick?"

"I am hesitant to choose Cedrick." The High King spread his hands. "Would that not appear to confirm Verun's claim that I meant to replace you with my own sons?"

"But to raise someone not from the royalty will encourage more trouble." King Petrus tapped his sword hilt. "My lords are not—quite—as ambitious as Otho's. But they will be, if a man of like status becomes king."

"Birnan," King Otho said, the tip of his braid swinging out as he turned to look hard at my brother. Birnan went another shade grayer under his scrutiny.

King Petrus waved a hand. "Birnan presents the same problem as Cedrick."

"No," King Otho said, his gaze still on my youngest brother.

"Birnan saved the High King. An entire hall of Brusterian nobles saw. He can be given Verun as reward for his actions."

"What say you, Petrus?" the High King folded one hand over the other, his elbows on the arms of his chair.

"We cannot raise someone from below the royalty," King Petrus said firmly. He paused, lips pursing as he considered. "Otho is right. Birnan is the best choice. He quelled the uprising. To give him Verun is justified. More importantly, justifiable."

The High King caught my eye and I realized from the glint in his, that winked and went out like a cloud-covered star, the discussion had gone precisely as he'd wished.

"Birnan, come forward."

Misery unrelieved on his face, Birnan knelt before the High King.

"Birnan, prince royal of Bruster, you have been called to the throne of Verun by the kings of Bruster. Do you accept this charge?"

His unhappiness was so complete he was shaking. "Lord, the kings honor me. But I am unworthy."

"Unworthy?" King Otho's eyebrows rose. "You saved your king!"

Birnan's head bowed. "I saw Verun draw. At the same moment, a man appeared at Utor's back with a knife. Utor..." he paused to steady his voice, "or Murrow, perhaps, could have thrown with one hand, and taken Verun with his sword in the other. I—I wasn't fast enough. Verun was so close. I was afraid I would not hit him with a killing strike if I tried to throw at the same time." His head sunk lower. "I am sorry. Give Verun to Cedrick."

The High King placed both hands on Birnan's head. "Son. You could not choose your duty. It simply was." He put one hand under Birnan's chin, turning his face up. "I say this, I who mourn Utor as my firstborn and Prince." He looked up. "Otho? Petrus? How do you judge?"

"Birnan was the High King's back-guard," King Petrus said promptly. "To risk protecting the King in an attempt to save the Prince would have been negligent."

"I concur." King Otho's voice was milder, edged with pity. "Birnan." He waited until the younger man turned towards him. "You could not have done differently. However much you wish it."

The High King leaned forward, his head close to Birnan's. "You *must* hear me, son. You feel you should have done more. I do as well."

And I. My eyes burned with weeping I could not yet allow. If I'd paid greater heed to the servers, listened to my instincts telling me something was wrong the first time the man had bumped me, Utor would yet live.

"But we must somehow bear things as they are." The King stood, grasping Birnan's hands and pulling him up. "What you must bear is that you will be king of Verun." He led him to the empty chair. "Birnan, prince royal of Bruster," he repeated, "you are called by the under-kings of Bruster to a new duty: to be king of Verun. Do you accept this charge?"

Birnan was still pale, but his voice had settled. "I submit to the kings' decision."

"Sit, then." The High King stepped back. "Under-kings. The king of Verun."

"Verun." King Petrus and King Otho dipped their heads in respect to King Birnan.

"Presence is power, Birnan." The High King returned to his seat. "I recommend you leave with all speed."

"Indeed." King Otho shook his head, his beard following the motion with a slight lag. "Verun has always been difficult. Keeping order after this..." He made a harsh, slashing gesture, accompanied by an obviously-vile Brusterian word—so vile even I did not know it.

The High King's eyebrows rose, but he did not contradict him. "You may want to consult with Dunstan and choose a troop of men to accompany you. Unquestionably loyal, the best fighters, with no family ties to Verun. Hopefully, some who have direct experience with you. Loyalty to Bruster and the High King is good. Loyalty to you personally is better."

Birnan was nodding. "Yes. There are several I have sparred with. But Dunstan may not want to part with them."

"He will give you whomever you request," the High King said. "One king's gift to another." Despite the night's wretchedness, he smiled at his son as he said it.

"Have my commander choose three men from our retinue," King Petrus said.

"You will need every sword you can bring," King Otho said darkly. "Speak to my commander too."

"That is well." The High King said. "Birnan will arrive with our combined forces at his back. That will signal this is a lawful replacement, not a coup."

"I see I have much to do." The new King of Verun rose. "If I may, my lords...?"

King Petrus laughed. "You are king, Birnan. You come and go at no one's pleasure but your own. But we *are* in counsel."

"Oh!" King Birnan looked as if he meant to sit again, guiltily.

King Otho yawned. "Are we finished? There are a few hours left until dawn. I would like to spend them sleeping."

I stared. *Sleep?* After this night? I could not imagine it. The High King's gaze slid toward Utor's body, and I knew my father would not be sleeping either.

King Petrus stood. "High King, under-kings, can we conclude?"

King Otho was on his feet almost before King Petrus finished. "Let us be done."

The door burst open like a breached gate. Cedrick and Hal rushed in, Murrow borne between them, his head bloody. All color drained from the High King's face at the sight of another son's limp body.

"She escaped," Cedrick panted as they lowered Murrow.

The High King was there in an instant, his hands running over Murrow's head. "He lives." He shuddered, control cracking at last.

I knelt beside them, wiping at the blood with Murrow's cloth, which I'd not yet returned after cleaning my knives. The hurt was not as bad as it seemed, a gash and a lump above his right ear, but it bled yet. I pressed the cloth against it. King Otho took a clean kerchief from his belt pouch and gave it me to use instead. Murrow stirred but did not waken.

"Cedrick is also wounded," Hal said.

"I'm fine," Cedrick jerked his chin up. One hand clamped over a wound on the other arm, blood seeping between his fingers.

The King turned to him. Cedrick tried to wave his father off but the King peeled back my brother's fingers. "It's not bad. But it'll need to be stitched. Maudlin?"

"I can do it. Can you take Murrow?"

My father shifted, his hand replacing mine on the kerchief. I went to fetch my needle and thread from my bag, stored—so long before, it seemed—in the King's cupboard. Birnan, who had been searching the cupboard for clean bandages, joined me at Cedrick's side as I returned.

"What of Yvein?" King Petrus asked

"Dunstan's men are chasing her." Cedrick picked up the bottle of wine I'd grabbed from the King's table, to clean the wound, and took a swallow. I took the bottle back and sluiced the cut. "Hold still."

Birnan held Cedrick's arm as I finished threading my needle, but for something to do as much as anything. Cedrick did not move his wounded arm even as his other swung out to retrieve the bottle.

"Don't drink it all," I said. "I want to wash it again once I'm finished."

He looked at the nearly-full bottle, then shared a glance of exaggerated disbelief with Birnan, shaking the bottle to demonstrate, and took another drink. "I don't know how she got her hands free." He looked at our father rather than my fingers, poking the needle through his flesh and pulling it closed. "As we were passing through the hall, she seemed to stumble. I tried to pull her up, but she rolled away, came up with a rock in her hand, and hit Murrow. Then she grabbed his knife, slashed at me, and ran." He shook his head. "I don't know if Dunstan had assigned new doorwards yet."

As if summoned by his name, Dunstan appeared in the doorway. "She is gone, lord."

The High King stood, Birnan taking over holding the cloth to Murrow's head. "She had help?"

"Rummell was waiting with a boat. My men saw them both as the ship rowed away. She was whipping the slaves."

The High King turned his head but I saw what word he mouthed. It certainly mirrored my thoughts. "Within the Keep?"

"I'm not sure, lord," Dunstan said. "We came when we heard Cedrick's shouts. We saw no one but her."

I finished stitching, and washed the wound again.

"Dunstan," the King said, "would you have hot water and more bandages brought?" Dunstan bowed and stepped out.

"I'd like to know where that rock came from," Cedrick said. "Stones aren't just lying around in the Black Keep."

"She put it there, of course," the High King said. "A weapon of last resort, hidden and safe because it is not a weapon. Rocks are not strewn on our floor, but if one appeared a few days could pass before someone cleared it away."

Murrow stirred. "She said her foot hurt. She fell. Then..." Birnan helped him as he struggled to sit up. "She hit me." His searching gaze stopped at Cedrick. "A rock?" His eyes went to the King. "She got away?"

"She did." The High King looked at each in turn. "Free, and I do not doubt, hating every one of us." His gaze rested on Birnan. "Possibly you most. Or will as she soon as she learns that you are now King of Verun."

"He is?" Cedrick said.

Murrow blinked, as if not certain he was fully awake.

"I urge you to gather your troop and leave with all possible haste. To hold Verun, you must hold the castle in Verten. To do that, you must get there before she does."

Birnan looked a question at Murrow. When he nodded that he could sit unaided, Birnan rose. "How?"

"Yvein will probably strike for the shortest route," the High King said. "But no matter how she whips them, slaves cannot row at full speed all the way to Verun. If your boats go south, around Punlan, the westward current should get you to Verten first."

Dunstan returned, bringing the water and cloths himself.

"Dunstan," Birnan said. "Come with me. We have a force to select."

Dunstan looked at the High King. "Lord?"

"Captain." The High King took the basin from him. "Please assist the King of Verun with assembling a troop of our best warriors. Any man but yourself is his to request." He jerked his head toward King Otho and King Petrus. "His fellow under-kings have given leave to choose from their men as well, with the guidance of their own captains." He went to Murrow and began washing the gash on his head.

Dunstan stood unmoving for a moment, taking this in. He turned back to Birnan and bowed deeply. "Lord. A better man now leads Verun."

"Not unless we can secure it," King Birnan said. He took his leave of the men, kissed my cheek, and went out, Dunstan following.

King Otho looked at the High King. "If Yvein holds Verten, Birnan will not take it with a troop, even of Reud's best."

The High King's face stiffened, clearly too weary and too distressed to smooth away his thought. "You need not tell me I have bet Birnan's life on Yvein choosing badly. I knew already."

Chapter XII

I was alone with my father. And Utor's body.

The under-kings had taken leave. The High King had asked Hal to go with Cedrick and Murrow, to watch over the injured princes as they slept. Hal, of course, agreed, and the arrangement was made—over the protests of both princes.

The King stood within the circle of chairs, his gaze fixed upward. "We will have the interments tomorrow." He walked back and forth, not looking towards the hearth. "Not the day dawning." He nodded towards the one narrow window, lightening as dawn approached. "The one following. Kimbur. I should talk to her. Make sure she understands what is required. And Dunstan. I need to ask him if the bodies have been burned."

I went to him. "Father."

He met my gaze, fearsome and bleak at once. "I want to watch his ashes strewn beneath my pigs' feet."

I held one of his hands in both of mine. "Father."

He pulled his hand free and strode to the door. "I forgot. How could I have forgotten? We must send word to Logan."

I hurried after him. "What for?"

"Utor's marriage. We finally found the perfect princess. Waited for her to grow up, more like. She's twelve years younger than he..."

His head tipped forward against the door.

I touched his shoulder. "Come. Sit." I shook him gently. "We will have plenty to *do*, Father. But none of it will change this. Come."

He allowed me to lead him to the hearth but refused a chair, letting himself drop to the floor like a frozen rope finally thawing and spilling in an untidy pile on the ship's deck. One hand reached to stroke Utor's hair. His face shuddered with what I realized a moment later was thunderous rage. "If she comes into my hands again, I will behead her myself."

He held out his free hand and I seized it as I would that of a man in peril of falling over the gunwale. "Birnan was right," he said at last. "Had Utor been back-guard, he could have taken Verun with his sword and flung a knife into the other. No one bettered Utor at knife throwing." His hand, held in mine, clenched. "Would I had seen Verun draw."

"I saw him. Too late."

"This is not your fault." He shook his head viciously. "Nor Birnan's."

"Nor yours."

His mouth twisted, his gaze unseeing.

"You hold us excused and keep the blame for yourself. Father." I touched his face, as he had Birnan's, and waited until his eyes focused on me. "Verun. Yvein. Ulton. No one else."

"After Utor is..." he drew a trembling breath, "given back to the mountain, we will plan. Verun is dead. Yvein and Ulton are not. I *will* have them."

"I know."

He sighed, drawing his other hand slowly away from Utor's head. "Murrow is Prince now."

"Yes." I did not loosen my grasp on his hand.

"He will grow quickly into his new role. A second son always knows what may be required." His free hand balled, pressed to his mouth, and when he spoke again his words were muffled. "Four sons! They all lived, and grew into fine men, worthy of their rank. They learned their duties, and did them, and behaved like gentlemen. Serving women in the Black Keep do not fear to encounter a prince in an empty room." He pulled a wet breath. "Even after your mother's death, and the babe with her, I knew I was fortunate. I had four sons. And you, of course, Maudlin. All of you lived."

I said nothing. Myriad dangers stalked the lives of children, and royal children faced human enemies as well.

He pressed his hand flat on Utor's chest where the heart no longer beat. "My son. My firstborn. My Prince. *Utor.*" The name burst from him in a shuddering heave. I clutched his hand, all— and nothing—I could do.

Some time later, he spoke again. "I sat here the night he was born. Close to the fire as I could get, cold with fear I never felt on a field of war." He glanced towards the cupboards and the hidden door to his room. "I could hear your mother in our chamber, sounding like she was fighting a battle of her own."

"I don't remember her very well," I said, my thumb rubbing warmth and sparse comfort on the back of his hand.

"Pity. She adored you. All of you. How proud she was of Utor, that night."

I listened as my father drew out his memories of his young wife and her dark-haired babe. How that infant hair had fallen out, leaving him bald until after his first birthday. How Utor, at three, had tumbled halfway down one of the staircases and their terror at the lump on his head. His comprehension, even as a child, of his role as Prince. How readily he learned to read and write. His insistence that he be taught knife throwing earlier than Anhud would have allowed, and his persistence in practicing once the Armsmaster agreed.

"Maudlin...would you..." My father's disjointed speech broke.

I squeezed his hand. "Of course. Whatever it is."

His parched swallow echoed in the quiet room. "Your mother...my sisters...are dead."

My heart chilled, knowing then what he asked. Brusterian women had made the dead ready for interment as long as Brusterian men had been fighting and dying. I had never done so alone. But, as he had told Birnan, you did not choose your duty. It merely was.

★★★

I prepared Utor as the older women had taught me.

I cut away his clothing. In a poor family the clothes of the dead would be reused. For royalty, they were burnt in mourning but not with the body. I steeped mullein in boiling water to wash him, fragrant steam billowing like a storm coming in over the sea.

There was almost no blood. The knife must have struck his heart. The wound was a small thing, barely a finger's width. It hardly seemed possible. All that was Utor, gone to a wound I could close with four stitches. I had not wept with my father, trying to help him with his grief, but if I wept now, it did not matter. I was alone with the dead, bathing him with water warmer than tears.

I cleaned and shaped his nails though they did not need it, immaculate as he had been for the Court feast. Then I took up my scissors and trimmed his beard. His face was disconcertingly calm, as if he were sleeping. I could not help feeling that my touch on his cheek might wake him even as my fingers knew his skin was too cool to be living flesh.

His braid was disheveled, hair escaping at his temples and above the ears. I hesitated. If I combed it out and could not force the memory of its creation back into my fingers, there was no woman in the castle who could help. Another of my brothers would have to come, breaking the burial custom.

Easing him onto his side, I loosened the leather tie and dipped my comb in the water. On my eighth attempt, the skill returned, sudden as summer rain. His hair slid like fine linen thread in my hands as I wove it into place. I took a silver bell no wider than my thumbnail from my belt pouch and fastened it to the tie at the end. Our mother had had four such bells, which she wore in her braid on festival days. They were all I had of her. I dried him with clean cloths, and rubbed his body with oil steeped with rowan berries.

Then I sat, reluctant to take the final step. Sprinkle him with dried rose petals and tansy, and sew him into his shroud.

Six years, Maudlin.

How often I had heard Utor in my mind since the Saradenian letter had come, speaking wisdom in the voice from which I was most accustomed to hear counsel and most likely to heed it. What a stubborn, witless, proud fool I had been. I had listened to his words when they had risen but uncritically, never asking myself why Utor—why all my brothers—crept into my thoughts more and more. I had wanted to come home at last, finally grown ready to return and make peace, and, perhaps, amends. But I refused to let myself hear what the still gray quiet at the core of myself had been whispering. Now Utor was dead, and I would never hear him again but in those thoughts.

I pulled the end of my braid over my shoulder, touching the leather tie he had put there.

At last I mustered my courage and threaded my needle. *Ulton. Yvein.* I stabbed the needle through linen. If I found either of them before my father did—

Realization struck, hot and sharp. Yvein wasn't rowing to Verun. She knew the High King would send a force there, and she wouldn't count on the loyalty of her husband's men after his death. She was going to Vere. To join Ulton and plot their next step.

I finished my stitching with more haste than custom would usually condone, and went to my father.

★★★

The under-kings' chairs had been cleared from the King's room by the time I returned. It was as it had been when I arrived. Only hours before? It seemed liked months. A lifetime.

It had been. Utor's lifetime.

The King was at his work table but rose when his guard admitted me. I stood before him once more, this time without the reassuring presence of Utor, and explained what I had guessed. He looked skeptical when I began, less so once I'd finished.

"Perhaps," he said. "It's possible." He picked up the quill he'd set down, cleaned the nib, set it down again. "I hope you're right. Birnan will have better odds." He pushed the cork back into the ink bottle. "How soon can you be ready to leave?"

"I—what?"

He frowned. "You know Vere. You alone of us know Ulton on sight. I've not laid eyes on him since he was a boy." He went to the high seat and lay a hand on one arm, letting me know what he would say next was a command, not a request. "You will lead a force to Vere. Find them. Bring them back. Breathing. Or not. As seems best to you."

I felt my mouth fall open. "Lord?"

"An hour? Two hours?" His eyes went upward as he considered. "No more than two. Take Master Carlson. A quiet one, I grant you, but he acquits himself well in difficult times."

I thought of returning to Vere, a band of warriors at my back. If we were fast, we could catch them before they fled or hid. The Pedagno might yet live. We might save him. I thought of Utor, pale and still in a shroud I had sewn closed. I looked down, and saw my knives in my hands. I had not realized I'd drawn them. *Ulton. Yvein.* One for each. "One hour, lord. I'll go tell Hal."

"Will a force of two dozen men be enough?"

"Yes, lord. Ample." I sheathed my knives. "Vere keeps no fighting men, and Yvein could not have gotten away with half so many."

He smiled. "I will order your boat ready."

***

Hal was doing as he'd been asked, keeping watch over Murrow and Cedrick, but my brothers were not. Neither were asleep, nor looked as if he had slept. All three of them were on their feet before I'd closed the door behind me.

Cedrick took one look at my face. "What's happened?"

I made soothing motions. "Nothing...else. But something is to hand."

Cedrick pulled a long breath. "Finally. There's something to *do*."

"What?" Murrow returned to his chair and folded his hands, the picture of a man about to be forced to renounce a deep desire. Which, of course, was certainly the case. The Prince could not be risked. Not now.

I explained for the second time why I believed Yvein was heading for Vere rather than Verun. The High King's assessment that it might be true, and the raid upon Vere he had ordered in response. Under my command. With Hal as one of the party. I flicked a glance in Hal's direction, wondering what he thought. Of making up one of a Brusterian warrior band. Of the delay in our search for Saradena. But he listened without speaking, his face as bland as any noble's

Cedrick turned an uncharacteristically grim expression upon me, his eyes narrowing like someone weighing where to strike. "I'm going."

"I have no objection," I said. The surprise that flitted across his face was almost amusing. I raised a hand. "If the King does not."

His face went rigid as the granite of the mountain. "He won't." He pivoted and strode towards the door, then paused, his hand on the latch. "I will be ready when the boat is."

Murrow was on his heels. "I'll go with him." He gave a lopsided, wan smile that did not touch his eyes. "To mediate."

I touched his shoulder as he went past.

The door closed, sealing in a silence that was not empty. Hal blinked slowly.

"I have to go," I said, as if answering an unspoken objection. "It is an order from my king."

He stood still as an oak on a windless day. "What of Saradena?"

"Just a delay. A short delay." I heard wheedling in my voice and pushed it away. "A week," I said firmly. "No more than a week."

"I doubt that very much, lady." His head tipped as he considered me appraisingly. "If we get to Vere and find them gone, only a day or even hours ahead, do you believe yourself capable of leaving their trail? Of not pursuing?" He shook his head. "I know better, even if you do not."

I did not dispute it. "If so, it would be a short chase. A month at most."

"A month!" He spoke harshly, his voice rougher than I'd ever heard it. "This hunt could easily go half a year. If not longer." His tone softened. "It is a worthy quest. But it is not *your* quest."

"I *must* go." I slashed at the air, as if warding off his objections. "The High King commands it."

"You *want* to go," he shot back. "If you go back now, you might still save the Pedagno. You picture yourself returning at the head of an armed group and triumphantly handing control of Vere back to your *maestro*."

That was so uncomfortably close to what I had imagined that I immediately shouted back, "*No*. That's not it. You don't understand. This is about loyalty. The High King is my liege-lord. My oath to the Roth excepted my duty to Bruster."

"What good will it do Bruster to hang Yvein and Ulton from the walls of the Black Keep but fall to Saradena?" His words snapped like a crossbow bolt.

I took a step towards him. "We do not choose our duty. It merely is."

"A pretty saying. And usually true. But not here. Not in this." He gestured towards the door. "Cedrick can take a troop to Vere. Or Dunstan. Or any number of your father's men. Only *you* can look for Saradena."

"What about you?" This time I did not shout. Not quite. I held onto that much of my hard-won mastery over my temper. But fury smoked and popped like grease in an over-heated pan. Who was he to speak to me in this way? "You can read. You can read Old Valenian. *You* go to Ferrant and beg Francis to search his books."

"Here we are." His voice was almost smug. "The center at last. You fear to face him and have seized a chance to avoid it, and pretend otherwise by calling it 'duty.'" He turned away as if unable to look at me.

"You—" I could get out no more around my outrage.

"Yes, I dare, lady." He gave me a hard look over his shoulder. "To tell you truth when you might profit from it, whether that truth be sweet or bitter. That is a difference between a friend and a servant. I cannot go to Ferrant alone. I could read the books, even if some are Old Valenian. But King Francis would not let me in."

"The Roth—" I clasped my twitching hands behind my back. Angry as I was with him, I did not want to momentarily lose patience and throw something—probably a knife—at him. He might not dodge as well as my brothers.

"Not at the Roth's request nor anyone else's. He will allow you. Not from kindness. Its opposite, in fact. He will not be able to refuse a chance to see how you are. Whether he has broken you utterly. You *know* this." He turned back to face me. "You *know* this," he repeated. "You must know."

"No." I felt my chin lift until I could glare at him down my nose. "I have heard enough. I am leaving for Vere in an hour. Less than an hour, now. You may come. Or not. As you choose."

***

I stood at my father's side at the shipyard, watching Dunstan prepare the troop of men and the captain prepare the ship. A crowd had gathered, nearly as large as the one that had said farewell to Princess Maudlin the day she left for Ferrant. I hefted my bag higher on my hip, shifting the weight of the books to a different spot. At my other side, Murrow noticed the move and interpreted it as impatience.

"All will be ready soon." He squeezed my hand.

I glanced back towards the castle. This time, Murrow understood the gesture correctly.

"He may yet come."

I lifted a shoulder in a half shrug. "Or he may not. I do not care. The High King wanted him along, but he has no authority to order him. Hal will do as he thinks best."

Murrow looked as if he wanted to say something more but I returned the press of his hand. "Peace. I will not quarrel with him further on this matter."

On Murrow's other side, Cedrick snorted. "We do not need

Master Carlson to take Yvein and Ulton."

"I agree," I said. "But I would have preferred it."

Cedrick shuffled his feet impatiently, a surprising breach of noble impassivity. "I hope they finish soon."

"Yes," I said.

Some of the boat slaves were inspecting the oars, while others lay the sail flat on the black sand well above the waves' reach. Unless one were in the direst haste, it did not do to head to sea without ensuring that your methods of sailing were sound. The oars would be checked for cracks, the sail for the smallest tears. A brisk wind could turn a sail with a snag the size of a rivet head into a tattered mass of rags within minutes. I understood, but I chafed at the delay. It left too much time for thinking.

You picture yourself returning at the head of an armed group and triumphantly handing control of Vere back to your maestro...You fear to face him and have seized a chance to avoid it, and pretend otherwise by calling it 'duty'...Cedrick can take a troop to Vere. Or Dunstan. Or any number of your father's men. Only you can look for Saradena.

I thought of Saradena. The books in Ferrant. The months that had passed. The few that remained. I remembered sitting with Mistress Baynor, frustrated at finding so little about Saradena, ready to abandon the search. What Hal had said was disquietingly similar to what she had. *Anyone can go looking for Saradena—and die of thirst and sunbake, lost at sea.* She had not touched me, but she might as well have been holding both my arms tight. Her face barely a hand's breadth from mine, she had glared, fierce and quelling. *Only you can do this. Read, search for shavings and parings about Saradena—and put them together.*

You do not choose your duty. It merely is. So our father had said to Birnan. To each of us, long before we were old enough to understand. But what if something lay beyond duty, or beyond the duty that was mere, unquestioning obedience?

I wanted justice for the Pedagno. It was true. Hal had spoken rightly.

Utor.

Six years, Maudlin.

I wanted also revenge for Utor. Not just revenge. Revenge at my hands. An unassailable target of my wrath, an object against whom I might release all the bonds of my anger, and let it burn and burn. Hal had been close—I did dread facing Francis—but he had not seen the darkest center. I wanted to slip my knife under Ulton's ribs, as he had arranged for Utor. I wanted to cut Yvein's throat with my own hand, as she had coaxed her husband to try to my father.

To find such desires in my soul did not surprise or distress me overmuch. Bruster was a hard, dangerous land, and the rest of the known world was scarce better. Fighting, dispensing death and avoiding it, were part of our lives from birth. Bitted and bridled, the fierce strength born of anger was not an evil but a good. And there *were* times and places—and people—for which wrath might be allowed to pull the reins loose and gallop free-headed. But to find that I was willing to risk the future of our world in order to ensure my hand was on the blade that took our vengeance…that could not be accepted.

Oh, my father. My King.

At last I knew where my duty lay. But I doubted he would agree. I touched his arm. "Lord. I…can't."

"Can't?" His voice pitched low, for our ears alone, was disbelieving. Dangerous. His eyes narrowed. "I do not ask. I command."

"Lord, please consider." I raised both hands, let them fall. "The letter. The book. I must go to Ferrant."

"That was before." His hand went to his sword, fingers tightening on the hilt. "Your first loyalty is Bruster."

Despite our whispering, Cedrick and Murrow had realized something was amiss, and were trying to watch us, curiosity and worry crossing their faces before being wiped away.

"I *am* thinking of Bruster," I said urgently. "Our new adversary means to strike." I would not say the name aloud in public, even in a whisper. "All of us, including Bruster, will fall if I don't find the cause of their grievance and how we might diffuse it."

He snorted dismissively. "Months from now. If at all. Verun has struck *today.*"

"I can tell Cedrick everything he needs to know about Vere to make this attack successful." There was urgency, desperation, in my voice, but I could not quell it. "But only I have the chance to thwart our unknown trouble."

The crowd's murmurs changed. They grasped that a discussion, and not an amicable one, was taking place among the King's company. One by one their faces turned from watching the boat slaves to watching us.

My father's gaze flicked to the surrounding faces. He blinked once, slowly. Then his attention returned to me, his expression now blank as he drew upon his noble's control. But he took a step closer, and I felt the shuddering rage within him, radiating like heat from a blazing hearth. "I charge you, upon your family loyalty, upon Utor's dead body still unburned and uninterred. Go to Vere and bring me back his killers."

"I can't," I repeated miserably, wishing I had heeded Hal's counsel earlier. I could have talked with my father in private, and he might have been more reasonable. Here, before the eyes of Reud, he would never—could never—countenance opposition. Rebellions had been born of less, and he was already vulnerable. Verun's usurpation attempt would make some suspect that the High King must have warranted such a move.

My father stood for long moments, so enraged he could not speak, looking at me, then away from me. When he did speak, his eyes were on the crowd and he pitched his voice that they might hear. "I am affronted, but perhaps not surprised, to find that Bruster...Utor...I...your own honor, your duty...mean so little to you."

"I *am* minding my duty," I hissed. "My duty as I see it."

"You do not decide your duty. Your lord does," he snapped back before his face smoothed as he mastered himself once more.

"I do as my lord commanded," I said, keeping my voice low and even. Now was not the time to match his anger with my own. But I found to my surprise I was not angry. Regretful, sorrowful, yes, to the brim and spilling over. I had no room for anger. Strange. "My formal oath of fealty to Bruster was set aside when I married. The Roth, in courtesy, gave me an oath of service that promised he would never order me to do anything detrimental to Bruster. I do as I was bid by my sworn lord." I was nearly whispering, not wanting the crowd to hear. "You know what he commanded. You know that it is in Bruster's interest I go on with that task."

He pulled a deep breath, his nose quivering with the force of his indrawn air. "I declare Maudlin of Bruster banished. He raised his voice, that he might be heard by every soul on the black sand shore. She is no longer *of Bruster.*" I felt the heat of his fury, now like a forge, hot enough to make iron pliable, but he did not look at me.

Murrow stared. Cedrick gasped. Our father silenced them both with a fierce glance.

"She is Elbish, perhaps. If they will have her. She may not return to Bruster. A Brusterian who aids her in any cause or any place should hold himself to share her exile." Now he did cast his gaze upon me, and it was like the hammer on the anvil. "Go where you will. Do not return. I will instruct Dunstan not to admit you for any cause."

***

I sat in the bow, watching the waves. A sudden gust blew whipped strands of loosened hair around my face, tugging Utor's braid away.

My bag and its precious books was in my lap. Hal, summoned with unseemly speed from the Black Keep, sat beside me, clasping one of my hands in both of his, the only brother I had remaining to me offering what comfort and support he could. It was about as effective as the comfort I had offered my father. Which is to say not at all.

My father had allowed Cedrick and Murrow to escort me to the longboat he had ordered to take me to Elbany. Immediately, without time for the boat slaves to check the oars or sail. It mattered not at all if we were lost at sea, so long as we were gone. I had hurriedly relayed to Cedrick everything I could think of about the layout of Vere, everything I'd planned about how to conduct the attack. With me, or without, Vere would have a company of Reud's warriors upon it soon. He nodded brusquely, looking as wrathful as our father. "You should have come with us." He strode away before I could say anything. Which was, perhaps, just as well. I'd said everything to our father, and it had not mattered.

Murrow had helped me into the boat. The boat slaves began to push the longship towards the water. Then Murrow ran into the ankle-deep water and grabbed my forearms. "Tell Elsbeth I'm sorry."

I had blinked at him in perfect astonishment. It was true that my mind was brimful of incomprehensible things from this wretched unending day, but this made less sense than any. When he'd sprinted out, I'd expected...something familial. Good-bye. An expression of regret. Something other than *Tell Elsbeth I'm sorry.* What had my brother to do with the Roth's wife? I had nodded automatically, and he'd stepped back.

I tried turning it over in my mind, but I was too far gone. I watched the oars slap the water until we cleared the bay and the slaves raised the sail.

"Well done, lady," Hal said. "The right choice. Difficult. But right."

"It does not feel well done," I said.

At length he slipped into an uneasy doze, still clutching my hand. We had not had a night of sleep since leaving Vere. The sea murmured in more kindly tones than the crowd at Reud. The sun warmed cordially but did not burn. Sleep, if sleep could still be found, would be welcome. But if I let my eyes close, I saw my father.

I kept them open.

How could I sleep? I had returned—by necessity, if not, as it had emerged, unwillingly—and learned, as I'd come to suspect, that I had imagined my family's rejection, seeing refutation and denial in all faces after finding it so stridently in Francis'. For a few hours, I had been home.

Now the estrangement was in truth, and in earnest. My father had disowned me publicly. The sea air stung my eyes. Not tears. I had left them all at Utor's bier. *No one can erase your blood,* Mistress Baynor had said, but that was not so. No one but the High King. My father. As he had. I was no longer *of Bruster.* Nor was I *of Elbany.* The Roth had accepted my service and a limited oath of loyalty, but I was not his subject. I was *of nowhere,* more lost than the slaves who rowed the longboat. When their time of service was done, they could return home.

Smoke rose, a tendril of gray uncurling like a scroll, from the distant smudge that I knew to be the Black Mountain. They had taken Utor to his pyre.

Then a brisk wind caught the sail and we raced across the water, fast as a hawk dives after a rabbit. I watched as Bruster slid into the sea, and I strained to distinguish the last crest of the Black Mountain from enveloping waves, trying to silence the dangerous murmurings of my heart that looked upon it yet and whispered *home.*

Acknowledgements

Lucky writers have encouraging but cogent beta-readers who keep you working but catch your most egregious missteps before you've gone too far. I have been very fortunate to have excellent beta-readers. Jessica read and commented upon all three, deeply varying, drafts. Anne, Eric, and Barbara read early drafts and gave both feedback and encouragement. My new critique partners Grace and Sarah read the last draft and still found a worrisome number of issues to comment upon. I owe a great debt as well to my editor, Bill Racicot, who both made the manuscript better with lucid suggestions and was very patient as we worked through the process.

ABOUT THE AUTHOR

Michelle Markey Butler holds a doctorate in English Literature, which is all Thomas Malory's fault. She blogs about parenting at www.heirraising.wordpress.com and is pleased to report that despite their best efforts none of the children have escaped. Recently.

Michelle's story "Little Hands" won an Honorable Mention in the Second Quarter 2010 Writers of the Future Contest, while her book-in-progress, *Lord Garland's Daughter,* was named an Honorable Mention in Textnovel's 2010 contest. More about Michelle can be found at: michellemarkeybutler.com.

Other fantasy titles from Pink Narcissus Press

COURT OF DREAMS
A comic fantasy novel by Stuart Sharp
"An engagingly fun piece... Getting a tone part-way between Pratchett and Rankin, *The Court of Dreams* is short, fast-paced, and well worth picking up." - *Drying Ink*
ISBN: 978-0-9829913-2-9

ELEMENTARÌ RISING
An eco-fantasy novel by Nancy Hightower
Starred review. "Interesting characters and an unusual world of deathless trees and common folk who are more than they seem make this a winner for fans of epic fantasy. With elements that should appeal to readers who enjoy Terry Brooks's 'Shannara' series and fans of weird fantasy." - *Library Journal*
ISBN: 978-1-939056-03-0

FEASTING WITH PANTHERS
A literary fantasy by Lyle Blake Smythers
"Like a concert pianist playing a favorite piece of music, Smythers conducts the reader through his fantasy world that's never boring. Future novels from this talented writer should be well worth reading." - *ForeWord Reviews*
ISBN: 978-0-9829913-7-4

RAPUNZEL'S DAUGHTERS
and Other Tales
Edited by Brown, Mambert & Racicot
"Any fairy tale fan will find something to enjoy in this collection." - *Publishers Weekly*
ISBN: 978-0-9829913-1-2